Barbara Metzger, a star of the genre, has written more than three dozen Regencies and Regency-set historicals and won numerous awards, including a RITA. Her newest title is *Ace of Hearts*. Visit her Web site at www.barbarametzger.com.

Edith Layton, critically acclaimed for her short stories and historical romances, has won numerous awards. She loves to hear from readers and can be reached at www.edithlayton.com.

Andrea Pickens was honored with a Career Achievement Award in Regency Romance from *Romantic Times* in 2004 and is a past RITA finalist. She also writes historical romances under the name Andrea DaRif. Visit her Web site at www.andreapickensonline.com.

Nancy Butler is the author of many Signet Regencies and is currently working on a romantic thriller. In 2004, she won her second RITA award, was inducted into the Hall of Fame by the New Jersey Romance Writers, and was nominated for the second time for Career Achievement by *Romantic Times BOOKClub*.

Gayle Buck majored in journalism and has written for magazines, newspapers, and radio. She has written more than thirty Regencies. Currently she advises high school students on how to find and secure free financial aid for college.

Regency Christmas Courtship

Five Stories by

Barbara Metzger

Edith Layton

Andrea Pickens

Nancy Butler

Gayle Buck

A SIGNET BOOK

SIGNET
Published by New American Library, a division of
Penguin Group (USA) Inc., 375 Hudson Street,
New York, New York 10014, USA
Penguin Group (Canada), 90 Eglinton Avenue East, Suite 700, Toronto,
Ontario M4P 2Y3, Canada (a division of Pearson Penguin Canada Inc.)
Penguin Books Ltd., 80 Strand, London WC2R 0RL, England
Penguin Ireland, 25 St. Stephen's Green, Dublin 2,
Ireland (a division of Penguin Books Ltd.)
Penguin Group (Australia), 250 Camberwell Road, Camberwell, Victoria 3124,
Australia (a division of Pearson Australia Group Pty. Ltd.)
Penguin Books India Pvt. Ltd., 11 Community Centre, Panchsheel Park,
New Delhi - 110 017, India
Penguin Group (NZ), cnr Airborne and Rosedale Roads, Albany,
Auckland 1310, New Zealand (a division of Pearson New Zealand Ltd.)
Penguin Books (South Africa) (Pty.) Ltd., 24 Sturdee Avenue,
Rosebank, Johannesburg 2196, South Africa

Penguin Books Ltd., Registered Offices:
80 Strand, London WC2R 0RL, England

First published by Signet, an imprint of New American Library,
a division of Penguin Group (USA) Inc.

First Printing, October 2005
10 9 8 7 6 5 4 3 2 1

Wooing the Wolf

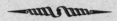

Barbara Metzger

Chapter One

*Women are frail and fragile creatures who must
be sheltered and guided by wiser, male heads. Remember, dear sir, that females' emotions are
boundless, while their intelligence is less so. You
must plan your courtship accordingly.*
—George E. Phelber, *A Gentleman's Guide to Courtship*

"The post, madam," Lady Bartlett's butler announced as he placed a silver salver beside his
mistress's plate at the breakfast table. As usual, the
tray was filled. Half the cards were invitations, which
the baroness would not accept for fear she would have
to reciprocate. The other half were letters filled with
gossip, which she devoured with her kippers and eggs.
As usual, bills went directly to her man of business so
Lady Bartlett did not have to ruin her digestion with
the cost of coal or candles.

Not nearly as usual, the butler turned to the older
lady's young companion. "And a letter for you, Miss
Todd."

Margaret seldom got mail. Her sister in India was
a poor correspondent, and her cousin, Sir Fernell
Todd, in Marionville, Suffolk, was a poor excuse for
a relative. This letter, however, was indeed from India,
but not addressed in Lily's neat copperplate. With

fingers trembling in dread, Margaret set it aside, and her breakfast also.

"Go ahead and open it, girl. Running off to India with that harebrained husband of hers was bad enough, but what has your fool of a sister done now?"

Margaret opened the letter and gasped. "She . . . she has died. Along with Harry, of an epidemic."

"What else did they expect, living in that heathenish country?"

Margaret ignored her employer, and the fact that Lady Bartlett had not expressed an iota of sympathy. Even if Margaret had not seen Lily in twelve years, she was still her beloved sister. With tear-filled eyes, Margaret read on. "The children—Lily had two daughters, you will recall—had been sent to the cooler mountains, and so were spared. This gentleman writes that they are being sent to England, to me, as Lily's last request, since Harry had no living relatives. The girls will arrive in London harbor before Christmas, he says, and he has notified our solicitor of the particulars."

Lady Bartlett snorted. "The particulars are that they are likely paupers. No matter, they are your cousin's responsibility. Head of the household and all that. Your solicitor will send a carriage to the docks to convey them to the baronet." She went back to reading her mail, oblivious to Margaret's distress.

Cousin Fernell had inherited Margaret's father's estate and baronetcy, but not his kindness or caring. Sir Fernell did not want Margaret or Lily, except as unpaid nannies for his own unruly children or maids for his overbearing wife. Lily had fled to India and Margaret had accepted a position as companion in London as soon as she could. At least here she was compensated, and away from the reminders of what used to be.

Mentally, now, she added up her savings, wondering if there was any way she could keep the girls with her, depending on what the solicitor had to say about the finances. She had been orphaned and unloved since she was sixteen. She could not let that happen to her nieces.

She arose early the next morning, far before Lady Bartlett would call for her to read the newspapers out loud or walk her pug dog. She took a hackney coach to the solicitor's office, only to find the establishment locked up tight, with a note on the door: CLOSED FOR THE HOLIDAY. WILL RETURN IN THE NEW YEAR. He had added a forwarding address in Cornwall and another solicitor's card, for emergencies. That lawyer knew nothing of any India correspondence, orphans or inheritances.

Checking the watch pinned to her dark gown, Margaret ordered her waiting driver to hurry to the docks. The clerk at the shipping offices proudly informed her that the *Belizar* had been spotted and was due in London in two days, two weeks early.

Two little girls losing both parents, crossing an ocean, facing a new land and relatives they had never met, was too sad to think of. Margaret could not simply put them in a coach by themselves and send them on to Suffolk where they would get a cold welcome, if any welcome at all. Lily had meant for her sister to raise the children, after all.

Lady Bartlett meant for Margaret to get back to her duties. "No, you cannot bring them here, missy, not for a whole month until some rackety man of affairs returns to his own business. I am not running a charity home, am I? Children mean noise and nuisance and nursery meals. Besides, they will take up your time, when I am paying for it. I need you to handle my correspondence and such. You have not forgotten about the Boxing Day gifts for the staff, have you?"

Margaret had hemmed half the handkerchiefs Lady Bartlett deemed suitable gifts for her servants. Margaret had intended to put one of her own coins into each folded square, but now she did not think she could spare the money.

"And I need you to look after Charlie. You know he does not take to just anyone."

Charlie the pug took a piece out of anyone foolish enough to get between him and Lady Bartlett, whose pockets were always filled with treats. Margaret had come to terms with the fat, surly creature by bribing him. The children would not be safe from his nasty temper, or Lady Bartlett's. But where could she go with them, and how could she support them if there was no bequest?

While her employer had her afternoon nap, Margaret went through the rear garden to Wolfram House next door, where she had befriended the housekeeper over the six years of her London employment in Berkeley Square. Perhaps Mrs. Olive knew of cheap but respectable lodgings somewhere, just until the solicitor returned. Margaret might lose her post by leaving Lady Bartlett's household, and without references at that, but she felt that neither she nor her nieces had any choice. They needed a loving home, and, at twenty-five years of age, Margaret thought this might be her only chance of gaining the family she had always wanted, perhaps a tiny cottage where she could be aunt and mother to the poor dears, if Lily and Harry had provided for their futures. Perhaps there was only enough to see to their schooling, in which case Margaret would find an academy in London for them, so she could visit on her days off from whatever new position she found. They were her kin, and they needed her. Lady Bartlett would simply need a new underpaid, underappreciated, overworked companion.

Mrs. Olive would not hear of Miss Todd taking the unfortunate orphans to a rooming house, not when Wolfram House stood nearly empty. Viscount Wolfram was traveling to various Christmas house parties across the country, and only Mrs. Olive, Dora the maid, Phillip the footman who was sweet on Dora, and a day cook remained to care for his lordship's home and his great-auntie. The small staff would all be delighted to have children running about the place, especially at Christmas. They'd have an excuse to decorate and plan a feast and make merry, just as they ought at the joyous season.

Nothing could be more perfect, since Margaret might still assist Lady Bartlett in hopes of keeping her position if needed, or at least getting that important reference. Leaving so suddenly, without giving her employer time to hire a new companion, was nothing Margaret could approve, no matter how beastly the baroness. But to move into Wolfram House without the owner's permission? That was nearly as rude and unprincipled.

The housekeeper shrugged. "No time to write to him if your girls dock afore the post leaves London."

"What about his great-aunt, Mrs. Bolton?" In all her years next door, Margaret had seldom seen the elderly lady. "Should I not seek her approval?"

Mrs. Olive shook her gray head. "She's naught but his lordship's pensioner herself, and she hardly leaves her apartment, except to walk in the garden. But the nursery is far away, and as long as she has her novels from the lending library, Mrs. Bolton won't care. Might even do the old lady good," Mrs. Olive added with a touch of disapproval, since she could have gone off to her own sister's for the holiday if not for the reclusive relic. While she was being critical of her betters, the housekeeper told Miss Todd not to worry her pretty head about his lordship, for while he was considerate and generous, he was also too busy sowing wild oats to tend to his own fields.

The viscount was not due back from his carousing until nearly February, the housekeeper said with a scowl, if the ladies in the country let him go then. "I know all about those house parties, I do. An excuse for prowling dark corridors and passing bedroom-door keys like they were calling cards. Flirtation and fornication, and him all of five-and-thirty, without an heir in sight." She clucked her tongue all the way to the all-too-empty nursery where Margaret and her nieces might stay until their affairs were settled. "Trust me, Miss Todd, taking his pleasure means more to our Lord Wolf than taking offense at any uninvited guests."

Contrary to his housekeeper's expectations—and his own—Wolf, as he was known, was not enjoying himself. John, Viscount Wolfram, was not called Wolf because of any gray hair. He still had his full head of curly blond locks. Nor did he have eerie, golden eyes. He had bright blue ones. Neither was he a predator, a sly hunter, for his prey came to him gladly. No, what earned him the sobriquet, other than his own name, was his lordship's elusiveness. One of the premier bachelors of his time, with a title and fortune and looks and charm, he had been damnably hard to catch by all the matchmaking mamas who had tried since he was one-and-twenty.

What, wed before he had to? Confine himself to one woman forever? One might as well tuck one's tail between one's legs and howl at the moon. Wolf was not ready, but his days were numbered, as he well knew. Was he truly thirty-five already? His friends were nearly all wed, assuring their successions if not their conjugal bliss. Even his faithful servant Paul, who acted as valet, secretary and confidant, had taken to putting pamphlets on Wolf's desk, silly twaddle about the proper way to court a real lady, implying that Wolf's successes were with lesser, unsuitable sorts of females.

Not so. Just look at his current mistress, the young widow of an elderly earl. Unfortunately, Lady Siddering was not half as appealing by the early morning light, when Wolf left her bedroom before the servants arrived. She slept with her mouth open, and she drooled. Well, a chap did not have to share a bedroom with his wife, Wolf reasoned. Most did not. And Martine was a real lady for all that.

Or she had been, until Wolf decided over breakfast that she simply would not do as his viscountess. He planned to end the affair with a ruby bracelet, then move on to the next invitation. If he had to wed in the new year, he was determined to celebrate the yuletide and his remaining bachelor days in high fashion, not listening to Martine's snores. Or her diatribes when she discovered him leaving after luncheon.

"But I never promised you a wedding ring," he said as she hurled the expensive bracelet at his head. "You had to have known that."

"Nonsense. It is time you married, everyone says so. And you have compromised me irreparably. You must do the gentlemanly thing."

Lack of sleep and an abundance of wassail had obviously addled Wolf's wits, unfortunately. He laughed.

Martine slapped him.

Which only confirmed his decision that she was not of the caliber of the future Lady Wolfram. Growing angry at the scene, the delay and his stinging cheek, Wolf told her, "Madam, since I was not your first gentleman, nor your last, undoubtedly, I shall not deign to address your absurd claims of compromise. But understand that I would not take to wife a female who is free with her temper, or her favors." Free? Martine had cost him a pretty penny in baubles and dressmakers' bills. A wife had to be less costly.

The lady was incensed. She was also in fear of growing older, losing her looks, having to live on the pittance her husband had left her. Her best chance of making a brilliant match was leaving this dull gathering where no other unwed gentlemen of means were attending. She could have gone to Lady Plannenbord's gathering, where the hunting was better. Furious, she raked her fingernails down his cheek.

Wolf bowed and returned to his bedchamber, where his loyal valet Paul was finishing the packing. Paul took one look at his master's face and his complexion turned as gray as his hair. Wolf looked in the mirror and felt his own heart clench. Blood was pouring from four parallel gashes down one side of his face, onto his neckcloth. Damn, he looked like he'd been at a bearbaiting, and lost! How could he go on to another happy holiday gathering? His hostesses would swoon at the sight of him. The females he'd been hoping to dally with would cringe away from him. Prospective brides would worry he'd be disfigured. Worst, his friends would laugh. Wolf could not even claim a riding accident—four sharp twigs hitting him at once?— for the gossipmongers at this party had seen him at breakfast with his phiz intact.

To add insult to the injury, or injury to the insult, the deuced thing hurt when Paul dabbed at it with spirits. Now Wolf did not even feel like celebrating Christmas, singing carols, cajoling another woman to his bed.

He wanted to hide. So that was what he decided to do, return to his empty London town house until the marks healed, his good humor was restored and he was resigned to finding a bride in the spring. Unless the bitch had scarred him for life.

Chapter Two

Every woman deserves to be courted, even the ones who are betrothed in an arranged match, the settlements signed before you so much as glimpse your prospective bride. She will be gratified at your kindness and consideration, and not feel like chattel. If your success is not thusly guaranteed, then you must strive that much harder to ensure that your suit is welcome. A pleasant character and a clean and neat appearance should be considered de rigueur, for both you and the young lady.

—George E. Phelber, *A Gentleman's Guide to Courtship*

Wolf rode through the day and half the night, leaving Paul to come with the carriage and his bags. The viscount would make better time that way, and take fewer chances of meeting people he knew. With his hat pulled low and his scarf raised high, Wolf rode into Berkeley Square.

Oddly, lights were lit on the ground floor of his house. For a moment Wolf wondered if Great-Aunt Bolton had finally decided to socialize. While the cat was away . . . ? No, the old lady was a mouse, and had no acquaintances in Town as far as Wolf knew. He let himself into the front door with his key and was again surprised, this time by the smell of evergreens, cloves and apples, and the sight of red ribbons trailing up the banisters of the marble stairwell. The few servants must have decided to decorate for the holidays, he thought, gladdened by the idea. Now his own Christmas would be a little brighter, if possible.

Then he heard noises from the music room—singing, laughing, tinkling notes. His great-aunt had never stepped foot in the music room to his knowledge, or shown any interest in attending concerts, the opera or musical recitals at his friends' homes, although he had asked for a year when she had first arrived, before giving up. He doubted the quivery, quaking old woman was raising her voice so merrily in the old Christmas carols now.

He did not mind the servants celebrating, or begrudge them the expense of a bit of greenery, but truly, they should not be in the formal rooms. And his pianoforte was a rare and valuable piece, not to be thumped by amateur fingers.

He strode down the hall and through the open door.

The songs, laughter and music all died. Mrs. Olive shrieked. Little Dora the maid threw herself into the arms of Phillip the footman. A child of about ten—a little girl, in his home?—pointed at his mutilated cheek and started crying. Another, smaller one—two little girls, in his home?—hid her head in the skirts of a pretty female in a faded brown gown who was standing by the pianoforte, her face as white as the ivory keys. Wolf instantly and expertly assessed the woman: young but not in the first blush of youth, even before the instant pallor. Too young, he thought, to be the little girls' mother, although the blubbering one that he could see had similar brown hair. The woman had large green eyes, a straight nose, soft lips, and a pleasing figure from what he could tell under the modest, unfashionable gown. And she was a total stranger.

"What the deuce is going on here?" he shouted.

Everyone started to talk at once, except the children, both of whom were bawling now.

Mrs. Olive was twisting her apron, not looking at
him. "She had nowhere to go, my lord, and I didn't
think you would mind. And they don't eat much."

Guessing that he was out of a position anyway, Phillip stepped away from Dora and said, "It's supposed
to be the season of giving, ain't it? Miss Todd brought
us a bit of cheer, that's all."

Her eyes downcast, but one hand reaching to Phillip
for comfort, Dora bobbed a curtsy and squeaked,
"And she is teaching me to read, along with the little
girls' lessons."

"Which tells me nothing!" the viscount yelled,
louder than he intended, causing the littler moppet to
wail. Maimed, his plans misfiring, with a mare's nest
at his doorstep—no, in his parlor—Wolf tossed his hat
and his gloves and his muffler onto the nearest chair.
He pointed with his riding whip at Mrs. Olive. "I need
an explanation."

Then he pointed to Phillip. "And a drink."

"And quiet." He jerked his head toward Dora, then
at the children in their white flannel night rails and
bare toes, indicating in no uncertain terms that she
should get the squalling infants out of his sight.

"What you need, my lord," a calm, quiet voice
spoke up, "is doctoring."

On her own, Margaret would have fled, mortified,
back to Lady Bartlett's house. She was not on her
own, however. She had sweet Alexandra and darling
Katherine to think of and protect. She had loved them
from the instant they had run off the ship into her
arms, crying, "Aunt Maggie! We knew you would
come for us! We do not have to go live with feckless
Cousin Fernell, do we?" No, she had loved them from
a distance as soon as her sister had written of their

births, and merely loved them better now. She would cherish her dear nieces as long as she lived. And she would not let anyone shout at them, frighten them, or toss them out in the middle of the night without a fight—even if he did own the house where she was trespassing.

And so Wolf found himself seated at a rough table in his own infrequently visited kitchen, where a kettle boiled temptingly on the hob, and a young woman's temper boiled in a quite tempting breast. He was warm and comfortable, with a glass of his finest cognac in his hand and, truly, the salve Miss Todd was applying to his face was easing the pain. Or perhaps her gentle fingers had eased his misery as she tenderly washed the wound, holding her pink tongue between her teeth in concentration, trying not to hurt him. He also appreciated the fact that she did not scurry away as Mrs. Olive and the footman had, or ask questions, as he heard the children whisper to the maid when she led them up the stairs. Either way, he was content to listen, for now.

Gentlemen hated scenes, tears and tantrums, Margaret knew, so she tried to compose her thoughts. She would not show her horror at his clawed face, her distress at his sudden appearance or her fear for the future. She would certainly not give way to her admiration for his broad shoulders, strong muscles and softly curling blond hair. She washed her trembling fingers, poured them each a cup of tea, and told her tale in as straightforward a manner as possible.

Wolf stared at the young woman, seemingly so composed except for her hand that clutched the teacup as if it were an amulet against evil—him. She did have long, graceful fingers, he noted, almost sorry he had no further injuries for her to soothe. He finally said, "I can see you found yourself in a deuced coil, Miss Todd, but surely there must have been an alternative."

Margaret set down her cup. "Have you ever met Lady Bartlett?"

He grimaced and took a sip of his own tea, now fortified with the cognac. "You might have sent a messenger to your cousin, rather than waiting for the post."

"Have you ever met Sir Fernell Todd?"

Wolf shook his head no. "I have not had the pleasure."

"It would not have been, believe me. And he would not have helped, not in time. But, my lord, have you ever had limited funds and great responsibility?"

Now Wolf stared into his cup, rather than into his conscience. He'd never known anything but a life of privilege, although he was painstaking in his duties as lord of a vast estate with scores of dependents. He also served in Parliament, supported numerous charities and went to church most Sundays. If one overlooked his lack of an heir and somewhat raffish bachelor existence, Wolf considered he was doing a decent job of being viscount, one to make his father proud.

He doubted his mother would have been proud to hear him shout at servants and children and a hired companion. He sighed, half in apology. "But still, there must be hordes of women right in Town with hungry infants and no means of support." He always tossed a coin to the poor unfortunates. "They do not invade a gentleman's residence because they have nowhere else to go."

"Of course not. They find women's shelters, or sell their bodies or starve in the streets. I was simply not that desperate, thank heaven. I was ready to find lodgings, I swear, but Mrs. Olive assured me you would not mind." Or find out, but Margaret did not add the last.

Wolf leaned back in his chair. "And I suppose I

would not have cared, if I had not come home. The situation is different now."

"But how so? We will stay out of your way, I promise, tucked in the old nursery. You will not even know we are in the house."

Wolf did not think he could ever forget that such a pretty young female was sleeping on the floor above his bedchamber.

"And it is not as if I am a thief or a revolutionary or a bedlamite. Everyone at Lady Bartlett's house can tell you I have led an exemplary, respectable life. Why, this is the first foolhardy act of impropriety I have ever committed, at least since leaving my cousin's home. And the children are angels, who are in no way at fault for our trespass."

"I am not blaming the children, or even you. I cannot like the circumstances, however."

Neither could Margaret, sheltering in the home of a known rake, with or without his permission. "I do apologize again, my lord, but this seemed the perfect solution to my dilemma. And it is temporary, I promise you. I am not asking you to assume responsibility for my nieces or their welfare, not in the least. As soon as the solicitor returns and informs me of the details concerning the girls' legacy and trusteeship, I shall of course make other arrangements. Meanwhile, I will ask Mrs. Olive to keep track of our expenses so that I might reimburse you."

Wolf brushed that aside. Take money from a poor female with two girls to support on who knew what monies from India, if any? He made a circle of the kitchen with his hand, indicating the full larder, the modern conveniences, the very luxury of the seldom-visited area of his home. "Money is the least of my concerns."

"I shall help with whatever chores need doing, so we will not burden your staff."

"My staff is well paid, and can be added to in a

moment's notice. You have enough work, looking after your nieces and Lady Bartlett's household too."

Margaret took hope from his words, but he was still frowning. "If you are worried about the proprieties, you need not be, not with your aunt in residence."

Wolf started to rub at his sore cheek, then winced. "No one remembers I even have a great-aunt. Half the time I forget the old woman is in the house at all."

"Yet the world will remember, and exonerate you of any wrongdoing," Margaret insisted. "Not that anyone would suppose I was your mistress."

He had to smile when the altogether proper female's cheeks turned scarlet, making him wish he could rub *them*. The woman had not resorted to wiles and guiles and come-hither smiles, with which he was all too familiar. She was a lady, deserving of his respect. Still, he raised one blond eyebrow in question, teasing her. "How so?"

Margaret hid her embarrassment at such plain talk in pouring out another cup of tea. "Gracious, anyone can tell you I am no kind of dasher. I am not of the *beau monde*, but I am not of the *demimonde* either, as anyone can plainly see. And I must care more about the conventions than you, if I am to find another post eventually, or see my nieces accepted in any kind of polite society. A woman in general must be more watchful of her reputation, especially one without face or fortune. Your aunt's presence protects both of us from unwanted gossip."

The viscount was still not convinced, Margaret could see. He was not yelling or pointing toward the door, but he was not inviting her to stay either.

"I beg of you—"

Now he did get angry again. A gentlewoman begging for aid that would cost him nothing but a bit of inconvenience? That was repugnant. Her cretin of a cousin ought to be shot for subjecting such a soft-spoken, well-mannered young lady to such dire straits.

With a bit of dressing and a touch of Town bronze, a fashionable haircut and a hint of a dowry, this baronet's daughter could have danced at Almack's, trying to snabble an eligible *parti*. Like him.

Perhaps she could read his thoughts, or interpret his muttered curse. "If it is your freedom you feel in jeopardy, my lord, please do not worry. I am nothing but a lady's companion with two nieces to raise. I am not a fortune-hunter or an adventuress looking to marry into the peerage. I came here only because you were away from Town, not to seek your attention. I swear on my mother's love and my father's honor that I have no designs on your title or fortune."

Ah, but the little girls did.

In all their short lives they had never known such luxury as at his lordship's house, with kind servants, plentiful food, a park across the street, attics and cellars to explore, all of London waiting to be visited. Nor had they ever known as much affection and attention as they had received in the few days since hurtling into their Aunt Maggie's arms. They wanted to stay.

Once they heard that his lordship had agreed to keep them until the solicitor came back, they decided they wanted to stay forever. Why, Lord Wolfram even apologized for shouting at them, when they passed him in the hall the next morning. Washed and shaved and smiling, he was a viscount, a hero, a god to the little girls, despite his scary face. That would heal, Aunt Maggie assured them.

They needed to be here, to make sure it did, and to make sure they were not sent away to school or to Feckless Fernell's. Prayers and wishes and stirring the Christmas pudding were not going to make it so. Getting his lordship to marry their aunt would.

He was bound to fall in love with Aunt Maggie eventually, Katherine and Alexandra decided, she was so pretty, besides being kind and loving and wise. That was not the problem. Time was.

They had less than a month, and Lord Wolfram was playing least in sight. He was resting in his room, going over his accounts in the office, reading in the library, playing the pianoforte in the music room and billiards in the game room, all by himself, as he had decreed. How was he going to come to care for Aunt Maggie if they never became better acquainted?

The girls had no money to buy her pretty gowns or face paint to catch his attention, no skills to teach their beloved aunt to flirt. What they had was a small pamphlet "borrowed" from his lordship's desk during one of their early morning explorations, while Margaret was at Bartlett House, busy with the old besom and her dog.

A Gentleman's Guide to Courtship ought to work just as well in reverse, the children reasoned.

So they found him a cat.

Chapter Three

When you go courting, do not go empty-handed. Tokens of your regard and sincerity are always welcome. Remember, you are selecting a bride, not pursuing a mistress. Jewelry and clothing are far too improper for a well-bred female. Small gifts are acceptable.

—George E. Phelber, *A Gentleman's Guide to Courtship*

"MISS TODD!"

If anyone in the neighborhood was not aware that Lady Bartlett's prim and proper companion was acquainted with the renowned rake, they knew it now. Margaret could hear Lord Wolfram's bellow from the street outside, when she returned from dragging Lady Bartlett's cur Charlie around the square.

He was waiting on the steps by the open front door as she hurried toward Wolfram House, anxious that her nieces had met with disaster.

"My lord?"

"Come."

He gave her no choice, grasping her hand and pulling her through the door and toward the marble stairs leading toward the upper storeys. No servants were in sight, which added to Margaret's dismay. Were they all attending the catastrophe, or merely hiding from his lordship's fury?

Margaret hurtled along at his side, trying not to let her fears make her stumble. Only when he tugged her in the direction of what she knew to be his bedroom did Margaret dig her heels into the thick hall carpet.

"My lord, this is unseemly and im—"

He threw open his bedchamber door and pointed at the velvet-hung bed. "What is that? And I do not mean my bed."

"A . . . a cat?" The animal in the center of the mattress had the shape of a cat, but was twice as big, with tufts in its black-edged ears, and a thick golden-brown coat and unblinking yellow eyes.

"A cat? More like a small lion without a mane. It is a very large, possibly ferocious, likely flea-ridden feline. If my man Paul were here, he would have . . . kittens to see the hairs on my bed and likely my clothing, if he survived the shock. Or the creature itself."

"Yes, but—"

"And what, Miss Todd, is that around the beast's neck, looping it to the bedpost?"

The cat wore a ribbon, a pink ribbon embroidered with green vines that matched Margaret's eyes, one of her few recent extravagances. She usually wore it in the morning instead of taking the time to put her hair up before walking the dog. "I wondered where that had gone to."

He answered his own question. "The beast is wearing your hair ribbon."

Now Margaret stopped wondering about the exotic animal, or how her ribbon got on it. She could only marvel that his lordship had noticed what she wore in her hair. He had hardly poked his nose out of his rooms, except for the minutes he spent with her in the kitchen for nightly application of the salve. He had been polite and pleasant and distant, unlike this morning, when he was rude, overbearing . . . and standing altogether too close for her comfort.

"And what does the note say?"

The note? Margaret was breathing in Lord Wolfram's spicy scent. She stepped forward with trepidation. It was a very large cat, bigger than any she had seen outside the Tower menagerie. Its yellow eyes were half shut now, as if it had lost interest in the newcomers, and it had not moved, but Margaret was used to the nasty pug. She was not taking chances. Gingerly she reached out for a piece of vellum propped at the foot of the bed.

Turning the paper this way, then that, she finally read, "To Lord Wolf, a small token of appreciation. Margaret Todd." She let out a nervous giggle. "Surely you do not think that I—"

"Not if you are managing Lady Bartlett's correspondence, not with that handwriting. We both know who is responsible. Your angels, whom you promised to keep out of my sight and my way! What is the meaning of this?"

Margaret could not imagine. But she would go find out.

When she returned, she could not meet his lordship's eyes. She did not really need to, for the large, handsome gentleman was bending over the cat on the bed, leaving a lovely view of the back of his form-fitting buckskin breeches. Margaret tried to steady her breathing while she tried to decide what to tell the viscount about the creature's arrival with her name on its calling card. She was certainly not about to tell him the truth.

Her darling nieces were playing matchmaker, for heaven's sake.

"But you like Lord Wolf, don't you?" they had asked when she demanded an explanation. "We want him to like you, too."

There would be more words about their behavior later, and their unrealistic expectations. For now, she had to make Lord Wolfram understand without embarrassing both of them.

"You see, the children knew they were not supposed to bother you, or come near your rooms."

"Hah!"

"So they used my name." For which Margaret would strangle the little dears. "But they were so thankful that you permitted them to stay on here that they wanted to please you. With no money or particular talents to create a token of their regard for you, they struggled to find a way to express their gratitude. And they did have a brilliant notion, actually."

The big cat was actually purring. His lordship was stroking it behind its dark ears. He slowly, carefully, sat down on the mattress rather than staying bent over, to Margaret's disappointment. At least now she could concentrate on her explanation. "You see, they worried that you were spending too much time indoors, and might be growing bored."

Actually, the viscount had been enjoying his solitude. He had not spent so much time alone in ages, and appreciated not having to run from dinner party to dance, from ball to boudoir. His own thoughts were more enjoyable than the tedious social drivel he heard so often. The few minutes of Miss Todd's ministrations were more satisfying than any mistress's touch. With his valet still out of town, taking a detour to visit his family, Wolf did not even have to wear tight, confining apparel or change his clothing thrice a day. The few servants were treating him like a king to win back his favor, and the day cook's offerings were ample and satisfying without all the sauces and stupor-inducing courses. The house was looking festive, more so every day, and the cold, rainy weather outside the windows made his own hearth still more inviting. Wolf was reacquainting himself with his books and his music, recalling the simpler pleasures he used to enjoy.

He frowned. "What, did they think a lion would enliven my days?"

"The animal is a young Punjabi hunting cat, and is

quite tame." Its rumbling purr could be heard across the room. "It was hand-reared and belongs to Prince Qu'inn, who traveled to England on the *Belizar* with the girls to attend university. The prince will take My-lo to Oxford after the holidays, but he thought the cat would be happier in a house than in a cage at his hotel. I think the hotel staff would be happier also, and the prince, who mentioned escaping his tutors in London. Prince Qu'inn was grateful to the girls for improving his English during the long voyage, so was glad to grant their request, especially since it matched his own inclinations so conveniently. Oh, and you will not have to worry about feeding or exercising My-lo, for its, um, native handler moved into an empty stall in your stable mews."

"So I get the feline and a foreigner for a month, in addition to your nieces? Does no one ask permission to invade a man's home? Botheration, what is next, a dancing bear knocking on my door?"

Margaret ignored his sarcasm. "The children meant well." And she meant to send the brats to Hades! Their mother had been a conniver, too, Margaret recalled, too late.

"They meant well for me or for the prince? By the way, what does My-lo hunt? Just so I know, of course. Servants, elephants, small children?"

"Birds, the children thought. So he should be safe in the park. On a leash."

"I am supposed to take a member of some royal menagerie to the park?"

"That was what the girls were hoping, yes." Before the viscount could comment on that harebrained notion, she quickly added, "Which is not so terrible an idea. If you are seen with the cat, people will suppose My-lo scratched you, not some . . ." She paused. "That is, you will not have to stay inside until the wounds heal."

Now that was indeed a brilliant idea.

* * *

They all went to the park as soon as the rain ended. Wolf did not choose the fenced-in area across the street, either, but Hyde Park, where the *ton* went to see and be seen, even with most of polite Society away at country homes. Wolf held My-lo close on the leash, to protect the park's pigeons, while Alexandra and Katherine walked slightly behind, holding their aunt's hands. Wolf raised his hat and bowed to several matrons, and introduced an old friend of his mother's to his party.

"My neighbor, Lady Bartlett's companion," he said, without revealing that Margaret no longer resided under her employer's roof. "Miss Margaret Todd and her nieces, and their royal but unreliable friend, My-lo." He touched his cheek, sending his tale out to the gossip mills for grinding.

Next met on the path—which was quickly emptied of squirrels, lapdogs and toddlers on leading strings—was Lord Salter, who fancied himself a wit. The man rudely inspected Wolf and his companions through his quizzing glass, then drawled, "My, what a charmingly domestic scene."

Wolf again touched the healing wounds on his face, then nodded toward the cat. With at least two or three meanings to his words, he said, "Still untamed, old chap. Still untamed." He led Miss Todd and the girls in another direction, away from speculation, delighted with the success of his mission and his miniature Machiavellis.

He was so pleased, in fact, and feeling such a new-found freedom from his exile, from his embarrassment, that he invited them all—except the cat and its Hindustani handler—to Gunter's for ices.

The children were delighted. They were also well behaved and adorable, Wolf thought, in their sweet giggles and new red capes. They should always be laughing, and they should have fur linings, he idly considered while they debated between raspberry and strawberry confections. The English climate would be far cooler than they were accustomed to. He would ask Mrs. Olive to see about it, as a Christmas gift.

Miss Todd ought to have fur, too, and jewels, he decided, although her pert little nose was shining brightly from the cold. Her wavy brown hair was tucked under a plain, limp bonnet, and her severe gray gown was worn at the cuffs. No matter. Wolf recalled her long flowing tresses and her appealing curves from watching her in the mornings exercising the pug next door. He imagined her in silks and satins, then out of them. His smile was not for the pastry on his plate, although that was one of his favorites.

The smile faded. Of course he could not buy the woman a new wardrobe, or an emerald brooch to go with her eyes. His warm thoughts were due to the hot tea, that was all, and his recent celibacy. Miss Margaret Todd was not mistress material. She was a gentlewoman, in respectable service, devoted to her new family. In fact, she was so good with the little girls, she ought to have babies at her breast, a loving husband at her side and a home of her own to bedeck for Christmas.

Those thoughts would not do, either.

Now that he could, Wolf decided to go to his clubs. Distance would remove the proper Miss Todd from his mind, and from his improper desires.

The little girls needed a new plan. Their last one had succeeded too well. How was Lord Wolfram going to fall in love with Aunt Maggie if he was never home? He was halfway smitten, they knew, because he looked at her whenever he could, but walks in the park with a cat on a leash were not going to bring the two closer. As for their aunt, she blushed whenever his lordship was near or his name was mentioned. She took to putting a sprig of holly in her hair, a dab of perfume at her wrists, a tuck in the neckline of her gown, and herself in the hallway when Lord Wolfram was heard stirring. Still, she insisted that their matchmaking was absurd and must cease henceforth. A viscount marrying a lady's companion? When pigs flew!

If an English peer could parade a Punjabi cat through the park, anything was possible. Alexandra and Katherine consulted the courtship guide. Then they picked a bouquet.

Chapter Four

Flowers are always a suitable gift when a gentle-man goes courting. Who does not like a bouquet, except those who sneeze at roses? Be it a small posy of violets or an armful of exotic blooms, flowers bring the hint of spring, the glory of na-ture, and yes, a reminder of the temporality of every living thing, so do not delay in your wooing. However, if you are contemplating the more fra-grant blossoms because the object of your af-fections is less than fastidious in her personal hygiene, perhaps reconsider your haste, and your choice.
—George E. Phelber, *A Gentleman's Guide to Courtship*

Ah, the glee in the nursery. Their new plan was working. Lord Wolfram had asked Aunt Maggie to have dinner with him that night.

Ah, the primping in Miss Todd's bedchamber. Mrs. Olive, Dora and the two girls all wanted to make Margaret into something she was not: a fashionable lady, the sort his lordship escorted to balls, to be mentioned in the *on dits* columns come morning.

Margaret had to laugh at her helpers. Her prettiest evening gown, a peach-colored velvet, was years out of style. Her thick wavy hair could only be arranged in staid plaited coils on top of her head or at the back of her neck, unless she was going to cut it, which she had no intention of doing. She had nothing but pearls for adornment, and her gloves had been darned. She was never going to be a diamond, only a slightly polished pebble.

This was merely a courtesy invitation from her host, anyway, Margaret told the others, and reminded herself. He was most likely tired of eating alone. Still, she did pinch color into her cheeks and she did tug her neckline a tiny bit lower.

She was glad she had, for his lordship was magnificent in evening dress. The dark blue of his coat made his blue eyes that much brighter, and the perfect fit made his shoulders that much broader. His neckcloth was a masterpiece; his valet had returned. Wolf was altogether a work of art—and Margaret tried to frame the image in her mind, for viewing after New Year's when she would never see him again.

Ah, the effort it cost Wolf not to stroke the velvet, taste the peach, uncoil the topknot of her hair so it flowed over her shoulders and down her back, through his fingers that ached to touch. She looked lovely gliding into his parlor, as if she belonged there, belonged to him.

She did not. This was no seduction, nor even a social event. This was a farewell, Wolf reminded himself, unless Miss Todd had a convincing argument. He simply could not have his life turned upside down by a paid companion and her kin. He would pay for their lodgings at a respectable hotel if he had to, but they would be gone by morning, along with the cat who had attacked Dora and her feather duster.

Wolf led his problem—his guest—into the dining room and seated her at his side.

"Your aunt does not join us?" Margaret asked, noting the two places at the long mahogany table. She started to rise, to leave. Dining *a deux* felt more improper than staying in his house, away in the nursery with the children. Lord Wolfram had to know how such intimacy appeared. He was a womanizer, but Margaret had not suspected him of such warm familiarity toward a respectable woman living under his roof. He could not be harboring evil intentions! He would not!

He did not. He did grasp her hand to pull her back to her chair.

"Stay. I wish to speak with you. My aunt usually has her meals on a tray in her bedchamber. I believe the stairs affect her joints. I could have requested her presence, but this is a personal matter."

Margaret could think of only one topic that needed such privacy. Her spirits sank while Phillip filled her wineglass. If Lord Wolfram was going to proposition her, offer his protection in return for her favors, she would have to leave. Not even for the children's sake could she remain in a house where she was considered no better than she had to be.

She had thought better of Wolf. Margaret raised her spoon, but did not even taste the soup Phillip served. Fear, doubt and sorrow stole her appetite.

His question, when Phillip left, stole her wits. "Are you acquainted with Colonel Brookstone?"

Confused but relieved, Margaret swallowed a spoonful of soup. "I never heard of the man."

"He is a recently retired army officer, just back from India."

"India? Recently?" Margaret had another mouthful. "On the *Belizar*."

She set her spoon down, her stomach suddenly rebelling at the taste and the trend of the conversation. Perhaps a dishonorable offer would be preferable.

"Yes, he returned to England on the same long, arduous voyage as your nieces. The colonel was quite busy on the trip, it seems, for he brought back with him a collection of rare, valuable plants seldom seen at his horticultural society. He had been in constant correspondence with his fellow members, who encouraged him to bring what he could for their observation, and advised him on how to keep the plants alive and thriving. Why, he would carry them onto the deck on sunny days, and he gathered his own rainwater to keep them moist. Your nieces helped."

"How lovely of them." At the mention of her nieces, Margaret wondered if it was possible to drown oneself in a bowl of soup.

"Colonel Brookstone thought so. And he thought their visit to his daughter's town house this morning was polite and charming."

Perhaps she ought to try the wine. "This morning? Impossible. The girls were at lessons while I attended Lady Bartlett."

He raised one golden eyebrow.

Margaret raised her wineglass. "Never tell me they went traipsing through London on their own! They promised me they would not."

Wolf waved one elegant hand, the light glinting off his signet ring. "The colonel's daughter lives directly across the square. They were in no danger. Then."

Phillip brought the next course and laid a small fish across each of their plates.

"The colonel came to visit me," Wolf said when the servant left.

Margaret thought she knew how the poor fish felt.

"The colonel was distraught. His best blooms had gone missing, cut off the plants a week before his presentation to the horticultural society. I naturally and honestly denied knowing anything about any flowers, and vehemently swore to the colonel that your nieces, my houseguests, children assumed to be my wards by most of London, were blameless. They are angels, are they not?"

"Most of the time."

"Today was not one of those times. When I went upstairs after the colonel's visit, I found a bouquet on my bed."

Margaret could not look the cooked fish in its one eye, or the viscount in his accusatory blue ones, so she studied the centerpiece, a pretty floral arrangement . . . of unusual flowers she could not identify. "This bouquet?"

"The very one. Odd, I never knew my valet enjoyed arranging flowers. He spent quite an hour achieving just the right effect, but then Paul has always been a perfectionist." Wolf touched his snowy white neckcloth, which was a marvel of intricate folds and creases.

"How . . . interesting."

"Yes, but not as interesting as the note attached to the bouquet." Wolf handed her a card, one of his own. "Turn it over."

On the back was written, TRUELY YOURS, MISS MARGARET TODD.

"What do you have to say about that?"

"That they should have been at their lessons, learning to spell 'truly.' "

"Miss Todd, I have never claimed to understand women or children. But this goes beyond mere incomprehension. Your brats escaped the house without permission, decimated a gentleman's greenhouse and forged your signature. Why?"

Margaret had to confess. She just did not have to say it loudly enough for Lord Wolfram to hear.

"I beg your pardon, could you say that again?"

Margaret took her napkin away from her mouth. "They want you to like me."

"But I do. I admire you greatly, surely they know that. I allowed you to stay on at Wolfram House because of your devotion to duty, your serious, intelligent nature and your competence. Anyone who feels loyalty toward Lady Bartlett must be a saint. And I do know how hard you work, which is totally unnecessary, as I have told you, trying to make my home more comfortable for me. If I have not expressed myself to you or the children, I am sorry."

Embarrassed at his praise, Margaret only whispered that she liked to feel useful, and that he was the one who deserved their gratitude and apologies.

Wolf was not finished. "You are calm in an emergency, restful to be around, soft-spoken and well-read. And lovely to look at, of course."

Ignoring the last, lest she turn the color of her peach gown, Margaret said, "I am the perfect lady's companion, in other words. Unfortunately, my nieces hope to make a match."

"They are too young. There is plenty of time to worry about your social position and their futures when they are ready to be presented."

"You do not understand. They wish to make a match for me. Now. With you."

Wolf's fork hit the floor. His feet almost did too, running. With effort, he stayed in his seat. "Damn."

"Damn, indeed," Margaret boldly echoed.

Wolf thought a moment, then asked, "They wished to win a wedding proposal by stealing flowers?"

"I am not altogether sure about the reasoning behind the flowers, except they are eager to please you. They desperately want to stay here with you. And they also want to stay with me. Regrettably, your aunt does not seem to require a lady's companion, which would have been an obvious solution. Besides, that is not a permanent enough answer for children who have been so uprooted. Your aunt could die—I apologize for the bluntness—or move to a cottage in the country, or you could find a replacement. A companion can be dismissed. A wife cannot. Katherine and Alexandra have their hearts set on our marriage."

"That is absurd."

"Absurd," she agreed.

Both of them were suddenly very busy cutting their meat served next, piling their peas, straightening the silverware.

"Is it?"

"Is it what, my lord?"

"Is the idea of a match between us so absurd?"

Margaret took a deep breath, taking a moment to think, as if she had not thought about anything else in days. "Of course it is. You can pick your wife from the highest families in the land, acceptable in your social circles. Your viscountess must be a woman who brings a huge dowry or acres of land or political advancement, if that is what you wish. All I bring are two possibly penniless orphans."

"And a borrowed hunting cat."

"And an irate retired army officer."

"Do not forget Lady Bartlett's ire."

She nodded. "Furthermore, I would never marry a gentleman with such a roguish reputation as yours, not even to secure my future or my nieces'. That way lies heartbreak for all of us. I would be miserable with an unfaithful husband, and you would be wretched with a jealous wife."

"So it is a silly, childish notion?" he asked, smiling.

"Yes," she said, not smiling, because he had so readily agreed with her. He might have argued a little bit!

Instead, he refilled his wineglass, and hers, his hand brushing her arm. "But if we were equal, and I not a rake, would you consider a proposal from me?"

If he touched her again, or flashed that smile, she might consider the primrose path after all. Margaret sipped her wine and considered. "If you were a clerk or a tutor or a vicar, say? Who promised to be true to his vows?"

He nodded.

"Then, yes, I would carefully consider your suit.

And what if I were a well-dowered debutante or a duke's daughter? Would you offer for me?"

He smiled again, showing dimples. "In an instant. I would be trampling all your other swains to seek your hand first. I would challenge any beau who stood in my way, especially a clerk or a tutor or a vicar."

"Ridiculous."

"Ridiculous," he agreed, but his smile faded at the thought of some clerk or tutor or vicar—realistic matches for a lady's companion—carrying her off. He waved away the footman with his tray of ashes and chaff. Apples and cheese, that was. When Phillip left, Wolf asked—and was angry at himself for doing so— "You do like me?"

Now she laughed. "What female would not?" He was so handsome Greek gods paled in comparison, although Margaret would not say so. "You are charming and generous, kind to animals and small children and elderly relations. I have seen how diligent you are about your estate duties, and your servants adore you, which is high recommendation indeed. You are chivalrous, not only rescuing us but keeping the colonel from retribution. You have a wonderful sense of humor." And a glorious smile that warmed her from her head to her toes, with a stop and a stay at her heart. Like him? Margaret liked his lordship all too well. She rose from her chair, forcing him to rise also. The dinner was over. "And there is always your title and your fortune."

Wolf set his napkin on the table. "I am not fond of the idea of being wed for my fortune."

"I doubt those debutantes are, either, my lord. Perhaps you should consider that when you finally decide to go courting."

"It would seem I have a great deal to consider."

"And I shall consider a just punishment for the flower-nappers, and how I am to make restitution to the colonel."

"Do not bother with that. His bouquet will be returned this evening, and I have asked his horticultural society to move their meeting forward to tomorrow afternoon, so they might all see the blooms. It will not be quite what the colonel had envisioned, but now the collectors will have funds for a small conservatory of their own."

"You did that? For us?"

Wolf shrugged. "It is Christmas. I could not see visiting your imps in Newgate over the holidays."

Before she could think, Margaret stood on tiptoe and kissed Wolf's cheek, then ran for the stairs. "I *do* like you, sir."

First Margaret closed her nieces in their bedroom, for a month, she swore. Then she lectured them on almost all of the Ten Commandments: lying, stealing, coveting, and dishonoring their parents—or their guardians, as the case might be. They had incited to blasphemy and possible murder—their own at Lord Wolf's hands—to say nothing of adultery, which last Margaret did not say, naturally.

Then she locked herself in her own room and cried herself to sleep.

Her nieces made gingerbread.

Chapter Five

In addition to flowers, sweets are suitable for a gentleman to bring when he goes courting. Sweets for your sweetheart, confections to convince her of your worth, comfits to convey your intentions, bonbons to win a bonny bride. Best of all, a mannerly female is bound to share.

—George E. Phelber, *A Gentleman's Guide to Courtship*

Wolf awoke to the smell of Christmas. If his memories of holidays past had an aroma, it was that of gingerbread. The scent pervading his house and his bedroom reminded him of his childhood, when holidays were always spent at Wolfram Hall in the north. His parents and his sisters would all be at home, along with all the friends and neighbors for miles around coming to help celebrate and decorate. The nursery was full of cousins and schoolmates, all excited by the games and surprises and promised treats. Everyone hoped for snow and finding a charm in a cake or a package with one's name on it. There was love and joy and anticipation in the air.

Wolf had not known that feeling in years. He'd thought it was for children, outgrown by adults who took their pleasures more seriously.

But gingerbread brought it all back. The spirit of Christmas was alive and in his own house, by Jupiter.

After the holiday came a new year and new possibilities, perhaps a few surprises. No, definitely a few surprises.

Wolf smiled, eager to start the day. Then he laughed out loud when he realized that he was indeed looking forward to another day of Miss Todd and her nieces, and the chaos they brought to his all-too-organized life.

Last night he'd decided to take up his old ways, now that the scratches on his face were not so raw and the gossip was not so personal. Back in his own milieu he could get his houseguest out of his mind, and out of his dreams.

First he'd gone to his club, thinking that if cards and conversation did not work, he could drown Miss Todd—the aching for her, anyway—in drink. Even with most of the gentlemen away at their country estates or house parties, the stench of cigars and unwashed linen still draped the rooms like a shroud. The pasteboards held no interest, and his fellow members had nothing new to say.

Wolf ordered a bottle of brandy, not a glass. Then he recalled that he had children at his house. He could not be staggering home at dawn, unshaved, unsteady. What if he met Miss Todd walking Lady Bartlett's dog?

He left the club and went to the weekly musical gathering at his friend Montague's. The soprano was too shrill, the chairs too hard, the room too warm. The listeners ought to be singing Christmas carols, anyway, instead of trying to hide their yawns. He reminded himself to tell Miss Todd that she could use his music room any time she wished.

The ball he attended next was full of silly twits and their self-serving sisters. All of the most attractive females must have gone to the country, Wolf decided. The ones who stayed used too much perfume, bared too much bony chest or bovine bosom. And they simpered at everything he said. Bah! None of them could hold a candle to Miss Todd.

He thought of going to a house of convenience or visiting one of his former mistresses. That would take care of those unwarranted and unworthy urges toward his houseguest. His head was convinced she was beyond his reach, off limits, but his body was still lusting. It was not lusting for a light skirt, though. Try as he might, he could not stir any enthusiasm for a paid companion—other than Lady Bartlett's, Miss Todd, Margaret, Maggie. Damnation, the only woman he wanted was the one he could not have.

He'd gone home and thought about her all night. And decided he just might be wrong, for once.

After their conversation at dinner, he thought they understood each other. A long night had told him he did not even understand himself. This morning everything was changed.

Christmas was in the air, along with the smell of gingerbread. He sniffed. Perhaps a batch was burned around the edges. No matter. And no matter that he and Miss Todd had politely agreed that there would be no expectations, thus no disappointments. Wolf had expectations aplenty, and refused to be disappointed again. He hurried through his dressing, not bothering to ring for his valet.

He had supposed the gingerbread would be served at tea, along with clotted cream. Instead, there it was on his plate at the breakfast-room table, and not a slice of cake, either. A large, lumpy gingerbread man, all decorated with currant eyes and icing mouth, smiled up at him. One of the chap's arms was longer than the other, and the feet had been too close to the fire, so it appeared he wore boots. Wolf thought he was handsome—too handsome to eat, although the viscount was hungry, having left most of his dinner last night.

Nothing else arrived. Phillip did not bring his eggs,

toast or coffee. Wolf broke off a tiny bit of the ginger-bread man's longer arm to eat while he waited. And waited.

"Phillip? Mrs. Olive?" No one answered. No one brought a muffin or a rasher of bacon. What, did they expect him to eat a gingerbread man for breakfast? He started to do that very thing, lifting the pastry, only to find a card underneath.

YRS., MT, it said. He was not surprised. The girls, of course. Wolf thought he might enlist the infant intrigu-ers to his cause, after he lectured them about forgery, naturally, and interfering in the affairs of their elders. They would be able allies, he knew. But were they able cooks? He looked at the gingerbread man, and then he looked at his bare table and empty sideboard. The pang he felt was no longer hunger.

He went to the kitchen.

He would be getting no breakfast this day. No din-ner, either, it seemed, for Cook had taken one look at her domain and given notice. Mrs. Olive was uncon-scious in the corner of the kitchen, while the Indian animal-trainer fanned her with a skillet. Phillip had his arms around Dora, who was weeping. Or maybe that was the smoke in her eyes. Wolf could barely make out the form of My-lo, lapping something off the floor.

A band of marauders must have invaded the prem-ises, flinging pots and pans to the ground, spilling every sack in the pantry, looking for treasure . . . or cooking gingerbread. Every surface was sticky, includ-ing the floor, except the areas encrusted with burnt batter. A bowl was broken, a knife was stuck in the table, flour dusted it all.

"MISS TODD!"

Being a mother was a great deal harder than being a hired companion. If her position turned untenable, a companion could leave. She could take her chances on another position, or another type of work. She could even throw herself on the mercy of her relatives, if she had any. A parent—or aunt, in this case—could not quit.

Margaret could not leave the children, so she could not leave Lord Wolfram's household, no matter that it was the wisest course. Her precious nieces would be miserable in the tiny rooms Margaret could afford, with no servants or luxuries.

Margaret was miserable now. She even thought, as she dragged Lady Bartlett's fat pug through the park, that she would be happier if she had fewer scruples. Then she could be Wolf's mistress. She knew he wanted her, and she knew he made her feel wantings she had never supposed, in places she had only suspected. She was five-and-twenty, and this was the first time she had ever wished she were not her mother's daughter. Someone else's child would have chosen a more lucrative means of support, and someone else's daughter would have taken Wolf's unspoken invitation. He could not marry her, but he could offer her a life of ease, in a small house away from Mayfair, or in the country. She would have a carriage of her own, an allowance, credit at the shops, and the company of the most attractive, appealing gentleman in all of London.

Margaret's mother was a lady, though, and Margaret was born and bred in her image and moral understanding. She carried her mother's legacy in her narrow, proper, righteous veins. She carried her sister's legacy on her shoulders. How could she think of becoming Wolf's mistress when the dear girls needed her? Margaret could never bring her nieces into a house of ill repute, even if she owned that house and was its sole resident.

Besides, the viscount would have to marry eventually. He would have children of his own, and Margaret and the girls would be sloughed off, as a snake's skin was shed. They would all be heartbroken—and in worse straits than they were now. Now only Margaret's heart was aching.

They ought to leave. The solicitor's return was too far away for her to batten on Lord Wolfram so long, or to tempt the fates and Margaret's tenets so badly. Her reputation would suffer, if nothing else. Her employment with Lady Bartlett was already in jeopardy, as that old crab grew more petulant by the day, left to her own—unpleasant—company so much. Margaret took it upon herself to add a line to a letter to her employer's ne'er-do-well nephew, suggesting a visit. Perhaps that would relieve the lady's boredom, for she could rip up at the nephew for hours, then revile his profligate ways for days after.

If Lady Bartlett could have found a cheaper replacement, Margaret was sure, and at no effort on her part, she would have sent Margaret to the devil, without references or a Christmas bonus. Not that Margaret expected much, not from the cheeseparing baroness, but every farthing would help.

For now, Margaret thought her part-time position was safe, at least until she finished hemming the Christmas handkerchiefs for Lady Bartlett's staff. The old woman would not want to finish them herself, or pay a seamstress for the work.

Of course, if word got out that Miss Todd was having private dinners with Lord Wolf, if gossip made the rounds that Margaret was residing under a rake's roof without proper chaperonage, Lady Bartlett would have no choice but to dismiss her companion. Then Margaret might as well be Wolf's mistress, for no one would believe otherwise.

She should leave. The girls were looking forward to Christmas at Wolfram House, though, and Margaret could not bear to disappoint them. As it was, their new warm capes had taken too much of her savings for her to afford lavish gifts, but she was secretly sew-

ing new frocks and matching doll clothes. There would
be a feast, Margaret was certain, and caroling and
good English traditions they ought to experience.
Then they really ought to be here on Boxing Day, to
give presents to Lord Wolfram's small staff in return
for their friendly, caring service. New Year's came
soon after, and then the solicitor would be back in
Town, with their fate and fortune in his hands.

Resolved if not happy, Margaret brought Charlie
the pug back to Bartlett House and went home, without pondering why she considered Lord Wolfram's
house home, instead of the place where she had resided these past six years. She was staying, that was
all that mattered.

Heavens, she should have left! For that matter, she
and her nieces would be leaving in an instant, from
the fury in his lordship's voice. This time Margaret
did not immediately suppose calamity had befallen her
little angels, but she raced up the stairs anyway, to
check. There they were, asleep in their narrow beds,
looking like cherubs. She tucked the covers more carefully around them before returning below to see what
had Lord Wolfram in such a state.

"You took your blasted time," was all he said.

Maybe she would not be so heartbroken after all,
Margaret decided, if he was as curmudgeonly in the
morning as Lady Bartlett.

"Your nieces made me a gingerbread man," was
all he said as he led her toward the service stairs, to
the kitchen.

Margaret sighed. "I suppose they signed my name
to it. I will have another talk with— Good grief.
What happened?"

"Your nieces, ma'am. Your nieces."

As punishment, Margaret made the girls clean the
kitchen, with no breakfast. Everyone helped, though,
including Margaret and his lordship, so soon the chore

was more like a party, with carols and laughter and cups of chocolate to make the task go faster.

When they were done, the kitchen and pantry nearly restored to Cook's standards, Wolf wanted to take Margaret and the girls out to a coffeehouse for a hearty meal.

"That would be a reward, not a penance," Margaret insisted. "How are they to learn from their misdeeds?"

So Wolf drove them first to where Cook and her sons lived, to apologize and beg her to come back. The children's apology was sweet and heartfelt. Wolf's gold coins were twice as effective.

Margaret made sure her nieces noticed Cook's tiny flat in a boarding house that smelled of cabbage, down a narrow, litter-filled street. They could be forced into such lodgings, her look told them, if they continued to wreak havoc on Lord Wolfram's house.

For good measure, she asked Wolf to drive them to an orphanage, where she made the girls deliver the rest of the gingerbread men. She made her point. Wolf made a generous donation, and said, "Good. Now we can put that behind us. What about luncheon?"

Margaret had to get back to complete Lady Bartlett's correspondence, though. And her nieces had lessons. She also refused his offer of dinner at a hotel, a visit to the theater or the opera, or a drive in the park.

"People will talk," was all she said.

So the children found her a chaperone.

Chapter Six

When a gentleman goes courting a young lady, he must remember that he is also courting her family. Their opinion will influence her choice of husband, so he must convince them not only that he is capable of adequately supporting their daughter; he must also show he can make her and them happy.

As often noted, a suitor is not merely marrying his chosen bride, he is also marrying her family. A husband can choose to keep his wife apart from his interfering in-laws, money-borrowing brothers, spinster sisters, and grumpy grandparents. Such a course, however, is bound to upset a sensitive young gentlewoman—and lessen the chances of any inheritance. Being kind to the relatives is a better bet.

—George E. Phelber, *A Gentleman's Guide to Courtship*

"Oh, dear. I am dreadfully sorry, but I cannot." Margaret stopped pouring the tea. "Chocolate, perhaps?" she offered her unexpected guest in the nursery sitting room.

"Tea is perfect. Especially in the winter, I always say. And the afternoon. And I do enjoy a cup before bedtime."

"Then you cannot have another macaroon?"

"Oh, no. They are my favorites," the white-haired old woman said, quickly selecting another from the dish before Margaret could set it aside. "I cannot . . . That is, I would if I could," she said, looking nervously over her shoulder and at the door.

Thinking the elderly lady might be fearful of the big cat, Margaret reassured her. "My-lo is out with my nieces."

"I know, that is why I came. I thought his name was John, though, not Milo."

Gracious, the viscount's aunt was daft. That was why he kept her shut up in her rooms. Slowly and softly, Margaret said, "Lord Wolfram's name is John, although everyone calls him Wolf, I understand. My-lo is the cat. They all went for a walk, the girls, his lordship, and My-lo's handler."

"I do love cats," Mrs. Bolton said, suddenly dabbing at her eyes with a lace-edged handkerchief. "I miss my little friends."

Margaret doubted the hunting cat was what she had in mind. "I am sure your nephew would not care if you kept a kitten in your rooms. He seems fond of animals."

"Oh, I could never ask. And now, when the dear girls ask me for a favor, I have to be so disobliging. It is quite distressing, I swear."

Margaret could see that it was, from the tears falling down the lined cheeks. She wished someone else were around, to tell her how to deal with the anxious, attics-to-let auntie. Then she realized what Mrs. Bolton had said. "You know my nieces?" Until this afternoon, Margaret had never met the viscount's Great-Aunt Glorianna. When she had scratched on the door the day they all moved in, a whispery voice called back that she was suffering the headache and could not be disturbed, ever. "I told them not to bother you! I am so sorry."

"Oh, no, they are no bother. I quite enjoy their

company, you know, and all their tales of India. I am teaching them whist and they have taught me spillikins." She leaned forward, lest her reedy voice be overheard. "I think the younger gal cheats. That is why I owe them the favor. I lost, you see."

Margaret saw nothing but red. Her darlings disobeying again? Gambling? Cheating a poor addled old lady? "I shall repay whatever they won."

"Oh, we do not play for money. And they already owe me an hour of sorting my embroidery threads, my eyes not being what they used to be, you know. This time I promised to act as your chaperone so you could attend the theater and the opera and dinners and perhaps"— she sniffled—"a ball or two with Lord Wolfram. But I cannot."

"Would you not enjoy getting out?" The entertainments sounded all too inviting to Margaret. She had attended the theater and the opera a few times with Lady Bartlett, but that woman was too frugal to keep a box of her own, and only went when someone else invited her. Seldom was the invitation extended to the lady's companion. As for the handful of balls Lady Bartlett chose to grace with her presence, Margaret had to stand beside her employer's chair, ready to fetch refreshments, warmer wraps, or a fan, while Lady Bartlett gossiped with her cronies. To go to a ball as a guest was beyond her hopes. To go with Wolf was beyond her dreams. To go because he actually wanted to take her was beyond wonderful! "I must admit the notion is appealing to me." Which might have been the biggest understatement of Margaret's life.

Mrs. Bolton blew her nose. "I know. And the children want you to get out to enjoy yourself, but it is impossible."

Margaret knew of an old woman back in her parish who was afraid to leave her house. Perhaps the viscount's aunt suffered a similar affliction. No, she did sit in the rear garden, Mrs. Olive had said. Either way, Margaret would not upset the overwrought woman further. "Think nothing of it. My nieces have a silly idea that his lordship and I— That is, a mere companion has no need for a chaperone, and no excuse to be jaunting about Town."

"Oh, but it is an excellent idea, and just the thing. Straight out of one of my Minerva Press novels. And I would help, I swear. But I cannot," Mrs. Bolton ended on a wail.

"But why not? Perhaps I can help overcome your fears. Or is it that you do not have proper attire? Neither do I, so we could be unfashionable together. Or that you do not have a circle of acquaintances? I assure you, your nephew knows everyone and can introduce us. If you are shy of crowds, I would stay by you. I am used to that, with Lady Bartlett."

The mention of Margaret's employer made Great-Aunt Glorianna wail louder. "None of that matters a whit."

"Then why will you not come out for rides or walks in the park or ices at Gunter's? Why will you not let Lord Wolfram escort us to all the entertainments London offers? Please tell me, so I understand."

"You cannot understand. How could you know of fear and poverty and having nowhere to turn?"

Margaret understood all too well the concerns of a woman on her own without funds. Granted she was young and healthy, but she knew the dread of a desolate future as well as Glorianna Bolton. "But you have your nephew to look after you."

"I am not his aunt!"

"His great-aunt, then."

Not that, either. *Gloria* Bolton, it turned out, was Wolf's great-aunt. His grandfather's sister, she was married to James Bolton, a country gentleman of no particular distinction or property or longevity. He died, leaving Gloria with little income beyond her widow's portion. James also left her his penniless spinster sister, Anna. When Gloria succumbed to an influenza epidemic, Anna was left with absolutely nothing, no home, no money, no family—nothing except the current Lord Wolfram.

With more daring than she had possessed before or since, Anna had sold her gold locket for coach fare and deposited herself and her few belongings on Wolf's doorstep in London. She had claimed to be his great-aunt, Glorianna.

Wolf, bless his kind heart, had taken in an elderly relative he had not seen in decades. He made her welcome, and he made her an allowance. Oh, the shops, the bookstores, the museums—and oh, the people who might recognize Anna Bolton. Why, Anna had gone to school with the gorgon next door, Lady Bartlett, which was why she seldom showed her face outdoors. Someone was bound to recall that James Bolton's wife Gloria was a short little dumpling, while his sister Anna was a tall, thin beanpole of a woman. Besides, Great-Aunt Glorianna felt guilty. She hated spending Wolf's money when he had no obligation to give a groat for her upkeep. She did not like making more work for his servants or disturbing the tenor of his bachelor existence. Let him waste his time with a lying old lady while he could be carousing with his friends? Mrs. Bolton refused his invitations. Take her meals with him? How could she eat, with falsehoods stuck in her throat?

So she stayed in her rooms, which were more spacious than any she had known in her lifetime. Her joints did ache and she was prone to headaches; that was no lie. Mostly, she lived in dread that Wolf would throw her out. She saved every shilling he gave her, for that rainy day she knew was coming. Her . . . gravest fear, though, was being buried under the wrong tombstone. "How will the angels find me if Glorianna is not on St. Peter's list?" she cried. "If they look for me at all, after my sins."

Margaret handed over a fresh handkerchief and agreed to speak to Wolf. The deception had to end, for all their sakes. Interfering in his family matters was nothing Margaret wanted to do, but she was already turning his house upside down. What was one more bit of effrontery? At the worst, she would have one more mouth to feed and house when he threw them all out. How much could an old lady eat, anyway?

She found him in his library after luncheon. His blond hair was mussed and his neckcloth was loosened. He looked wonderful to Margaret, less like the perfect London nonpareil and more like someone who could be a friend to her. His welcoming smile gave her the confidence to sit across from his desk and ask, "Did you know your aunt was afraid of you?"

Wolf sat down again and poured them each a glass of wine. "I swear, I never yelled at her. I believe you are the only woman I have ever shouted at, for which I apologize. I cannot promise never to yell again, considering the brats. That is, the little beauties."

Margaret smiled and accepted his apology graciously. "You had just cause to raise your voice. But about your aunt. She is immensely grateful to you, but she also fears your wrath, you know."

"Is that why she will not come out of her rooms?"

"No, she is more afraid of being revealed as an imposter."

"What, is she one of Napoleon Bonaparte's spies then, hiding out from the War Office in my guest wing?"

"She is not your aunt."

"Of course not."

Margaret almost choked on her sip of wine. "You knew."

"How could I not? The solicitor naturally notified me of Great-Aunt Gloria's death, as a relative, and also since her annuity ended. I did not know of Anna Bolton's existence, since she was not living with her brother the one time I visited. I do not recall if she ever came to Wolfram Hall with my great-aunt and uncle when they came for my father's funeral, or holidays before that. I swear I did not know of her, or I would have made provisions."

"I am sure you would have."

He smiled again, inside and out, that she trusted him to do the right thing. "Then she appeared on my doorstep here in London, and it seemed easier to let the old girl satisfy her pride than take her in as a pauper who was no true relative whatsoever. When she avoided me and the rest of London, I assumed she was simply old and ailing and perhaps grieving for the life she had known. I asked if she would rather go to the country. Wolfram Hall is three times the size of this place and always fully staffed. She refused."

"She was afraid of being recognized there, too."

"By whom? Aunt Gloria had not been to the family seat in ages. She never came to London that I knew of, at least since I came into the title. Besides, after all those years Miss Anna Bolton could not possibly resemble the schoolgirl she might have been. And her friends' memories cannot be all that good, at their age." He sighed. "I did not wish to embarrass the skittish old dear by forcing her into the public eye, and she seemed content to stay in the house."

That was about to change.

Aunt Bolton, as they decided to call her, used her own money to refurbish her wardrobe, and Margaret's too, out of gratitude. She could, now that Wolf had raised her allowance, which he'd done hoping for precisely that outcome. He could not purchase fashionable apparel for Miss Todd without raising eyebrows. His great-aunt could. Wolf also insisted on establishing an annuity for the old lady, so she never had to worry about the future, no matter who was viscount. Aunt Bolton wept, then went shopping.

While her new clothes were being sewn, she went to call on Lady Bartlett, so that the baroness—and her wide circle of gossips—would know that Miss Todd was well chaperoned. That was how she was repaying dear Wolf and Margaret and the children.

To Aunt Bolton's surprise, as well as Margaret's, the two old ladies had a comfortable coze, spending hours reminiscing about their school days and deceased friends, and made plans to meet again and often.

Aunt Bolton also befriended My-lo, once she stopped trying to pick up the big kitty. She went for walks with the children, offered Wolf her novels for his library collection, and helped Margaret with the handkerchief-hemming.

Then she declared them ready to face London society. There was nothing like a new gown to give a woman confidence, she told Margaret. In her new green velvet, Margaret could only agree. She had never owned such a pretty frock, or one so revealing of her bosom. She had never had a generous fairy godmother, either, or such a handsome escort.

Wolf was disappointed. Not in Margaret's bosom—hell, no. He was disappointed there were so few places he could take her. And his great-aunt. Most public entertainments were closed for the holidays or shut for the winter, leaving fewer nights of music or dramatic offerings. He could not take them to Vauxhall, balloon ascensions or fairs because of the weather. Fewer people in town meant fewer balls, not as many dinner parties or Venetian breakfasts. Some of those hostesses were too high in the instep to entertain an unknown old woman or a paid companion or a rake. Others of the party-givers were too low-minded.

Wolf found a few gatherings where his womenfolk

would be welcome and comfortable. He also found that one dance with Miss Todd was not enough, that his fists clenched every time another gentleman approached her and that he could not eat when she was seated far down the dinner table from him. Then again, he could not eat when she was next to him, for staring down the neckline of her new gowns. His hungry gaze kept her safe from other rakes. Her lack of a dowry kept her safe from other gentlemen.

Wolf did not forget the children in the new round of gaiety before Christmas. On a nice day they all drove to Richmond and the maze, where Aunt Bolton got lost. One night they visited Astley's Amphitheatre, where she fell asleep during the trick riding. But she was there, and no one could slander Lady Bartlett's erstwhile companion, who seemed to be working for the viscount's aunt now . . . or working on bringing the Wolf to heel.

The gossips noted that the companion was looking better every day, and that Lord Wolfram was constantly looking at her, for her or after her. Miss Todd was looking at his lordship as if he had hung the moon. Mrs. Bolton was looking at both fondly, and with great care for their reputations. Everyone quickly consulted his or her Debrett's and Lady Bartlett. A baronetcy in Miss Todd's background? Then it was not an entirely ineligible match for the viscount. No money in her family? Then it was a brilliant match for the pretty companion. Luckily Lady Jennifer Camden ran off with her butler that week, so no one cared that the wolf seemed to be in the trap for sure.

The trap was not yet sprung, to the little girls' despair. Their plan was not working, or it was working all too well. Aunt Maggie and Wolf were out and about, enjoying each others' company . . . and Aunt Bolton's. How was Wolf going to ask her to marry him if he never had a private moment? How was Aunt Maggie going to accept if they were never alone?

Alexandra and Katherine skipped the parts in their guide about poems and serenades. Wolf seemed to like Aunt Maggie's singing just fine when they joined in the caroling, and he complimented her playing on the pianoforte, but that was no proposal.

So they ran away from home.

Chapter Seven

The object of a chaperone is to keep a fellow honest. The object of a courtship is to win one's beloved's hand. These two goals are not necessarily complementary. Sometimes a bit of privacy is needed to express your affections. You will also wish to be certain you and your chosen bride suit in character and commonality of goals. Remember, a proposal is irrevocable, marriage is forever, and eternity is a long time to discuss nothing but the weather.

—George E. Phelber, *A Gentleman's Guide to Courtship*

"Miss Todd!" Wolf was waiting in the hall when Margaret returned from listening to Lady Bartlett complain about her nephew, Oscar. The young fribble was expensive, lazy and lacking in sense, but between him and Aunt Bolton, the baroness was too busy to require a new companion.

Margaret did not rush through the door in a panic this time when she heard Wolf's call. For one thing, he was not shouting. For another, the girls were at needlework lessons with Aunt Bolton. Finally, the house was not burning. She doubted Wolf would toss them out for anything less. The question was whether he would keep them after the new year. She'd tried not to think about that question these past days, deciding to enjoy herself while she could. She even warned the girls not to make too much of his lordship's attentions, for he was being polite to a houseguest, Town was thin of company, and she was still a nearly impoverished lady's companion. Fine feathers and flying high did not make her a member of his elite flock. But, oh, how he made her heart soar. No, she was not going to think about that, or how handsome he looked in his dark blue coat and buckskin breeches and gleaming high boots. "Yes, you were looking for me?"

He led her into the Rose Parlor and shut the door. "Margaret," he began again, but changed that to "Maggie." He cleared his throat. "Maggie, I do not know how to tell you, but the girls have disappeared."

"Nonsense. I left them with your aunt."

"She fell asleep. When she awoke, they were gone."

"Then they are in the kitchen bothering Cook, or at the stable annoying your groom."

"We looked there. And in the attics and the cellars and every room between. We searched every corner, the staff and I. I am sorry, my dear, but your nieces are not in the house, nor the garden."

"The cat must have needed a walk."

He shook his head sadly. "No. I was out in the park with My-lo and the handler, watching them train with feather decoys."

Margaret would not cry or swoon or throw herself into his lordship's arms, although the last was tempting. As calmly as she could, she tried to think of places where her poor lost lambs might have wandered. "Perhaps they wished to apologize to the colonel, although I know they were not supposed to visit him."

"That pair does a great many things they are not supposed to. The colonel would not admit them to his house, though, and would likely call the magistrate if they did get in. Either they would be home, or the constables would be calling here."

"Then they went to visit their friend Prince Qu'inn."

"I thought we got the cat because His Highness was going traveling, but I was going to go ask at his hotel anyway as soon as you came in. I did not want you to hear about the disappearance from anyone else, or think I was not doing my best to return the girls to you. I already sent for the curricle."

"I shall go with you."

"My aunt is so distraught that Mrs. Olive gave her laudanum. She cannot accompany us and there is no time now to call out the closed carriage."

"It makes no nevermind if people see me alone with you. What is my reputation compared to finding my nieces? If anyone is so mean-minded as to find fault in such an emergency, then a pox upon them. They are not worthy of my concern. The girls are. You don't think they have been abducted, do you?"

He took her hands and held them between his, trying to ease her fears, "I pity the poor fool who tries. He'd have returned them long since, tossing them back like undersized fish."

"Do you think they are injured, then, and that is why they have not come home?"

"Hurt? I pray not, not before I get my hands on them anyway."

Margaret took her hands back, reluctantly, to retie her bonnet. "After me, if they are merely out playing somewhere."

Wolf brushed her hands aside and tied the bow, then caressed her cheek. "More like playing another of their tricks on us. I am sure of it."

Margaret felt her skin tingle where he had touched. He was merely being sympathetic, she told herself, nothing else. She stepped away. "Do you know, I think I might have been wrong about the girls."

"What, that they are not the perfect angels you imagined them to be? I doubt I have ever met a pair of more mischievous, manipulating brats in my life, and I pray I never do again." They were almost troublesome enough to make a man reconsider his plans for the future.

"Could that be why my sister sent them away with nothing but nannies and servants? I have been wondering about that, a mother parting from her babies."

"The girls are not babies, being all of what? Eight and ten? Women regularly send their youngsters off to school at that age. Furthermore, I understand most of the prosperous English in India do retreat to the mountains in the summer. Your sister saved her children's lives. So I can strangle them."

Margaret smiled, as he'd intended. "They are only children."

"And no worse than I was as a boy, I suppose, although my illicit adventures usually included big horses and broken bones. I merely hate to see you so distressed."

As if Wolf weren't. Lud, anything could happen to two innocents in London. But Maggie was being brave, so he had to be. Wolf wanted to take her in his arms for comfort—hers and his—but the curricle was brought to the front door just then. Leaving instructions and an itinerary with his man Paul, Wolf helped Margaret onto the carriage and set off.

First they stopped at the colonel's daughter's house, because it was closest. As suspected, no one had seen the children. The butler was under instructions not to admit them, but looked in the greenhouse anyway. Nothing was missing, which meant the girls had not paid a call.

The prince had left the hotel days before.

The guard at the Royal Menagerie knew the children well from their recent visits and pestilential questions, but he had not seen them that day.

No one in Hyde Park recalled two little girls in red

capes. No one at Gunter's had served them. Wolf was running out of places to look.

"I know you gave them money to purchase Christmas gifts. Perhaps they went shopping on Bond Street?"

So Wolf drove up and down, asking acquaintances—and stirring the scandal broth by having a pretty, windblown woman up beside him. Neither of them cared.

Margaret could not help noticing the unkempt ruffians on the streets, the former soldiers begging for alms, the shifty-eyed women. Any one of them could have recognized an opportunity in two prosperous-looking little girls.

She shivered.

"Are you cold?"

She was chilled to the bone by her dire thoughts. "Maybe we should go home in case there is a demand for ransom."

"My man will know what to do. And I will pay it," he added, "so do not worry about the amount."

Margaret bit her lip. Now she'd lost her heart as well as her nieces.

The girls had not disobeyed her, not by much anyway. They had not crossed the street, had not gone exploring London on their own. They were right next door, in fact, with a proper escort. Well, not quite proper. They were picnicking in Lady Bartlett's carriage house, in her carriage, with their new good friend, Oscar, Lady Bartlett's profligate nephew. Oscar was just as eager to be out of his current temporary abode and the current lecture as the girls were to be out of theirs, if for different reasons.

Yesterday the hugger-mugger had sounded like a lark to Oscar, but yesterday he had been foxed. In truth, most days he was foxed, or suffering from the effects of being castaway the night before. He'd thought he'd play the hero to the adoring girls. Better, he'd claim to be rescuing them from some dread fate, slavers or procurers, he had not decided which. He'd be a hero indeed, and Lord Wolfram would reward him. Miss Todd would reward him. Auntie would reward him. Then he could pay his debts and be gone.

Today, a shade more sober, he was nothing but a blasted babysitter. After eating the provisions they had brought, and drinking from his own supply that he kept stashed in the little-used coach, he was bored. Teaching the infants how to play at dice took up an hour. A nap while they read storybooks took another. He woke up with a stiff neck from sleeping against the side of the carriage, cold, out of sorts and out of spirits in his flask. This was a bad idea, he decided, almost as bad as the silly little twits thinking they could wrest a proposal of marriage out of that downy bird, Wolfram.

"You might as well go on home, brats, 'cause a top-of-the-trees goer like Wolf ain't never going to marry your aunt. A viscount and a penniless nobody? Hah! He could have his pick of the heiresses and beauties and ladies of title. He's been diddling you all along, and you are too young to realize it. He'll make her an offer, all right, to be his ladybird. If she ain't already."

Katherine kicked him in the shin. Alexandra bashed him over the head with the picnic hamper.

In one way, Oscar was right. The children's disappearance was not bringing Wolf and Margaret any closer. Distress was not conducive to tender feelings, and a crisis was no time to be thinking of matters of the heart. Right now, the would-be lovers were barely speaking to each other. Margaret wanted to call in Bow Street, positive her nieces had been kidnapped. Wolf wanted to wait until nightfall, certain the girls would return on their own without scandal or public knowledge. Margaret was shredding her damp handkerchief. Now she would have to hem yet another one, dash it. Wolf was pacing in front of the window, staring out at the street. Soon he'd need a new carpet, damn it.

"Oh, where can they be?"

"Don't you think I would have them back if I knew?" he snapped.

"You have no need to speak so harshly. I am not blaming you."

Wolf was blaming himself. He should have hired a nanny. He should have packed them all off to his country place. Hell, he should have sailed to the Antipodes while he had the chance.

Margaret was blaming herself. What did she know about children? She should not have left them with ancient Aunt Bolton. She should not have tried to be a mother while still being Lady Bartlett's companion. She should have taken the girls to Cousin Fernell's, where there were nursemaids and governesses and strict rules of behavior. They might have been miserable, but they would have been safe. She should—

"Here they are!" Wolf yelled, after rushing to the hall and flinging open the front door. Lady Bartlett's nephew was dragging Alexandra by the arm while he carried Katherine, kicking and pounding on his back, over his shoulder.

"Here they are," Oscar echoed, "all safe and sound. I found your chicks hiding out in m'aunt's carriage house, don't you know. I brought them back as soon as I discovered they were runaways. I knew you'd be worried."

Wolf reached for his purse.

Safe in her aunt's embrace, Alexandra spoke up. "You liar! You told us yesterday where to hide, and you ate our luncheon. And you called Aunt Maggie bad names and you said Wolf only meant to—"

Margaret clapped a hand over the child's mouth.

"And you cheated us." Katherine tossed a pair of

dice at Oscar's feet. They landed with a three and a four showing.

Wolf put his purse back. "You knew the brats were next door all along? You thought we *might* be worried?" Wolf would never strike a child, but Oscar was not as lucky. Nor was he as handsome, when Wolf's right fist rearranged his nose. "That's for upsetting Miss Todd." Oscar's expensive clothes were not quite as elegant either, when Wolf kicked him down the stairs and out to the street. "And that is for besmirching her name."

Oscar ran away before Wolf could recall the loaded dice.

Then Wolf turned to the children.

They ran faster than Oscar.

They were almost out of time, with Christmas just days away. A week later the solicitor would be on his way home, so the girls knew they had to act now to get what they wished.

They did not really want the fur muffs Wolf was giving them, the ones that were supposedly hidden in Mrs. Olive's rooms. They did not want the new dresses Aunt Maggie was sewing when they slept, nor the doll clothes Aunt Bolton was making for them. Katherine and Alexandra did not want Aunt Maggie to go back to work, or Wolf to go back to his lady friends. Most of all, they did not want to have to live with flea-witted Cousin Fernell and his fusty family.

What they did want for Christmas was a pair of parents. Loving ones, healthy ones, permanent ones.

By hook or by crook, fair means or foul, they meant to see their aunt and Lord Wolfram wed. They had to be betrothed before the solicitor returned and made other arrangements. They must be promised, and promising to keep Alexandra and Katherine.

This time the girls had money to finance their latest strategy. Wolf had given them a handful of coins to buy presents, but they were giving him their father's pocket watch for Christmas, and giving Maggie their mother's diamond earbobs. The kitten they were giving Aunt Bolton was free, waiting in the stable mews, and Maggie had bought small gifts for the servants from all of them.

Wolf's generous sum was not enough, not for what they intended. So they borrowed from Aunt Bolton, and begged Mrs. Olive for a bit of the household funds. It was for the good of the house, wasn't it? Even Dora and Phillip tossed in a coin, and Wolf's valet just happened to find a pound note in one of his lordship's discarded coats.

So they took all the money and they bought . . .

Chapter Eight

*As the last stage in a successful courtship, having
dispensed with the duenna, bind your dearest to
you with stolen kisses. Remember, however, you
are wooing a bride, not a bedmate; do not frighten
an innocent young lady with your lust. For the
sake of your would-be sons, beware the miss who
gives her favors too freely or returns your passion
too enthusiastically. Alternatively, if the female
kisses like a dead fish, run as if the devil were
nipping at your heels.*
—George E. Phelber, *A Gentleman's Guide to Courtship*

"MISS T—" Wolf began to shout, on finding that
one of the colonel's exotic vines had run amok
in his entryway. Then he made a closer inspection of
the rampant vegetation, peering into the parlor, then
the library. "Mistletoe? My entire house is dripping
with mistletoe?" Wolf started laughing. Then he
started kissing the children and Aunt Bolton and Mrs.
Olive and Dora, all of whom had been hiding behind
doors to see his reaction.

Kissing balls hung from every door frame, strands
of the vine dangled from the chandeliers and the wall
sconces. Shiny green leaves and white berries decorated every chair back and banister rail and drapery
rod. Picture frames, mantelpieces and bookshelves had

nosegays of the stuff tied with red ribbon. "I did not know this much mistletoe existed in all of England!"

"Everyone helped," Katherine proudly explained. "Mrs. Olive wove the balls and Aunt Bolton tied the bows. Mr. Paul climbed the ladder."

"What did Dora do?" Wolf asked, although he thought he knew, by the maid's blushes.

"Oh, she and Phillip tested the mistletoe to make sure it worked," Alexandra told him.

"And did it?"

Dora's face was as scarlet as the red ribbons. "Like a treat, my lord, like a treat."

He would have to have a talk with young Phillip, it seemed, and promote him to under butler so he could afford a wife. "I see. And I see that I am going to be busy as a bee going from flower to flower. Why, my lips might wear out before Twelfth Night at this rate."

"Oh, no," Katherine said. "You are supposed to pick a berry for each kiss. When there are no more berries, you cannot claim any more kisses."

Wolf looked around, pretending to count. There were enough berries to last a philanderer until next February. "Hmm. I better not waste any more on little girls, then. Do you know any big girls waiting to be kissed?"

"Silly, you are supposed to be kissing Aunt Maggie!"

"I am?" He feigned surprise, while Aunt Bolton laughed. "I suppose this means I have your permission to pay my addresses?"

The little girls looked at each other in confusion. This was Wolf's address, and he paid the bills without asking anyone.

He asked the same question in different words. "You approve of my suit?"

The results were the same incomprehension. His clothes were fine.

"He wants to know if he can court your aunt," Mrs. Olive bent down and whispered to the girls.

"Oh, yes!" Katherine clapped her hands together, beaming until her older sister kicked her.

"Only if your intentions are honorable," Alexandra told Wolf, with her two years of added maturity. "Our Aunt Maggie deserves nothing less."

"She deserves a prince," her sister chimed in, "but Qu'inn is too young, and he'll go back to India anyway. Prince George is too old. You'll do."

Wolf solemnly thanked the precocious poppets and assured them that his intentions were indeed aboveboard.

"That means you are going to ask her to marry you, doesn't it?"

Wolf took a deep breath. "It does." The world did not end with that admission, so Wolf repeated it. "Yes, I am going to ask your aunt to be my wife, and you, my fine conspirators, to be my family. Now all I have to do is convince our Maggie that I will, ah, do."

"You are a rake, aren't you? That's what Aunt Maggie said."

"Why, so I am. Between my skills at seduc—at romance, and your mistletoe, she is bound to say yes."

She didn't at first. Kissed breathless and witless under the guise of Christmas kisses, Margaret did not hear the question. Her bones were bending, her muscles were mush, her scruples were strained. She would have fallen to the floor in a heap—a panting, yearning, open-armed heap—if Wolf had not been holding her up against his strong, hard body.

His body growing too hard, he sat down with her in his lap. Luckily a bunch of mistletoe was pinned to the back of the chair, so they could continue the season's best greetings. Wolf forgot to pick the berries. He forgot the question. He forgot he'd forgotten to lock the library door, dash it.

Lady Bartlett charged in, poor Phillip in her wake, trying to stop her. He might as well have tried to stop the fog from rolling in. The lady was incensed at the damage to her nephew, the crumbs in her carriage, and the surgeon's bill she was forced to pay for Wolf's handiwork.

Now she was incensed at the lack of morals, the audacity in the afternoon, the misbehavior under a mistletoe excuse.

"Why, I never!"

She had been married. She had, presumably, once at least. Still, Wolf stood and set Margaret on her feet behind him, where she could pull her skirts down and her bodice up. Nothing could be done about her gloriously loose hair and reddened lips, or his discarded neckcloth. Fortunately—or not—the old shrew's entrance had instantly shriveled the most blatant evidence of their activity.

She shook her fist in Margaret's direction. "You are dismissed, Miss Todd. I would not have a woman of such low character in my home. As for you, Wolfram, it serves you right, you libertine. You'll have to marry the nobody now, you know."

Margaret inhaled sharply, but Wolf spoke first: "Miss Todd is a somebody who serves me precisely right. Further, you are already housing a cardshark and an ivory tuner in your house. I would not think of permitting my betrothed to return there. Good day, madam. Oh, and you had better keep your dog close. Without Miss Todd to walk the beast, your pet is at risk. Our Punjabi hunting cat took a fancy to a poodle in the park today. Who knows but that he is even now out stalking plump pigeons, or pugs."

Lady Bartlett gasped and fled.

This time Wolf locked the door behind her and an interested audience of children, servants and distant relatives.

"You do not have to marry me," Margaret said when he returned.

He stood in front of her, clasping her hands. "Of course I do."

"But your honor is not at stake, not over a mere companion. As Lady Bartlett said, I am a nobody, so no one will care. And my reputation no longer matters. If the solicitor does not have news of an inheritance, I shall take the girls to our cousin's house. He will have to give us shelter, so I will not be seeking another position."

Wolf ignored her, kissing her into silence. Despite her brave words, Margaret knew she would miss her good name. Feckless Fernell would make her life a misery if he got wind of her fall from grace. She would miss Wolf's kisses more, though, so did not protest when she found herself back in Wolf's arms, back in a daze.

Wolf feared consummating the marriage before the engagement. Lud, those shiny mistletoe berries—and his radiant beloved—were hard to resist, but he did. He stepped back and said, "To the devil with Lady Bartlett and her gossip-mongering. I do have to marry you, though, because I will not be happy without you. I might not even survive without you. For certain I will not take another bride, so my entire line will die out, without you. I cannot imagine how I lived before you tumbled into my life with your imps. It was no life, and I do not want to return to that empty void."

"But—"

"Sh. Let me finish. I love you, Miss Margaret Todd, and I want you for my wife, forever and ever." He let out his breath. "There, now I am done. You are supposed to say you love me back and are honored at my offer and yes, you will make me the happiest of men."

"I do love you, Lord Wolfram. And would gladly be your bride, but . . ."

"But you have doubts."

"I love you so much, I would die if you looked at another woman."

"You have ruined me for other women. I cannot

imagine wanting a female who is not you, and your nieces would make my life wretched if I did. But I always intended to honor my wedding vows, which is why I never took that step. I never found the woman I thought I could be faithful to. Now I have."

"People will say mine is cream-pot love, that I would marry you for your money."

"Shall I give it all away, then?"

She laughed. "Of course not. The girls need an education, and our sons—"

"We are going to have sons? Then we had best marry for their sake." He led her to the chair and seated her. Then he took a ring out of his pocket, a single diamond set in a gold band. "I was going to wait until Christmas to give you this and ask for your hand in return. Will you accept it now, and me?"

Margaret held her hand out for him to put the band on her finger. Through tears of joy she admired the beautiful ring, and the wonderful man who was kneeling at her feet.

"I have nothing for you but a handkerchief with your initials embroidered on it."

"I am going to need it to mop my brow, dealing with your nieces. Zeus, that makes them my nieces too, doesn't it?"

"Yours to raise and love and teach how to avoid rakes."

He looked at the ring as if he wanted it back. "I am not sure about that last."

"You have a few years to get used to the idea. But you have made me so happy, I would give you so much more."

"More than a family, more than a love I never thought to find?"

"I dreamed that you might love me, but never dared hope. But I am not what you were looking for, a well-bred young lady of means and polish, one who could make you a comfortable match. I am not of your world, not well dowered and not all that young. Worse, I fear ours will not be an entirely comfortable marriage."

"I will try not to shout."

"And I will try not to turn your house into Bedlam."

"No matter. Our marriage will be a joyous one."

"Just like the season."

"Like every season, with you."

Thank heaven for mistletoe . . . and little girls.

The Dogstar

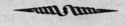

Edith Layton

For Georgie Girl, my own tricolored miracle,
forever in my heart as I was in hers.

They were born in a tumble of rags at the back of an alley in the oldest section of London town. They didn't notice their low surroundings. They had a devoted mother and enough sweet milk to drink, and when they weren't eating or sleeping, the pups played. That is, they did until one morning when they woke to find their mother gone. They looked for her, and then they played, and then they stopped and sat and waited, ears pricked up and tongues hanging out. They didn't have long to wait.

Before the sun had set each of them knew, in the way this uncanny litter had of knowing what was important, that it was time to move on So they parted. One made his wobbly way west; one went south. One meandered toward the park. One went due north to where the remnants of the old gates to the city still stood. Two played together until they cocked their heads as though they heard far-off whistles. Then they went on alone down separate, new, but certain paths.

Soon they were all gone from the only home they'd ever known. It was time for them to do the tasks they were born to; it was time to meet their destinies. After all, Christmas was coming to London, and everyone else in town was headed home too.

Alexander Malcolm Grenville, fifth Marquess Grenville, Baron Trent, last in a proud line of aristocrats, had everything a young gentleman could want: looks, money and position. Everything, that was, except a place to go for Christmas.

He sat by the window and brooded. He would not cry. He was, after all, seven years old now, and if his jolly classmates didn't pummel him for weeping, they'd certainly mock him. At least, those few who were still at school would. Still, a young gentleman had his pride to consider. It was a good thing an early winter's dusk was coming on. That way, if treacherous tears did happen to appear the way the evening stars were doing, slowly, one by one, the room was so dim no one would see it. Alex was feeling wretched and alone, and would have wished for happiness upon the brightest star he saw now, but he was too old for that, and anyway, his wishes never came true.

"Alex? Is that you?" a nervous voice inquired.

Alex sat up straight. He could see only a dim outline in the gathering gloom. Nevertheless, he hastily wiped away treacherous tears.

"Alex?" the voice asked again, hesitantly.

Only one boy Alex knew had a voice that quavered that way. "Simon? That you?" he asked in return.

"Yes. It is," the other boy said in a rush. He stepped into the room and came closer to the window. He was a slight lad, with a pale freckled face. "I'm so glad you're still here. Almost everyone's gone. The place is so empty, it echoes. I don't leave until the morning, but I must know, are you coming home with me?"

Alex hesitated. He wiped his nose with the back of his hand, and hoped it looked like it was itching. "Well, I dunno," he said, because, in truth, he didn't. Simon was a friend, but a friend made the way strangers get to know each other when they're taking shelter from a storm together. In their case, the storm was the attitude of the other boys at the school. Simon was a weakling, and a fearful one. Alex was only a newcomer. He'd been ill and so had come to this new school two months late. That was all it took to make a fellow an outcast.

"Y'know," Alex added with what he hoped sounded like the casual drawls his mama's elegant gentlemen friends affected, "Perry asked me too."

"Oh, Perry," Simon said with a sneer. It was unpleasant to hear an outcast sneer at someone even lower in status, but that was how everyone reacted to Perry. Fat fellows could have friends, but not fat lads with ghastly manners and a total disregard for cleanliness. Soap was the common enemy here. But to Perry, it was entirely alien.

"Well, let me know before bedtime," Simon said. He hesitated. "Actually, you can let me know in the morning too. I'd love for you to come," he went on eagerly. "You could see my collection of tin soldiers. I have battalions, and we could play Waterloo. Of course," he said, in a quick recovery, because though he was a pariah, he wasn't stupid and had learned a thing or two at school this first year—"*I'm* far too old for them now. But you might find them interesting."

"Might," Alex agreed. He could think of few things more deadly, but he was a kindhearted boy. Still, it would be better than staying with Perry and watching him eat. But apart from those two invitations, there was only the unknown. He squared his narrow shoulders. He would face the unknown. "But, y'see," he said, deciding on the spot, "I think I'd better go where my mama wishes. Or, maybe, where my papa did."

He unclenched a hand and showed Simon the two crumpled pieces of paper he'd been rereading until the light went. "My mama asked her old friend to watch over me for Christmas, seein' as how she can't be home in time for it. So her old friend wrote and asked me to stay with her, in London. She wasn't planning much otherwise, and she lives alone anyhow."

It wasn't a thrilling invitation, but sounded like a sincere one. It would be better than staying at home alone except for the servants, as he'd done so many times in the past. Alex's mother seldom came home. Now it looked as if she never would again. Presently she was in Italy with her new lover, who didn't speak much English. And so she'd written that she didn't know when she'd get back home again, and wished Alex a happy Christmas. They'd never been close, but Alex remembered Christmases at home before his father had gone riding off to war, never to return. He remembered the house dressed in evergreens, lots of company coming to stay, festive dinners and dances, and being allowed to stay up at the top of the stairs with his nurse to watch the festivities until his bedtime.

"An' I've got this invitation from my papa's old friend," Alex said, producing the other rumpled letter. "He says he got a letter from my man-at-law, saying as to how it was time for him to take up some of his responsibilities for me. He's my guardian. I mean, he would be if something happened to my mama, because my papa wanted him to be. I guess he didn't know it 'til now, no more than I did. So he invited me to stay at his London town house. He says he's got lots of servants to look after me, and he lives near the park."

Alex looked at the two letters. In spite of his resolve, he sniffled. "So," he said with forced heartiness, "seein' as how both of 'em asked me to meet them at the Bull and Mouth—that's a coaching stop in London—and as to how they both sent me tickets to get there, I s'pose I will."

"How can you use two tickets?" Simon asked.

"Won't," Alex said quickly, hoping Simon wasn't hinting about how a trip to London would be a deal better than staying home and playing Waterloo with his tin soldiers. "I'll go by mail coach 'cause it's faster. They set their horses to a prime clip. Those are the tickets Viscount Falconer sent. I'll give Miss Lockwood her tickets back when I get there."

"Who will you stay with?" Simon asked, fascinated.

"I'll let them decide," Alex said with a shrug.

Because in truth, he didn't much care. And if his two hosts were anything like most adults he'd met, he doubted they did either.

Alex enjoyed the ride down to London enormously. The headmaster saw him into the mail coach, instructed the driver and the guard to keep an eye out and let no one interfere with Alex, and then left him. It was a bit daunting. But then the sheer speed of the coach as it bucketed down the roads, the spanking teams of horses, the chance to get off at stops and drink hot cider and then swagger back to the coach in perfect imitation of the lordly driver and guard, all served to chase away his fears and doubts. It was grand.

He wished he could speak to the coachman or the guard, or some of the other passengers, but he'd been trained not to talk to strangers. Still, he was too excited to feel lonely.

Now he was approaching London, driving under a gray stone arch, slowing as the coach clattered over cobbles and into a wide inn yard. The Bull and Mouth, his destination. The coach rolled to a stop. The other passengers readied themselves to leave, and all Alex's worries came flooding back like stormclouds before a high wind. He was in a strange place, going to stay the Christmas holidays with strange people.

Having been left with a succession of nurses and governesses all his life and then sent to school was one thing—or rather, several awful things. But this! Alex's courage faltered.

But he wasn't a Grenville for nothing. His ancestors had faced wild barbarians and greedy kings, or so he'd heard. He could do this. He gathered his carpetbag, waited for everyone else in the coach to leave, and then stepped down into the weak winter sunlight, and blinked.

The inn yard was vast, noisy, crowded and so colorful he was dazzled. It was filled with people greeting new arrivals, and those waiting to board. Alex heard shouts and conversations, the neighing of horses and the rattling of their brasses. He stood near the mail coach and waited. The passengers who had been with him left. It didn't get less crowded.

Alex stood and watched. There was no one waiting for him. Or so it seemed. He realized he didn't know what either Miss Lockwood or Viscount Falconer looked like. Nor did they know what he looked like. And there was always the possibility that they might have forgotten him. In fact, he might be entirely on his own in London. Surprisingly, this didn't worry him as much as being with his hosts did.

He was trying to decide what to do, trying to gather up courage to do *something,* when a coaching guard approached and hunkered down to speak to him. "Be you the Marquess Grenville, lad? I mean, my lord?" he asked.

Alex nodded. "I am."

"Well, there's a relief. You're to wait inside the inn. We got word." He squinted at a note he held. "Viscount Falconer, well, he's late, and this Miss Lockwood, she sent to say she'd be here presently. I'll show you a place to wait, and you're to stick there until they comes for you, understand?"

Alex nodded, relieved yet newly nervous.

The private room he was shown to looked dim after the brightness of the courtyard. Dim, and reeking of beer and ale and smoke from the tap next door. Alex waited for what seemed like ages, sitting and swinging his legs, until he grew more bored than worried. Then he got up and walked to the one window. It looked out at the rear of the inn, and showed a grand vista of garbage and trash bins out back of the kitchens, as well as an alley that led to the stables. Alex's bored

gaze sharpened. Because there in the center of the
narrow alley sat one lone, lovely, fat little puppy.

Alex stared. He loved dogs, but only got to see the
miniature creatures his mama's lady friends wore like
muffs to complement their clothes. He wasn't allowed
to touch them any more than he was allowed to speak
to their owners, beyond wishing them a good day. He
wasn't allowed to play with the hunting dogs in the
stables at home, either.

At first he thought the puppy was some child's discarded toy. It looked small as his mama's friends' or-
naments. But then it shook itself and bumbled closer
to the inn and Alex realized it wasn't as small as he'd
first thought. It was a sizeable creature, and yet clearly
a baby, so stout and fuzzy he knew it would be plush
to the touch. And there was no one to stop him from
touching it.

Alex left the private room he'd been stowed in and
crept down the hall to the back door. He slowly
cracked the door open. The pup was still there. It
looked up, saw him, and smiled. He would swear on
anything that it actually smiled.

It had that kind of a face. It was a plump, fuzzy,
tricolored puppy with a black body, four white paws
with rust socks over them, and a broad white chest.
A white line started between the ears and widened as
it ran down the middle of the humorous face, showing
up the black button nose, broadening at the neck and
ending in that shining white chest. A pair of rust eyebrows wriggled over bright brown eyes when the pup
was interested, which it was now, as it looked at Alex.
He looked back at the puppy with delight.

The two met in the middle of the alley, and though
Alex didn't have a tail to wag, an observer would have
had a hard time knowing which of the two was happier. Alex picked up the puppy and hurried back into
the room where he'd been told to wait. Now he didn't

mind the passage of time. He held a fragrant puppy that chewed on his buttons and teethed on his thumbs, licked his face and fell asleep at last in his lap.

Alex didn't care if anyone ever came for him. No one had ever given him such complete and loving attention as this wonderful puppy . . . *his* wonderful puppy. On that, he was resolved. He might be a lost boy in a strange town, but he was still the Marquess Grenville, and some things weren't negotiable. Wasn't that his family motto, on all the family documents?

What I have, I hold.

Alex did.

Miss Laura Lockwood was breathless when she finally got to the Bull and Mouth. She again consulted the watch she had clipped to the inside of her pelisse and stifled a groan. She was very late. But she couldn't afford a hackney, and so had taken a public horse bus. It had run late because of traffic and the other stops it had to make before it got to London's most famous coaching inn. Laura's already-shortened breath caught when she saw no sign of a seven-year-old lad in the inn yard. There were ragged boys holding horses, of course, and a boy in livery standing on the back of an elegant curricle, but she saw no young boy with bags or cases, and certainly none who looked well-bred.

She went into the inn and waited to speak to the man behind the desk there. Several people were waiting to see him too, as he was selling tickets and answering queries about the coaches coming in and out.

"Excuse me," she said to him, when she could, "I was to meet a young boy who rode down on the *Flyer*, from Warwickshire. It was due in at eight o'clock."

The man nodded, without looking up. "Came in then too."

"Oh," she said, her hand on her heart. "But I don't see him anywhere. Whatever happened to him? He was traveling alone, I thought he'd be safe! But I'm late, whatever shall I do?"

He looked up at the note of anguish in her voice. Then his gaze sharpened. He stared at her, and gave her a slow, reassuring smile. She didn't take heart. Most men smiled at her. "Hold on," he said. "I'll find out." He raised his head and shouted. "Geoff! Know anything about a lad traveling alone, who came in on the *Flyer* this morning?"

"His name is Grenville," Laura said quickly.

A hefty coaching guard ambled over, eyed Laura, and also smiled. "Aye. You his mum?" he asked her.

She flushed. "No, I'm Miss Lockwood, his mother's friend. I sent a note. Where is he?"

"Oh, a note. Aye, that rings a bell. The Royal Mail came down from Warwickshire too. There was a lad named Grenville on it, but he's a noble lad, a marquess, no less. And a regular little gent, he is too."

"Where is he?" Laura asked.

"Safe'n sound. Got him stowed safe in a room to the back. Come with me and I'll show you."

She hesitated. One thing living on her own these past years had taught her was to never go off alone with any man, anywhere. But he wore a guard's uniform, this was a public inn, and she had no choice. "Thank you," she said, and followed him.

The guard took her to a small room at the back of the inn, and opened the door with a flourish. Laura stepped into the room and gasped.

There was a child inside, a slight pale blond youth. But he was not alone. He was standing, staring up at a very angry, very elegant gentleman who was looming over him. The gentleman's elegance only occurred to Laura as a second thought. Her first thought propelled her into the room, where she immediately took a stand, interposing her body between the boy and the man.

"What is the meaning of this?" she asked the gentleman in her strictest governessy tones. "And who are you, sir?"

Both man and boy seemed nonplussed. The man recovered first. "I am Falconer," he said loftily.

That meant nothing to Laura. But now his clothing and his presence registered with her. Though not much above thirty, this was a man born to command. He was tall and lean, and his dark hair was expertly barbered. He wore a spotless high white neckcloth and she'd give a month's wages if his jacket wasn't tailored by Weston. His brown half boots shone, and his long legs were clothed in immaculate dove-gray breeches. He was a swell, top-of-the-trees, a Tulip, a Corinthian—she wasn't sure which, but she was sure that whatever he was, it cost a great deal of money.

But she, of all people, knew that money didn't mean manners or moral right. She met his cold gray gaze directly.

"I am Miss Lockwood," she said. "And I've come to take the marquess home with me for Christmas, on his mama's express request."

The gentleman frowned. He had a lean face: cold gray eyes, a blade of a nose, and his frown was thunderous. It was a formidable sight.

Laura held her ground. "If this young person is not the marquess," she added hastily as the thought occurred to her, "then please accept my apologies, Mr. Falconer."

"Viscount Falconer," he corrected her absently, his eyes never leaving hers.

"Very well, Viscount Falconer," she said. "But if he is the Marquess Grenville, I tell you I won't have him interfered with by anyone."

"Interfered with?" the viscount said incredulously. "My dear woman, I do not interfere. I am here to take the marquess home for the Christmas holiday, at his papa's express wishes."

"His papa," she said in awful tones, "is dead."

"As I know," the gentleman said with a show of exasperation. "But before he died, he made his wishes known to his man-at-law."

"And his mama, who is very much alive," Laura said sweetly, "made her wishes known to me, and so I believe they supercede the ones you claim his father made. Do you wish to see her letter?"

The viscount found he wished to see a lot more from this strange and strangely defiant young female. She had dark gold curling hair under her simple bonnet, framing a lovely face. Her anger made her cheeks blush pink, but her mouth was pinker, and her eyes were golden brown. The only problem was that the lovely mouth was held in a thin line now, and she looked at him as though he were a villain. But doubtless she was that, or worse. She was the feckless widow's friend, after all. She'd just announced it loud and clear.

"His mama's wishes don't matter," he said. "She is abroad, and even if she weren't, her husband, deceased or not, made his wishes known, and they come first."

"I will not argue this with you here and now," Laura said. "But I won't let you waltz off with the boy, either. Why, when I walked in, it looked as if you were threatening him."

"Was I threatening you, Alexander?" the viscount demanded, looking at the boy.

Laura did too. She saw him fully for the first time. He was a handsome boy, who resembled his mama. But his large blue eyes held more sincerity than his mama's ever did. And his expression was that of a desperate man. Now Laura realized he held a fluffy toy in his arms. She was taken aback. Surely he was too old for such a plaything? Maria hadn't said there was anything wrong with her son. Still, mothers, even neglectful ones like Maria, often didn't admit such things about their children. . . .

That put a different complexion on the matter entirely. Laura's heart sank. How could she cope with a slow child? Well, she would, she thought, straightening her shoulders. A promise was a promise, after all.

The boy's toy stared at her as glassily as she stared at it. Then it blinked, and she realized that the young marquess held a live puppy in his arms.

But Alex was looking at the viscount. "Were you threatening me?" he asked the viscount, cautiously echoing his question. "Well, yes, my lord. You were."

Now the viscount blinked.

The boy's fair face colored up, but he maintained his poise. "Well, y'did," he said, in a curiously adult drawl. "I mean to say, I said we should wait for Miss Lockwood, and you said to come with you straightaway. And then you said I wasn't to take my dog with me, and that I cannot do."

"*Your* dog?" the viscount said through gritted teeth. "I heard nothing about a mongrel. I doubt you clapped eyes on him before today. They don't let students take their pets away to school with them, unless things have changed very much since my day."

"Well, maybe they have," the young marquess said in a voice that started to waver. "He slept in the stables, and I took him home on holidays."

Laura winced. Anyone could see the dog wasn't old enough to have celebrated any holiday yet, except for its birth. And she too knew that exclusive young gentlemen's schools did not supply house or stable room to a student's dog. But no matter how brave his words, the boy's eyes were stricken, and he looked so small and courageous that she knew she had to defend him, no matter what.

And too, she didn't like being reminded that a dead man's wishes mattered more than his live widow's. That cut too close to the bone. Her own mother had lost the roof over her head when her husband died. And that simply because he'd had a distant male cousin, and he, in the eyes of the law, was master of all her father had possessed, not her mother. Laura wouldn't be working as a lowly governess now in order to support her mama if it had been otherwise.

"Well, you can bring your dog when you come with me," she told the young marquess, shooting an angry look at the imperious viscount.

"That will not happen," the viscount said grimly. "And if you're so easily gulled, even more reason not to allow you to take the lad. *If* he's your dog," he suddenly asked the boy, "what's his name?"

"Pompey," the boy said promptly, his face getting even pinker.

Even the dog stared at the boy.

"Pompey?" the viscount asked, with a growing smile. "Ah yes, studying Julius Caesar now, are we? Nice try at a recover, but it won't hold water. Well then, young Antony, I suggest we settle the matter here and now. Put the pup on the floor, and I'll call to him. I'll eat my hat if he answers to Pompey."

"He don't like you," the boy said desperately, "so he won't come."

"A well-trained dog comes when called," the viscount said. "I don't think he's yours and I don't think he's trained. I think he's a stray you picked up on the way to London. Put him down, and prove me wrong."

Alex looked at Laura. She sighed and gave a tiny shrug.

Alex sighed too, and then gently set the dog on the floor and stepped away from it.

The dog sat on his plump bottom and looked around the room. It was an adorable pup, Laura thought sadly.

"Here, Rags," the viscount called sweetly.

The puppy sat.

"Here, Brownie," the viscount wheedled.

The dog lifted a hind leg and scratched behind his ear.

"Here, Pompey," the viscount called in such sarcastic tones that Laura wanted to swat him.

The pup looked up, and then, his plume of a tail wagging, immediately trotted to the viscount's side. He sat there and looked up expectantly, his bright eyes fixed on the tall gentleman who had called him.

Everyone looked shocked. Especially Alex.

Alex and his puppy were settled in a deep chair near the hearth, both nearly dozing. Laura and the viscount sat at the table in the private dining parlor at the Bull and Mouth, and argued in low voices over their now-cold cups of tea.

"Again, Miss Lockwood," the viscount said wearily, "I was asked to foster the lad over the holiday and I cannot not do it. His father went to school with me; he was a good man and my friend. I owe him that."

"Again, my lord," Laura said, equally wearily, "his mama went to school with me, and though we have lost touch since, still she remembered me when she realized she couldn't come home for the holiday. I promised her I would take him, and *I* cannot not do that."

"I have a huge town house," the viscount said. "More room than I need, and I can hire him a governess for the duration."

"I . . . don't have that," Laura admitted. Then her face lit up. "But I don't need to hire a governess. I have time off. . . . That is to say, time on my hands, and I've already set it aside for him. I can take him everywhere all the time."

"You live alone?" he asked, incredulously. A proper female didn't live by herself. Still, he thought . . . Maria's friend, after all.

She cast down her eyes, obviously distressed. Then she looked up at him, and told him what she'd decided she must, which was some of the truth, slightly altered, and none of the facts she feared he'd disapprove of.

"I live with a friend's family. They're gone to the countryside for Christmas, and I decided to stay in London. I know you might think it bold of me to come for Alex by myself. But the time was running late and I acted impetuously. Still, I didn't feel I needed an escort. After all, I cut my eyeteeth years ago. I reached five-and-twenty at my last birthday."

She hated to tell her age, but had to explain why she was unaccompanied by a maid or a footman. She prayed he wouldn't ask more.

He didn't. "Well, I suppose Alex makes a suitable chaperone," the viscount said. "But you don't have a family to pass the holiday with? Or any special . . . friends?"

He couldn't believe she didn't have a gentleman friend, given how lovely she was, especially given that she was Maria's friend. She was, after all, five and twenty, unwed, and staying in London by herself for the holidays. And so she was also probably not uninvolved. If she had a man she planned to be with for Christmas, Falconer could certainly claim the boy on moral grounds.

He himself was discreet about his liaisons. He was three and thirty, a man, and expected to have affairs. Still, he found himself holding his breath. He didn't want to see her disappointment. He didn't want to keep on arguing. Most of all, he found he didn't want to know about her gentleman friends.

She shook her head. "I have my mama, but she's up in the Lake District and I . . . hadn't planned to go there this year. It's such a long journey," she said quickly. "I don't have anyone else. Do you have a family you intend to spend the holiday with?" She held her breath. If he had a wife or a large family, she'd be lost. She couldn't offer anything to compete with that.

"No," he said, a shadow of sorrow passing over his face. "That is to say, no longer, as such. My parents are gone. I've a brother, but he's in the army, in Spain, with Wellington's staff. My sister is married to a diplomat, and they're in Brussels."

"Then why can't we settle this amicably?" she asked, almost pleading. "Why not let me take him? Surely you'll agree that a woman is better suited to entertain a boy his age. And I've been looking forward to this time with him. I like children, and would provide him with a cozy Christmas at home with me."

The viscount paused. "I can't provide that," he admitted. "I haven't had one of those since I was a lad myself. But I can buy him all the gifts and treats for the holiday that he wants."

"That's not Christmas," she said softly. "You can't buy Christmas."

"Sometimes," he said, thinking of his greedy mistress, "you can."

They looked at each other, each preparing new arguments.

"Why don't I spend half of it with you, Miss Lockwood," Alex said suddenly, from his quiet corner, "and half with you, sir?"

Laura looked at the viscount. He looked at her. But then, he'd been doing little else since he met her. Now, for the first time, his smile was real and warm. It made him amazingly attractive, Laura thought. Amazingly more attractive, she corrected herself.

"Why not?" the viscount asked her.

Her lips curved into a smile as well. "Yes. Why not?" she said, and laughed.

The viscount loved the sound of it.

Alex did too. He sighed into his puppy's warm, wide neck. "But the dog, I mean, Pompey, comes with me," he said quickly.

"Of course," Laura said.

"Well, then . . . yes," the viscount said.

And tomorrow, Alex thought, as he rubbed his chin

on the soft fur beneath it, will take care of itself. But I, he silently vowed to the sleeping pup, will always take care of you. I don't know how. But so I shall do.

"I'd take you home, but I only brought my light curricle," the viscount told Laura as they walked out into the inn yard again. "It won't hold three . . . and a half," he added, glancing at the enormous ball of fur trotting at Alex's feet. Damned if the pup hadn't grown since he'd first set eyes on it. "At least, let me call a hackney for you."

Laura nodded, and silently bid farewell to the few coins in her purse. In for a penny, in for a pound, but she hoped it wouldn't come to more than that.

"And you must give me your direction," he told her, raising a hand to signal to a hackney, "so I can come to see how Alex and Pompey are doing."

She stopped and went white.

"At least that," he said, taken aback and vaguely insulted. "After all, you have the first week, and I did promise to watch over him."

"So you did, and so you shall," she said gaily, as the hackney driver reached down and pulled open his door. "I thought to give the boy a day of rest today, and then take him to Astley's Amphitheatre tomorrow to see the horses perform. We can meet there."

"Excellent idea," he said. "But let it be my treat. I'll meet you outside before the performance. Take care until then," he added as she, the boy, and the dog got into the hackney.

He waited.

The hackney driver waited.

"Great Irvington Street," Laura told the driver.

"Here," the viscount said, handing coins up to the driver. "This should cover it."

"Aye, and handsomely, thankee," the driver said, tipping his hat.

"But I can't let you pay!" Laura protested.

The viscount looked at her curiously. "Why not?" he asked. "It is what a gentleman should do."

"So it is," she murmured, because she hadn't remembered that. "I don't know what I was thinking. The excitement today has addled my wits."

The driver raised his whip. The viscount raised his hand in farewell. And the coach drove off.

Laura sank back to her seat. Great Irvington was a fashionable street. Fortunately for her, it was also a long one. When they got there, she'd tell the driver her house number, which was much less fashionable. The boy wouldn't care, but the lofty viscount certainly would have. Her rooms were in a house in a district that barely hung on to respectability, since it was on the spreading skirts of a slum. But they were all she could afford.

Her employers were off to the family home in the countryside. They hadn't seen the need to take their governess with them because there'd be so many other children visiting with their own nurses and governesses. They especially hadn't seen the need once they realized that not taking Laura would also save their paying her two weeks' salary. So they'd told her she could take the Christmas holiday off, to spend on her own. Literally.

Laura had to spend her own money to finance her unexpected vacation. She didn't have much, since most of her pay went to her mama. Still, she'd saved, so she'd have enough to feed and fete the young marquess. Sightseeing only cost coach fare, and they could buy most of their meals from vendors in the streets. A boy would love that. And boys didn't care how fashionable a district the room they slept in was in, nor did their dogs. . . .

Dog! Laura sat upright. She'd spoken in haste to spare the boy's feelings, and the dog had looked so little then. Now, here beside her, she saw the beast took up wholly half the seat. How could she have been so mistaken?

Pompey looked at her, his tongue lolling in what looked like a dog laugh.

Her landlady might not think it was funny. She'd let the attic rooms for a pittance. That had come after Laura had done a great deal of bargaining. Still, getting two rooms had been necessary after she accepted the responsibility of boarding Maria's son. But she hadn't told her landlady a thing about pets.

"Alex," Laura said, "let's try to make this the best holiday ever! It may be a little difficult at first. You see, my landlady mightn't care for dogs. So, do you think we can take Pompey up to my rooms without her knowing?"

"Absolutely," Alex said. "If he won't walk up, I'll carry him."

Laura sighed. She was glad Alex didn't think it odd that she had rented rooms, but it looked like he might have to ride on Pompey's back in order to get the dog up the long flight of stairs that led to them. She decided she'd face that when she came to it, and her rented rooms. There was suddenly something more on her mind. How could she keep the viscount from taking her back to her rooms after their afternoon at Astley's? How could she keep him from seeing where she lived, and how meagerly?

Maybe she wouldn't have to, she thought desperately. The viscount had seemed haughty at first, but they'd come to an amicable agreement. Maybe he wouldn't mind where the boy stayed, so long as he was happy and well looked after. That was the crux of the matter.

But she didn't want to test her theory. Noblemen lived by different rules. She was the daughter of a knight, and she'd known her share of snobs at school. She also knew the fierce pretentiousness and awareness of class distinctions that her middle-class employers lived by. If she was wrong about the viscount's reaction to her living situation, she might lose the boy. She couldn't bear that, not after she'd so looked forward to her unexpected Christmas guest.

Alex seemed to be a good boy, and a clever one. Laura genuinely liked children, and thought she'd enjoy his company. She sensed he was as lonely as she was. Well, of course he'd be, with a mama like Maria.

Maria had been a good friend when they'd been girls. A good friend, that was, until she'd become a young woman and realized how much more amusing life could be with young men. At that same time Laura's father had died. She'd had to leave school, and so had lost all contact with Maria. If things had been different they might still have been friends. Maybe they were. After all, after years of silence, Maria had written to ask her to watch over her only son at Christmastime.

Laura determined to do it. It was the right thing, and too, this way she wouldn't have to be alone at Christmas. She couldn't afford the trip up to the Lake District to see Mama; she could barely afford this treat. But taking care of Alex was an obligation, even though it was one she suspected she'd enjoy. She wouldn't be alone at Christmas, and she could see the holiday through a child's eyes again.

And if, in the process, she got to know a dashing viscount, that would be fun too, so long as she remembered it was only for a week, and she didn't get too involved with either the boy or the man. When the bells announcing the New Year rang, she'd be like Ella in the cinders, and go back to being a servant.

She felt a sudden weight drop onto her lap. Pompey had laid his great head on it, and was gazing up at her with deep brown, sad, preternaturally sympathetic eyes.

Laura sighed and stroked the dog's silky head. She corrected herself. She'd have a fine holiday if she remembered to keep her head, and her heart, safe from all three of the males she'd just met.

When they finally arrived at her rooming house, after stopping at Great Irvington Street and then telling the driver to move on, Laura beckoned to Alex and his dog.

"Here we are!" she told Alex as they left the coach. "Let's be quiet as mice as we go up to my rooms. We'll break the news of our furry guest to Mrs. Finch, my landlady, at another time, shall we?"

Alex nodded wisely as he and Pompey followed her.

Laura opened the door to the narrow hallway and walked lightly and quickly to the long stair that led up to her rooms. She held her breath as the dog approached that stair—and then let it out in surprise. Anxiety must truly magnify one's problems, she thought. Because when Alex put down the pup, she realized it really was a small dog. And a quiet one. Though it was still remarkably hefty-looking, it moved like a fat little shadow, its plump footpads ensuring its nails didn't even click on the steps as it hopped all the way up to the very top flight.

She eased open her door and ushered the boy and dog inside. For a moment, Laura was ashamed. The lad might be used to austerity; she'd heard that the more historic the school, the more meager its accommodations because the upper classes believed that privation shaped a boy's character. But surely he'd be disappointed, if not appalled. Her rooms were beyond meager. They were downright poverty-stricken.

The larger room had small windows, a wooden floor, a chair and a stool, a threadbare settee, and a table. The small room had a bed and a table and a window. She'd planned to give that room to the boy, and sleep on the settee herself.

Alex looked around the bare rooms. Then he went to a window, his dog following him. "Oh, this will be fun!" Alex said, leaning on his elbows and looking out. "We're so high up we can see all the chimney tops! Aren't there a lot of them? We're higher than the birds. This is capital!"

That was when Laura realized that, in spite of her resolve, she was well on her way to loving him.

Sebastian Falconer, Viscount Falconer, saw Miss Lockwood and his old friend Harry's son off in their hackney. Then he clapped on his high beaver hat and stepped up into the driver's seat of his curricle. He flicked the whip, and his perfectly matched team trotted off toward his town house. He raised his head and took a deep breath. Christmas was already literally everywhere in London.

The streets actually smelled of something other than horses, because the street vendors were selling steaming hot cider, spicy apple and mince tarts, and freshly baked gingerbread along with hot soups and stews. The better shops had their doorways hung with freshly-cut evergreen boughs. The cold air was bracing, the holiday was coming, and all the shoppers who thronged the pavements seemed to be smiling.

So was Viscount Falconer. Things hadn't turned out as he'd expected, but he felt unusually happy, because he was unexpectedly pleased.

He could now admit that he'd had no idea how he would entertain the boy. He'd expected to leave that to his servants. He'd also expected to feel guilty about it. After all, this year his holiday would have been a ramshackle thing to offer a young boy. His best friends were married and off to their country homes. Though he'd been invited, he couldn't share in their domestic bliss. He wasn't eager to be entertained by cooing newlyweds, or pass his time praising their drooling infants.

Instead, he supposed he'd pass the holidays with other friends, playing chess and discussing politics with the staid ones; going to gaming hells and sporting events with the boisterous ones. And then, of course, for domestic bliss of another sort, there was his new mistress. None of which were amusements fit for a boy.

But now the boy had a lovely young companion, and Sebastian could also get to know the lad before he took him for his week. Plus, he thought with a slow smile, he could get to know the lovely young companion as well.

But was she a lady? He didn't know, not really. Nor did he know where she lived, or who her family was. She'd charmed the good sense out of him. That wasn't like him.

Still, Sebastian counted himself an astute judge of character. He'd had to be. Coming into the title young, he'd met a score of people who had tried to charm the money from his pockets. Some had succeeded. It had taught him to take his time and measure his judgments.

Since coming of age, he'd also met a score of women who'd tried to entice him into marriage. None had succeeded. Instead, he'd grown up with a healthy skepticism and an appreciation of females who dealt plainly with a fellow, offering what passed for love for money. He knew that was crass, but at least it was honest.

And yet, just now, he'd let a remarkably pretty young woman ride off with a boy who was supposed to be his charge, because she'd shown him a letter asking her to, and a pair of beseeching golden-brown eyes. He allowed she'd also behaved in a well-bred fashion. But that didn't excuse his hasty decision.

He didn't think Miss Lockwood was a kidnapper, or that she meant any harm. Her letter was genuine, as was, he'd swear, her concern for the boy. But she was, after all, Maria's friend. His old friend Harry Grenville had been a sensible fellow until he'd met

Maria. She'd been a giddy flirt before and after their marriage, and after Harry died she'd carried on even more, taking up with one marginal fellow after another.

Sebastian frowned. He turned his team.

"Changin' in midstream, guv?" called out the raffish boy who acted as his tiger and perched on the back of his curricle. "What's up?"

"Time to see that man-at-law again," he told the lad.

He had to reassure himself that though he'd made a quick decision, it hadn't been a rash one.

Whatever the man-at-law said, Sebastian vowed to be sure to take a longer and harder look at Miss Laura Lockwood when they met the next day. Then, however charming she was or pretended to be, he'd make sure he'd made the right decision.

"That was capital!" Alex caroled as they left Astley's. "Wasn't that splendid? Thank you, sir," he told the viscount, looking up at him with sparkling eyes.

"I confess I enjoyed it too," the viscount said. "And you?" he asked Laura.

She smiled up at him. There weren't words for how she felt. But still, she said, "It was wonderful."

"And Pompey loved it too!" Alex announced.

Both adults turned to look at him.

He opened his coat, and two bright eyes looked back at them.

"You carried the dog under your coat?" Laura gasped. "To a horse show?"

"Astonishing," the viscount said. "A dog who didn't bark or so much as squeak for all those hours as the horses trotted by."

"He's a daisy," Alex said proudly.

"But . . ." Laura said, "I thought he was too big to fit under your coat."

"He's just the right size," Alex said comfortably, setting the dog down on the pavement beside him.

"But he *is* too big," Laura murmured, eyeing the fat puppy.

"Evidently not," the viscount said. "But I'm afraid he's far too big to take out for the treat I'd planned. I'd thought we'd go for pastries next."

Laura's eyes grew wide. Of course, the afternoon was still young. But they couldn't go to a shop or a bakery, not with the dog in tow. And so then the viscount would probably expect her to invite him back to her home for tea. She couldn't.

After a moment in which no one spoke, the viscount did again. "We could go to my house," he said. "But I've no respectable female living with me, and Alex cannot be considered a suitable chaperon." He said that with one dark eyebrow raised, as if in expectation. His gray eyes weren't flinty now as he gazed at her, but rather warm and soft as fog when it flowed over the meadows at dawn.

Deep waters best left untested, Laura thought uneasily, and said, too brightly, "Oh my. My oversight, I'm afraid. I thought it would be acceptable for me to come with Alex, especially at this hour, without another escort for propriety's sake. But of course, you're right. So then," she said on an inspiration, "why don't we make it a true London holiday treat for him? Can't we eat *alfresco*? There are so many street vendors out today. We have a grand selection laid out before us. We can buy pasties or pastries, cakes and gingerbread, tea or hot lemonade and more, as we stroll toward the park. But I insist on paying for the gingerbread, at least."

"Never," the viscount said, and they argued about it pleasantly as they strolled down the street toward the park.

They ended up buying gingerbread and hot cider,

and they ate and drank while sitting on a bench in
the park watching Alex and Pompey romp on the wide
lawns. The sun was out and the air was mild, for December. The park was crowded with nannies and their
charges, well-dressed people strolled the lanes, and
dashing gentlemen rode by on horseback, expertly
threading their way through the line of elegant, slow-
moving equipages.

Laura hadn't been at leisure in this fashionable section of the park in years, and she enjoyed it immensely. Nothing was as delicious, though, as the
experience of sitting beside a handsome gentleman
and flirting with him. Because that was what they were
doing, and she hadn't been able to flirt with a gentleman as an equal since she'd been seventeen. It was
headier than the mulled cider; it was intoxicating.

The viscount wasn't handsome in the classical sense
of the word, but he was surely a wildly attractive male.
It wasn't only his elegant clothes or his air of certainty.
He had perfect manners, a sly sense of humor, and a
deep voice, which thrilled Laura, and not only because
she didn't hear adult male voices too often. He also
had the tiniest suggestion of a cleft in his firm chin.
She noted it when she dropped her gaze to avoid his
searching eyes, after she found herself shocked by her
reaction when she looked at his well-shaped mouth.

Laura sighed. A week of this and she didn't know
if she could ever be happy in her small room with
her small charges, in her small world, again. Then she
realized she was being foolish. She'd have Alex for
the week, not the Viscount Falconer. She might never
see him again, except for when she delivered Alex for
his week with him.

"So where shall we take Alex next?" the viscount
asked her.

We! and *next!* Laura thought with a surge of glee.
But, "I was thinking of the museum for tomorrow,"
was what she said.

The lofty viscount made a face that made him look about Alex's age. "Ancient crumbling statues and stuffed birds? Sad stuff for a boy, I'd think."

"I also thought about taking him to the Tower," she said quickly.

"That's more like it. Show him where heads were lopped off. He'll be enchanted."

"Yes, exactly," she said. "That will be for when he's older. I was thinking more along the lines of showing him the crown jewels."

"Glitter attracts you ladies," he said. "I wasn't joking. Give a lad a bucket of blood to make him happy, and throw in a few instruments of torture for an unforgettable day."

She laughed.

He admired the way that made her face light up, the line of her throat as she tossed back her head, the way the sunlight made her eyes glow when she looked back at him.

"I'll come along to show him the gory details, if you'd like," he said.

She smiled. "I'd like that very much."

He wondered again what to make of this charming, intelligent young woman. Maria's man-at-law had confirmed that Laura Lockwood was an old school friend of the merry widow, and that she was a respectable young woman, daughter of a deceased knight. Her London address was in a district that had known better days, but it too was respectable. So what the devil was she about going out with him without a maid in tow for propriety's sake? And why should the unmarried daughter of a gentleman wear unfashionable clothes? She looked charming in them, but they weren't the latest mode. And most of all, why didn't she invite him to call on her at home, as a proper young female should?

. . . Unless, of course, he thought, like her friend Maria, she *had* been a respectable young woman, and

now was something very different. It might be that
the absent friend she shared her home with was more
than that. It might be that the *friend* was a male. She
was lovely; she had manners as well as upbringing.
And so if she needed funds and for whatever reasons
had no prospects of marriage, she might well have
found herself a protector. She wouldn't be the first to
have done so. And if her protector was no longer
living with her, it could be he had left her forever and
not just for Christmas. That would explain why she
was alone now, and why she didn't live with her
mother. Such an arrangement could well have made
her family cast her out. It would also explain why she
hadn't the funds to dress in higher style, and relied
on public transportation.

Yes, Sebastian mused, it might well be. In any case,
the situation warranted a closer look—just as she did.
Even if his conjectures were true, he supposed she'd
done young Alex no harm, as yet. If he found out that
it was possible she could, the boy would pass the rest
of the holiday with him.

"It's growing late," he said. "So where shall we
dine tonight?"

Her eyes widened. She consulted the watch she kept
clipped inside her pelisse. "Oh my! So it is. It's already
growing dark. But I'm too full of gingerbread and
cider to even think of dinner," she added, lying, because she already felt the pinch of hunger.

"I didn't mean now, at sunset," he said, laughing at
the thought. "No one dines out before nine."

She bit her lip. She'd forgotten that was how the
ton dined. She ate her dinners at sunset because she
ate with her charges, and they had to go to bed right
after that.

"Exactly," she said, with a brittle smile. "And Alex
must be in bed by nine. I'm afraid my dinner will be
some soup, tea, and buttered toast tonight—and at a
most unfashionable eight o'clock. But thank you for

the invitation." She rose from the bench and called, "Alex, time to go!"

"What time shall I come get you tomorrow, then?" he asked.

He could see the look of dismay that flashed across her face even in the lowering light.

"I think it would be best to meet you at the Tower. We might dawdle over breakfast, you see," she added in a forcedly bright voice. "Then we have to walk Pompey so he doesn't embarrass us at the Tower. So to be sure, why don't you meet us there at noon?"

He bowed. "Perfect," he said. "Come, let me get you a hackney."

He saw Laura and Alex, and Pompey, who seemed to have grown a few inches since they'd arrived at the park, into the hackney, told the driver, "Great Irvington Street," paid him, and smiled as they waved good-bye when the coach rattled off.

But he was lost in thought as he walked through the park toward his own town house.

"Lud! We meet by daylight," a female voice trilled. "It is my lucky day!"

Sebastian looked up. A petite young dasher had paused in his path and was smiling up at him. Her pelisse was as red as her painted lips, her cheeks were as blushed with color as her red-gold hair, and her smile was as practiced as any actress's. Which was only fitting, since the young woman had been an actress on the stage before she discovered that acting for an audience of one, in bed, was easier and much more lucrative.

"Hello, Miss Lane," he said, and sketched a bow to his mistress.

"Oh, la!" she said, tapping him with one gloved hand. "So formal! But here I was out for a stroll, and who should I meet up with but the man I've been looking for all week! What luck!"

He doubted that. They were close to his house.

She'd likely been waiting for him. "And why were you looking for me?" he asked.

"Why, you know better than that!" she said.

He hadn't realized that she always spoke with such emphasis. It probably was what had defeated her career on the stage. He realized it was also probably what made her so successful at her present career. A man did like encouragement, and there were times when fervent enthusiasm wasn't questioned. But it seemed his ears had lately become accustomed to softer tones.

"I'm flattered," he said. "But unfortunately, I can't spend any time with you now. I'm promised to someone else this evening," he lied. "No one as lovely as you, I assure you," he added, to stop her pouting. He used to think those red lips were adorably kissable when she pouted. Now they made him think of a trout out of water. "In truth," he added, speaking as the idea occurred to him, "I was going to send you a note."

She didn't live in apartments he rented for her; he wasn't that firmly fixed as her sole protector yet. Last week, the notion had tempted him. Now he was delighted it would be so simple to disengage himself.

"I'll be gone for the Christmas holidays," he went on. "I can't say when I'll return to London. It would be wrong to keep you expecting me."

All traces of coquetry fled. "I see," she said flatly, eyeing him with dislike. "Giving me the boot, are you?"

"Not in so many words . . . Well, I am, I suppose," he admitted. "I won't leave you without funds, though. I'll send a generous sum to tide you over until you make new arrangements."

"Didn't think you wouldn't," she said with a shrug. "You're a gent, and a nice one, at that. Mind telling me if it's anything i did—or didn't? I've got a reputation and a future to worry about, you know."

"Nothing you said or did or didn't," he said truthfully. "It's just that . . ." He found himself searching for words because he himself didn't know the real reason why. It had just been an irresistible impulse that once acted upon seemed very right.

"Another female?" she asked.

He cocked his head to the side. "Let's say, the idea of one," he said truthfully.

"Well, it's Christmastime," she said with a shrug. "Men get sentimental. If you change your mind, let me know. Don't forget my address in either case," she added, "seeing as to how a generous settlement would give me a vacation, and be a real holiday treat."

It was a slap at him but he decided not to take offense. He owed her a chance to get her own back. "I'll see to it," he said, and meant it. He bowed and watched her walk away.

Sebastian felt a little disquieted because the whole thing meant so little to him—and to her. He also felt a little more than annoyed at himself. He'd campaigned to secure her affections, and had been pleased with them until today. The truth was another woman was to blame. He felt a surge of expectation and desire. It wasn't because his mistress was walking away with such a jaunty swagger, causing her bottom to sway so he could see the last of what he'd just given up. It was because he realized he'd like a Christmas treat too. And that led him to thinking about Miss Laura Lockwood again.

Pompey paused at the foot of the stair to Laura's rooms, even though Alex was quietly urging him to follow. Laura frowned. The puppy had really been remarkably obedient, making her forget he was just a pup. He was quiet as a mouse all night, where he lay curled up at the foot of Alex's bed. He didn't bark or play loudly when he was in her rooms. In the park he'd played with all the abandon a boy could want, but always come back to Alex at a whistle.

He was clearly a dog of contradictions. Well-behaved as he'd previously been, he now sat and refused to budge his bottom. And though he'd been small enough to hide within the folds of Alex's jacket at Astley's Amphitheatre the day before, it was just as clear now that he was too large for the boy to carry up the stairs. Puppies grew quickly, but Laura believed this dog must surely be setting records. It couldn't just be all fur. Alex would surely hurt himself hauling the beast up all the stairs.

Alex had started off whispering encouragement, but now his exhortations were getting louder. The last thing Laura wanted was for her landlady to clap eyes on the dog.

"I'll carry him," she whispered, and bent to pick Pompey up.

Her landlady's door opened.

Laura froze. Alex stood stock-still. Pompey looked up at the landlady and started to thump his tail on the floor.

The landlady stared. Then she smiled. "Oh my! Just look at this fine little fellow!" She bent to stroke the silky ears, and then, with ease, lifted Pompey up in her arms.

Laura gaped. If she hadn't seen it, she wouldn't have believed it, but the dog fit as comfortably in Mrs. Finch's skinny arms as a baby spaniel might have done.

"Mmm," the landlady said, rubbing her chin in Pompey's fluffy fur, "he reminds me of the pup I had when I was young. The best dog I ever owned, even though he was small as a squirrel. I used to dress him in baby clothes and carry him everywhere with me. I love dogs, but they made my late husband sneeze, so I haven't had one in years. But just look at this little fellow! *'Oo's a clever little mudgekin?''* she asked Pompey in a high squeaky voice. *"He is!''*

Pompey licked her face.

"And oo's ittu baby are you?" she asked him.

Alex took a step forward. "He's my dog, ma'am."

The landlady looked down her long nose at Alex. "And who is this?"

"This is Alexander, the Marquess Grenville, son of a dear friend of mine," Laura said. "He's visiting me for the holidays."

"Marquess?" the landlady said. "And I'm Queen of the May. What would a marquess be doing staying here, eh? No matter, we all have dreams and fancies. But this," she said, stroking Pompey, "is truly a fine little doggy you have, young fellow." Her smile erased most of the lines in her careworn face. "Don't suppose you'd care to sell him? Got a shilling here that would fit right in your pocket. He'd make a grand Christmas present—to myself."

"No, ma'am," Alex said in a worried voice. "He's mine, you see."

"Aye," she said in a softer voice. "I remember. I was only funning." She reluctantly set Pompey on the ground again. "Be sure to take him out regular, so my floors stay clean, you hear?"

"Oh, yes, ma'am," Alex said as he scooped Pompey up in his arms.

"Well then, good day," the landlady said, and went back into her rooms and closed the door behind her.

Laura looked down at Alex. She could hardly see his face now. Pompey was bigger than the boy who held him.

"Alex," Laura said slowly, "did it ever occur to you that Pompey is a very strange dog?"

"He's perfect," Alex said staunchly.

"Come, you can tell me," she persisted. "How long have you had him?"

"Not long enough," Alex said.

"Where did you get him?"

"He was . . . a gift," Alex said.

Laura sighed. "Well, put him down now before you do yourself an injury, and let's go upstairs."

But so he was a strange dog, she thought pensively. Not only did Pompey's size appear to be as variable as most puppies' moods, he was obedient and well mannered. And unlike any other pup she'd ever seen, he never chewed on furniture or slippers.

The trio went up to Laura's attic rooms. Laura was thoughtful, wondering if it were her eyes or her mind playing tricks. Alex took the stairs as fast as a young lad could. And Pompey came lumbering after.

The day was fine, cold, but the sun peeking through scudding clouds gave an illusion of warmth. Laura wore her best gown. It wasn't very different from her worst one, but she knew it was newer and that made her feel better—at least, until she saw the Viscount Falconer. He was dressed so splendidly she felt as though she ought to walk a few paces behind him. He didn't seem to notice her shabbiness, or care. She thought that might be just his excellent manners, but after a few moments in his company she didn't care either.

She placed her hand on his proffered arm, feeling like a lady again for the first time in a very long time.

Alex and Pompey walked the grounds at the Tower beside them, Pompey now on a lead that the viscount supplied.

"I know the lad has fine manners," he told Alex, as he clipped the new lead onto the new collar he'd also brought. "But the guards at the Tower might not."

Whether the guards did or did not, Laura never knew. The coins the viscount gave them ensured their smiles as they let Pompey pass through the gate, just as though he were a pug carried by a lady of the court and not a big, bumbling bear of a puppy, romping alongside a young boy.

The cells and the chopping block and its bloody history interested Alex. The medals and royal artifacts on display clearly bored him. But his ears pricked up, along with Pompey's, when the viscount declared the menagerie their next destination.

The sun glistened on the wide waters of the Thames, making it sparkle brighter than any of the crown jewels as the trio paced along the bank toward the compound where the exotic animals were housed.

Laura heard the howling and trumpeting as they got closer, and grew nervous. "Do you think this is wise?" she asked the viscount. "Do you think the animals will react badly to seeing Pompey?"

He patted the hand that lay on his arm. "It's being locked up that disturbs them, not seeing those that are free."

Indeed, Laura was amazed because the animals actually quieted when they saw Pompey. And they saw him, that was obvious. The humans that looked into their cages seemed to be transparent to them. But the glazed and desperate looks in their eyes sharpened and then focused on Pompey whenever he appeared before them. Whenever he did, they fell still.

The dog himself behaved strangely. He paused and sat for a moment before each cage he passed. He seemed to be communing with the beast inside, whether elephant or tiger. And each beast appeared to be listening to whatever silent thing he said.

"Pompey is the strangest dog I ever met," Laura whispered to the viscount as they watched a threadbare lioness stop pacing, her mad yellow eyes growing calm and sane as she stared at the dog.

The viscount nodded. "I agree. But there's no question he's devoted to the boy. I don't know where Alex picked up the creature, but now I begin to believe Pompey picked him. That's not at all bad for him. He needs the devotion." He hesitated. He studied Laura's face. "I don't know how close you are to Alex's mother, but surely you know she's not very close to him."

"I know," she said sadly. "We, she and I, aren't close anymore either. We haven't been for years, actually."

"And yet you agreed to take the boy for Christmas. No, you fought for the right."

"So I did."

"And why is that?" he asked.

"Were you close to his father?" she asked in return.

"No, not after he married Maria."

"And yet you fought for the right to take care of Alex too."

He smiled. "Yes, and now I'm glad I did. Think what I might have missed if I'd just handed the boy over to you and forgotten my promise. Sometimes," he added with a teasing smile, "good deeds bring their own rewards."

Because she couldn't think that he could really think befriending her was a reward, Laura looked away. Just in time to see that Alex and Pompey had proceeded to the next cage, where a huge black bear was almost touching noses with Pompey through the bars of the cage.

She gasped. The viscount dropped her hand and sprinted forward. He ran to the dog, prepared to snatch him away, and then paused. There was no animosity shown by either creature.

"She must think he's a cub," Alex whispered excitedly. "See how gentle she is with him? He looks like one too, doesn't he?"

"So he does," the viscount said softly, gently easing Alex back from the cage. "Pompey is a strange beast, altogether. Where exactly did you find him, Alex?"

Alex's smile vanished. "He's my dog, sir," he said stiffly.

"And that's that, eh? Well, it's all right with me, and obviously it is with Miss Lockwood too. But you do know you must give him up when you go back to school."

Alex grew still. Pompey nudged the boy's hand. "He wants to walk on," Alex said abruptly. "May we?"

"Of course," the viscount said. "That's what we're here for."

It was in all a glorious day. But it grew colder as the sun sank in the west.

"Time to go," the viscount finally said when he noticed how Laura pulled her pelisse tighter as a chilly wind began blowing in off the river. "Today I brought my carriage so I can take you home in style."

Laura grew even colder at his words.

"How kind," she said, trying to conceal her horror. But she was prepared. She'd sat up in the night thinking about what she'd do if this happened. "But we're not going straight home. I have to buy Alex's Christmas present and so I thought we'd go to a toy store and I'd watch and see what he wants most of all."

"That's a good idea. I'll come along with you, if I may, because I'll have the same problem when Christmas comes."

He saw her tear and dismay and realized that whatever her game, he didn't want to hurt her. But now he knew she would always refuse to let him see where she lived, or with whom. She only had Alex in her care for a while longer, but that might be too long if her behavior in any way jeopardized the boy physically, or, more likely in her case, morally.

The viscount suddenly realized that it was far too long a time for him to wait to know what her circumstances were. He meant to find out what she was up to once and for all.

"You can't bring Pompey into a toy shop," he said.

"I know," she said miserably.

"And the shops will be closing soon in any case."

"I know," she said, her eyes searching his.

"So you might as well go home."

"True," she said, "but you see, the thing is . . . the point is . . ."

"That things at your home aren't what you'd wish?" he asked softly. "And certainly not what you'd wish me to see?"

She caught her breath. Then she nodded and looked down at the pavement as she sought all the well-rehearsed words she'd thought up in the middle of the night, things she'd meant to say to him if and when her secret was finally discovered. She didn't know how he'd done it, but he'd obviously found out the truth about her circumstances.

"But I'm a man of the world," he went on gently, taking her hand in his. "I understand that reversals of fortune can make people do things they mightn't otherwise do."

She looked up, hope springing into her eyes as they searched his.

His smile was tender, his handclasp strong and warm, his gaze soft as his voice. "Please don't take offense. I am, as I said, a worldly fellow. But your circumstances may be . . . difficult for a child to live with. I only worry that Alex might be exposed to things beyond his understanding if he stays with you. That would be a thing I couldn't countenance. He has only seven years to his name, after all."

"Oh no!" she cried, and said in a rush, "I promise he's in no way compromised, or in need, or unhappy or likely to be, no matter my present living accommodations. There's enough for us, and there's just the two of us, and as for me, I find him good company and think he feels the same about me. I *promise* my circumstances can in no way reflect on him. I wouldn't have taken him in if it were so. That, I vow!"

"Hush," the viscount said, "don't fret. I believe you.

I'm glad we spoke of it though." He cocked his head to the side and studied her. "You have no one with you but Alex and Pompey now?"

She nodded sadly. "Yes. As I told you."

"Your position is unenviable."

She couldn't answer. That was nothing but truth.

"But I think I may have a solution," he said.

Her eyes widened. Could he help her achieve her dearest secret hope? He was after all a nobleman with money and influence. If he'd found out about her financial difficulties, maybe he also knew of a way she and her mother could recoup some of her father's assets. When her father died everything had gone to the nearest male heir, but Laura always believed there had to have been something that wasn't entailed. She'd been sure there were things their greedy cousin had taken that he'd no right to. She was convinced he'd done so because he'd known his distant cousin's impoverished widow and daughter had no money or recourse to do anything about it.

"A solution?" she breathed. "Really? Oh, that would be wonderful."

He looked down at her parted lips, so shapely, so near, and bent closer to her . . . until something bumped his leg, almost toppling him. He righted himself and looked down. Pompey looked up at him with a dark, searching gaze.

"Done with the beasts already?" the viscount asked Alex.

"Yes. They don't look happy," Alex said. "But the guards said they'd all get a treat for Christmas. The best one would be to free them."

"Lions in Pall Mall?" Laura asked. "A tiger in Parliament Square? I don't think so, Alex, but I agree. No one can be happy in a cage or trapped in a life they'd never have chosen."

"That's true, but this will never do!" the viscount exclaimed. "It's too close to the holiday to be so sad.

Let's make plans for our Christmas treats. I'll have your company on Christmas day, Alex, because it will be my turn to house you then. Maybe you can help me think up some wonderful surprises for you and for Miss Lockwood, because certainly we should all celebrate the holiday together. What do you think of that?"

"Yes!" Alex said happily. "I think that would be good."

No, Laura thought, looking at the smiling gentleman. That would be better than good, because this attractive, clever gentleman is also the kindest man I've ever met.

No, Sebastian thought, watching Laura's glowing face, that would be beyond good, because good has nothing to do with it.

He'd have his Christmas treat after all. It was hasty decision on his part, but he'd just disposed of one mistress on just as quick a whim. It had been the right decision too. How much time did a man need? His body had decided on Laura Lockwood long before he'd consciously brought the matter to mind. Now she'd as much as admitted his theory about her had been right. That wasn't the only thing that was.

He saw the way she looked at him. He knew the way she'd lived, how she had to live now. It was clear. He needed her. She needed him. He could hardly wait to get Miss Laura Lockwood alone to make his proposal and get matters under way.

But the viscount couldn't get Miss Lockwood alone the next day, or during the days after. They did not have two seconds alone together, much less a chance for a serious talk. They'd gone to the park again and watched a cricket match until a thin sleet chased them to their separate houses, since a dog couldn't go to a pastry shop, and a tavern wasn't the proper place for a child, and Alex wouldn't go anywhere without his dog.

They went back to the park the next day and watched a Punch and Judy show until the snow coated them over and sent them back to their own homes again.

They watched a game of rounders the following day, cheered for their favorite players, and ate hot chestnuts and drank hot soup that they bought from vendors and held in their gloved hands. But they went their separate ways when the sun sank low.

They walked and talked, and the days sped by. They attended a special holiday children's performance of the ballet one afternoon, but had to part immediately after, because Laura and Alex had to walk Pompey. And then it would be Alex's bedtime.

As he walked home that evening, the viscount realized they never met any of his acquaintances. He supposed that was because they always went places meant for children, and all his friends who had children had left town for the holidays. He didn't see any women he knew, highborn or low-. He supposed that was because they never spent time with their children. It made him pensive.

He couldn't invite Laura to the theater or a restaurant by herself. Or rather, he did, but she never accepted. She didn't mind spending time with him and Alex without a proper chaperon, but shied at seeing him alone, day or evening, and refused to leave Alex, saying he was only her responsibility for a little while, and she would watch over him for every moment of that time.

Sebastian couldn't go to her house, because he wasn't invited. And he never had single females visit him in his own home at night. Having a proper young woman there would signal his desire to marry her. Having an improper one . . . Well, it just wasn't done.

Still, Laura saw the viscount, and he saw her, and they enjoyed each other's company more each day. They spoke about any number of things, and laughed about even more. They watched each other, and each hoped to see more of the other, albeit in very different ways.

Then Alex got a letter from his mama. So did Laura, both letters having been forwarded to them by Maria's man-at-law.

They sat near the windows of their attic rooms late that snowy afternoon, reading their letter. Alex finished first, and folded his letter neatly. "Mama says she hopes to see me in the spring," he said somberly.

Laura finished rereading her letter. "Yes. She tells me the same thing. She misses you very much."

Alex shrugged.

Laura felt both bad and better for having read her letter. Maria had never been so forthcoming, and she'd explained many things. She'd thanked her old friend for taking her son for Christmas, and then added that she was lonely and discontented, although not so much as she'd been when her husband had been alive. Still, she'd confessed, none of the diversions she'd sought had healed her from the experience of having a husband who had always preferred warfare to his wife's company, and foreign adventure to the adventure of raising a family.

Maria also wrote that she was lonely and felt guilty, and that nothing had worked out as she'd planned. She hoped Laura would understand, because all she'd done had been done out of a desire for friendship and love, and she really hadn't changed that much since they'd been girls.

Laura understood too well. How could she blame her old friend for lusting after adventure and pleasure, when she herself did the same, if only in vain? She hadn't known what desire was until she'd met the Viscount Falconer. She'd met few eligible men, and none like him. But since she had she could think of little else but his face, his form, and his touch, even though she knew she'd never find pleasure in anything but looking at him and hearing his rich deep voice. And though nothing could or would come of it, now she found herself less puritanical, less judgmental, and, most of all, less content with her lot.

Because it simply wasn't enough to have his friendship, not once she'd realized she'd never know his embrace, or hear him whisper love words to her. And even if she could be content with mere friendship, that was also impossible. The bridge between their worlds existed only now, in these last few days before Christmas, because only now did a small boy bring them together.

So certainly she understood her unhappy friend Maria. But there was no need to make Alex unhappy too.

"So!" Laura said with a show of brightness. "There's cause for celebration. Your mama will be home along with the violets in the spring. Then, she says, she wants you to live at home with her. Seven is, after all, very young to be away at school."

Alex's smile was uncertain. He lowered his eyes. Pompey roused himself from sleep and waddled over to the boy. Alex petted the dog and said nothing.

"Aren't you glad?" Laura asked.

Alex raised his eyes to her. "S'pose it will be good, though I don't much know my mama. And it will be nice to be home. But, see, thing is"—he hesitated— "well, the thing is that I don't know what to do about Pompey until then."

"Oh," Laura said. She was surprised he actually admitted that he hadn't had the dog with him at school.

"So, thing is," Alex went on resolutely, "I wondered if you could keep him for me until then. I mean, until Mama comes home."

Laura looked at the two pairs of eyes watching her: one blue and filled with sadness and hope, the other pair brown and filled with even more.

"Oh, my," she sighed. "I'd like to, I want to, but

Alex, I don't *have* a home of my own. I don't really live here; I'm just renting these rooms for the holidays. My mama lives up in the Lake District, and I must work to pay for her lodgings. I'm a governess, usually, that is, when it's not Christmastime. I haven't room, or permission, to keep so much as an ant of my own when I'm working. Which I'll be doing when the holiday is over."

The boy's expression broke her heart, because it looked as tragic as Pompey's great sad drooping eyes did.

"My landlady loved Pompey," she said. "Why not ask her?"

"She won't want to give him back," Alex said simply.

Laura fell still. That was entirely possible.

"But what about the viscount?" she asked on a sudden inspiration. "I'm sure he has enough room to house that elephant we saw at the Tower! Why not ask him?"

"I lied to him," Alex said simply.

"Well, yes. You did, to be sure. But sometimes if a lie is told to help another person . . . or animal," she corrected herself, "it's not quite so reprehensible. He's a kind man, I'm sure he'll understand."

Boy and dog looked at her curiously. The boy spoke. "Will you ask him, for me?"

"Of course. Tomorrow. We're promised to meet him at the lake in the park. He said he'll take you skating. The snow will have stopped by then. Even if it doesn't, we can dress up warmly. Won't that be fun?"

"S'pose," Alex said, and buried his face in Pompey's neck.

"I'll ask," Laura said seriously. "I promise. We'll find a good place for Pompey until your mama comes home. I promise you that too."

But she wondered what she'd do if the viscount

couldn't take the dog because of previous commitments, or whatnot. She knew very little about his private life. He never spoke about his plans for the future either, nor did she expect him to. What was she to him, after all? To be fair, she'd never been entirely candid with him either. They seemed to have made a silent agreement. They both lived from day to day in an artificial bubble of Christmas cheer for Alex's sake, and never discussed what they planned for the new year.

She looked at Alex, who had his arms wrapped around Pompey. The dog watched her with dignified sorrow.

Whatever the viscount's answer, Laura vowed then and there that she'd pay for Pompey's upkeep and boarding if she had to. She'd put away money for Alex's holiday and had saved a considerable bit of it since she'd met the viscount, because he insisted on buying their treats and hackney-cab rides. If she did pay for the dog's board, she'd have nothing left for herself. But then, she thought with newfound wisdom and sorrow, there was never too high a price to pay for love, was there?

The lake wasn't entirely frozen. Signs had been posted to that effect, and anyone could see that only the center was thick white ice, while the rest of the lake was translucent, with only a thin glaze over the dark water at the banks.

"It's like my heart," the viscount said dramatically, putting his hand on his chest, "cold on the outside, but warmth beneath."

Alex grinned. Laura laughed out loud.

"So I'm afraid we can't skate today," the viscount continued. "Still, we can give Pompey some exercise." He eyed the dog. Pompey looked the size of a small pony, although he supposed most of it could be an illusion, because the dog's fur was so thick. "Lud!" he exclaimed. "What are you feeding him? I swear he's twice the size he was when we went to Astley's."

Pompey wagged his great plume of a tail.

"Doesn't he look grand?" Alex asked nervously. "And he's trained to live in a house, truly he is! He never makes a mistake. And he barks if anyone comes near the house, but not too loud or too long. Truly, sir, he's the best of puppies."

"Puppy?" the viscount asked. "I daresay he would be, if he were a puppy. How long have you had him?"

"Not long enough!" Alex said quickly. "But it's just that puppies grow fast. I don't think he'll grow any bigger, truly I don't, sir."

The viscount raised an eyebrow. "He needs some exercise, whatever size he's going to be." He bent, picked up a stick, and threw it. "Fetch!" he called.

Pompey went bounding after the stick, Alex at his heels.

"Why is he praising the dog so much?" the viscount asked Laura, as they slowly paced along the border of the lake, following the boy and the dog. "What's he done wrong?"

"Nothing," she said. "The dog is, as he said, a remarkably amiable creature. But Alex admitted he can't take him back to school with him, and asked me to ask you if you could house him until his mother comes home. Oh! That's the best news," she said excitedly. "We both received letters from Maria yesterday. She's coming home in the spring, and she's resolved to turn over a new leaf."

The viscount sneered. "Like Pompey vowing to give a lecture, I'm afraid."

Laura drew herself up, her expression suddenly chill. "No, it's not. Maria had reasons to act as she did. She wrote and told me."

"Did she?" he drawled, his voice dripping ice. "Interesting. *I*, however, saw how she behaved. She flirted shamelessly, even when poor Harry was alive and by her side."

"Was he?" Laura answered as coldly. "Interesting, indeed. I had heard that he was seldom by her side. He was far more often with his comrades in the army, whether he was at war or not. Or if not, then he was off hunting or riding, more comfortable with his friends than he ever was with his wife. She flirted to get a man's attention, I'm sure. But she says, and I believe, that that man was her husband."

The viscount's head went up higher than his stiff white neckcloth could account for. He looked down his nose at her. "I can see that you would like to believe that," he finally said.

"And I," Laura said, equally haughtily, "can easily see how you would like to believe that your friend was a model husband."

They stared at each other for a moment.

She saw a tall, imposing, imperious gentleman of fashion, breathtakingly attractive and equally imposing. His clothing was as impeccable as his breeding, and she knew he was proud of both. He said he'd found a solution for her difficulties. He'd obviously forgotten the entire matter. She wondered how she could ever for a moment have believed he could understand her.

He saw her curls peeking out from under her unfashionable bonnet, and wished he could give her a finer one, to suit her charming face. He wanted to buy her gowns to show off her deliciously curved form. He wanted even more to take them off that deliciously curved form. Her speaking eyes looked into his, her lips were soft and appealing. He saw a lovely, desirable, proud young woman, and wondered why he was arguing with her.

"Come," he said suddenly, his expression easing. "Let's not fight about what neither of us can ever really know."

Laura sighed. "I suppose you're right. Instead, let's think of where we can board Pompey for Alex, until Maria comes home in the spring."

"No," he said softly, tenderly, his eyes searching hers. "First, shouldn't we be thinking about where *you* should be boarding until spring, and summer, and next winter?"

She blinked, then, embarrassed, looked away. He had indeed discovered her circumstances. "So, you know," she said as softly, though there was no one near to overhear them.

He nodded. "Yes. So, Miss Lockwood, what shall you do?"

Her spirits rose, but she didn't want to beg for his help. She shrugged. "If I can't prove my cousin cheated my mother and myself out of our rightful inheritance? Go on, I suppose, as I have begun. I have obligations: my mother, my future. I have to earn money and save it for both our sakes."

"I thought as much," he breathed. He stopped walking, turned to her, and took her mittened hands in his gloved ones. "But, as I said, I have a solution."

She stared up at him with breathless hope.

"There's no need for you to go on alone," he said with a curious half smile. "Not when I am here."

But this was more than help he was offering! She could scarcely believe what she was hearing. She saw him nod, as his smile grew. "But if I'm not mistaken . . . it's far too soon for such an offer," she protested. "You hardly know me."

"What more is there to know?" he asked. "I see your beauty, I hear your voice and never heard anything foolish fall from your lovely lips. Unless you want to make me laugh," he added tenderly. "Then, you always succeed. I know you have a care for me; I'd bet my soul you haven't been pretending that. Your misfortunes kept us apart until now, otherwise we might well have met sooner and under happier conditions. But now fortune has brought us together.

"Let's not rue the past, or waste what fate has given us," he said. "I've met society misses as well as wantons, women from all walks of life, but I swear I've never met your like before. Nor am I apt to do so. What more could I want? I'm comfortable with you, I desire you, I need you. Come, let me take the burden of your future off your shoulders."

Laura searched his face to see if he was joking. But he was sincere. He'd never uttered a word of love, but she supposed that was because he was a proud man and probably wouldn't until he knew how she felt about him. Still he, the lofty Viscount Falconer, was offering for her!

Laura breathed a silent prayer of thanks. He was everything a woman could want in a husband, and she'd known it since they met. His proposal of marriage had been her one most secret wish, the one she'd never let herself seriously dream of.

Still, as she tried to frame her answer, she remembered she mustn't be overwhelmed with gratitude. That was no basis for a good marriage. She wasn't entirely beneath his notice, after all. As he said, they might have met long before this if her father hadn't died, and if he'd left her anything but the will to go on. She was well-bred; she'd once been considered a lady. She didn't know if she deserved him, but she knew he had no need to feel ashamed of his choice.

She gazed at the devilishly attractive male before her, seeing that he was breathlessly watching, waiting for her answer.

She smiled shyly.

"Excellent!" he said fervently, taking her hand to his lips. "I see your answer in your eyes."

She closed her eyes and waited for him to take her in his arms.

He didn't. "But for now," he said quietly, clasping her hands tightly, "this must be our secret. I can't move you to better lodgings until after Alex returns to school. We can't even speak of it until then, much less act on it. But be sure, I can't wait until we do."

Her eyes snapped open.

"Don't worry," he added quickly, "I'll make adequate provisions for you. More than adequate," he went on, noting her eyes narrowing. "A handsome flat in a good district, a generous allowance for clothes, and jewels, of course. Be assured, you'll have a liberal amount of pocket money too. Even if we find we don't suit, you'll be well provided for, but I don't envision . . . Why are you looking at me like that?"

"You," she said carefully, "are offering to make me your . . . mistress?"

"Well, yes, though I wouldn't put it that bluntly."

"How would you put it?" she asked.

"Well, I suppose that's what it is, though there are ways to say it more obliquely. But where's the need? Alex is nowhere near. And why are you so surprised? You're no blushing miss. After all, isn't that what you were before we met?"

She glared at him. "Why should you think so?"

"You said you had to support yourself," he said patiently, wondering what more she wanted him to promise. "You have no chaperones, no family I ever saw, indeed, no friends either, though you said you lived with them. What was I to think?"

She paused. "Anything but that, I suppose, if you believed me a good and decent person. Obviously you do not."

"Good, of course, yes. But decent?" he asked. "That depends on your interpretation of the word. I don't consider Maria decent, but you do. Come, what is this?"

"This," she said furiously, "is a refusal. No, never, ever!"

"And why not?"

"Because I am no man's mistress, I never was, and would never be!"

"Then what the devil were you talking about?" he asked in confusion.

"I was talking about my working to fulfill my obligations," she said angrily.

"Well, just so."

"So you assume that means a female who works for her livelihood is a prostitute?"

"I never said such!" he said, frowning. "But you do—or did—work at something you never specified. And too," he said, affronted, "you never invited me to your home. What else should I think?"

"Ah," she said. She snatched her hands from his. "I see. Or rather, I don't, but I see what you mean. Well, it's simple. I didn't invite you to my lodgings because I've been living in an attic, in rented rooms."

His eyes widened. He took a step back. "You work at a house of assignation?" he asked incredulously.

Her head went back as though he'd slapped her. Her color rose. "Worse," she spat. "Or so I suspect it would seem in the eyes of a man such as yourself. *Worldly,* are you, my lord? I think not. You do know your own world. Oh yes, that I do believe. But you're a man who never saw the world as it exists beyond his own riches and privileges. Because, my dear sir, I am not a whore. In fact, though I work for my living, and live in my employer's house and must obey her every command and put up with my patrons' whims, that is where the similarity ends. You see, sir, I'm alone at the moment, and in rented rooms, because I was granted a vacation for the holidays. Otherwise, I'm employed as a governess! And I'm a good one."

She looked over his shoulder at the romping boy and dog. "Moreover," she said stiffly, "as such, I don't think you're the sort of man an impressionable lad like Alex should be associating with. Good day, sir.

Alex!" she called, "*Pompey!* To me, please. We're going home."

The dog reached her first, and crowded close to her side.

The viscount was amazed to see the dog had such big white teeth, which were suddenly bared as it stared at him.

Alex merely looked from one adult to the other in confusion.

"We're going home," Laura said, taking Alex's hand. She turned on her heel and began walking.

"Good-bye, sir," Alex called as they marched back the way they'd come.

They'd only gone ten steps when the viscount came running up to them. "I hope you remember that I get Alex on Christmas day," he told Laura in clipped tones.

She bit her lip. That had been agreed. But she'd hoped they would all spend that day together. Now, even in her rage at the man, she realized she'd be alone on Christmas day; more alone than she'd been in years. She gave a curt nod.

"So we agreed," she said. She hesitated, then looked down at Alex and Pompey. Both were looking at her with big, sorrowful eyes. She swallowed her anger. There were some things more important than a foolish spinster's shattered dreams. She looked up at the viscount, her eyes bright with unshed tears. "But things have changed. Can't Alex stay with me for just that one more day? I was going to have a fine goose from the cookshop, an entire dinner, actually. I've treats planned for him.

"I was going to tell you everything on that day," she said, trying to keep from sounding as if she were pleading. "Because it would scarcely matter any more then, would it? You'd see for yourself, after all. I waited because I was afraid you might be just as appalled at my circumstances as you are, and would have taken Alex from me if you'd seen how I lived. You must admit that I did him no harm, whatever you think of my financial state. My lodgings are meager, but entirely respectable. I am entirely respectable too."

She tried to keep her pride, without offending him. She tried to state her position without letting Alex guess what had just happened between herself and the viscount. "We've all had fun together these past days, haven't we?" she asked. "Soon, it will be over. I'll have kept my promise to Maria. Please let him stay with me for Christmas day."

"I'd planned to take you all out for a Christmas dinner at a fine restaurant I frequent," he said, gazing at her steadily. "I was going to engage a private room. The owner knows me; he said he'd allow the dog. I thought we'd have a feast."

She shook her head. "That's not possible now," she said softly. "But may I please keep Alex for that one more day? I'll have him at your house the next morning, I promise."

He stared at her.

She stared at him.

Pompey looked up suddenly. His ears pricked forward, as though he heard someone call him. He looked around and suddenly took off, dashing down the road. As he ran, he crashed into Laura and knocked her off balance. She fell, toppling down the slight embankment and landing in the turgid waters of the semi-frozen lake.

The viscount was in the lake only moments after she landed there and sat sputtering and shivering. He scooped her up and strode back to the road with her. She was icy cold and soaking wet. Nevertheless, he thought her body felt just right in his arms.

Laura looked down as best she could from under the limp and dripping brim of her bonnet, and saw her drenched gown and pelisse. She realized she was clinging to the viscount. She hated him in that moment. She was embarrassed, hurt and frozen. But his arms were strong and his body held all the warmth she wanted, and she never wanted to stand on her own again.

Even so, she knew what she had to do. "Put me down, please," she said through chattering teeth. "I'm all right."

He set her carefully on her feet.

She winced at the icy water sloshing inside her ruined half boots.

"He didn't mean it!" Alex cried, his hand on the now-returned Pompey's collar. "He just ran after a squirrel and his shoulder bumped into you, but he never meant it, just look at him!"

Indeed, the dog looked penitent. He was a big tricolored heap of misery, his eyes grown huge and sad.

Laura felt even sadder. "I know," she said. "My fault for not watching where he was g-g-going." She realized she was stammering with cold. "But I think we should g-go home now."

"Yes," the viscount agreed. "And get you out of those dripping clothes. And no," he added in her ear as he picked her up again and strode to the entrance of the park with her in his arms, "I don't intend to divest you of them myself, only to make sure you're out of them as soon as possible."

He called a hackney cab, and they all piled into it. Laura gave her address to the driver. They drove to her rooms in silence. The viscount didn't let her out of his arms, even though her drenched clothing had thoroughly soaked his own.

But her curved little bottom was warm in his lap, and her body heated his own to furnace heat as the ride went on.

The hackney stopped, and the viscount bade the driver wait for him. He lifted Laura in his arms again, and stepped out of the coach, frowning when he saw the house. Harry's man-at-law had told him where she lived. It was a respectable neighborhood that had known better days. But he hadn't realized until now how long ago that must have been. He scowled and stared up to the top of the narrow house when she told him where her rooms were located. But he said nothing as Alex raced ahead to open the door for him, and not a word as he strode in through the doorway.

The woman he carried didn't say another word either.

But, "Oh, lord! What's happened?" the landlady cried as she opened her door and saw the viscount and his drenched burden come into her hall.

"She fell through the ice at the park," he told her tersely, because now he too was chilled to the bone.

"Well, then, bring her in here!" Mrs. Finch commanded. "I've a nice fire going, and I've a tub, and the poor thing needs to get out of those clothes and into a hot tub. Then she needs to sit before a fire, and there's no hearth in the attics. But how is the dear doggy?" she cried, looking for Pompey.

Pompey poked his head out from behind Alex, and wagged his tail.

The viscount blinked. In his condition, the dog seemed smaller, puppylike again.

"Let the dear doggy in," the landlady commanded, "and the boy too. . . ." She stopped, hands on her hips, and looked the viscount up and down. "And who, sir, are you?"

"Falconer," he said, "Viscount Falconer."

"Certainly," she said. "A viscount and a marquess in my house, is it? Well, I'm the Queen of Sheba, but get Miss Lockwood in here immediately anyway."

Then, and only then, did Laura make a sound. She giggled.

Laura didn't have much to laugh about in the days that followed. She didn't develop a cold, as her landlady had feared. But she didn't feel very well, either. She was still bruised and shaken, in heart and body, and couldn't get out much because a fiercely cold winter wind had begun to roam London's streets. Though she ventured out to buy Alex books and paints to keep him occupied, and spent every hour with him, she worried that he'd find his last days in her company sadly flat.

Still, she was determined that Christmas day, at least, would remain ever bright in Alex's mind, and set out to make that so. She hadn't heard from Viscount Falconer, apart from his sending a basket of out-of-season fruit after her mishap. And so she believed that meant he'd agreed she could keep Alex until Christmas.

Well, why not? she thought. What could a bachelor, even a rich and titled one, do for the boy that she couldn't?

"I've bought a few gifts," she told Mrs. Finch as they sat in the landlady's flat before her blazing hearth the night before Christmas. "And we've decorated my rooms with fresh evergreen boughs, as we used to do at home. Don't worry, I'll be sure to sweep up any needles that may fall. *And* I've ordered a fine goose from Mr. Benson, the poulterer," she added proudly.

"Well, won't we be stuffed then?" Mrs. Finch said. "Seeing as to how I ordered a fine turkey from him myself. And if you try to have your Christmas dinner anywhere else, Miss Lockwood, I'll turf the two of you out into the streets, rent paid or no. Of course," she added with a twinkle, "in that case, Pompey stays with me."

"Oh, Mrs. Finch," Laura said, and hugged her.

Alex smiled, and Pompey, at his side by the hearth, opened one sleepy eye and beat his tail on the floor.

"So," Laura said, "we'll have ourselves a happy Christmas tomorrow then, won't we?"

The others remained silent, and avoided her eyes.

Until that moment, Laura had thought she'd hidden her sorrow. "Well, then," she said with forced gaiety, as she stood, "thank you, Mrs. Finch. Come along, Alex, it's past time for bed."

They trooped up the stairs to their rooms. She waited until Alex and Pompey had crowded into Alex's bed. Laura blew out the lamp and went into the front room. But she didn't go to sleep. She sat gazing out the window, looking out over the chimney-pot-peppered rooftops of London.

A full moon appeared and disappeared as it sailed through wind-driven storm clouds; it looked as though the rooftops would be covered with snow by dawn.

Laura's expression was as distant and cold as the moon's. She'd endured a lot since her fortunes changed, going from pampered young lady to faceless servant. But she'd done it without a complaint. Now, however, she felt all the anger and regret that she'd suppressed. She felt sick with envy and a need for revenge—upon the cousin who had taken her old home, and now, too, upon the man who'd taken away her heart.

She knew she couldn't live the rest of her life that way.

And so she looked at the matter practically, and decided to endure.

After all, she reasoned, there was no saying he'd have courted her seriously even if they had met when she was still a lady. She had no title, and no entrée into London society. And she'd never had a fortune, at least not what a viscount would consider an adequate dowry.

Still, he'd wanted her in his bed, which was, although demeaning, also rather flattering, in a strange way.

So what if she never saw him again? she asked herself. His loss.

. . . And hers, she thought, as tears, translucent as

the silvery pre-storm light, at last trickled down her cheeks.

Laura sat at her window and waited for the great clocks of London to strike the Christmas hour, knowing that her greatest gift, her love, would probably never be given to any man. And that the love she wanted most in return would also never be hers. She only became aware of the lateness of the hour when she felt a furry head bump into hers, and felt a velvet tongue trying to lick away her tears.

"Oh, Pompey," she whispered as she hugged the enormous dog, finding comfort in the solid warmth of his great body, "what am I to do?"

"Sleep," must have been what he said, because with the great beast herding her like a wooly lamb, she left the window seat, stumbled to her bed, and did just that.

Mrs. Finch woke early the next morning and went out to sweep snow off her steps so she and her tenants could go to church. Alex walked in the door before she could get out. He was covered with snow.

"What's amiss?" she asked in sudden fright. "You're up and about so early."

His eyes were bleak, his expression stark.

"Is it Miss Laura? Has she taken a turn? I told her not to go out yesterday! Look at the snow piling up. Not gone to the doctor for her, I hope?" she asked fearfully, her hand going to her heart.

"No," he said bleakly. "I was looking for Pompey. He was gone when I woke up this morning. I can't find him anywhere. He's never done this before."

But neither had Laura gone coursing through the streets of London at dawn before either. She was looking for a dog that wasn't hard to find. Except that no one had seen him. And she was having a hard time describing him.

"A pup the size of a pony? Or one the size of a

lapdog? Come, miss," the watchman on the corner
said. "I can't say I seen the animal if I don't know
what he looks like."

"His looks are deceptive," Laura said, "but singular.
He's tricolored, with a white chest and a black coat,
white shoes and rust-colored socks. And rust eyebrows. He's very handsome, with floppy ears. If you'd
seen him, you'd know him."

"Then I ain't seen him," the watchman said, tipping
his hat to a resident who could be counted on to tip
him handsomely this Christmas too. "Sorry."

There weren't any vendors out, and Laura saw
fewer and fewer people to ask. It was, after all, Christmas morning. She retraced her steps back to the lodg-
ing house. Maybe Pompey had already returned; he
seldom left Alex's side. Fine Christmas this would be
for the boy if the dog left him! Fine Christmas, she
thought sadly as she trudged through the deepening
snow, for them all.

The goose was on the table, as was the turkey, both
done to a turn by the cookshop. They weren't alone.
They were surrounded by dishes of potatoes and peas,
creamed onions and sprouts, savories, chutneys, dressing, mince tarts, and rich sauces. Between that and the
scent of the evergreens hung over the hearth, and the
apple wood snapping in it, the landlady's flat smelled
like heaven.

But Alex sat fighting back tears, because he wanted
to keep searching.

Laura sat silent, worried for Pompey and Alex, and
herself, because she couldn't stop thinking of yet another male she'd hoped to see on Christmas day.

And Mrs. Finch sat sighing, because Pompey had
been a fine dog, and the boy was a good lad, and Miss
Lockwood had the worst luck.

So they all leapt up in sudden hope when they heard
the door-knocker fall. They raced to open the door

and had to sort themselves out so they could see who was there when it was pulled open.

"Pompey!" Alex called, and fell upon the dog as the dog fell upon him.

Laura could say nothing, because she saw who had brought Pompey home.

"Is everything all right?" the viscount asked. "I worried when Pompey arrived at my house alone."

"Everything's all right now, sir!" Alex cried. "I don't know why he ran away, but see how clever he is? He ran to you!"

"How did he know where you live?" Laura asked.

The viscount shook his head, and snow fell on the landlady's shining floor. "I have no idea. A footman heard barking, opened the door, and there he was. But not for long. Pompey knocked the fellow over and upended my butler in his mad rush to find me." His lips crooked at the memory of how his staid household was suddenly scrambled. "I must say I was happy to see him."

The viscount smiled at Alex. Clever lad, he thought, to bring the dog to me. The exuberant pup had also upset his bleak mood. In fact, Pompey's boisterous appearance had thrown the prospect of his usual cold Christmas into sudden cold perspective. It made him remember what he'd so briefly had, and what he was about to lose. And most of all it gave him the perfect excuse to come here.

Laura looked at Alex in exasperation. Had the boy somehow discovered the viscount's address and brought the dog to his door in a childish attempt to get the two adults together again? If so, she was profoundly embarrassed.

Alex, who hadn't known where the viscount lived, or cared, was too delighted at getting his dog back to notice what was happening with mere humans.

"I must get some toweling," Mrs. Finch said. "The beast's all over snow, and so are you, sir."

The viscount doffed his hat and even more snow fell on the floor. But he only had eyes for Laura. "He hit me like a furry avalanche," he told her. He smiled.

Laura didn't. Alex and the dog had gone into the landlady's flat, and now they stood in the hall, alone.

"I was going to dine with friends today," the viscount went on, noting she wore a pretty rose-colored gown for the holiday, and thinking how lovely she looked in it. "I was going to dine at my club. I was going to ride west and sit alone in my country house. The truth is, with all the things I had to do, I didn't know what to do with myself. I knew what I wanted to do. But I didn't know how to apologize, because I so seldom do, you see. I couldn't do anything because I couldn't think of anything but you, and how I wronged you. Miss Lockwood," he said, bowing slightly, "I'm trying to say I'm sorry."

"Apology accepted," she said quietly. It was shameful that she could be so affected by the sight of him, she thought, especially since all he could offer her was his apologies for offering her the only other thing that he could. "Should you like to come in?"

"I'd like more than that," he said earnestly. "I've been trying to think of a way to tell you that ever since we parted. Thank God the dog forced my hand, or I'd still be trying. Now I believe the best thing to do is to say it outright. Though you accept my apologies, I still can't have you to my home. You still can't invite me to yours. And you certainly can't once you go back to work. I miss you. And I'm not used to being deprived." He smiled again.

She had the sudden terrible notion he was going to ask her to be his mistress again.

"So the only way to mend matters," he said, his soft gray gaze never leaving her, "is to marry me, then we never have to worry about the proprieties again."

She stared.

"Marry me, Miss Lockwood," he said. "Marry me,

Laura. I'm of an age to know my mind, and you showed me my heart."

"But we haven't known each other very long," she protested. Her protest was weak, and only because she was afraid to believe what he'd said, and needed to hear it again.

"Many of my friends proposed to their wives after a few morning calls and two dances. Others did so after a party, or a night at the opera. One friend did after a carriage ride. I've been asking them, you see. But us! We've spent whole *days* together. How long are any of our class permitted to get to know each other, after all?"

"But . . ." she said.

"But I know my own mind," he said, stepping closer. "And my own heart—once you showed me where it was. Now the only question is: do you know yours?"

"Oh, my lord," she said.

"Sebastian," he urged her, "my name from your lips, at least that."

"Oh, Sebastian," she said, "I do know my own mind, as well as my heart, and you have filled both, but . . ."

She never got another chance to protest, because then he took her in his arms and got more than his name from her lips. He kissed her. And she kissed him back, thoroughly.

Mrs. Finch stood smiling in the doorway, holding both hands to her own heart. Alex grinned from ear to ear. And Pompey flopped down by the hearth.

The Christmas dinner was every bit as tasty as Mrs. Finch had claimed it would be. Viscount Falconer, who had dined at the finest restaurants in Paris, and at the prince regent's own table, agreed. He vowed he'd never tasted anything so wonderful, even though his hostess would swear he never tasted a thing because he was too busy feasting his eyes on his fiancée's face.

"Pompey will stay with us until your mama comes home," he told Alex. "We'd like you to as well, if your mama agrees. We plan to marry soon, and you, Mrs. Finch, are invited, of course. Oh, as Pompey is already spoken for, Mrs. Finch, if you'll tell me the sort of pup you favor, I'd like to present you with one, as a Christmas gift. You," he told Alex, "shall have your pick of toys, even more than I've already bought for you. Pompey shall have a bone, or a whole roast, whatever he wants. And you," he told Laura with a tender smile, "must have been a bad girl all year, my dear. Because all Father Christmas has for you—is me!

"I'll have your ring tomorrow," he whispered in Laura's ear, under cover of the laughter he'd provoked, "and jewels to complement it."

"All I need," she whispered back, "is you."

"And that," he murmured, "you shall have in full."

He stood and raised his glass again. "A happy Christmas to us all," he said, "and every year from now on."

Pompey had dined on turkey and goose, and then settled back by the hearth. He curled up and closed his preternaturally wise eyes. He sighed, and dreamed, in the manner of dogs, twitching and muttering as he did.

But then he stilled. He felt a warm hand on his head, and heard the sweet voice that had always commanded him. He moved his mouth as though to lick that invisible hand.

Good boy, the voiceless voice said in his ear. *Good dog. Well done. Now you may be a dog again.*

When Pompey woke, he yawned, stretched, and then ambled into the next room. There, ears cocked every time he heard laughter, which was often, he nevertheless set about the business of discovering what a real puppy was. He finished shredding the slipper he'd found under a chair, and then, ever obedient to a command, got on with the task of gnawing a leg off the chair.

Lost and Found

Andrea Pickens

A curse on Christmas."

Lord Nicholas Moreton was not in the habit of blaspheming, but he tacked on a rather colorful epithet as he squinted through the pelting sleet and fought to keep his phaeton from running off the road. The night was black as Hades. Which, at the moment, was just the place he wished to consign his father, along with Lord Castlereigh and the entire Foreign Service of England. Tugging up the sodden collar of his driving coat, he tightened his hold on the ribbons, trying to keep a grip on his growing anger.

He had, after all, been well schooled in reining in his feelings. From the time he was in leading strings, his father, a distinguished diplomat, had stressed the importance of being guided by reason rather than raw emotion.

Duty over desire.

It was a lesson Nicholas had learned well, having an admirable example to emulate. The Earl of Evergreen was esteemed as a man of great principle as well as privilege. Ever since he could remember, Nicholas had wanted to march in his father's footsteps. He had applied himself diligently to his studies, and had accepted a position—granted, a very junior position—with the Home Office while most of his peers were larking about Town. He was aware that a number of them considered him rather a stick in the mud for never kicking up his heels. But the weight of government responsibilities and family expectations kept his feet planted firmly on the ground. He felt he must toe the line . . .

Even when that line seemed, at times, to be awfully narrow and unbending.

Which served to explain why, curse the holidays, he was racing toward London in a freezing rainstorm, feeling cold, wet and miserable, when he should have been stretched out before the fire of his best friend's country estate, snug, warm and pleasantly foxed on the case of excellent vintage port that had just been brought up from the cellars.

He shifted on his perch, uncomfortably aware of his father's missive—its elegant parchment and copperplate script now reduced to a sodden squish—tucked in the pocket of his waistcoat. Or rather, he corrected himself, his father's order, for despite the sugared coating of the words, the note of command oozed from the paper like the filling of a Christmas sweetmeat.

Nicholas still had a sour taste in his mouth from rereading it during the brief stop he had made at an inn several hours ago. Not that the text needed any elaborate analysis—its message was quite straightforward. The younger Moreton was urgently needed for a special assignment of great importance. He was expected to present himself without delay for a whirl of holiday festivities and pay court to the ward of an influential foreign count. The match was perfect on paper, assured his father. The young lady's lineage and looks were of the highest order, and a union would ensure a crucial alliance between the two countries. And seeing as Nicholas had shown no particular preference for any of the young ladies on the Marriage Mart, what possible objection could he have to the proposal?

What possible objection indeed! Nicholas's exasperated snort echoed the complaint from his tired team of greys. Just because he had been too occupied with his duties to give any thought to choosing a wife did not mean he wished to relinquish the right to conduct his own personal affairs. Perhaps, for once in his life . . .

His mood turned even grimmer as the rain changed to thick, wet flakes. *This was courting disaster,* he thought darkly, as a gusting wind lashed at his face. He had better come upon some sign of civilization soon. His horses were starting to stumble, and his own limbs were fast turning numb. He blinked, trying to see through the swirling snow, but ice clung to his lashes, turning the surroundings to naught but an ominous blur. Still, it soon became clear that the road was taking a steeper twist and drifts were slowing his progress to a mere crawl. Worst of all, he was beginning to fear that he had taken a wrong turn back at the last fork.

A pox on Edmund for suggesting a shortcut to the London road.

And a pox on himself for allowing himself to be spurred into such an ill-judged journey. Nicholas let yet another oath slip from his lips. He did not normally embark upon any endeavor without the proper preparations but the note of urgency in his father's letter had prompted him to abandon his usual sense of caution. Urged on by his friends, he had decided to dash down to Town alone, leaving his valet and luggage to follow along in the much slower—and safer—travelling coach.

With a shake of the frozen reins, he tried to coax his team to a brisker pace. However, the phaeton was having more and more trouble ploughing through the snowdrifts. As the front wheels hit a deep rut, throwing it into a sharp skid, one of the exhausted horses stumbled and pulled up lame.

Jumping down from his perch, Nicholas quickly

freed it from the tangle of the traces. Though tired and shivering himself, he took a moment to calm both animals, then readjusted the harness for their strait-ened circumstances. He would go on for another mile or so, he decided, taking hold of the bridle and setting off on foot. If he did not come to some sort of shelter, he would have to consider an alternative. It would not be the first time he had been forced to rough it in the wilds. While most of his acquaintances assumed he did nothing but sit behind a desk and shuffle papers, his diplomatic mission to Lisbon had actually entailed several forays to meet with partisan fighters. If he was unlucky enough to find himself trapped in the storm, he was confident he had the practical skills to survive.

However, it appeared that luck had not entirely abandoned him. Rounding a bend, he caught sight of a faint light up ahead. With a muttered prayer of thanks, he stepped up his struggle through the deepen-ing drifts, and a short while later managed to limp into the cramped courtyard of a ramshackle inn.

A rap on the stable door roused no response. Though miserably wet and thoroughly exhausted, he saw that his horses were rubbed down and fed before trudging to the tavern entrance. There, his knock still went unanswered. His temper, now frayed to a thin thread, suddenly snapped.

"Damnation!" Smacking his shoulder into the door, Nicholas took hold of the latch and slammed his way inside. "Is there no one to give a gentleman a hand around here?" he shouted, stamping the snow from his boots. That his toes felt like blocks of ice did not improve his mood.

A moment later, a balding man bustled out from a side room, wiping his hands upon his apron. "Forgive me, sir," he mumbled. "We rarely get much traffic from Quality at this time of night, and I was just seeing to serving a hot meal to another unexpected guest."

Nicholas doubted the isolated inn got many visits at any hour of the day. And judging by the rough planked floor and rustic furnishings, he imagined his short stay was going to be an awfully unpleasant one. "I will be wanting a room," he snapped. "Preferably one tolerably free of fleas."

The innkeeper cringed as Nicholas added mention of his name. "I—I shall do my best to see you are comfortable, milord. Shall you be wanting a meal as well, sir?"

"Just a bottle of brandy—assuming it has not been watered down with horse piss."

"Yes, milord . . . no, milord." Confused and clearly intimidated, the man edged back a step before recalling his duties and returning to snatch up the small valise by Nicholas's feet. "If you would care to follow me upstairs . . ."

Feeling a bit ashamed of himself, Nicholas fell in step behind him. Though he was tired and frustrated, there was no call to be rude. "I apologize for my outburst of temper," he said, on reaching his room. That the spill of candlelight showed it to be quite neat, with freshly ironed linens on the narrow bedstead, only made him feel more of a prig. "What with the hellish weather, the journey has been a nightmare and I fear my nerves are rather frayed." The one consolation, he thought to himself, was that things could not get any worse.

"I quite understand, sir. The snowstorm blew in out of nowhere, but I daresay it will clear up by morning and you shall be able to continue on your way."

He devoutly hoped so—Christmas was only two days off and from the way his father had phrased it, he would be cooked along with the traditional holiday goose if he did not show up at Evergreen House for the gala ball.

"Are you sure there is nothing more I can get for you, milord?"

"Thank you, but no. Just the brandy." Nicholas barely managed to stay awake long enough to toss back a glass of the warming spirits before crawling beneath the coverlet and falling into an exhausted sleep.

Arrogant man.

The young lady taking her meal in the private parlor could not help but overhear the snappish exchange. *And odiously ill-tempered to boot.* Why, the stomp of his foot had nearly rattled the closed door off its hinges. Had she been the innkeeper, she would have been tempted to respond with a kick of her own—aimed right at the pompous prig's posterior. But then, Anna Wintergrove Federova was not feeling in charity with *any* overbearing male at the moment.

Setting aside her tea, Anna looked down at her uncle's letter. How dare he order her back to London, as if she were a mare to be put up for auction at Tattersall's? The answer, of course, was staring her right in the face, the bold black script a mocking reminder of how little control she had over her own life.

If only she had her independence. She would gladly trade her vast fortune, august pedigree and celebrated looks for a bit of unfettered freedom. For months she had been looking forward to escaping her regimented life in Town and spending the holidays with an old school friend.

But duty, in the form of her rigid guardian uncle, had suddenly called, and no one dared disobey Count Yevgeny Gilpin Federov.

Anna made a face. The English acted as though he had a great black bear chained in his study, ready to eat anyone who dared disagree with him. The count certainly looked liked a predator of the steppes, with his black beard and fierce Cossack eyes. Granted, the beard was neatly trimmed, and the roar was a cultured baritone that could converse on art and music in seven

different languages. A confidant of the Tsar, he had
been in London for months handling a series of delicate and demanding negotiations between England
and Russia. Not that she had seen much of him. Save
for the occasional small evening soiree at their town
house, where she served as his hostess, the count was
rarely at home.

What with his travels and his duties, Uncle Yevgeny
had been a rather distant figure of authority since the
death of her English mother and Russian father had
left him as her legal guardian. But then, he had not
really been required to give her much attention. Her
life was already well ordered—she was enrolled in an
exclusive boarding school for young ladies outside
London, and summers were spent with her grandmother on the family estate near Moscow.

But now that she had been out of the schoolroom
for several years, his attitude was becoming decidedly
less *laissez-faire.*

After two whirlwind Seasons in St. Petersburg,
where she had driven him to distraction by rejecting
marriage proposals from a number of extremely eligible noblemen, he had threatened to put his foot down.
If she could not make up her mind, he would do it
for her.

Anna sighed. Uncle Yevgeny meant well, but he
was of the old school, for whom marriage was a matter
of strategic alliances. *Money. Power. Land.* His long
and distinguished government career had only rein-
forced the importance of tangible assets. He simply
did not seem to understand that happiness could not
be negotiated in quite the same way as the settlement
of a border dispute. Dispassionate reason was all very
well when it came to compromising over slivers of
dirt. But when it came to matters of the heart . . .

Her own gave a tiny lurch. She did not wish to settle
for a match because it tallied up well on paper. She
had been courted by the book, with fancy flowers,

sentimental poetry, effusive compliments. It was all so . . . expected. As were the gentlemen themselves. They were all perfectly proper, perfectly polished, perfectly suitable.

Perfectly boring.

Not one of them had showed a spark of unique character. Or of spirit.

And so she had begged her uncle for more time, and he had grudgingly agreed that she might accompany him to England for the winter months. In March it would be on to Vienna, by which time he had made it quite clear she was expected to make a decision.

But then the arrival of his letter had abruptly revoked the reprieve.

Its message was as cruel a Christmas gift as a lump of coal. She must return immediately to London, in order that she might be courted over the holidays by a perfectly proper English lord. If she refused, she would have to return on the new year to the rigid household of her imperious grandmother, where the family would take charge of arranging a traditional match.

Anna folded a sharp crease in the paper—not that she had any hope of altering the stark black-and-white note of command. Oh, to be sure, her uncle had penned an apology for changing the terms of their treaty, explaining that the possible advantages were so great, for both country and family, that it was worth . . . improvising. He had added that he would not force her into marriage. The final decision would be left up to her. However, she knew how difficult it was for anyone, even someone as determined as she was, to stand up to the count. His last line was an ominous portent of just how intractable his will on this was.

. . . You will thank me for this, bebinka, for I have a great deal more experience in life than you do . . .

Pressing a palm to her forehead, Anna fought to

hold back bitter tears. She did not want to be trapped in a conventional match, no matter how convenient to her guardian and her government. Indeed, it was a sign of how desperate she had become that on catching sight of a star through the threatening clouds earlier that evening, she had found herself wishing for a Christmas miracle. If only she might conjure up a Shakespearean spell or a Baba Yaga to forestall her fate . . .

What she got was a snowstorm, which was not going to alter the course of her life, save by delaying the inevitable for a day or two.

Anna consoled herself with the thought that a courtship could drag on well into spring. Much could happen during that time, though the start of this particular journey did not augur well for things going her way. In the first swirling of snow her coach had been driven off course, and while it had arrived at this refuge in time to miss the brunt of the storm, her abigail had come down with a fit of coughing. It had taken most of the evening to see the poor girl settled enough to fall into a fitful sleep. A glance at the battered clock perched on the mantel showed it to be nearly midnight. Only now had she finally been able to slip downstairs and seek a belated supper.

Her lips pursed in a rueful twist. What she needed was a guardian angel to help her counteract the strictness of a guardian uncle. But it seemed that even angels were allowed a holiday respite to make merry with friends. While she was alone, caught in the midst of a raging storm.

Chin up, she told herself. Over the years, she had learned it never did much good to give way to disappointment and despair. She had weathered other storms in her life. Somehow, she would find her way through this one.

Finishing off the last morsel of cold apple tart, she gathered her shawl and rose. No doubt her unsettled musings had been exacerbated by fatigue and hunger. In the morning her situation would not seem quite so bleak. After all, there was an old Russian proverb that said things always looked brighter in the light of a new day.

"The snow may not be so deep, but what with the ice and frozen ruts, it will be rough going, milord." The innkeeper eyed the blue skies with an arch of skepticism. "And there is no promise that we have seen the last of the bad weather. If I were you, I would not be in such a rush to be on the road."

"No matter, I intend to be off within a quarter hour."

"Begging your pardon, sir, but how do you mean to manage that? I thought you said your horse was lame."

Nicholas frowned, suspecting he was about to become the victim of highway robbery. But however outrageous the demand, money was no object. "I saw another team in the stables."

"Aye. But they are not for hire."

"What do you mean, they are not for hire?" Nicholas fought to keep control of his voice as he pulled his purse from his coat. "Don't worry, I intend to pay you very well for their use."

"You could offer me a king's ransom in gold, milord, and it still wouldn't do any good. I told you, they ain't mine to be offering. They belong to the other guest. And there are none others to be had. Not with this weather."

Of all the cursed luck.

"But I simply must be in London by Christmas Eve."

The man lifted his shoulders. "Perhaps your horse will be fit to travel after the night of rest."

Nicholas knew enough about horses to have little hope of such a miracle, even if it was the Christmas season. But seeing there was no point in further argument, he jammed his hands in his pockets and started for the stable. *Damn—as if he did not have enough to worry about!* Perhaps there was a chance he could convince his fellow traveler to give up—

Whomp.

The snowball hit him square in the back of the head. Knocked off balance, his feet flew out from under him and he fell back on his rump.

"Oh, I am terribly sorry, sir! I was just playing a game of fetch with the dog and somehow my aim went dreadfully off."

Nicholas looked around to see an elfin young lady, muffled in furs and high felt boots, cavorting with a terrier in the snow. Despite her words, she did not look a whit contrite. Indeed, she appeared to be biting back laughter.

Scowling, he picked himself up and retrieved his hat. "Hoyden," he muttered, not deigning to dignify her apology with anything more than a frosty nod.

"I beg your pardon?" Twirling a graceful series of spins through the snow, his erstwhile assailant moved toward him. A peek of raven curls had escaped from her ermine-trimmed shako, accentuating the porcelain perfection of her fine-boned features. That a rosy flush suffused her cheeks and a mischievous sparkle lit her sapphire eyes added a bewitching vitality to her beauty.

Nicholas gave himself a rough shake, ostensibly to dislodge the flakes still clinging to his coat. *What dark magic had cast its spell over this Christmas?* A time of warmth and good cheer was quickly turning into a slippery slide into the depths of Hell.

"Don't bother," he growled, mortified to realize he had been staring like a lackwit for the last few moments. "I do not suppose that a schoolgirl can be expected to behave with any decorum." In truth, he had quickly revised his initial impression, realizing appearances were deceiving—the minx was no mere schoolroom chit but rather a stylish young lady. In no humor to court any further humiliations, he turned on his heel and continued on his way.

His mood suffered a further set-down when a cursory examination of his horse's right fetlock showed the swelling had not gone down. It now appeared his only hope of escaping this debacle was to seek out the fellow who possessed the two glossy chestnuts in the neighboring stall and try to negotiate a deal.

Or, if diplomacy failed, he might just have to resort to groveling in the snow.

Again.

That option appeared even less palatable when Nicholas returned to the taproom and sought out the innkeeper. "Oh, they don't belong to a gentleman, sir," said the man in response to his inquiry. "But rather to a young lady who is traveling alone, save for the company of her servants . . ."

A queasy feeling suddenly came over him.

"Perhaps you caught a glimpse of her outside? She said she wished to have a short stroll before her breakfast." The innkeeper shook his head. "No accounting for the queer taste some folk have. Imagine wanting to walk about in the cold and snow for the fun of it." A thump of the teapot punctuated his inability to fathom the odd quirks of Quality. "As for you, sir, shall I lay out some toast and a plate of shirred eggs and gammon?"

Nicholas made a face. "No, if I am going to have to eat humble pie, I had rather do it on an empty stomach."

That had knocked a bit of the starch out of the gentleman, thought Anna as she tossed another snowball. The dog barked into delight, and she allowed a burble of laughter to echo the animal's merriment. Lud, he had looked madder than a wet hen at being taken down a peg or two.

Her chin rose a fraction. He had richly deserved the set-down. Perhaps her prank had been a touch childish, yet how dare he accuse her of bad manners when he had been unconscionably rude to the innkeeper, a poor fellow who was doing the best he could.

But then, gentlemen were loath to admit to any fault.

She blew out a puff of breath and scooped up another handful of snow. Why was it that most of them were puffed up with a sense of their own consequence? They seemed to have no sense of humor. Or serendipity. That anyone could look so horribly stiff and serious when the icicles sparkled like diamonds and the trees looked as if they had been coated in spun sugar—

"Might I have a word with you?"

The snow had muffled the sound of his approach, and as Anna spun around, she nearly lost her footing.

"Forgive me for frightening you." He caught her elbow and she was surprised at the firmness of his grip and the hint of muscle beneath his tailored sleeve.

"Very little frightens me, sir," she said tartly, shaking off his hold. "I assure you, I am not easily intimidated."

He looked at her rather thoughtfully before inclining in a small bow. "Then accept my apologies for approaching you without a formal introduction. However, given the pressing circumstances, I hope you will consent to dispensing with the usual formalities of polite society."

Having made up her mind to dislike him, Anna responded with deliberate sarcasm. "You act as though a simple snowstorm is cause for grave concern."

"It is."

He was quick with a rejoinder, she gave him that. And oddly enough, his voice was quite pleasant, deep and mellifluous, with none of the affected little mannerisms she so loathed in most Tulips of the *ton*.

"But before I explain, please allow me to introduce myself. I am Lord Nicholas Moreton."

Lord Nicholas Moreton had very nice eyes as well. Jade green, flecked with hints of amusement. She looked away, not wanting to see anything good about him. Still, she could not quite bring herself to be so rude as to snub him completely. "And I am Lady Anna Federova."

"Ah. I imagine that explains why you feel so at home in the wilds of winter." His gaze fell on the lump of white cradled in her mitten. "I must say, your English is as impeccable as your aim."

Was he implying that all Russians were uncouth savages?

"I should hope so, seeing as my mother was the daughter of the Marquess of Middleton," retorted Anna, happy to have reason to renew hostilities. "And were they still alive, she and my father would be sadly disappointed if the goodly amount of blunt spent on educating me at Mrs. Rusher's Academy for Select Young Ladies had been all for naught."

Lord Moreton had the grace to flush. "I meant no offense, Lady Anna. I was merely trying to break the ice, so to speak. We did not exactly get off on the right foot during our earlier encounter."

"It was not I who slipped and fell on my . . . derriere."

If he heard her murmur, he chose to ignore it. "Might I ask how you came to be stranded in this out-of-the-way place?"

"Most likely in the same way that brought you here. My coachman took the wrong turn." Her lips gave a wry twitch. "By the by, the stableboy tells me the signpost was knocked askew weeks ago by a stray ram, but no one has bother to fix it."

"D . . . drat it."

"Come now, it could be much worse. The inn may be simple, but it is quite comfortable."

After a small start, the gentleman actually smiled,

revealing a peek of teeth that was as white as the surrounding snow. "Then perhaps you would have no objection to spending another night here."

A hint of humor? Anna blinked. That was not the only thing that took her aback. Lord Moreton was actually very attractive when he was not scowling. His earlier spill had tumbled his carefully combed locks into an unruly shock of gold. The tangle around his ears and collar softened the chiseled cut of his aquiline nose and square jaw. The contrast was intriguing— as if beneath the starched formality and stiff-rumped manners there was still a bit of spirit eager to break free. His lips seemed to hint at that as well. They had a most interesting curl . . .

And his temper had a most atrocious edge, she reminded herself, quickly averting her eyes. His shout could match that of Uncle Yevgeny, which was certainly not a mark in his favor.

"W—whatever are you talking about, sir?" she asked.

"The fact that in my experience, a small delay never matters overly much to a female. While I, on the other hand, have a matter of serious business in London that cannot be put off." His smile stretched a bit wider. "If you would allow me to continue on with your team, I shall see to it that new horses are sent here from the nearest coaching inn. The inconvenience would be ever so slight, and I would, of course, insist on covering the additional expense."

"Absolutely out of the question." Anna fixed him with a cold stare. *To think she had imagined he might be different.* It was just like a gentleman to assume his affairs were more important than hers. And that a female would step aside without a whimper. However, in this case, the gentleman in question had no right to ride roughshod over her. Despite the fact that she was in no hurry to reach her destination, she took a measure of satisfaction in standing her ground.

"I, too, have a pressing need to be in Town," she replied, angling her chin in a defiant tilt. "My uncle would be seriously upset if I failed to arrive at the appointed hour."

Lord Moreton looked as though he had been struck dumb. No doubt he was rarely denied anything. Well, disappointment built character—or so said another Russian proverb. It would do him no harm to cool his heels for a bit. Squaring her shoulders, she prepared to face the expected explosion of ire without giving an inch.

"Forgive me. I had forgotten that it is Christmas," he said quietly. "Even if it were not a special time, I would not have asked you if my haste were only for personal reasons. It is not, but I shall think of some other way."

His thoughtful response softened her stance. Feeling somewhat childish, she reminded herself that however depressing the holidays were for her, the Season was meant to be a time of caring and sharing. "Well, seeing as it is Christmas, I suppose I could take you along in my carriage until we come to the main road. From there you can catch a mail coach to Town."

An instant later she was regretting her spur-of-the-moment offer. The expression of icy hauteur was back on his face, and rather than express appreciation for her Yuletide generosity, Lord Moreton looked appalled at the idea of having to travel in a public conveyance.

"I suppose I have no choice but to accept," he said grudgingly.

"Not unless you wish to walk." Anna gave a toss of her curls, causing the plume of her shako to tickle her cheek. She slapped it away. "Or you could consider strapping blades to your boots and skating there."

"I could—"

"Or you *could* say thank you, Lord Moreton."

His mouth thinned to a grim line. "I am much obliged. However, rather than waste precious time in exchanging social niceties, might I point out that it would be prudent to be on the road as soon as possible."

"I am well aware of that, sir. But as my abigail was feeling poorly last night, I did not wish to rouse her at first light. Be assured that we will be ready to depart within the hour."

"Thank you," he said, the exaggerated politeness edged with an unmistakable note of mockery.

So much for the prospect of peace on earth and good will toward men.

Anna gave an inward groan. Yet another overbearing male to make her last little bit of solitude miserable. This most certainly did not promise to be a very merry journey.

Nicholas gave a baleful grimace as he watched her march away. Judging by the performance he had just put on, the only diplomatic position he could ever aspire to was a posting to Siberia. Polar bears and seals had thick enough hides that his gaffes would merely bounce off them.

As for the elegant young lady . . . no doubt she thought him an ass. She had hinted as much with her reference to falling on a certain part of his anatomy. Both his bottom and his pride were a bit bruised from the uncharacteristic show of awkwardness. He did not like looking the fool.

A swish of skirts drew his eye from introspection as she paused to pat the dog. *Lady Anna Federóva.* Like her name, she was an intriguing mix of the familiar and the foreign. She had the creamy complexion of a young English miss, but her blue eyes—their exotic slant accentuated by the pert arch of her raven-dark brows—flickered and danced with a strangely compelling light. *Fire within ice.* As if that made any sense.

Nicholas pulled his muffler a bit tighter. He had no business allowing her looks, however alluring, to distract him from his duty. Which was getting to London without further delay.

Pulling out his pocket watch, he grimaced. Immune to the vagaries of weather or women, the minutes were ticking away. He sincerely hoped that unlike many of the pampered young ladies of the *ton*, Lady Anna did not think it fashionable to keep a man waiting.

But true to her word, the young lady descended from her room well within the allotted time. Nicholas was quick to put down his teacup and grab his valise; however, the look on her face brought him up short.

"I am afraid my abigail has taken a turn for the worse. She is in no condition to travel."

"You need not worry about her receiving the proper care, milady," ventured the innkeeper, who had come over to clear the table. "My missus is well-known in these parts as a skilled healer. In a few days, I am sure the girl will be fully recovered."

Anna murmured her thanks, then hesitated. Turning to Nicholas, she indicated an alcove by the mullioned windows. "Might I have a private word with you, Lord Moreton?"

The reflections from the snow cast a pattern of light and shadow across her profile, accentuating the hollowness under her eyes and the pinch of worry around her mouth. She looked very small and very vulnerable standing all by herself. Despite their earlier hostilities, Nicholas had to fight off the urge to enfold her in his arms.

"I find myself faced with a very awkward dilemma. I have offered you a ride, sir, but without my maid, it would be terribly improper for us to travel together."

"Of course." He took a moment to swallow his disappointment. "You may think me an ass, Lady Anna, but I assure you I am not a cad. I would never seek to force a lady into risking her reputation."

She lowered her lashes, the thick fringe a dark flutter against her pale cheek. "Now it is my turn to apologize. I did not mean to imply any such thing. Indeed, you . . . you seem a real gentleman."

His mouth crooked up at the corners. "If you wish, I can give you a list of my credentials."

"Are you going to pull out the stud book and read off your pedigree as well?"

It was not only her snowballs but her quixotic character that had him strangely off balance. *Fire and ice.* He sensed that both were used to mask a far more fragile part of herself.

"That was just a joke, sir," she said quickly, before he could reply. A sigh escaped her lips. "Perhaps an ill-timed one, but I don't suppose you would understand how often we ladies are treated as if we are no different from hunters or hounds. Sometimes I cannot help but rail at the unfairness of it."

"When you put it that way, I can see how you would feel angry."

Once again Anna seemed surprised by his faint smile. "N— not many gentlemen do."

Nicholas reached out and tucked an errant curl behind her ear. She seemed to shiver as his touch grazed her cheek. While he felt a spark of heat tingle on his fingertips. "Far be it for me to add to your discomfort. But I feel I ought to point out that travelling alone, without your abigail, will also give rise to unpleasant rumor."

"Yes, I had thought of that, too."

"I know this will sound self-serving, but the obvious solution is for you to remain here with the girl until she recovers, or until your uncle can send someone else to escort you to Town." After a stretch of silence, he added, "I know how terrible it must seem to think of missing a family Christmas."

She turned, angling her profile even deeper into the shadow. "Like yours, my reasons for returning to Town are not personal. They relate to a matter of important business for my guardian, so I . . . I cannot delay."

He did not miss the tautness in her tone, and though it was no concern of his, Nicholas felt a flare of anger at her uncle. Her earlier outburst made it obvious what sort of business she was talking about. So she, too, was being shoved from here to there, as if she were naught but a pawn on a chessboard. The irony of their similar situations would have been rather laughable had not he caught the glimmer of pain in her eyes.

"Then let me think how I can help you." Nicholas rubbed at his chin. "Perhaps the innkeeper knows of a local girl who could be hired to accompany you."

"I—I had not thought of that." She paused a fraction. "What about you, sir? You seemed to imply your presence in Town was of great import."

"It is, but that is not your concern. I shall figure out something." Wishing to wipe the pinched look from her face, he essayed a note of humor. "If you would make me one of your snowballs, mayhap I could roll my way to the next coaching stop."

Her lips gave a small twitch before falling back into place. "Perhaps there is another alternative."

"Yes?"

"That we keep to our original plan. It is not as if any gossip is going to reach Town from here. And if we employ a modicum of discretion, we ought to be able to drop you at a coaching inn with no one being the wiser." She forced a smile. "It would be in keeping with the spirit of the holidays. Surely no harm can come of offering kindness to a stranger."

"The risk does seem small," he mused. "But still, it is not something either of us ought to take lightly."

His note of caution rekindled the fire in her eyes.

"Are you always such a stick in the mud, Lord Moreton?" she demanded. "Don't you ever wish to shake free of the rules, if only for a fleeting interlude?"

"Sorry to disappoint you. If you are looking to encounter a dashing hero on this journey, read Byron." He had thought himself long past caring about such snide comments about his lack of color. Yet for some reason her criticism hurt more than he cared to admit. "With all that expensive education, I would have thought you smart enough to realize that this predicament is nothing to make light of. Surely your instructors taught you that Society does not forgive or forget a mistake, however innocent."

"To hell with Society and all its strictures," she muttered, the angle of her chin defying him to remark on her unladylike language. "If you are afraid of risking your own reputation, I will go on alone. Even if there were a local girl willing to leave her family at Christmas, it would take too long to make arrangements."

"You appear to enjoy courting disaster," he said through gritted teeth. "I cannot in good conscience allow you to continue on your own. But let us pray this lapse in protocol does not come back to haunt us."

"Don't be so pessimistic."

"I prefer to think of it as being realistic. In my line of work, I cannot allow emotion to cloud reason."

"I shudder to think what it is you do," she countered. "Hopefully it does not involve dealing with people."

Stung by her note of scorn, he reacted with equal heat. "For your information, Lady Anna, I am accorded to be quite skillful at settling quarrels and bringing about a meeting of minds."

"Is that so? Well, it seems you will get a great deal of practice in honing your abilities during the next few hours."

* * *

The sun was still shining, but the trip was certainly starting out on a stormy note. Anna tugged at the cords of her reticule as she leaned back against the squabs and listened to the creak of her coachman loading the boot of the coach. Somehow her mood was proving more difficult to untangle.

Why could she not put thoughts of Lord Moreton out of her head?

He was an oddly infuriating gentleman, arrogant and overbearing one moment, only to show an intriguing glimmer of sensitivity the next. *Don't be a goose,* she chided herself. Just because he showed a flash of wit and an attractive smile was no reason to imagine he actually possessed some real depth of character.

His own words had warned her not to expect anything out of the ordinary from him.

Several minutes later, the gentleman himself climbed into the coach. Without a word, he settled himself in the opposite corner and cracked a book. A surreptitious glance showed it was *not* Byron, but a thick tome on the history of the Byzantine Empire.

No wonder he looked so glum if that was the sort of reading he chose for relaxation.

She returned to her own book, the latest work by Miss Austen. Her teachers had frowned on such novels for young ladies—and no wonder, for with a sharp eye and dry wit, the author exposed of the frailties and foibles of Society. Which was, of course, exactly why Anna found them highly entertaining, even though her laughter was often tempered by a twinge of pain as the observations cut close to home. The truth hurt at times. She was not so vain as to think her uncle and her acquaintances were the only ones with faults. Like Elizabeth Bennett, she had her own prejudices, and a tendency to be headstrong and highly opinionated.

Still, Anna took heart that she was not alone in seeing the absurdities and unfairness in life. At least, with her nose buried in the pages, she felt she was in the presence of a kindred soul.

Lord Moreton's grumble reminded her of another, more unwelcome presence. "Now what is the delay?"

"John Coachman is quite thorough in checking that all is in order before setting out," she replied, not looking up from the page. "I imagine he has found some buckle or bolt that needs attending to."

Her amusement over a particularly pithy observation was interrupted by a low snort of air. One that sounded suspiciously like a word that should not have been uttered in front of a lady.

"Really, sir, you have a devil of a temper," she observed without shifting her gaze.

"Me?" His response bristled with indignation. "Hah! I am known for my even disposition."

"Right—you are *always* horribly irritable," she countered.

Nicholas drew in a sharp breath. "What makes you say that?"

"To begin with, from the moment you stormed into the inn last night, you have been loud, rude and overbearing, expecting everyone in your path to bow to your needs."

Leather crackled as he shifted uncomfortably on the seat. "I was not aware you overheard my arrival. I . . . I cannot blame you for thinking me an oaf. I have not been at my best of late," he admitted.

Surprised at the unexpected frankness, Anna found herself curious. "Is there a reason?"

She half expected him to tell her to mind her own business, but after a stretch of silence, he cleared his throat. "If you must know, I would much rather be spending Christmas in the country, so I am not particularly pleased at having been summoned back to Town."

A sidelong glance showed that his grip on his book was in danger of splitting the spine.

"However," he went on tightly. "When duty calls, I have no choice but to come running like an obedient hound."

"I thought only females were on such a tight leash."

"There is much about the real world that they do not teach you at Mrs. Rusher's Academy for Select Young Ladies." The note of mockery was directed more at himself than at her. "Males may appear to have the freedom to roam at will, but trust me, the collar, however subtle, can be just as choking. I—" Nicholas abruptly snapped his book shut. "I shall just have a look at what is holding us up."

Between the jangle of the harness and the whisper of her own conflicted thoughts, Anna could not make out the muffled exchange between Lord Moreton and her driver. Whatever it was, the discussion did not last long. The arrival of hot bricks and extra blankets finally signaled that they were ready to leave.

"I brought along the last of the meat pie, along with some bread and cheese, in case it takes longer than expected to reach the main road." Nicholas added several oilskin packets to the items the innkeeper had brought out. "Hardly the sort of fare a refined young lady is used to, but it will have to do."

"I am not one of those sheltered misses who has never had a taste of life outside of the schoolroom," replied Anna tartly. While she did not want to be thought of as a wild savage, neither did she wish him to view her as just another pampered aristocrat. "I have traveled extensively through Europe and Russia, in far harsher conditions than these, sir, so there is no need to be . . . condescending."

"My apologies." He did not sound overly contrite, and wasted little time in raising his book as a barrier to any further conversation.

She stared at the tooled leather, silently mouthing a rather unladylike word of her own. Lord Moreton was one of the rare gentlemen she had ever met who had shown a hint of introspection, yet just when the topic of discussion was taking an interesting direction, he had retreated behind stiff confines of convention. Her disappointment was hard to swallow. How she longed to talk about real feelings with a gentleman rather than engage in a stilted exchange about banal subjects, like the state of the weather.

Which was, she saw, threatening to turn as dark as her mood. An ominous line of leaden clouds hovered on the horizon, their gathering force a warning that another storm might be headed their way.

"The sky is now the color of pewter," she said a short while later, unable to concentrate on her reading.

"Do you wish to turn back?"

Anna stared out at the fairy-tale forest, then looked away as her sigh fogged the panes of glass. Feeling hemmed in on all sides, she blurted out, "If I had my wish, a Baba Yaga would appear to turn the horses into reindeer and fly the coach to the North Pole."

"Surely it cannot be that bad." The scowl softened to a rueful smile. "It would be awfully cold atop the world, not to speak of awfully lonely. There would not be another person around for thousands of miles."

"So much the better," she muttered. "But I doubt you know what it is like to be bound by duty, convention, always at the beck and call of others, with no freedom to make up your own mind. Parents, teachers, guardians—Lud, at times it feels as if even the gardener and the groom may growl orders at me." Her breath had turned to ice on the window, and with a gloved finger she traced the random patterns. "I assure you, there is little difference between me and a mare put up for auction. Neither of us is ever given free rein. Instead, we are expected to submit docilely to a pair of spurs or a whip."

"Gentlemen are not quite as free as you might imagine to run neck and leather through life."

"No?" A bitter note crept into her voice. "Judging from the gossip that flows as freely as champagne at the balls and soirees, I find that hard to believe."

Nicholas did not answer right away, his attention seemingly caught up by his own view out the window. "If it is any consolation, not all English are gentlemen of indolent indulgence."

The fact that he did not respond with a lie or a platitude gave her the heart to continue speaking honestly. "No doubt you are once again thinking me childish. Here I am bemoaning what I do not have, rather than counting my blessings." She fingered the thick sable trim of her cloak. "Believe me, I am not such a selfish creature as to be unaware of how much I have to be thankful for. I have every comfort imaginable. And yet . . ."

"And yet, not all happiness can be measured in terms of material possessions."

"You . . . you understand."

"Lady Anna, I have a feeling we are more alike than you think."

The coach was gliding smoothly through the powdery snow, and yet her insides were giving the oddest little lurches, as if they were spinning cartwheels along her spine. Confused, she braced herself against the squabs and sought to shift the conversation to a more even ground. "I have no parents or siblings to spend Christmas with. But you, sir—surely you have a family who shall miss having you there with them to share the joy of opening presents and feasting on roast goose and plum pudding."

"I, too, am an only child. And while my parents are alive and well, there is little these days that draws us together as a family. My mother is quite happy to potter about the family estate in Devonshire, raising her exotic hothouse roses. Indeed, there are times when I wonder whether she cares more about pistils and stamens than flesh and blood." It was said with a smile, but the humor did not stretch wide enough to reach his eyes.

"As for my father . . ." Nicholas exaggerated a wry shrug. "My father does not allow either heavenly or earthly concerns to distract him from his work," he said dryly. "Indeed, if the Savior were to be born today in his stables, he would react to the news with a vague frown, then go back to his government papers, admonishing the servants not to disturb him unless something truly important had happened."

Anna laughed in spite of everything. "He ought to meet my uncle. It sounds as if the two of them would get along quite well."

"That—or murder each other." Nicholas's chuckle sounded a rich counterpoint to their amusement. "In my experience, two strong personalities either love or hate each other."

"I have noticed that as well."

"Does your uncle live in London?"

"No. He is just visiting for several months." Hoping to forestall any further personal questions, Anna began thumbing through her book to find where she had left off. "On business."

Nicholas proved to be as persistent as he was perceptive. "And what sort of business is that?"

"I—I am sorry, but I really can not discuss his affairs. They are highly confidential."

"What about the reason he summoned you back to Town?"

"I would rather not discuss that either, if you please. It is . . . very personal."

"And obviously very painful. You have my sympathy." He accepted the rebuff without batting an eye. "Seeing as I, too, am traveling under duress, perhaps the less said about the subject the better. Shall we make a pact not to press each other on the matter for the duration of the journey?"

"You will not find your skills at negotiating tested

in this case." Grateful for the suggestion, she was quick to reply. "I gladly agree."

"Then I will return to the world of Byzantine intrigue. Whatever your uncle is involved in, it could not possibly rival the Greeks and the Turks for cunning or intrigue."

Hah! Anna wished to say it aloud. Instead, she cleared her throat. "Before you do, I have yet another apology to make. I was not only very rude earlier with my remarks on your temper and your skills at dealing with people, but also very wrong. You are very good at putting a person at ease."

"It is already forgotten. As you witnessed, I am all too aware of how easy it is to suffer a lapse in judgment when one is upset." He turned a page. "I take a bit of solace in the fact that some of Miss Austen's characters behave even more foolishly than we have."

They settled into a companionable silence. Cozy beneath the soft folds of her merino blanket, Anna picked up the thread of the story, and was interested to note that, on paper at least, closer scrutiny of the individuals involved did not always magnify their foibles.

The sound was deceptively mild, a soft flutter, something akin to the beating of a moth's wings against the glass. Nicholas pulled back the drapery only to find the view was of naught but vague shapes obscured by swirling snow. A gust of wind rattled the door.

"It looks to be getting worse."

Anna yawned and stretched her legs. "I wonder how much farther we have to go. It feels as if we have been travelling for hours."

"I fear the miles have not rolled by as quickly as the minutes. If we—"

A cracking lurch cut off his words and sent Nicholas skidding across the smooth leather. The sound of splintering wood exploded in his ears. The coach rocked back, flinging him up into the air where he hovered for an instant before landing in the young lady's lap.

"Damnation!" His curse echoed the cacophony of confusion outside. As he struggled to untangle his limbs from the twist of blankets and clothing, the wind whipped pellets of ice against the windows and the horses set up another chorus of frightened whinnies. From his box, the coachman cried for help.

To her credit, Anna did not panic. She wriggled out from under him and set to freeing his boot from her knotted skirts.

Brave girl, he noted, though aloud he snapped only a brusque "Stay here" as he dove for the door and wrenched it open. Fighting his way through the driving flurries, Nicholas caught the driver as he fell from the icy perch.

"T-tree fell across the way." Blue with cold, the man's lips were having difficulty forming distinct words. "M-managed to steer the team clear b-but I fear the w-wheel . . ."

The wheel was trapped by the broken branches of a large spruce.

Nicholas took hold of one of the shattered stumps, but abandoned the effort after several heaves proved there was no way he was going to dislodge it on his own. "If we back the coach up," he yelled above the howl of the storm, "I think we can manage to pull the wreckage free."

"Aye, sir." The coachman made a game try at returning to his seat, but his awkward fumblings quickly showed his wrist had been injured in the accident.

"I had better do that. It will take two good hands to control the team."

The man winced. "And it will take at least that to clear the branches."

Nicholas took a moment to assess his options, which, he decided, were extremely limited. "We will have to make a stab at it. There is no other choice—"

"Actually there is, sir." Anna appeared by his side, a muffler wound expertly up to the tip of her nose, its ends tied over her hat to snug it in place. "Let me handle the ribbons, while you help John."

"Too dangerous," he replied gruffly. "Go back inside."

"*Balvan!* I have a great deal of experience in driving a coach in these conditions."

"Did you just call me a . . . horse's arse?" he demanded, stifling the urge to laugh.

"Yes—but if you wish to ring another peal over my head for hoydenish behavior, I suggest you do it later."

"She is a dab hand on the box, sir," volunteered the coachman. "I can attest to her skill."

As a frigid gust nearly swept him off his feet, Nicholas gave a grim nod. "Very well. We won't stand on ceremony." Directing the two others to take up their places, he maneuvered the skittish animals into position to straighten the coach. "Ready?" he called.

Anna readied the whip.

"NOW!"

After a few slippery moments, the horses responded to the tug of the reins and dug in. The coach inched back, slowly but surely, until they were able to extricate the trapped wheel. Though several spokes were cracked and the rim bent, it looked as if it would hold up for a few more miles.

The same could not be said for the coachman, who was trying to mask his pain with a thin smile. Ignoring the weak attempt at argument, Nicholas bundled him inside the coach and tipped a flask of brandy to his iced lips. It was a moment or two before he realized he had left the young lady to fend for herself.

"May the devil's arse be buried in ice," he swore, reaching for the door latch.

It snapped open with no help from him. "Hell just might freeze over in this weather." Anna sounded almost cheerful as she scrambled in and slapped the snow from her mittens. "I trust you have saved a sip for me."

Thick flakes clung to her fur hat and ice rimmed her dark lashes, giving her the look of a storm-tossed ermine. A very adorable storm-tossed ermine. And a very brave one. Of all the young ladies he knew, Nicholas could not think of a one who would not be on the verge of a dead swoon by now. While Lady Anna seemed about to succumb to . . .

Laughter?

It was a sweetly musical sound that seemed to lighten the confined space with a note of sunshine. Nicholas found himself smiling in spite of the circumstances. "Well done," he murmured, passing over the spirits. "I would never have imagined a highborn lady could take hold of adversity like that."

"I would never have imagined a proper gentleman could carry his own weight," she retorted, but with a twinkle in her eye. "And if you are about to remark that a highborn lady ought not imbibe in anything stronger than ratafia punch, you may bite your tongue."

"If I could, I would be offering you champagne," he murmured. Strangely enough, he found he was developing a taste for her effervescent spirit. In comparison, all the other young ladies of his acquaintance suddenly seemed flat.

Anna took a tiny taste of the brandy, then handed it back. "Actually, I would prefer vodka."

"I shall ring for one of the footmen and ask him to fetch a bottle. Along with a jar of caviar."

Another laugh. He was sorry to hear it die away more quickly than the first one.

Her expression turned serious as she rooted around in her reticule and drew out a length of linen. "Let me have your hand, John. That wrist needs to be bandaged."

"But milady, you ought not have to tend to me—"

She already had hold of his sleeve and was folding back the cuff. "Don't be foolish. This should help stave off any further swelling." Her gaze angled up, looking for Nicholas's eyes. "However, you won't be in any condition to drive."

"As to that," he replied. "I will take his place on the box."

"And I will spell you."

Before he could argue, the coachman voiced his own reservation. "Sir, with the wheel as weak as it is, it might not be wise to risk pushing on. The snow and ice has become awfully treacherous on this narrow road. Another accident might turn out to be far more serious than the one we just escaped."

Nicholas frowned. "What are you suggesting?"

"That I go ahead on foot and fetch help. We have traveled some distance, and by the innkeeper's direction, the next village cannot be far off."

"Out of the question," exclaimed Anna. "I'll not have you run such a risk."

"The storm is letting up," replied her servant, pointing out a sliver of blue in the slate gray clouds. "And there is nothing wrong with my legs, milady. The way is clear enough that I am in no danger of getting lost. I should be back in a short while with a safer vehicle. If I am not, then his lordship can attempt the drive."

"He has a point," mused Nicholas. A more prolonged look out the window showed that the snow had stopped and the dark clouds appeared to be blowing off to the east. "All things considered, the plan is a prudent one."

"There must be another way," she protested.

"If you have a better proposal, I am willing to hear it."

Her lips parted, but remained frozen in silence.

Nicholas began assembling some essentials for the coachman to take with him. "Lady Anna, like it or not, we must be . . ."

"Practical." A sigh blunted the edge of irony.

"Sometimes, discretion is the better part of valor," he murmured, adding a pair of extra mittens from his valise and the muffler from his neck to a packet of cold meat pie. "Your courage and concern are commendable, but pushing onward might only end up being far more dangerous for all concerned."

She signaled her surrender with a small nod.

"That goes for you, too," he was forced to add as the coachman tried to refuse the food and clothing. "Now be off with you. Stick to the road, and if you encounter any difficulty, do not hesitate to turn back."

Looping the length of merino wool up over his ears, the man snapped off a brisk salute and slipped out into the cold.

"Do you always remain so calm and unrattled in the face of an emergency?" asked Anna after the door fell shut.

"Being a stick in the mud, it takes a great deal to make me budge."

She colored. "Oh, dear! Must you remind me of all the regrettable things I have uttered over the course of the day?"

To keep such a becoming shade of pink upon her cheeks, he would consider repeating their conversations word for word. In Latin and Greek, if need be.

"You no doubt look on me as a hopeless hoyden, now that I have shown my true colors."

"I do not see you in quite so harsh a light, Lady Anna."

She shied back from the window as the sun scudded out from behind the clouds. In a moment it was gone again, dimming the uncertainty in her eyes. What inner turmoil drove her to seek refuge in shadow? Nicholas had an inkling he knew its cause, which seemed confirmed by her troubled reply.

"Then you are the rare exception. Most gentlemen expect a lady to resemble bleached muslin—soft, pliable, leached of all texture and hue." Abruptly changing position, she leaned back up to the panes of glass and cupped her chin in her hand. "I have always loved winter, and the way the world appears after a snowfall. The pristine white blanket is so pure, so perfect. It covers a multitude of flaws, hides the imperfections, softens the jagged edges . . ." Her voice trailed off as she stared at the pale trees. "Everything looks so hopeful and full of promise, as if life itself were a blank canvas, on which one could start afresh."

"But it melts away."

"Yes, I know." Her voice was sad, subdued. "It's only an illusion."

He thought for a long moment. "In many ways, what you are speaking about is really the true spirit of Christmas. It seems to me that it is a time to remind ourselves that there is always hope, always a chance for the rebirth of light and laughter, no matter that the days are at their darkest."

"Why, Lord Moreton, you are . . . a very wise man."

"Sorry, I have no frankincense, gold or myrrh to offer you, just a piece of rather moldy cheddar." From within another square of oilskin he produced half a loaf of dark bread. Cutting off a slice, he topped it off with a crumble of the cheese and presented it to her with a flourish. "Along with a crust of stale rye."

Her mouth quivered, then slowly curled up at the corners. "I think it quite the most lovely Christmas gift I have received since . . . since I was a child."

Nicholas was too well attuned to the nuances of language to miss her last minute change of words. A shapely figure was not the only thing hidden beneath the fur-trimmed coat. *Secrets.* She had secrets too personal, too painful to share.

Didn't everyone? he thought, uncomfortably aware of his own inner conflicts, and how carefully he tried to keep them under wraps. Lud, what a pair they made—two prickly strangers, forced to travel by the call of duty, thrown together by chance. Her problems were not really any of his concern, and yet he felt an inexplicable bond between them.

Trying to lighten her bleak mood, he kept up his show of humor. "What! You mean to say a porcelain doll can hold a candle to this exquisite delicacy?"

"It was a rocking horse, painted bright yellow, with a flaxen mane and tail soft as spun silk." She shivered as she nibbled at the morsel of food. "I used to imagine I could ride to the moon and back if I wished to. But like all childish fantasies, such dreams soon came crashing back down to earth."

Sympathy only seemed to be making things worse. He tried another strategy. "And here I was thinking you had more bottom than most highborn young ladies. But I see I was wrong. A tumble or two and you run for cover, feeling egregiously sorry for yourself."

Her eyes blazed, just as he had hoped, burning away the look of dull despair. "I never succumb to self-pity! Why, I have faced plenty of hardships that would send any of *your* cosseted female friends into a paroxysm of . . ." Anna's indignation trailed off as she caught sight of his twitching lips. "Wretch—you were trying to make me angry."

"I would rather hear fire in your voice than such a note of defeat," he admitted. "Trust me, we all experience times when our dreams soar a bit higher than reality allows."

"Even you?"

"Even me. The fall may leave a few bruises, but the trick is to dust yourself off and get back on your horse."

She nibbled at the last bit of cheese while digesting his last words. "I don't imagine it happens often. Gentlemen are so rarely knocked from the saddle."

"You saw me land flat on my . . . back. A rather lowering experience, I might add, that put several distinct black-and-blue marks on my pride."

"At the time, you appeared to need a set-down. But I was wrong, and owe you yet another apology." Her gaze dropped, dragging her along with it. "My judgment seems greatly askew these days."

"But not your aim."

"Which is hardly a mark in my favor."

"On the contrary, I think it quite admirable that a young lady possess practical skills, and the spirit to use them."

Anna cast him a doubtful look. "You are teasing me again, I expect."

"No, I am not. You are right in remarking that, in many ways, young ladies of the *ton* are indistinguishable from one another. In a ballroom, they do have a tendency to blend together into one blur of pastel silks. A very pretty blur, to be sure. However, up close, pastels tend to look a trifle insipid. I often find myself wishing for some sort of show of real color."

Nicholas watched as her eyes deepened to an indescribably unique shade of blue. Deep, mysterious and rippled with subtle shadings ranging from turquoise to indigo. A man could drown in such a hue. And die happily.

"Even if it takes the form of a snowball smack to the back of your head?"

He found himself grinning. "You certainly leave a lasting impression, Lady Anna. A number of gentlemen might not like it that you have strong opinions, as well as a strong arm, but you also have a unique pluck and courage. I cannot think of another female with whom I would rather be trapped in the wilds."

His observation stirred an unfathomable reaction. It

was gone in the blink of an eye as her lashes lowered. "That is nice of you to say, sir. Most of the time, I hear only florid compliments on my looks or shameless flattery of my mediocre skills on the pianoforte."

"And you do not like that?"

"No. In truth it is very wearisome."

Anna made no protest as he tucked another blanket over her lap and settled her head on his shoulder. "Try to get a bit of sleep, then. There will still be a long way to go once your coachman returns."

"Perhaps you could come on with us to London after all," she murmured into the folds of his coat.

Dangerous. That road could only lead to trouble. "It is probably best that we go our separate ways."

In her dream, she was being chased by a big black bear whose gaping jaws stretched into an uncanny resemblance of her uncle's smile. *Snap. Snap.* The teeth were coming ever closer, threatening to swallow her into a maw of darkness.

Shrinking back with a small cry, Anna found herself sheltered inside something reassuringly warm and solid. Her lashes fluttered and she was vaguely aware of a dark shape swooping in to ward off the danger.

"No need to be alarmed." Nicholas brushed another tangled curl from her cheek. "The howl is just the sound of the wind picking up."

Now fully awake, Anna sat up. "How long have we been sitting here? It looks dark as midnight outside."

"Not more than an hour, but I am afraid the storm has come back with a vengeance." The wood paneling shivered as another gust slammed into the coach. "I don't think we can expect a rescue party anytime soon. We are going to have to fend for ourselves."

Even with her nose pressed up against the glass, she could make out naught but an impenetrable white shroud surrounding them. "Lud, the temperature is dropping as well. If it gets much colder, we will have to consider abandoning the vehicle and digging a snow cave."

"A snow cave?"

"In Russia, it is a common practice when travelers are stranded in a storm. The snow provides much more insulation than a drafty vehicle. It is actually quite cozy, and can make the difference between life and death."

"How very interesting." She had half expected Nicholas to dismiss the idea as far too outlandish, but he looked rather intrigued. "Do you speak from experience?"

No doubt it would only add to her image of being a very foreign sort of female. Not that she really cared what Lord Moreton thought of her. She had grown accustomed at school to being considered different from the other girls.

"Yes." Her chin rose a touch, as if to deflect any derision. "My grandmother and I were caught in a snowstorm while traveling from Moscow to her country estate in Obuchovo. I was only fourteen and a bit frightened, but she had braved many a winter and made it seem like a grand adventure." Her tone turned slightly wistful. "She kept me entertained through the night by recounting traditional Russian folk tales, with their fearless *bogatyrs,* enchanted ice maidens and magical firebirds. I was disappointed come morning, when a search party found us and dug out our sleigh."

"I can well imagine. 'The Feather of Finist the Falcon' was a particular favorite of mine when I was a schoolboy."

"You are familiar with Russian wonder stories?"

"I usually had my nose buried in a book while the other lads were out playing cricket." He made a wry face. "You are not the first one who has thought me a stick in the mud."

Wishing that her tongue had not been so well aimed as her snowball, Anna said as much.

"No need for remorse," came the cheerful reply. "Such boring habits came in quite handy when I met up with a partisan band in Portugal—"

"You were in *Portugal* with the *partisans*?"

"Just for a short time. I was delegated to make a rather minor delivery to one of the less important chieftains. Luckily for me, I had read an arcane Moorish text on mountain warfare, for when we were set upon by a regiment of French dragoons . . ." He went on to tell a pithy anecdote that she suspected did not give full credit to his actions in fighting off the enemy.

Anna was thinking on how to respond when a jangling of the harness rang out above the din of the storm. "Lud, I have forgotten the poor horses! In Russia the sleighs carry horse blankets for just such an emergency. Unless the storm abates . . ." Wiping the frozen vapor from the windowpane, she tried to peer outside.

He was already buttoning up his coat. "I saw a small stand of pine trees close by. They should provide an excellent shelter from the snow and wind."

"Lord Moreton, wait! I should like to come help."

"And turn into a real-life Snow Queen?" Hand on the latch, he paused. "I much prefer you as a flesh-and-blood young lady—so please, do me the great favor of staying here for the nonce."

Her flesh and blood were suddenly suffused with a flush of heat. Which made no sense, seeing as ice crystals clung to her mittens. "Well, then . . . do be careful."

A flurry of snow nearly obscured his grin. "Don't worry. I have no desire to transform from a stick in the mud to an icicle in the snow."

As it turned out, the wind soon died down and it was not necessary to go the extreme of seeking refuge in the drifts that had all but buried the coach wheels. Layered atop the fur carriage throw, the extra blankets ensured that her makeshift bed was quite comfortable. Anna wiggled her stockinged toes, finding she could almost stretch out full-length on the narrow bench. While on the facing seat, Lord Moreton must be feeling like a *matryoshka* doll, with his limbs crammed tightly into a confined space. He had refused all but one thin covering, and must have been half frozen as well.

After a restless few minutes, guilt weighed too heavily on her for sleep to come. Sitting up, she was about to insist he take one of her blankets when a soft yet unmistakable buzzing stilled her lips.

The man was snoring.

It was an oddly intimate sound. And strangely comforting. Anna lay back and stared up into the darkness. Come to think of it, a great many things about Lord Moreton were surprisingly reassuring. Far from being an arrogant prig, he had shown himself to be thoughtful, well-read and funny, while at the first sign of trouble, he had assumed command with a cool calmness that had saved them from further injury.

She blinked, aware that she was seeing him—and herself—in a whole new light. Though its flicker and sway still left much in shadow. It had been some years since she had taken any real joy in Christmas, but now, this chance encounter with a stranger had made her feel less alone in the world.

That gift, however small, however fleeting, kindled a tiny flame of hope that she might once again share a feeling of closeness, of kinship with another person.

Listening to the slow, steady rhythm of his slumber, she was soon lulled into a peaceful sleep.

It was the resinous curl of wood smoke that tickled her senses back to consciousness. Throwing off her covers, Anna tugged on her coat and boots. Her hair-pins proved a more daunting challenge.

"Good morning." Nicholas had cleared a small patch of ground to the bare earth and was fanning a spark from his flint and steel to life. "Do you always sleep so soundly?"

"Only when I stay awake half the night listening to a strange gentleman's snores."

"I should have warned you." He didn't look around. "Several of my friends have likened it to a dull saw cutting through the keel of a forty-gun frigate."

Another point in his favor that he could make fun of himself. And the score inched a notch higher as he turned in profile, the snow reflecting a dappling of silvery light across his chiseled features.

"It wasn't quite *that* bad."

She watched him strip off his gloves and carefully arrange the thin curls of wood into a small pyramid. A great many gentlemen of her acquaintance were quick to boast of their skill at shooting or dancing or choosing the cut of a waistcoat, but she could not recall a one admitting to knowing how to fix an axle or coax a fire from damp shavings of wood. But by now, she was not at all surprised that he did not kick up a dust about getting his hands dirty.

"You do not seem to mind doing menial tasks."

"Not when it is necessary." He dusted his palms, then picked up the knife and began cutting more fuel for the fire. "I would rather shed my dignity than my life."

"Ever practical, sir?"

"Practical, prudent and pragmatic," he agreed. "I warned you not to expect the Corsair as your companion on this journey."

He did look very raffish with his uncombed locks grazing rumpled linen and a gleam of golden whiskers stubbling his jaw. Trying to put such thoughts out of her mind, Anna stood up and hugged her arms to her chest. "Speaking of journeys, we should probably be harnessing the horses and starting off."

Nicholas threaded a morsel of bread onto a sharpened stick and held it over the meager flames. "I am afraid we are not going anywhere." At her start, he waggled the piece of toast at the snowy silhouette of their coach. "I checked earlier on the wheel, and what with the weight of the ice and snow, the damaged spoke had cracked clean through."

"We could ride on to the next inn."

"Too dangerous." The bread angled heavenward. "With the clouds as thick as they are, I won't chance it." After one last pass over the coals, he held the stick at arm's length. "Have some breakfast. It's hardly a mouthful, but we had better conserve what we have."

A nibble of the toasted crust caused her to cough.

He plucked a tin cup from the coals. "Sorry, unlike the wizard in 'The Frog Prince,' I am not able to conjure up a spell to turn frozen apples into a pot of steaming tea."

"This is magical enough, sir." Anna sipped at the cider, feeling an extra warmth tingling through her limbs. Lord Moreton had a most delicious sense of humor—dry and spiced with a whimsical irony. As she swirled the last dregs, she felt an odd sort of emptiness in the pit of her stomach. *Strong. Capable. Modest.* Adding on a number of his other attributes, Anna realized she had never savored a gentleman's company quite so much. Yet quite likely their paths would never cross again.

Her fingers tightened around the cup, suddenly chilled to the bone.

"Your cheeks are looking pale as ice, Lady Anna. We had best not linger here too long, exposed to the elements, lest you succumb to frostbite."

It was her heart, she feared, not her face, that was in danger of suffering some irreparable damage. The cold had seeped straight to her core.

Not that she could quite explain why. Lord Moreton would probably have some insight to offer on chance and fate. But she felt awkward, unsure. Unsure of what, she asked herself. Of whether he would laugh? Of whether she would cry?

Better to keep silent than risk breaking the fragile camaraderie that had formed between them.

Eyeing her with growing concern, Nicholas tucked the blanket more snugly around her shoulders. "I had a look around while you were sleeping. The ruins of an old abbey are not too far off. The walls are crumbling, but there is a roof overhead and room to move about. If we bring along the blankets and a few essentials, I daresay the place will be a bit more comfortable to wait out the weather than a cramped, drafty coach. That is, if you are feeling up to the journey."

She nodded. "Of course. It is a sensible move to take leave of the coach." Would that she could also take leave of the regrets for what might have been.

After strapping their luggage atop one of the horses, Nicholas turned to the other animal and arranged a blanket in place as a saddle. "Let me give you a hand up." Worried at her pallor, he tried to tease a bit of color back to her face. "You show a very pretty ankle, Lady Anna," he murmured, as he laced his gloves beneath her boot.

"Lord Moreton, my leg is presently covered by something resembling a small furry animal."

"Yes, but were it not, I am sure it would be a most delightful sight."

"How very improper of you to say so."

Her burble of amusement encouraged him to go on. "Yes, well, considering our present predicament, I think we can safely say that propriety has long since flown out the window. Let us hope our necks have not gone with it."

He meant it as a joke, but the smile froze on her

face. "If you are worried that you are going to find yourself ensnared by the circumstances, don't be. I promised that you would suffer no consequences because of this journey. Your reputation shall remain unsullied." If anything, her voice turned colder. "And your leg unshackled, if that is what is bothering you."

Hell's teeth. What perfidious fairy dust had been mixed in with the snow? In the past, he had always maintained a rigid correctness in any conversation with a female. But Lady Anna had made him feel at ease. As if he might be himself.

Hah. And pigs might fly.

"That was *not* what I meant at all. I was merely . . ." Frustrated, he kicked at the snow. "To the devil with reputations and rules! Would that I could shake off all the dratted chains of convention."

A powdering of flakes shot up, sparkling like jewels in the peekaboo sunlight. So, too, did the first notes of laughter lighten the air. The sound grew richer, more brilliant as it caught in the breeze. "Why, sir! If you raised your voice an octave you would sound exactly like me. However, as you wear boots and breeches, it is termed 'letting off steam' rather than 'falling in a fit of vapors.' Call it what you will, would you like the loan of my vinaigrette?" She gave a small shake of her reticule. "I am sure it is in here somewhere."

His shoulders stiffened, and then he caught a glint of the merriment in her eyes. "Minx! Are you . . ."

"Teasing you?" Her peal of laughter rang delightfully musical to his ear. "Yes, I suppose I am. I have never dared do so with a gentleman before, but when you let yourself unbend, you are . . . different. So do not turn too starchy, Lord Moreton."

"Do not turn too saucy, Lady Anna."

She stuck out her tongue. "What is good for the goose is good for the gander."

Grinning, he made a last check of the luggage and

took up the reins. *Different.* It was a start in the right direction. Though where it would lead, he could not hazard a guess.

"Let us hope we do not end up burned to a crisp."

They set off through the windblown snow, and for a time, both of them seemed content to let their thoughts drift, like the swirl of flakes kicked up by the horses. As he trudged through the knee-deep powder, Nicholas found himself simply enjoying the soft sounds of a winter's morning. The muffled swoosh of his steps . . . the stirring of the snow-coated pine boughs . . . the musical tinkle of the brass harness fittings, which echoed of faraway church bells. It was peaceful. It was . . .

It was Christmas! Or nearly so.

"Good Lord!" His exclamation formed a whispery cloud around his lips. "Tonight is Christmas Eve. The holiday festivities will have to go on without us—it goes without saying that we will never make it to Town in time for our engagements." He angled a look over his shoulder. "I hope that is not too bitter a disappointment."

Anna's eyes were downcast. "In truth, I did not feel much like celebrating."

"If you were in Spain, your eyes would be all aglitter on this eve as you wrapped sweetmeats in gold foil." Wishing to lighten the look on her face, he said the first fanciful thing that popped into his head. "It is a tradition that all unmarried young ladies of the land prepare treats for the elfin folk who fly in on storks to leave a gift on the pillow of every sleeping child."

Her lashes lifted ever so slightly. "How do they get into the houses?"

"They, er, fly down the chimneys." A gust whistled through the trees. "While in Denmark, the North Wind blows in through the cracks in the windows and leaves an ice crystal on the mantel for every member of the family. When the morning comes, the fire is kindled to a great flame and the frozen gift melts into a wish."

Her gaze had regained a bit of sparkle. "In Russia, a Baba Yaga is said to fly in on a mortar and pestle, leaving gifts for those who have behaved all year and lumps of coal for those who have been bad."

"Ah, that is nothing compared to the monkeys of Malta, who according to an old Templar rite are allowed to pelt miscreants with rotten oranges from dawn to dusk on Christmas day."

A burble of laughter cut off any further fantasies. "Really, sir, how do you come up with such outrageous bouncers at the drop of a hat?"

"As a government official, I am expected to be creative with language."

"You mean to lie through your teeth?"

He managed to assume an expression of mock indignation but it quickly quirked into a grin. "Well, if you put it that way . . ."

"What I will say, Lord Moreton, is you have a wonderfully whimsical imagination. As well as a gift for putting people at ease." Anna toyed with the end of her muffler. "Thank you for lifting my spirits. I know everyone is expected to be happy at Christmas."

Her attempt at cheerfulness fell rather flat.

"If you are thinking that something is missing, Lady Anna, you are not alone." Nicholas cut around an outcropping of rock. "No doubt it sounds blasphemous, but the season has always left me cold. There is so much jolliness all around—the cheerful laughter, the festive decorations of evergreen and mistletoe, the smells of sugar and spice perfuming the air. One feels guilty about not getting into the spirit of things. And yet so much of the celebrating feels forced, or superficial. It sometimes seems the true meaning of the holiday has been lost."

"I *hate* Christmas," she blurted out.

Nicholas halted, ostensibly to give the horses a rest. "May I ask why?" he said, his hand lingering on her knee after he had smoothed out the folds of her coat.

"Because it used to be a magical time of light . . . and love."

"What happened to change that?"

"I was in school here in England. My parents had been called away to St. Petersburg, but they had promised to return in time for us to share the holidays, as we always did. The passage through the Baltic was a rough one, and by the time their ship reached Antwerp, it was running several days late. They should never have set sail that night, but the harbormaster said my father was so anxious to reach Dover without further delay that the captain relented. A winter gale . . ." Her voice, which had grown brittle as ice, finally cracked.

His glove found hers and clasped it tightly. Through the thick wool he could feel her fingers. They were clenched together, as if seeking solace from each other. "If your uncle were here, I would hit him with a thumping right cross, rather than a snowball. He must be as hard and unfeeling as a lump of coal to have you traveling on your own so close to Christmas."

"He is not uncaring, merely unaware. At the time, he was away in the Far East. I don't think he ever knew the exact date of the shipwreck. Or if he did, the significance did not quite sink in. You see, he is of the Orthodox faith, as are most Russians. By their calendar, Christmas comes in early January." Her lips quivered. "In any case, he is too busy ordering the affairs of the world to think about such small tragedies."

Without saying a thing, Nicholas pulled her down from the makeshift saddle and into his arms. He sensed she did not need words, just the unspoken warmth of a heartfelt hug.

Ice crackled in the branches overhead. From a nearby stump, a solitary raven flapped up into the sky. Finally, at the sound of a frosty snort from one of the horses, Anna lifted her cheek from his collar with an answering sigh. "You are immensely kind to offer a shoulder to lean on, Lord Moreton. Though I fear with all my sniffling I've left your line rather wilted."

"We both agreed it was better not to be too starchy. I would much rather you call me Nicholas."

"Very well . . . Nicholas." Blinking away a last tear, she straightened her fur hat. "We cannot stand in one place forever. The horses are growing chilled. We really must move on."

Though loath to let her go, Nicholas let her pull away. His gaze moved across the pastureland, to where the ruins of the abbey were just visible above the crest of a hill. "Would that I could make the journey an easier one for you." Like her he was speaking of more than mere physical distance.

"I'm not sure how far I could have come without you," she murmured as he helped her back onto her mount.

"Tell me," he said, once they had gotten under way again. "What are the things you recollect most about Christmas with your family?"

"Lud, I have a myriad of marvelous memories." She thought for a moment, a wistful smile curling the corners of her mouth. "I recall how Papa would search the woods for the biggest Yule log he could find. How Mama delighted in playing Christmas carols on the pianoforte—from English to Russian, and all the languages in between. How she would have Cook decorate the dining table with cherubic angels carved out of ice, their chubby little arms filled with candles and sugared plums."

"It sounds truly wonderful."

Looking as though she did not quite trust her voice, Anna nodded.

He let the conversation trail off into the rhythmic crunch of snow. As the abbey walls came into sharper focus, an idea began to take form in his head. A crazy one to be sure, seeing as they were stranded in the wilds, with barely a crust of bread and bit of cheese between them.

Miracles could happen, Nicholas reminded himself, if one believed them possible. To go along with the cherished memories of Christmas past, he determined to make the advent of Christmas present an evening that Anna would not forget.

Magic. Her wish upon a star must have bounced off Antares, gathered momentum as it circled Polaris and finally reached the ear of some powerful wizard or warlock. For nothing short of unearthly enchantment could explain the sight that now greeted her gaze.

Eyes wide with wonder, Anna looked around the remains of the ancient chapel. Barely half an hour ago it had been a dark, damp space, with wind whistling through the crumbling mortar and mouse droppings sprinkled liberally over the dead leaves that covered the worn stone floor.

And now?

Fatigue and hunger did strange things to the brain, and she *was* awfully tired and hungry. That, of course, had not stopped her from demanding to help make their temporary shelter habitable. So when Nicholas had asked if she would chip through the ice of a nearby stream while he gathered kindling, she had gladly taken up the old bucket they had found and stumbled off.

Setting down her load, she pressed an icy mitten to her brow, wondering if she was dreaming. But no, a peek through the wool showed that the vision was still there.

In the far corner a blaze of merry flames danced up from a massive log whose rotund girth matched that of a brandy cask. Above it, a garland of evergreen branches festooned the entire length of the weathered wall, its needles perfuming the air with the fragrance of fresh-cut pine. Her breath then caught in her throat as she spied a flickering of light set off from the main fire.

"It's not quite finished." Knotting a strip of linen around a twig of white birch, Nicholas smeared the cloth with sticky resin and added it to the other wooden candles he had fashioned. It burst into flame, illuminating the blocks of ice he had hollowed out to hold the display. "They are not the most elegant tapers, and my skills as a sculptor leave something to be desired, but—"

"But they are beautiful," she whispered. "Simply beautiful."

"Come, let us make the last few ones together."

Anna sat down on the blanket and took up a remnant of cloth. "How did you ever manage the Yule log?" she asked.

"With the help of the horses. I rigged a length of the reins as a crude sling."

"You . . ." A shower of sparks shot up as she lit her candle from one of his. "You have worked miracles, Nicholas Moreton."

"Abracadabra!" Making a wry face, he waved a branch at the burning log. "Now if only I could make a Christmas goose appear for a holiday repast."

The fluttering in her stomach had nothing to do with hunger. Not for fowl. Or fish, for that matter. Lud, she could feast on his smile alone and never feel an emptiness inside her again.

"I fear it will be the same sorry supper of bread and cheese—save for one small treat." With a flourish he produced a tin of tea from his coat pocket. "I found this in my valise. In my haste to take leave of my friends, I forgot to leave behind the blend of Oolong that William requested from Town."

"Any more magic up your sleeve?"

He made a show of looking up his cuffs. "That's it for now. I shall just kindle a very ordinary fire for cooking, and use our tin cup for boiling water."

As he stacked some branches and struck a flint to tinder, Anna began to rummage in her reticule. "Ah," she exclaimed a moment later, extracting several mashed pieces of gingerbread. "I, too, have been carrying around some forgotten treasures." A second plunge brought up a handful of honey drops wrapped in brightly colored paper.

His brows rose. "I have always wondered what females carry in those things. Aside from vinaigrette, of course."

"A great many useful things. Like . . . a spoon . . . a coil of twine . . . a pair of scissors . . ." She laughed as she added a tiny tin trumpet to the growing pile. "Oh, I had quite forgotten about *that.*"

"Good Lord, what else do you have in there? A regiment of hussars? We could arm them with shovels instead of sabers and be out of here in a trice."

Turning the reticule upside down, Anna gave it a shake. "No soldiers," she announced, as a jumble of items spilled from its depth. "Would a bear do?" The wooden toy was painted a whimsical blue, with spots of scarlet for the eyes and nose.

"One of its arms is broken," he pointed out.

"Yes." Anna picked up a bit of engraved silver. "So is the ring on this watch fob. Still, it is a very pretty design." She hesitated, then reached for his hand and placed both the bear and the fob in his palm. "It is a rather hodgepodge assortment of presents, but it is the spirit that counts. Merry Christmas, Nicholas."

His fingers closed around her offerings. "Thank you," he said softly. The candlelight reflecting off his whiskered jaw seemed to ignite a thousand sparks of fire. "Your gifts, and your spirit, are quite special."

Anna suddenly felt hot all over. "They are just . . .

flights of fancy." To hide her burning longing to press her cheek to the stubbled gold, she ducked away and began refilling her reticule. "Surely gentlemen must collect lots of serendipitous things during the course of their travels."

Nicholas cocked his head to one side, setting off another flare of fire. "I never really thought about it. Let us see." Fetching the leather document case from his valise, he emptied it on the blanket. Along with a flutter of papers, out fell a filigree penknife, a small book whose marbled cover had seen better days and a Spanish gold coin.

"This is from a tiny artisan's shop in Lisbon," he mused, fingering the silver blade. "And the coin . . . after escaping the French patrol, I considered it a lucky charm."

"And the book?"

"Dante's sonnets. Italian is a lovely language." He opened it and angled the page to the fire. "Here, I shall read one aloud."

The words were like warm honey. Anna closed her eyes, savoring the sweetness of his voice. "How beautiful," she whispered, when he was done.

A rustle of wool, and suddenly the book was in her lap, along with the knife and the coin.

Her lashes flew open. "Oh, I couldn't—"

"The gift of friendship is what Christmas is all about." His fingers twined with hers. "As is sharing. And caring."

"And wishing good will to all men."

He chuckled. "A sentiment you did not hold dear when first we met. With good reason I might add. Though I hope we are now . . . friends."

"I—I have come to think of you as that."

Nicholas snuggled her a bit closer. "I have read you poetry, now won't you sing me one of the carols your mother played on this eve?"

"S—Silent night, holy night . . ." At first the words

were hardly more than a zephyr of breath, but they grew stronger as he added a bass note to her soft soprano.

"I should like to hear one in Russian," he encouraged.

"Now it is your turn," she said as the melody died away.

"Hmmm." He rubbed at his chin. "How about 'God Rest Ye Merry Gentlemen' in Dutch?"

When she was done giggling at his off-key rendition, she had her own suggestion. "Would you care to hear 'Good King Wenceslaw' in Polish?"

The winter night was long, but the hours passed quickly as they filled them with songs in a gaggle of other languages. Shared laughter filled the gaps of missing words or melodies. Anna did not quite realize how quickly until Nicholas pulled out his pocket watch and thumbed open its case.

"Good Lord, it is a few minutes past midnight. This calls for a holiday toast." He found the flask of brandy in his bag and passed it to her with a wink. "We must keep the body as well as the spirit warm."

Anna did not need strong drink to feel a delicious heat curl down to her toes. Still, she took a small swallow. And shivered as fire filled her mouth.

Would a kiss from Nicholas taste . . .

Handing it back, she scrabbled to her feet. "I—I should like to see if I can spot the Christmas star."

Overhead, the sky was a canopy of black velvet alight with the infinite sparkle of hope. "I wished on a star the night of the storm," she said, as he came up behind her.

"Make another wish."

She bit at her lip. It was cold. "You aren't supposed to say such dreams aloud."

"Tell you what—let us both make a wish, and keep it secret."

Silence stretched for several moments. Drawing in

a deep breath, Anna spun on tiptoe and kissed his cheek. "May all your wishes come true, Nicholas," she whispered, then turned and hurried back to the abbey.

But not before slanting a last, longing look at a certain point of light that seemed to twinkle just a bit brighter than all the others.

Anna awoke to early morning sunlight filtering in through the crumbling stone. She smiled as its pale warmth suffused her face, recalling a memorable night.

"Good morning, Nicholas. Now we can truly say merry Christmas," she called softly.

Hearing no answer, she rubbed the sleep from her eyes and turned to the fire. The coals, rekindled at some point during the night, crackled with a cheery red glow, but the rumpled blanket where he had slept looked stone-cold.

Perhaps he had gone to fetch more water, or forage for food . . .

The sheet of foolscap, stark as snow against her folded cloak, told her otherwise. Her name was scrawled in the same leaden hue that had recently darkened the skies, and she had no doubt the words inside would weigh just as heavily on her heart. She knew, of course, what they would say.

Nicholas was gone.

Drawing the blanket around her shoulders and coaxing the last of the firewood into flames did nothing to ward off the chill seeping into her bones.

Dear Anna, it began. The lettering was smudged and looked to have been written in a hurry. *I am truly sorry that you will awake to find yourself alone on Christmas morning. I should like to have shared one last carol and . . .* He appeared to have crossed out a word or two. *However, having spent most of the night mulling over the situation, it became clear that I must be gone before anyone saw us together. As soon as I reach an inn, I shall see to it that a rescue party is sent. Stick to the following story, and I am confident you will weather any threat to your reputation. Your servants will support whatever account you give, so there is no worry there . . .*

She slowly read over the advice, which detailed how she was to tell everyone, including her uncle, a carefully edited version of the truth. *Say only this—you tried to beat the storm, but the coach suffered a mishap and the storm caught up to you. Your driver went for help, leaving you stranded in the wilds. The snow forced you to take refuge in the abbey ruins, where you decided to wait for the weather to clear and a search party to find you. No one, not the highest stickler or the strictest guardian, will find fault with such actions.* Anna looked up. Not if she remembered to never, ever make mention of a male companion. Skimming the last few lines, she looked for the ending.

Your friend, N.

A dear friend indeed, she thought, blinking back the beads of moisture clinging to her lashes. If she had been thinking clearly, she would have realized long before now that the solution he had come up with was the only way to avoid a terrible scandal. But her reason had been clouded by more than a passing snowstorm.

She knew she ought to be very grateful for his unassailable logic and his practical skill at putting a plan into action. Yet a small part of her could not help but regret that he had moved with quite such a show of efficiency. A tiny voice in the back of her head echoed the disappointment, whispering that there had, in fact, been one other alternative to his sudden departure. But seeing as he had not proposed it, there was no point in dwelling on what might have been . . .

It would only make the future harder to bear.

No, he had been right—it was best that the parting be swift and sure. Her fingers closed around the small gold coin in her pocket. She would treasure the memory of this Christmas, and the coin's burnished hue would always be a special reminder of a certain blond gentleman. For a glimmering interlude, they had warded off the bleakness of winter with shared sorrow, joy and friendship.

How could anyone wish for a better gift than that?

Anna smiled through her tears, hoping that he took away with him something more meaningful than a chipped wooden bear and a broken watch fob. She wanted very much to believe they did not lie discarded by the roadside, along with all thoughts of the time they had spent together.

However, the truth was, she knew so little about his personal life. For all she knew, he had a fiancée waiting to welcome him back to Town. Or a *chère amie.*

Before her spirits could sink any lower, a shout from the distance recalled her to the present. "Lady Anna!"

Her coachman's familiar voice. True to his word, Nicholas had wasted no time. "Yes—I am here."

Gathering up her things, she stood and began to stamp out the last flickerings of the fire.

The letter, he noted, was still in her hand.

"A slight change in plans—I hope you don't mind." Nicholas could feel that his smile was slightly lopsided. So were his nerves. The beating of his heart had knocked them all to flinders. "I found I could not bear the idea of leaving you alone on Christmas." His feet shuffled in the snow. "Or on any day, for that matter. That is to say, the idea of a future with you . . . and me . . . together . . ." He cleared his throat. "For a diplomat supposed skilled in the nuances of language, I am making a real hash of this."

Anna let out her breath. "I think you are doing just fine. Please go on."

Encouraged, he pulled her into his arms. "Then I shall stop beating around the bush. I love you, Anna.

More dearly than words can ever express." His lips feathered a gossamer kiss to her brow, her cheek, and then slanted across her mouth.

It was several minutes before he spoke again. "Will you marry me, *liebe?* You have hinted that your uncle has other plans for you. And as a matter of fact, my father wishes for me to . . . well, never mind. It doesn't matter now." His arms tightened around her. "To the devil with the expectations of others. We have been given a great gift in finding each other, one too precious to let be taken from our grasp."

Tears, like ice jewels, sparkled on her cheek. "I love you, Nicholas. I wish with all my heart to be your wife." Her chin took on the defiant little tilt he had come to adore. "And if my uncle seeks to make an international incident—"

"Leave the negotiations to me, my dear. I will take care that our two countries do not come to blows."

"You are late."

"Yes, well, I ran into a spot of difficulty." Biting back a more acid comment, Nicholas settled for a retort that was only mildly sarcastic. "Next time you wish to summon me during the depths of December, kindly negotiate a truce with the weather gods so they do not interfere with your plans."

"Hmmph." Without looking up, the Earl of Evergreen opened another portfolio and fanned the contents across his blotter. "Was that, perchance, meant as a criticism?"

"With all due respect, sir . . ."

His father shuffled a sheaf of documents into order. "Yes, it bloody well was."

The earl put down his pen. And let out a chuckle. "That was not the most diplomatic of replies."

"I was not speaking as a diplomat." Nicholas did, however, moderate his tone to something less than a shout. "Sir."

Leaning back in his chair, Evergreen quirked a silvery brow and fixed his son with The Stare. It was a look the earl had perfected over the years, using it with ruthless regularity to reduce friend and foe alike to quaking in their boots.

Unmoved for once, Nicholas stared back.

"Well, well, well. It appears you have a bit of fire in your belly after all." Steepling his fingers, the earl tapped at his chin. "I was beginning to wonder whether there was any sort of spark there, or merely a lump of ice."

"I was under the impression that you considered cold reason to be the cornerstone of duty and diplomacy."

"So I do." The corners of his father's mouth twitched ever so slightly. "But that is not to say one must always appear a Stoic. There is nothing wrong with showing a bit of passion from time to time."

"I am very glad to hear it, sir." The conversation, like his Christmas journey, was taking all sorts of unexpected twists and turns, but Nicholas refused to be sidetracked. "Then you will not have any objection to my telling you that I have decided not to pay court to some stranger."

The humor disappeared from Evergreen's face. "Now, now, there is no reason to be hasty—"

"I have had a rather prolonged time in which to give your request careful thought," he replied. "And the answer is no."

"If we discuss this in a calm and rational manner, I am sure we can come to an acceptable compromise."

"You may as well save your breath, Father. I cannot, in my wildest dreams, imagine any argument that could change my mind." Nicholas angled his gaze to the portrait over the mantel. Lud, did all Moretons look so imperious? "You see, I have made other plans."

The earl's brows angled higher and The Stare took on a more pronounced squint. "The count would be deeply disappointed were I to tell them you will not attend the ball in the young lady's honor. Indeed, he might take it as an insult, not only to his family, but to Mother Russia."

"Russia?" His head jerked around.

"A very large chunk of frozen tundra to our east, populated with bears, beards and boyars," came the dry reply. "Need I remind you that the alliance is of strategic importance to our country?"

"No, I am fully aware of how much is at stake. But the truth is—" He was saved from having to explain himself by a muffled roar from just outside the library.

"Step aside, lest you wish your spindly shanks to be fed to the wolves! I tell you, the earl will see me, regardless of the hour."

The family butler, who did have rather reedy legs, had a hunted look on his face as opened the door a crack. "Milord, I tried to tell the, er, gentleman, that you could not be interrupted, but he would not take no for an answer—"

"Nyet indeed!" thundered the intruder.

"It is quite alright, Belmont, your limbs are safe from snapping jaws for the time being. You may allow the count to come in."

The butler pressed his frail shoulders against the paneled oak to avoid being flattened by the onrushing figure. With his greatcoat kicking up a swirl around his high top boots and the capes flapping about his shoulders like raucous ravens, the count appeared even larger than he really was.

"Merry Christmas, Yevgeny. Won't you join me and my son in a toast to good cheer and—"

"Nyet! I cannot be merry at a time like this! I am, how you say, dis . . ."

"Distraught?" suggested Nicholas. His own nerves were none too steady at the moment.

"Yes! Distraught! Otherwise I would not descend upon your home and your holiday like a ravening bear. Of all my English acquaintances, you are the man I have confidence in, Evergreen."

"I will help in any way I can. What is the trouble?"

"My niece was due to arrive in London the day before yesterday, but she has gone missing!"

The earl's expression sobered considerably. Setting aside the decanter of brandy, he sought to allay his visitor's agitation. "I am sure there is no real cause for alarm. I know for a fact that the bad weather has delayed a number of travelers."

"Father . . ."

Neither man paid any heed to Nicholas's quiet murmur.

"Nyet!" The count's composure took a sharp turn for the worse as he started to pace before the fire. "One of the men I sent out in search of her discovered her coach, abandoned on a stretch of desolate road."

"We—" began the earl.

"We were just coming to tell you that all is well, and that your niece is quite safe." He fixed the earl with a steady gaze and waggled a brow. "Weren't we, Father?"

The Stare took on a peculiar tilt, but years of diplomatic experience allowed the earl to reply without missing a beat. "Indeed. We were. But seeing as Nicholas deserves all the credit, I will defer to him in explaining all the details." Folding his hands upon his blotter, the earl added dryly, "I confess, I am as anxious as you are to hear exactly how he managed the feat."

Count Federov, who had been rendered momentarily speechless, recovered enough to sputter, "You mean to say my Anna is with you?"

"At the moment, sir, she is downstairs with our housekeeper, freshening up from her ordeal."

An odd rumble started deep in the count's throat, and his hands began to twitch. It was, decided Nicholas, a reaction that did not bode well for peace and harmony. In one fell swoop both his limbs and any prospect of a treaty between England and Russia looked about to be ripped asunder.

"Grrrr . . ." With two quick strides, the count crossed the carpet. "Grace to God, I am eternally grateful to you, *tovarich*." Nicholas found himself enveloped in a bear hug and lifted off his feet. "Evergreen," called Federov, his craggy face wreathed in a joyous smile. "You told me that your son was a remarkable young man, but you were too modest by half. Ha! I do not know how he discovered my plight, but to have acted so quickly and decisively . . . it is a miracle!"

"Sometimes even I am astounded by my son's resourcefulness," drawled the earl. "Er, perhaps if you allow him a breath of air, we may hear all about the dramatic rescue. It promises to be a fascinating tale."

"Yes! Of course."

Nicholas hit the floor with a thump. His knees wobbled, but he kept his balance and cleared his throat. He did not need to look at the earl to know that he was treading a very fine line. One small misstep and he would go from being a hero to a goat.

A goat staked out on the Siberian steppes for the wolves to devour.

"It was a dark and stormy night, Count Federov . . ."

The earl gave a small cough. "Forgive me—something lodged in my throat." A laugh, unless Nicholas was much mistaken. His reproachful glance was met with a nod of contrition. "Do go on," murmured Evergreen, after swallowing a sip of his brandy.

"Through the swirl of the snow I happened to spot a wink of light . . ." His secret delight in the novels of Mrs. Radcliffe and the Minerva Press was now proving quite useful in cobbling together a suspenseful narrative. "Then, above the howl of the snowstorm, I heard a faint cry for help . . ."

Jaw slightly agape, Federov perched his bulk on the edge of the desk and leaned forward.

"Half frozen, and on death's door from the blow he had suffered trying to stave off the falling tree, the coachman lay unconscious inside the coach. The stalwart young lady had braved the elements to save him from a certain demise, but with the weather worsening, things were looking very grim . . ." For the most part, Nicholas was able to adhere to the spirit, if not the letter, of the truth, with just a few omissions and embellishments to gloss over the sticky parts.

His father's brows crept fractionally higher as the tale went on, but he remained silent. The count was a good deal more voluble, interrupting every few moments with a gasp or a mutter in his native tongue. "Extraordinary!" he exclaimed, when Nicholas was done recounting the arrival in Hanover Square.

"Extraordinary," echoed the earl.

"With such admirable talents, I think your son is destined for a brilliant career in your foreign service, Evergreen."

"Yes, well, I have always stressed to him that one of the keys to success in diplomacy is creativity—along with the ability to think on one's feet."

"Actually, I am not quite finished," said Nicholas.

Federov looked slightly perplexed. "There is more?"

"I have left until last mentioning that I have asked Anna for her hand in marriage." He was rather amused by the stunned silence that followed the announcement. It was not often that two such gentlemen could be rendered speechless.

"She has accepted?"

"Yes, sir."

"Without . . . how you say . . . fireworks? Or your having to call in a regiment of the Preopresanski Guard?"

"As you know, sir, the use of force is always the last resort for a diplomat," replied Nicholas, a twinkle lighting his eye as he clasped his hands behind his back. "I was able to persuade your niece to say 'yes' through the means of rational discourse."

The count made a wry face. "Perhaps you have rescued the wrong young lady." An instant later the grimace was gone, replaced by a grin. "I think I shall accept that drink after all, Evergreen. It seems we have much to celebrate on this most joyous of your holidays."

Turning to the younger Moreton, he inclined in a low bow. "It may not yet be Christmas in my country, but you have given me a most wondrous gift, Lord Nicholai. I believe Anna shall be happy with you. For that I thank you with all my heart."

"Rather it is I who should be thanking you, sir." He turned to his father. "And you. I consider myself blessed with miraculous good fortune. Who would have dreamed that in the midst of darkness and storm, I would come upon the light of my life." He raised a glass, savoring the blazing fire and beaming smiles through the warm glow of the spirits. "To family. Both present and future."

The clink of crystal had not yet subsided when the count proposed another round of toasts. "It seems that tomorrow's ball will take on an extra note of good cheer as we will be able to announce a pair of alliances between our two countries." He winked at the earl. "After much discussion, my delegation agreed to your latest proposal and the papers were signed this morning."

Nicholas stifled a laugh. "I trust they plan to award each of you a medal for your consummate skill at handling delicate negotiations."

His father maintained a straight face, save for a tiny waggle of his brow. "Oh, I believe Yevgeny and I have reward enough."

It was not snow, but a blur of bright silks and satins, that swirled through the ballroom, and the brilliant sparkling of light came from a myriad of crystal chandeliers rather than ice.

"It is like a scene from a fairy tale," whispered Anna as Nicholas spun her through another series of twirls.

"Our journey most certainly had a storybook ending, my love," he replied, his eyes dancing with a depth of emotion that made her heart skip a beat.

"Complete with a dashing hero who sweeps the maiden off her feet." How had she ever viewed him as just another pompous prig? Now she saw only his kindness, his strength, his humor. His chiseled features, softened by the curl of golden locks and a devilish smile, were not bad to look at either. "You had that part of the narrative wrong. Along with a few other small details. Your father is not such an ogre after all."

The Earl of Evergreen, resplendid in ivory silk waistcoat embroidered with a forest of fir trees, appeared not at all perturbed to be holding a glass of champagne instead of a sheaf of government papers.

"He dances quite beautifully and told me several funny stories about you and your first pony."

Nicholas gave a mock wince. "Yet another instance of me falling smack on my rump."

"As for your mother . . ." Anna touched the pale peach flower pinned to his lapel, then glanced at the countess, who was dancing with Count Federov. "To think she spent the summer and fall creating a new species of roses specially for you. And it was very ingenious of her to design a portable greenhouse so that several of the bushes could be transported from Yorkshire."

"Yes, I have learned much these past few days, not only about myself, but about those around me. We all have facets we have grown used to keeping under wraps. Sometimes what we need is a challenge to bring them to light."

"And sometimes what we need is a miracle from

above." Anna could not help but think back on her own doubts and fears. "When I saw that first star in the heavens, I wished for a guardian angel instead of a guardian uncle. What I got was an even greater blessing—you."

"We have both been blessed. I trust that we shall look out for each other. I hope I shall always be a guardian of your happiness, my love, and you of mine. But I do not mean for this to be a one-sided match. You have my solemn promise that your opinions and wishes shall always be as important as mine." He grinned. "After all, my experience in the art of diplomacy has shown me that the prospect for harmony is always best when both parties have an equal say in things."

"Be careful what you wish for," teased Anna.

"Truly, I have nothing more to ask for." The curl of his lips sent a sizzle of heat right down to the toes of her dancing slippers. "I have been given the most precious gifts of all. Love, hope, happiness. Christmas is truly a time of miracles." His smile turned a touch more tentative. "I know that for you it has been a time of sorrow, but—"

She pressed the palm of her glove to his cheek. "I think I have come to understand another message of the season. Loss is part of life, but we must never allow its darkness to extinguish the light in our hearts. From now on, Christmas will always be a season of great joy, as long as we share it together."

He suddenly spun to a stop in the middle of the ballroom and swept her up in his arms. "Nicholas! People are staring—"

"Sometimes it doesn't hurt to bend the rules, remember?" he murmured, cutting off her laughing protest with a long and lingering kiss. Anna arched into his arms. When at last his lips released hers, he murmured, "Speaking of protocol, would you be opposed to having our nuptials on Christmas?"

"Christmas?" Her face fell. "Y-you wish to wait a whole year to be married?"

His eyes lit with unholy amusement. "Indeed not. I was thinking of Russian Christmas. Which is less than two weeks away. I have procured a special license, and your uncle has assured me he has no objection."

"Considering that ours has been a very unorthodox courtship, it seems a very fitting day for a celebration."

"What a lucky family we shall be—having Christmas come twice a year!"

"Every day will feel like Christmas with you by my side, my dear Nicholas."

"Amen to that."

Christmas with
Dora Davenport

Nancy Butler

Chapter One

Elnora Nesbitt sat scribbling away at the large walnut desk in her study, mindless of the jumble around her. The flotilla of crumpled pages that littered the floor might be expected from a writer whose thoughts arose in a frantic and disordered stream, but it also appeared that her entire winter wardrobe lay strewn over the furniture behind her.

She'd paused to gaze out the window, wondering if the slate-colored November sky held the threat of early snow—and shuddering at the cost of ordering more coal—when someone scratched at the door.

She'd been expecting her cousin August Bonvilliers and so was not surprised, or shocked, when a Tulip of the *ton* sporting a coat of cerulean blue and applegreen stripes came sauntering through the portal. Bemusement enlivened his bland face as he made his way delicately around the balls of foolscap.

"How goes the revolution business?" he inquired, and then raised his quizzing glass to study the tangle of velvet, taffeta, and satin that adorned the furniture. "Giving up your gowns for the downtrodden masses? Admirable if a bit unpractical. It's deuced cold outside to be going about in your petticoats."

"I'm not likely to be in the revolution business much longer," Elnora muttered, impatiently brushing back one unruly black tendril that had, as usual, escaped from her topknot. "Subscriptions for *The Fire-brand* have fallen off, I'm afraid. My publisher informs me that fiery rhetoric is no longer in vogue. Readers want calm, thoughtful essays . . . especially at this time of year."

"You could go back to writing 'Dora Davenport's Domestic Delights.' I was quite partial to her, if you must know."

She raised one hand. "*Please*, don't even mention Dora. Those wretched articles have turned out to be such a millstone. It's Kittredge, you see."

Of course, August did *not* see what a syrupy column on the homey pleasures of country living had to do with his cousin's stuffy beau, but he trusted she would soon illuminate him.

From a teetering pile of reading matter on the desk she tugged out a dog-eared copy of the *Ladies' Fire-side Companion*. She opened the gazette to a piece entitled "A Joyful Christmas in My Country Home" under the byline of Dora Davenport.

"This," she said, stabbing an accusing forefinger at the inoffensive page, "this paean to stuffed goose and figgy pudding, to kissing boughs and sleigh rides and rosy-cheeked carolers has got me properly in the suds."

"*Because . . . ?*" he coaxed. Obliqueness of speech was a family trait he shared with his favorite cousin, but even he was rarely this obscure.

"It turns out Kittredge's mother was a devoted follower of old Dora," she explained at last. "She was bereft when the articles ceased this summer. I, on the other hand, recall doing a rather lively jig at the thought of never again having to spoon such treacle onto the page."

"Mmm, I agree that you're much better at incitement and agitation."

Elnora beamed at him. Then she glanced again at the byline, and her face fell.

"Last week Kittredge told her my secret, that *I* wrote those articles. She was so ecstatic, she insisted he wangle an invitation from me to spend the holidays at Merrivale Chase. I believe her exact words were, 'What could be more perfect than Christmas in the country with Dora Davenport?'"

"He must be serious about wooing you if he wants you to meet his mother," August pointed out as he flicked back his coattails and settled on a chair draped with a green velvet cloak.

"I *have* met her," Elnora said. "At the theater, when she came up to town last month. She's frightfully high in the instep and examined me through her lorgnette as though I were an opera dancer."

"Ah, but that was before she knew you were Dora," he said with a twinkle. "She's more apt to treat you like royalty now."

"August, you *know* we never go to Merrivale Chase for the holidays. Aside from its having been leased to a tenant, I dislike the country enormously. When I am away from London, I find it difficult to breathe. No, don't laugh at me."

"It's just that most people find it the other way round . . . country air being so much more *airy* than the general London soup. Still, you've got a legitimate excuse for refusing her ladyship's request. Simply tell Kittredge the place is let." He cocked his head. "And if the old dragon is so set on Christmas with Dora, make Kittredge invite you to *his* country house in Devon."

"It's not let," she muttered under her breath.

"What?"

"We've lost our tenant at Merrivale Chase. You recall me mentioning Mr. Spackler, who moved up to Merrivale for the fishing? It turns out he departed earlier this month—just hared off with all his endless casting rods—leaving the rent three months in arrears. He apparently also left the place in some disrepair, and our leasing agent hasn't been able to find another tenant. Mama and I were depending on that money to get us through the winter."

Elnora felt the uncharacteristic sting of tears starting up. She rubbed violently at her eyes, having little use for women who turned to watering pots at the slightest provocation. Only this wasn't a small setback, but a blow of major proportions. Her mother had taken to her bed earlier in the week and did not look to be recovering her spirits anytime soon.

August was tapping the head of his walking stick rhythmically against his pointed chin and gazing into space. "Now that's got me to thinking."

"There's a novelty," Elnora drawled, but then softened her snipe with a fond smile.

He grinned back. "Taxing work. But it occurs to me that you can kill two birds with one stone. Go up to Merrivale Chase for December . . . you know, spruce things up a bit, and then have Kittredge and his mother there for Christmas. You win him over *and* fix up the place for the next tenant."

"I don't want to spend December in the country—particularly in the shambles left by a fishing-mad loose screw. Besides, after ten minutes in my company, Lady Kittredge will realize those Dora Davenport stories were total fabrications. Borrowed, as it were, from your London cook, Ada, who actually did grow up in the country. *I* wouldn't know a figgy pudding from a cocked hat." She leaned her cheek on her palm. "Oh, I do prattle on to Kittredge about a youth spent rambling in the bosom of Hartfordshire, but I don't think he's buying it. And I believe it really matters to him. He spends a great deal of time at his own country estates, doing Lord knows what."

As a landowner himself, August could have edified her. Instead, he reminded her that she'd first met Kittredge at a house party in the Dorset countryside.

"And as *you* will recall," she retorted, "it rained

nearly every day. Kittredge never discovered that I loathe tramping across fields and picnicking out among the ants and stinging insects. Though being cooped up in the house for a whole week was no thrill, either. I vowed I would never play another game of charades or endure another round of whist. I believe the guests were working their way toward choosing a human sacrifice by lots . . . they were that desperate to relieve the tedium."

"Fortunately for me, the grooms had a merry dice game going at all hours." He smoothed the Belgian lace at his cuff. "But then, I am rarely bored."

Elnora knew it was true; in spite of his fashionable air of ennui, her maternal cousin was always in the middle of some intrigue or other. She took a moment to wonder if there wasn't an ulterior motive behind his social call today.

"You didn't by any chance know about the Spackler disaster, did you?" she asked warily.

His mouth tightened. "Actually your mother did drop me a rather disjointed note. And now that I understand the entire situation, I really think you ought to go up there."

At her mutinous expression, he added more forcefully, "Look here, Ellie, I don't begrudge you the use of this town house. I've got my tidy little place on Cavendish Square, which suits me fine. This old tomb still echoes with the ghost of my pater"—he gave a theatrical shiver—"and I'd just as soon family lived here as careless strangers. Mr. Spackler being the perfect case in point. But you need to do something about Merrivale Chase before you can lease it again."

"Mama would hate being up there."

"On the contrary. Aunt Nesbitt was happy living in Hartfordshire, in the days before your father . . . well . . ."

"Frittered away all his inheritance," Elnora finished for him. "Thank goodness I've been able to bring in some money with my writing. But now with the imminent demise of *The Firebrand*, I don't know what we are to do. How am I to write 'calming' essays, when my thoughts are all in a pelter?" She gave a profound sigh. "We are living on borrowed time unless I can bring Kittredge to a declaration. I fear I have been very cavalier with him lately and wouldn't blame him if he went off in pursuit of more amiable . . . game."

"Then you've got no choice but to invite him to Merrivale. Christmas used to be your favorite holiday. . . . Why, just think of the jolly times we had at the Chase."

"Did we?" she asked blankly.

"It's a splendid old house, more so with the windows all frosty, the doorways hung with pine boughs, and a fire roaring in the hall."

"Roaring fires cost money," she reminded him.

"Tell you what," he said. "Last week I won a monkey off that silly Filbert Dunlop . . . he bet me he could stand on his head for five minutes. Only made it to three, and he's been listing like a sailor ever since. At any rate, you're welcome to my winnings, Ellie. Help defray the cost of making the Chase presentable. I promise you, Kittredge will tumble into a declaration when he sees you playing hostess in your ancestral home, framed by the ancient stones—"

"—covered with soot from unclogging the chimneys with a broom—"

He chuckled. "You'd look charming in soot, cuz. What is not charming is this hodge-podge collection of gowns. Have they migrated down from your dressing room for a reason?"

"Aunt Tibby had them brought in. . . . She's been after me to rework them and decided I would be more likely to do so if they were under my nose."

"How long ago?"

"Four days," she said, unrepentant. "I've been too busy with an article for a new gazette, *Modern Al-*

chemy. I'm dissecting the philosophies of Bacon and—"

"Your *gowns*," August reminded her firmly. "If you want to bring Kittredge to his knees, you're going to need to dazzle him." Using the tip of his gilt walking stick, he reached forward and hoisted the skirt of a sapphire-colored gown from the chaise. "I recall this one, you were wearing it the night you waltzed with his lordship at Lady Larrabee's party."

"And again at Ariana Spencer's Ice Palace ball."

"I wager he's seen all these gowns a half dozen times."

"I daresay. But surely Kittredge is not so shallow that he would condemn me for such a trifle. He is a man of principle, a man of ideals, a man—"

"Lord Kittredge is a pompous, self-impressed bore," August interjected. "Still, one cannot overlook a bore who's rolling in the ready. He's not precisely what I would have chosen for you, but he isn't a bad sort . . . no real vices that I've heard."

"He's a virtual saint," she said, in a tone somewhere between praise and lamentation. "He drinks in moderation, gambles not at all, and spends every free moment in London at the War Ministry, mustering supplies for our troops. Papa would have adored him."

August's brows rose a notch. "I might point out that your father was not the soundest judge of character. Every bamboozler and trickster in Britain made free with his purse."

"He also did a great deal of good," she said staunchly. Now was not the time to admit to herself that most of her father's charitable works had benefitted people outside his own family.

"Peace, cuz," August said. "I simply want you to remember that Kittredge has a certain stature to maintain in society and therefore, by association, so do you."

"He knows I've never cared for any of that. He sees me as someone above the petty concerns of the *ton*."

"He may also see you as above the petty concerns of matrimony," he observed dryly. "You've got to look to your laurels, my girl. The eccentric Nesbitt charm and your own not insignificant appearance might not be enough to tip the balance in your favor." He leveled a surprisingly steely look at her. "And as for this 'he appreciates me just as I am' nonsense, let me tell you, I've seen him subtly molding you into the perfect cabinet minister's helpmate—attractive, but not seductive . . . witty, but always diplomatic."

"That's unfair," she protested. "He merely offers the occasional word of guidance."

August grunted. "Have it your way. Lord Kittredge is none of my concern, thank heaven. Now as for these outmoded gowns, let's put our heads together and find some clever way to disguise their venerable age."

When he held out his hand to help her to her feet, she took it and squeezed it warmly.

"*You* are the saint, August. I'm sorry to be so vexing. I don't know how we would have managed without your kindness. But you've watched over us long enough . . . I am determined that Kittredge shall take us off your hands. And if that means catering to his mother and playing the country miss, so be it."

"So you will go to Hartfordshire?"

She nodded. "Everything you said makes sense. Mama's spirits will improve once we have begun to set things to rights up there." She paused to examine an amber satin gown that had lost some of its beadwork. "And you'll be there, of course," she said without turning. "Mama's quite useless at present and Aunt Tibby's gone off on another mad bout of painting. I can't bring the Chase up to Lady Kittredge's demanding standards without someone sensible to aid me."

When he made no answer, she craned around. "You are coming, aren't you?"

He fidgeted with his neck cloth. "Of course. The

thing is, I have a houseguest at the moment. The son
of an old family retainer who joined the navy some
years back. Poor chap was swept overboard in a storm
and ended up on a barren Mediterranean island. Stuck
there for months living on seaweed. He was finally
rescued by a Greek fishing boat, a veritable wraith by
then. I found him convalescing in a shabby military
hospital near the London docks and whisked him off
to Mayfair."

Elnora's eyes had gone wide, but all she could manage in the face of this wrenching tale was to echo,
"Seaweed?"

"I can't very well abandon him—he's barely
recovered—so you'd better not expect me until closer
to the holiday."

"You could bring him along," she said. "Is he capable of traveling?"

"He made it from Greece to Greenwich," August
observed. "I'll give it a thought. Lord knows the fellow could use a bit of holiday cheer."

"Lady Kittredge would approve," Elnora said with
sudden enthusiasm. "What better testimonial to my
domestic abilities than offering Christmas in the country to an ailing sailor?"

"Not to mention the serene company of Dora Davenport," August added with a wink.

Chapter Two

The Nesbitt barouche was a relic from the past century, so August allowed Elnora the use of his own elegant coach for the two days' journey north. His coachman saw her mama tucked into a corner with a hot brick and a lap rug, so that she'd fallen into a light doze before they even left London. Her Aunt Tibby, replete with feathered turban and layers of gauzy scarves, also soon nodded off.

Elnora was far too unsettled to sleep. There was scant hope she'd be able to convince Lady Kittredge that she was the font of homey knowledge portrayed in her articles. In the city she was the model of self-sufficiency, but put her into a rustic setting and she felt like a lost soul. Fireplaces backed up, plumbing was poor to nonexistent, one had to walk miles through a given house to get fed, and meals were usually ice-cold by the time they arrived from distant, cavernous kitchens. And that was just indoors.

Outside, the sky was too wide, the landscape too vast, and large animals, both wild and domestic, roamed at will. And if one dared to leave the muddy lanes for the open fields, there were burrs and nettles, thorns and thistles, and evil, poisonous weeds that left one with a disfiguring rash.

London might be a crowded, dirty, odoriferous place that combined ramshackle dwellings that threatened to collapse into each other with cold, stately edifices that put off more people than they attracted, but it had been her home for the past twelve years—and she missed it already.

When the coach reached the gates of Merrivale Chase late the following afternoon, Elnora's doubts over the success of her charade escalated drastically. The Tudor-style house, set in a picturesque valley of the Chiltern Hills, was accorded to be a charming addition to the neighborhood. But the dwelling that appeared beyond the coach window appeared quite derelict. The lawn had given way to high, tasseled weeds, while the drive and courtyard were littered with leaves and fallen branches. Mr. Spackler had clearly done nothing to keep the place up.

Lady Kittredge would likely order her coachman to turn about and head back to London before they even reached the front door.

Tibby, who was gazing out over Elnora's shoulder, hissed, "*That* sorry sight is bound to set off another of your mother's attacks. *Goodness,* I'm having a bit of a palpitation myself."

Elnora gently roused her mother as they drew up at the wide stone steps, and then she and Tibby efficiently bustled her into the house before she could glimpse the condition of the property. Unfortunately, the front hall was an equally distressing sight.

The three women stood gaping in shocked silence, taking in the denuded walls where paintings and armaments had once hung. Watery sunlight filtered in through begrimed mullions, glancing over the few piddling pieces of furniture that remained on the flagstone floor.

"Where is everything?" her mother cried. "I thought we let the place with all the furnishings."

"We did," Elnora muttered darkly.

She thought she had few feelings left for the old

place, yet something inside her twisted at the sight of it stripped bare. She was going to kill that leasing agent. He'd implied that Mr. Spackler had left a mess behind, not that he'd actually absconded with their furniture.

There was a stirring in an adjoining doorway, and an old man came forward. Elnora recognized him after a moment—Wills, the butler—and was shocked at the appearance of their once-elegant majordomo. His sparse white hair was unkempt, his waistcoat misbuttoned, and his gaunt face showed far too much of the skull beneath the skin.

"Ladies . . . I fear this is a sorry welcome for you."

"I don't understand," her mother whimpered. "Has that man taken everything? The leasing agent made no mention of it in his letter."

Wills sighed. "I imagine he was trying to spare you more grief. He's got men trying to trace Mr. Spackler, to force him to return anything he hasn't yet sold. But the truth is, that Spackler, he's been selling things out of the house for the past year or more. Had a carter here only last month taking out the dining table and sideboard. Fortunately, the piano wouldn't fit in the man's wagon."

"Why didn't you write to tell us of this?" Elnora asked a bit sharply.

Wills hung his head. "He had a legal paper, miss, signed by Mrs. Nesbitt. It said he was to sell the furnishings and send the money to her in London. I knew you were a bit strapped for funds, so it seemed all right and proper to me."

Tibby, who was still goggle-eyed, looking like an oversize, beturbaned carp, turned to Mrs. Nesbitt. "I wager you never signed anything of the sort, did you, Polly?"

Her mother shook her head slowly.

"I know that now," Wills said. "You see, that Spackler, he sent us all to the village on Guy Fawkes night. A treat, he said, an evening off. But when we came back to the Chase, he'd disappeared, and everything he hadn't already sold, all the paintings and candlesticks and silver, was missing. That's when I knew he'd never sent you a penny of the profits."

Mrs. Nesbitt was crying now, soft little sobs, but Elnora felt her dander rise. She slid an arm around her mother's shoulders. "We'll make it right, Mama. You're just tired and hungry. We've plenty of cast-off furniture in the attics, and I doubt Mr. Spackler ever bothered to look up there. Not when there was such bounty at his fingertips."

Wills patted his waistcoat pocket. "I have never parted with the key to the attic . . . or to the wine cellar. I'm happy to say your father's stock is untouched."

"But what of all our beautiful things?" her mother cried, not noticeably consoled that her husband's collection of vintage port was intact.

"I'll write to August directly," Elnora stated. "Perhaps he can hire a Runner to track down our furniture."

Elnora then insisted her mother go upstairs for a nap, neatly preventing her from investigating the other rooms on the ground floor. To Elnora's relief, the bedroom was much as she remembered it, bed and highboy and dressing table still in place, though a pair of Sevres vases had disappeared from the mantel.

After her mother had settled on the bed, she gripped Elnora's hand and drew her close. "They mustn't come, Elnora. You must write to Lord Kittredge and rescind the invitation. We should look a laughingstock to a man of his refinement. Two silly women robbed and duped and Lord knows what else."

That had also been Elnora's initial reaction. But no longer.

She gently released her mother's hand and stood upright. "No, Mama, I won't be beaten by a scoundrel.

Kittredge *will* come and he will see that we are not shabby gentry but women of property."

"*Property*?" her mother echoed. "That Spackler's got most of it by the look of things."

"We'll make do with whatever remains," she assured her. "We have no choice, because Kittredge simply must come to Merrivale. He needs to believe I will be completely at home in his own country estates."

Her mother's eyes narrowed. "He thinks otherwise?"

"*Mmm*. He often teases me, says he can't picture me away from the hurly-burly of London. So you see, it is essential that he discover my . . . bucolic side."

Mrs. Nesbitt gave a tiny snort. "Why, I doubt you've once muddied your slippers in a country lane over the past decade. Furthermore, Ellie, I can't say I like this business of trying to be something you are not, just to please a man of precise expectations. Most of us love you for who you already are. I . . . I hope you aren't making a mistake."

"Kittredge and I should suit admirably."

"Promise me you aren't sacrificing yourself on the altar of daughterly devotion for my sake. I believe I could learn to live simply if it was required of me."

Elnora nearly rolled her eyes. The woman existed to be coddled. And though she would never admit it aloud, her mother's delicate sensibilities had been a factor in Elnora's decision to encourage his lordship.

"Mama, I could hardly ask you to live like a pauper. You are the daughter of a baron, for which I am ultimately thankful, since it makes me less of a goose girl to Kittredge's prince."

She watched her mother snuggle under the quilt, relieved that the shocking state of the house hadn't brought on another of her attacks.

"Now I'd best go and talk to Wills about hiring a few local men to see to the lawn and the drive. As for the interior, I'm afraid we shall have to do most of the work ourselves."

"I'll help," her mother murmured, then added mournfully, "though the house will be a pale shadow of what it once was."

Elnora calculated that she had roughly two and a half weeks before Lord Kittredge arrived—though she had no idea when August and his ailing sailor would make an appearance. If she focused on the public rooms, she just might meet the deadline. The bedrooms, which Spackler had fortunately not plundered too greatly, needed only to be thoroughly cleaned. But as she feared, the ground and first floors were a daunting sight.

The following morning she walked through the house, wide-eyed and open-mouthed. The dining parlor had been stripped of everything, even the large Venetian mirror. The drawing room contained only a shabby sofa and a tea table with a mended leg. The fine Persian carpet that had once lain there was now only a memory. She held her breath before she went into the library—her favorite room as a child. She cracked open the door, barely containing a grimace, and was relieved to see that most of the books were still there. She took a moment to search out a copy of *The Compleat Guide to Furnishing the Country House.* Since she barely knew a sideboard from a settle, it wouldn't hurt to have a primer of sorts.

The music room was next, the rosewood piano still in place as Wills had indicated. But the tapestry her mother had brought to the family with her dowry was missing from the wall opposite the windows. That was going to be a blow. Elnora jotted it down on the list she was preparing for August. She'd already written to him with news of the theft.

Each time she added another item to her list, she grew more dispirited. She was acutely reminded of one of Tibby's favorite maxims—that you often didn't miss something until it was gone. In each room she faced anew the unhappy realization that so many of the familiar and, she had to admit, treasured links to her childhood had vanished.

It was odd. She didn't recall particularly minding when they'd left the house twelve years earlier, after her father had come home from yet another unsuccessful business venture and removed them all to a suite of rooms in London. In fact, she barely remembered that day at all.

They'd frequently changed lodgings as her papa's finances rose and fell—from Chelsea to Mayfair, from Mayfair to Bayswater. And in each neighborhood, whether stylish or shabby, Elnora found something to enchant her. Her country sensibilities soon fell away as she became a happy foster child of the great metropolis.

She'd gone to school at a respectable academy in Kensington, but the year she left, her father died. That was when August, nominally their guardian, installed the three women in his own vacant town house and made sure Elnora had a proper come-out.

When it became clear that she was too outspoken and bookish to appeal to the young gentlemen of the *ton*, Elnora had turned her energies to aiding the family's finances with her writing. Her sharp-eyed insights on the world around her were soon providing them with a small but steady income. In some oblique manner her father had set her on this road in childhood by always talking to her as though she were an open-minded adult. A pity the treacly Dora Davenport canon had paid more bills than her heartfelt essays on the soaring potential of the human spirit.

Now, walking through each room, Elnora felt something stir inside her—deep-seated memories of the happy times she'd shared there with her parents. They'd had a good marriage, a strong marriage. Her mother, not yet turned into the whimpering widow, had never berated her husband for his wild schemes and ill-thought-out investments. She seemed to understand that he was a dreamer, a man who needed to take risks.

Elnora often mentally compared her father with Lord Kittredge, finding comforting similarities in their profession of noble ideals. Although lately she'd begun to wonder if his lordship wasn't something of a shirker when it came to taking risks—such as marriage.

When she emerged into the hall at last, her inventory—or lack thereof—completed, it was nearing two o'clock, and her mother still hadn't emerged from her room. Elnora decided to give her this one day to recuperate from their journey. By tomorrow she would expect her to pitch in.

Unfortunately, when Tibby came downstairs that evening, covered with splotches of paint from the studio she'd set up in the nursery, it was to inform Elnora that her mother had contracted *la grippe* and would be unable to do anything strenuous for a week at least.

Elnora, who was dining in the drawing room, seated at the rickety tea table, wanted to put her head down and weep.

"I'd like to help out in some way," said Tibby, clearly not insensible to Elnora's distress. "Perhaps I could paint a mural in the music room, try to duplicate your mother's lost tapestry."

Once she had wandered off again, Elnora was struck by the sheer foolhardiness of her plan. There was no way under heaven she could restore the house by herself.

This dire fact was brought home to her when, after several days of cleaning, she went up to investigate the attics. There were furnishings aplenty up there, the castoffs of generations of Nesbitts, but most of the pieces hailed from an era before the current mania for delicate, almost feminine furniture had taken hold. They all appeared monstrously heavy. The few servants, the butler, cook, and two housemaids, were in their dotage. It wasn't fair to ask them to do any heavy lifting. August's strapping coachmen had returned to London, but the groom who tended the lone horse in the stable was a possibility.

When Elnora went out to the stable the next morning, however, she discovered him lying in a drunken stupor. *Splendid,* she thought.

The lean bay horse looked over the top slat of his stall and then at his empty manger. Elnora had no idea where the grain was kept, so she gathered up an armful of hay and dropped it onto his bedding, quickly stepping back out of range.

That was another aspect of country life she didn't care for—horses. She would never admit it, but they frightened her. Kittredge would doubtless expect her to have a seat like an Amazon, but until now she'd managed to dodge his invitations to ride with him in London.

"You are a charleton," she muttered as she strode out of the stable. "And a coward, to boot."

She took a moment to observe the men from the village who were clearing the drive and scything the lawn, thinking she could enlist a few of them to help with the furniture. When her gaze wandered to the house itself, she felt a tiny bit encouraged. At least the old Tudor manor had good bones. Even with the windows fouled and the rain gutters full of muck, Merrivale Chase was pleasing to the eye. The pale buff stucco and dark brown timbering had mellowed with the passing centuries.

She realized with a start that upon her mother's death the place would come to her, the Chase being unentailed, by some stroke of good fortune. August had promised to give her a token dowry when she wed, but she saw now that he needn't bother. She would ultimately bring property to her marriage—and she determined to make it positively shine for Lord Kittredge.

Once back inside, she donned her oldest gown and tucked her hair under a paisley kerchief, hoping to finish cleaning the downstairs rooms today. The house-maids were busy in the guest bedrooms; she heard them humming and singing as they worked.

Christmas carols, she thought wonderingly. It hardly felt like Christmas, but the season would soon be upon them.

She made her way to the dining parlor, where she scrubbed the parquet floor, degrimed the windows, and polished all the woodwork. When she'd begun cleaning earlier that week, it had quickly become apparent that her chief activities in London, walking and dancing, had not prepared her for rough domestic chores. Today, again, her arms trembled and her back ached, but she refused to let up.

There was only room for one malingerer in her family.

After four hours she stood back to study her progress, and then frowned. The remains of a large charred log had fallen half onto the tiled hearth, leaving a scattering of ashes. She stooped to heft it into her arms, nearly fumbling the heavy piece of wood. She could have certainly called on Wills to do this bit of dirty work, but she was a woman with a mission now. Grunting and grumbling—but strengthened by her zeal—she lugged it out of the room and down the stairs, then crossed the hall to the front door. She managed to get the door open, and staggered out onto the porch.

She was scanning the courtyard, wondering where to dispose of her burden, when she noticed a dark-haired man walking up the drive. He was looking directly at her, and she knew how odd she must appear standing there clutching a charred log. With a gusty *oomph* she tossed it onto the grass beside the steps, then quickly snatched off her kerchief. Unfortunately, most of her hair came tumbling down from its knot.

The man came right up to the foot of the steps and nodded in greeting. "Miss Nesbitt?"

"I assume you're here about the lawn," she said. "But we have our fill of workers." She thought a minute. "I don't suppose you know anything about horses."

"A bit," he said. "But—"

"Well, there's a horse in the stable who's not had his grain today. I'd be happy to pay you for looking after him. And if you happen to tread on that drunken sot of a groom who's lying in the stable aisle, I'll give you a bonus."

The stranger smiled. It was like the sun coming out on a dark winter's day.

"I'll fetch him a nice kick if you like," he said in an odd, lovely, singsong sort of voice.

Elnora assessed the width of his shoulders and the lean, rugged look of him and decided he was more than a match for the groom. "And then put him under the pump."

The man nodded again, started toward the stable, but then pivotted crisply and came back to her. "Pardon," he said as he drew out his handkerchief, "but you've got a bit of soot on you. Hardly gilding for the lily."

Before Elnora could protest, he dabbed lightly at her cheek. "Better," he said before he went off.

"You're entitled to a meal in the kitchen," Elnora called out. "At seven."

Without turning, he acknowledged her with an offhand salute.

Elnora was breathless and trembling slightly when she went back into the house. Probably from all the unfamiliar exertion, she told herself. It certainly had nothing to do with the new workman. Why, she barely recalled how he looked or what he'd been wearing. There was just a hazy image of broad shoulders, dark hair . . . a blazing smile.

From the peculiar way he spoke, she doubted he'd come from the village. More likely he was a tinker or Gypsy who had heard of work at the manor.

She went off to clean the drawing room next, mentally tallying the pieces of furniture she'd need from the attic to accommodate seven or eight people. She had a fleeting notion that the new workman might be the ideal candidate to carry the heavier pieces down. She'd have Wills send him to her after he'd had his meal.

Back in her own room to change for supper, Elnora was aghast at her reflection as she passed the mirror — one of the few Spackler had not filched. She looked like a charwoman, her dress smudged and wrinkled, her hair coming down in curling tendrils from beneath the kerchief. Yet there was something about her face she'd not seen before, a spark of vitality that lit her complexion from within. Her eyes glittered and her cheeks glowed. Barring the tatty gown and the tangled hair, she had never looked better.

Perhaps this country life agreed with her after all.

Chapter Three

Elnora was just finishing her apricot duff, and por-
ing over her book of country furnishings, when
there was a soft knock on the drawing-room door. It
opened a crack.

"I believe we need to have a talk, you and I," said
the dark-haired man as he pushed the door wide and
came across to her. He peered down at her dinner
tray. "Ah, that looks to be a fine pudding. Cook fed
the workers a sort of molasses mush for our pudding.
Not that I'm complaining, but—"

She looked up, about to rebuke him for such familiar behavior, and felt a sinking sensation as she took
in his appearance for the first time—the fine broad-
cloth coat, sueded buckskins, and polished riding
boots. She'd miscalculated somehow. This was no tinker but a gentleman down on his luck.

"I think you'd better have a seat," she said, waving
him to the nearest chair.

There, she was right! He lounged back in the arm-
chair, boots crossed at the ankle, completely at his
ease. There was not a scrap of forelock-tugging defer-
ence to the fellow.

"I believe I have a clearer understanding of who
you are now," she said. "I'm sorry I sent you to the
stables."

"It was no hardship," he said. "The horse is fed,

the stall is mucked, the groom is sober, if a bit damp, and likely to remain so. Sober, that is, not damp." He smiled that wide, slightly crooked smile, and Elnora felt her brain go all muzzy.

"Though all things being equal," he added, "I'd have preferred to dine upstairs. I'm quite partial to apricot duff."

"That's as may be," she said, trying to muster a composed expression. It was difficult, because when this man looked at her, he really *looked* at her, dark eyes intense and probing. "But regardless of your background, if I am to hire you, I would expect you to take your meals with the other workers."

His cheeks narrowed. "That was not my understanding of the situation, but then again, your cousin is famous for all the things he leaves unsaid—"

"My cousin?" she echoed blankly. "Do you mean August Bonvilliers sent you?"

He nodded slowly. "I came from London and took a room at the inn in the village. Knowing August, I wanted to make sure this wasn't some grand hoax he'd hatched to amuse himself. But when I saw you on the steps—a dark beauty, just as he'd told me—I knew you had to be his cousin."

Elnora wanted to sink into the carpet, if only there had been one. The awful truth was rapidly dawning on her, that she'd sent August's ailing shipwreck victim off to labor in the stables.

"You're . . . the sailor?" she asked in quivering tones.

When he nodded, she pressed her hands over her face and moaned.

"I am so sorry," she said through her fingers, peering at him with open distress. "You must forgive me. From something he said, I assumed you would be arriving together. Plus he led me to believe you were bedridden, still very much an invalid."

He winked at her. "And when he's not leaving out

important details, August can be counted on to embellish with a vengeance. Don't fret yourself, Miss Nesbitt, I'm getting fitter every day. I actually walked here from the village, though I wouldn't mind the use of your gig to get back tonight."

"Of course," she said, relieved that he was being so gracious. "But you must come to stay tomorrow, if you don't mind that the house is in such disarray. My mother is something of an invalid herself, and she would welcome the company."

"Ah, we can sit side by side in the sunlight on the terrace and compare ailments."

"She would adore that, truthfully. But you'll run screaming down the drive after about ten minutes. Trust me."

"What I'd rather do," he said haltingly, showing a trace of diffidence for the first time, "is help you with the house. August told me what that Spackler fellow did and how you need to get things in order for your Christmas party. You need a strong back or a steady hand, I'm your man."

Elnora wished he hadn't phrased it in such a way. It made her all too aware of his compelling physical presence, as well as leaving her with a pang of unaccountable regret that he was *not* her man.

"I don't want you taxing yourself, Mr.— Oh, I'm sorry, August never told me your name."

He rose and bowed from the waist. "Merthyr, Lieutenant Gowan Merthyr."

A name as musical as his voice, she thought. And he was Welsh, of course, which explained the lilting cadence of his speech.

"I'm very pleased to meet you," she said.

When she held out her hand, he took it and raised it briefly to his lips. "And I'm so pleased you really do exist . . . *dark beauty*," he added, so softly she wasn't sure she hadn't imagined it.

"But why isn't August with you?" she asked, once

her head had cleared enough for logical thought. "You were the reason he was delaying his trip north."

Her guest shrugged. "All I know is that he put me in a carriage with orders to stand at your right hand in every possible way."

"Well, it's all very puzzling, but it's also what I've learned to expect from him." Her expression of consternation faded and she gave him a wide, relaxed smile. "The main thing is, I'm delighted that you're here. My mother has taken to her bed and my Aunt Tibby, *who paints*, is not proving very useful."

"I'll earn my keep, Miss Nesbitt, never fear. We'll have the place shipshape in no time. It's the least I can do in return for your generous invitation. I'd have languished for certain if I'd had to spend Christmas in that festering hole they call London."

After he had gone, Elnora sat staring into the fire, wondering why she still felt light-headed and churned up inside. Lt. Merthyr was no more attractive than half the young bucks in the *ton*, less so if one considered his unfashionably tanned complexion and his shaggy crop of black hair. He also lacked polish and address, two things Lord Kittredge had in spades.

And then there was that scathing remark he'd made about London, which had not endeared him to her one bit. No matter that most of the *ton* fled the capital over the winter, an outlander Welshman didn't have the right to cast aspersions on her home.

Still, he was extremely amiable, this sailor of August's, and Elnora decided that what she needed most right now was a friend. And as for August, well . . . when she recalled the faradiddle he'd told her about Lt. Merthyr's condition, she decided she was going to skin him alive when he showed his pointy-chinned, conniving face in Hartfordshire.

Barely recovered, indeed!

*　　*　　*

The next morning, as Elnora allowed herself a few stolen moments under the covers before springing into frenzied action, she found her thoughts drifting, quite against her will, to the dark-haired Welshman. She was sure her cousin had told her he was the son of a family retainer. Which made no sense. Gowan Merthyr was obviously a gentleman, a ship's officer, no less. Not, thank goodness, the rough-and-tumble tar whose arrival she'd been facing with some trepidation. Typical of August to mislead her. And, furthermore, where the devil was he? She'd written to him several times, and he surely knew she had a mountain of work to get through.

"Vexing man," she muttered as she forced herself to fling back the covers.

The cold assaulted her like a bludgeon. She danced gingerly across the icy floor to stoke up the fire, wistfully imagining that in Lord Kittredge's numerous homes, the servants actually came into the bedrooms and lit the fires *before* one got up.

She dressed hurriedly, again donning one of her older gowns—well, they were all *old*—and twisting her hair into a simple knot before going down to breakfast.

While passing the dining parlor, Elnora thought she heard someone moving inside. She opened the door and grew instantly lightheaded. There before her was a lustrous walnut table sitting on an aged but beautiful floral carpet and surrounded by a half dozen Queen Anne chairs. She blinked several times, sure she must still be deep in dreamland.

"We've had a busy morning," said Gowan Merthyr from beside a pine sideboard, where Wills was setting out breakfast in gleaming chafing dishes.

"I am astonished," Elnora said as she drifted into the room. "It's like a miracle."

"I got here quite early," the Welshman said, "and quickly saw the state of things. I asked some of your workmen to help bring the table down from the attic. The rest Wills and I managed on our own."

"You should have woken me," she chided him gently. "I ought to have been here to help."

"I wanted to surprise you," he said simply.

He's an angel, Elnora mooned silently. Lord Kittredge might have been akin to a saint, but Gowan Merthyr was surely a bona fide member of the Heavenly Host.

"Thank you," she said, trying to focus on the renovated room and not on the dark intensity of his eyes as he watched her. "There are no words . . ."

"It's a trifle," he said with a shrug. "Your cousin said I was to aid you, and I thought this was a good start."

"An excellent start," she assured him as she took the plate of shirred eggs and kippers he held out.

He led her to the head of the table and seated himself at her right hand. He did not speak while he ate, digging into a plate heaped with eggs, sausages, mushrooms, and tomatoes.

"No kippers?" she asked, if only to get him to look up at her.

"Ah, no," he said in that musical voice that turned every phrase into a song. "I'm afraid I overdid the fish while I was castaway."

He went back to his meal, and Elnora covertly studied him. His table manners were excellent, another sure sign that he was no servant's offspring. She admired his strong, elegant hands and the crisp lines of his profile—pleased beyond reason by the imposing, slightly blunt nose and by the manly jut of his chin.

"It's fortunate that in the navy I learned to dine under severe scrutiny," he drawled without looking up. "My first captain used to say he wouldn't brook sloppy table manners any more than sloppy seamanship."

Elnora fought down a blush. "I . . . I didn't mean

to stare. It's just that you look remarkably well for a man who recently endured such privation. I'd like to hear about your . . . adventure, if you don't mind talking about it. August said you had to eat seaweed." She made a sour face when he glanced up at her.

"Seaweed's not so bad if you rinse it in fresh water. I was fortunate that my rocky prison had a spring. And a few stunted trees, which allowed me to whittle a spear for fishing. The water was so blue, yet so clear, it was no trouble to spot the fish." He sighed. "Still, I hated to kill them, they were that beautiful."

"You had to survive," she pointed out reasonably.

"I used to wonder why," he said in a low, musing voice. "Why was my life more valuable than another creature's? A man gets to having strange notions when he's alone for weeks on end."

Elnora was intrigued. "What other insights did you experience?"

"I pondered over how much time we fritter away on silly worries, how little money or possessions mean when you are faced with basic survival." He reached for the bread basket. "It seems that when your world becomes very small, you begin to think large thoughts."

Elnora liked that enormously. She could almost hear the essay beginning in her head.

"Mostly, though, I missed my home in Wales. While I was on shipboard, I was too busy to think much about *Llantri*. But stranded there on that little island, I was overwhelmed by the fear that I would never see my village again, never again put my arms around my mam, never share a drink and a song with my da down the pub . . ."

Another man, especially a beau of the *ton*, would have looked sheepish after making such a sentimental admission. Gowan Merthyr appeared quite at ease.

"I wonder you didn't go home to Wales for Christmas."

"The doctors advised against such a long coach journey. Though my family begged me to come."

"And your sweetheart?" she prompted impishly. "Surely she added her pleas for your return home."

"In truth, all half dozen of them were pining for me," he said with a sly grin.

"And yet after all the soulful revelations you experienced on your island, you've no stirring desire to single one out?"

"Not at the present," he said. "But I understand I am to offer *you* felicitations. August told me that you and Lord Kittredge—"

"Oh, nothing's been decided," she interjected quickly. "That is, the gentleman has not yet declared himself."

He sketched a wave around the room. "I take it you are hoping to urge him along with a rustic Christmas in your family home."

"Something like that," she said, hating that it made her sound so conniving and cold-blooded.

"Well, then," he said, pushing back from the table, "we've got work to do."

"Are you sure you're up to it? You've done plenty already."

He held the door for her as she passed out into the corridor. "You'll be the first to know when I've reached my limit. And the oddest thing is, I have a notion this isn't going to be work at all, but rather a great deal of fun."

The next few days passed quickly. Elnora had finished the cleaning, so they were now able to concentrate on bringing the furniture, draperies, and rugs down from the attic. Gowan Merthyr proved a born organizer, conscripting the outdoor workmen to help with the heavier pieces and with the laying of the larger carpets. He also rallied the maids to polish blackened silver, freshen musty draperies with fuller's

earth, and clean the grime of decades off Chinese porcelain and Indian brass by unreservedly pitching in
himself.

"All shipshape?" Elnora asked with a chuckle as
she came upon him in the butler's pantry, shirtsleeves
rolled up, tackling a nasty-looking epergne awash with
sea creatures.

"I'd have never gone to sea," he muttered, buffing
a fearsome octopus, "if I had any idea of the hideous
monsters lurking below the surface."

She went on her way wearing a smile, wondering
how she ever would have coped if he hadn't come
from London. There was a lightness in her step now,
a certainty that everything would, indeed, be shipshape by the time the Kittredges arrived.

In the evenings, after Elnora had dutifully spent an
hour with her red-eyed, sniffling mother, she, Gowan,
and Tibby would adjourn to the drawing room. It had
been refurbished with Queen Anne needlepoint
chairs, a Jacobean bookcase, and a Persian carpet with
a mustard-colored ground, which complemented the
green-and-gold damask draperies Elnora had found in
a trunk.

The room seemed to have eased back into an earlier
age, and Elnora found it not only comfortable, but
somehow more compelling than when it had been ar-
rayed with spindly gilt pieces.

They would sit in a semicircle before the fireplace
of deep red marble, Elnora busy with her stitching—
several of her dinner gowns still needed updating—
while Tibby dabbed at a watercolor of the family crest
for the front hall and Gowan immersed himself in a
book.

They would converse only occasionally, the silence
almost too convivial to break.

We're too weary to talk, Elnora realized one night.
Still, she was more than content when the exertions
of the day gave way to relaxed, mellow evenings with

her aunt and her dear new friend. It made her wish they could go on forever, stitching and dabbing and reading, each happy with his or her own thoughts.

Nevertheless, as much as she might value their quiet evenings, each morning brought the giddy anticipation of another day spent working beside Gowan Merthyr. She purposely did not dwell too much on why this might be.

By the time he'd been there a scant week, the house had already begun to take shape. Every room was partially furnished, and some, like the drawing room and dining parlor, were to all intents ready for guests.

One morning, during their daily treasure hunt in the attic, Elnora found a stately oak desk beneath a spattered sheet of canvas.

"What about this for the sitting room?" she asked him, one hand at her hip. "A bit of beeswax and turpentine should bring out the grain," she added in her best Dora Davenport voice.

"Aye, Admiral. An excellent choice." He gave her a mocking salute.

She stuck out her tongue. "Have you a better idea, then?"

"I'm thinking that pale wood writing table, this being a house of ladies at present, and that oak desk just reeking of masculine superiority."

She eyed the table. "It *would* go nicely with that delicate lyre-back chair we found yesterday." Her gaze shifted back to him. "Are you sure you aren't dreadfully bored by all this fussing about with odd bits of furniture?"

He settled onto a high, banded trunk. "In truth, my mother would be beaming over me. House-proud, she is. But she could never get me to take an interest in anything that didn't have masts or an anchor." His expression darkened. "Though those days appear to be behind me now."

"You're not going back to sea?"

"They've offered me a job at the Admiralty—in London." He made no attempt to hide his distaste.

"London's not such a bad place, you know."

He growled softly. "Pardon me for saying it, Miss Nesbitt, since I know you live there, but it is the most unwholesome city I've ever seen. Reeking streets with pitiful urchins at every corner wanting tuppence to sweep a path for you through the dung and debris."

"That is true," she admitted. "But the city's also teeming with commerce and culture."

"August told me you write essays advocating for the common folk, criticizing various civic policies and encouraging reform. Most people have put on blinkers where the poor are concerned. But if you are *not* blind to the conditions those people endure, I cannot understand how you could live in London and not be full of horror over them."

"To be an effective writer, I need to witness those things firsthand," she said. "I suppose I've learned to observe the world around me without becoming incapacitated by horror—or growing indifferent, for that matter."

He sketched a motion around an attic still cluttered with furniture and trunks. "Perhaps it is easy for you to remain objective, since your life affords you a great deal more comfort than the wretched poor."

She paused, uncertain of how much to reveal. Still, the man invariably invited confidences.

"I fear my family and I are nearly destitute," she said in a low voice. "Our house in London belongs to my cousin, and the Chase is normally leased, the monies from which my mother and I manage to squeak by on."

"Then Lord Kittredge must seem something of a savior to you."

Her eyes grew frosty. "I may one day find myself in the happy circumstance of marrying into a wealthy family. But my first concern is to wed a man I admire and esteem."

"And what of love, Miss Nesbitt?" he asked bluntly, with that direct look she had come to expect—and often dreaded.

"Love is the province of silly schoolgirls," she stated.

"So you would not consider the suit of a man who stirred your heart, even if he were not so plump in the pockets as his lordship?"

"It's a moot point, Lieutenant. Kittredge is the only suitor I've managed to attract. Most men find me too bookish and radical for their taste."

"Then *most* men are fools," he said under his breath, then added in an odiously polite voice, "I must congratulate the baron on his discrimination, for seeing the jewel that all the others overlooked."

"Don't," she said at once. "You needn't serve me up platitudes, Lieutenant Merthyr, or idle flattery. I thought we were well on our way to becoming friends."

"Friends, is it? Then I should very much like it if you would call me Gowan. Every time you say 'Lieutenant Merthyr,' I snap to attention like a quivering midshipman."

She grinned. "Very well, but then you in turn must call me Elnora. Whenever you address me as 'Miss Nesbitt,' I look around for Tibby."

He held out his hand. "Done . . . Elnora."

She took it, praying he couldn't feel her trembling. Lord help her, he'd made her name sound like an endearment, drawing out the syllables and rolling the last one on his tongue.

She felt an overwhelming urge to keep hold of his hand and tug him toward her. For an instant she imagined every sensation of embracing him—the strong, corded muscles of his back, the firm planes of his chest, the lean suppleness of his waist and belly. She felt his arms tighten around her, heard him whisper her name—

"Elnora?"

She realized she'd been standing there transfixed for goodness knew how long. What must he be thinking? She was so unnerved, she quickly made some feeble excuse and went skittering down the attic stairs.

Since her mother was still laid up, she sought out Tibby in the music room. Her aunt wasn't the most wide-awake person, Elnora well knew, but she had a surprising intuition about certain things.

"I need to talk to you," she said breathlessly. "Something's happening."

"Of course it is," said Tibby, not looking away from her mural. "When you alter your routine, things are bound to happen. Something interesting, I should hope."

"Mmm . . . interesting, but puzzling. And disturbing."

Tibby studied her palette, awash with deep jewel tones, then said, "I don't suppose it's anything to do with that delicious Welshman who's come to stay."

Elnora wanted to blurt out a denial, but opted for the truth instead.

"I'm not at all sure who or what it is," she said as she sank down onto the piano bench. "I've never felt so happy and lighthearted. But then everything shifts in an instant, and I feel the weight of doom pressing on me."

Her aunt's eyes lit up. "Oh, bless me, I was hoping for something like that."

"Whatever do you mean?"

"Sounds to me like you're forming a *tendre*. He quite likes you, you know. Goes on about you endlessly when he stops by to keep me company. He's not much for talking when we three sit of an evening, but he's quite the magpie when it's just the two of us together."

"You talk about *me*?"

"Among other things, and sometimes he sings for me." She nodded toward the piano. "But, yes, we do discuss you."

"I don't want to hear this," Elnora cried as she leaped up and began pacing vigorously around the room. "It's very confusing, this talk of Gowan Merthyr, when I'm supposed to be doing all this for Lord Kittredge—"

"And who's been helping you?" Tibby interrupted brusquely. "If his high-and-mighty lordship is to be your helpmate in life, then why in heaven isn't *he* here lugging two-ton sideboards down those narrow attic stairs?"

Elnora opened her mouth to argue, but realized there was nothing she could say. Spackler's theft had made her ashamed of the Chase, and she'd felt she had to hide that shame from the baron. Oddly, she'd had no such scruples where Gowan Merthyr was concerned.

"You take my point," Tibby said more gently. "And I'll tell you something else. That Welshman's a bit of an idiot for helping to pave the way for another man's suit."

"He's simply kindhearted," Elnora said. "I'm sure you're wrong about his feelings for me."

Tibby merely shrugged and went back to her painting.

Elnora glanced at the mural, which she'd only seen in its early stages, and was shocked to discover that Tibby was re-creating the battle of Agincourt—the subject of the lost tapestry—with an army of doughty English mastiffs and armor-clad poodles.

"That's a novel approach," she said, flailing for a compliment.

"Lieutenant Merthyr pronounced it a complete original," said Tibby with a little sniff. "Kittredge hasn't got a particle of his charm."

"That's the problem," Elnora said. "Kittredge writes to me every other day, but his letters are not especially . . . warming. It's all *this* statesman and *that* general. I sometimes fear he views me as a comrade in arms, not as a future wife."

Tibby turned to her, brandishing a paintbrush. "You might point the finger at yourself, Elnora, for that. You do natter on about such ponderous topics with his lordship. I vow, I never hear you laugh when Kittredge comes to call."

Elnora sighed. "He appeals to the serious side of my nature. Gowan Merthyr, on the other hand, appeals to something quite different."

"I daresay," Tibby murmured.

"He's playful and amusing . . . and would it be so wrong to be . . . well, flirtatious and a bit silly for a change? And who knows? After spending time being *not* ponderous with Lieutenant Merthyr, I might even manage to leaven things with Kittredge."

Her aunt gave a gusty exhalation. "Now who's being the idiot? Do you honestly think you can give in to your feelings with one man as an *educational experience*, and still find yourself heart-whole with another? Let me tell you, my girl, it's not an ailment you get over in a week's time like *la grippe*."

"Then you're going to have to abandon your mural, Tib, because I believe I need a chaperone."

"Why? Has the Welshman forgotten his manners?"

"No," Elnora groaned, "but if I spend so much as another half hour alone with him, I might very well forget mine."

Tibby duly promised to guard Gowan's virtue against Elnora's budding attraction, but she managed to play least in sight most of the time, running off to fetch restorative tonics or giving in to the sudden need for a walk on the terrace. It was almost as though she were intentionally throwing them together.

Elnora kept thinking about what Tibby had said, that Gowan was the one pitching in and not his lordship. How could she marry a man who made her feel embarrassed over her family's troubles? To be fair, she'd never even attempted to tell Kittredge of the Nesbitts' shaky finances. Maybe he would have shrugged it off as inconsequential. Then again, maybe he'd have headed straight for the door.

The one thing that she could not deny, no matter how she tried, was that Gowan Merthyr had become her champion. He was the person she turned to with her troubles, and who buoyed her up when she felt blue-deviled. It was Gowan who made her laugh with his sly teasing, and who nearly brought her to tears with his warm consideration for everyone around him.

He had slipped right past all her defenses.

And yet, he'd not given her any sign that his own feelings were engaged. There was only that dark intensity in his eyes whenever he gazed at her. If only she knew what was in his heart, she might be free to let her own feelings soar.

Because Tibby was right—she had formed a *tendre* for the man. A simmering attraction that needed only the tiniest encouragement to fan it into longing and desire.

The situation had her confounded, especially since she thought she'd managed to overcome her biggest problem, restoring the house. Who could have predicted that a whole other problem would arise, one that could not be solved by turning to the trusty pages of *The Compleat Guide to Furnishing the Country House?*

Chapter Four

Elnora and Gowan were in the hall, wrestling a heavy oak settle into place, when the two elder ladies of the household came bustling through the front door.

"I have never been so mortified in my life," Mrs. Nesbitt cried, throwing herself onto a padded bench and fanning herself violently with one hand. "Never!"

"I'm sure it was all a terrible misunderstanding," Tibby said, hovering over her.

Elnora, who'd abandoned the cowardly notion of hiding behind the settle, finally came forward, her eyes wary.

"Ah, Elnora," her mother called out. "Come console your mama. We have just been rudely thrown out of every shop in Merrivale, if you can imagine such a thing."

"It was that Spackler creature," Tibby explained. "He left unpaid bills in every establishment in the village, with the butcher, the greengrocer, the baker, the mercer, even the chandler."

"But I *gave* you money," Elnora said. "My latest receipt from *The Firebrand*."

"They didn't want *our* custom," her mother declared in ringing tones. "They didn't want anything to do with us, not until we paid off Mr. Spackler's debt. As if that were our responsibility."

Elnora shot a beseeching glance at Gowan. He motioned her aside, and she followed him to a shadowy corner of the hall.

"This is a disaster," she hissed. "However can we entertain guests without food or candles or new table linens?"

"There's a good question. But it's my understanding that your butler's been forced to buy household staples outside of Merrivale. He's now run up bills in every outlying hamlet. I would have warned your mother, had I known she intended to go into the village."

At hearing that, Elnora wanted to pound her head against the wainscoting.

"She rose from her sickbed this morning," she explained, trying to stay calm, "and asked what she could do to help, so I sent her off to Merrivale to order supplies." She looked up at him with a frown. "Why didn't you tell me about Wills' excursions?"

"You had enough on your plate."

"But how are we to pay off Spackler's debt *and* the money Wills owes?"

He said a bit crossly, "Well, where did you think the food on your table was coming from, Elnora? The last household money your butler received from Spackler ran out weeks ago."

"Wills never said a word. Everyone's been trying to protect me, and look what it's come to—Mama embarrassed, and the Nesbitts digging themselves even deeper into debt."

"Perhaps you do need to call off the house party," he suggested a bit more gently. "You're gambling that Kittredge will propose, but the expense of it will beggar you in the end if he doesn't."

"Of course he'll propose," she insisted, tamping down the unruly thought that she no longer gave a figgy pudding for his noble lordship. She added somewhat combatively, "He is my *only* hope."

"Is he?" Gowan inquired gruffly.

Elnora looked up at him, wanting so much to believe that there was salvation in his dark, glittering eyes. But then he dashed her dreams by drawling, "Surely there are other men in the *ton* who would have you to wife."

Disappointment added clipped annoyance to her tone as she shot back, "I told you, the baron is the only man who ever gave me a second glance."

Again, he looked as though he wanted to say something, but then her mother called out from across the hall, "You must write to implore August for funds. Surely he will not like it that his family is become the neighborhood disgrace."

"Hold off on that," Gowan said. "Let me see what I can do to smooth things over in the village."

Elnora was about to object, suspecting that the Welshman was going to dig into his own pocket to bail them out, but he put her firmly aside and went striding toward the door.

She stood unmoving after that, thinking furiously, oblivious to her mother and Tibby, who were still clucking and moaning over their collective mortification.

Suppose she did call off the party. Kittredge was bound to have other options for the holidays, even at short notice. Gowan would likely stay on, and her cousin would, she assumed, eventually join them. Christmas would become a gathering of friends and loved ones instead of a beastly, stressful showcase of her nonexistent domestic talents.

Still, a niggling little voice reminded her, *what if you've misread Gowan's attention? The holiday will end, you will have no suitors and no prospects.*

Worse yet, she'd be nursing a broken heart if the Welshman didn't return her regard. She'd end up both poor *and* pitiful.

She wondered if she should keep Kittredge around as a sort of reserve beau.

No, came the answer in the next instant. A loveless marriage, however financially comforting, would be emotionally excruciating. She couldn't imagine why she'd thought she and the baron would suit. It was clear she'd been wearing blinders until the moment Gowan Merthyr walked up her drive.

So she would cancel the house party, fabricate some excuse to keep the Kittredges at bay, and maybe, just maybe, once Gowan knew the baron was out of the picture, he might feel free to tell her what was in his heart.

She was congratulating herself on sorting things out, when her mother piped in, "I hope you don't mind, Elnora, but we met the vicar and his wife on the road to the village. They're coming to share Christmas dinner with Lord Kittredge. And I asked the vicar to pass the word to Sir David Parkhurst, our local magistrate. It's going to be such a distinguished gathering, just like the old days."

Elnora winced, not up to the task of explaining to her mother why the house party now must *not* take place. She'd just have to think of another way to convince Gowan that she no longer had any interest in his lordship—or his fat purse.

The day before the Kittredges were due to arrive, Gowan proclaimed that Elnora had been cooped up inside for far too long. He insisted she accompany him in the gig while he went to forage for greenery. Elnora resisted at first but her protests were all for show— she considered herself a budding countrywoman these days and had even been making friends with the bay horse.

She hurried upstairs to fetch her green velvet cloak, which she'd smartened up with a black fur collar and black silk frogs. There was no point in going driving with one's heart's desire, if one was going to look like a dowd.

A few miles from the house they came upon a large stand of fir trees growing behind a rail fence. Gowan drew up, and then climbed down to fetch the handsaw from the back of the gig. Elnora sat there clutching the big ball of twine she'd brought for binding the greenery.

"Aren't you coming to help me?" Gowan called out from beside a stile.

"I am completely useless in the woods," she said, then added with an airy, dismissive wave of her hand, "You go on. I should be nothing but a burden to you."

Before she knew it, he'd scooped her off the seat and carried her over the stile—exactly as she had hoped he would.

"Remember," he admonished, as he took up her hand and tugged her among the trees, "this is supposed to be *fun*."

Elnora had to admit it was quite lovely among the evergreens. It had come on chilly the night before and the tips of the fronds were adorned with white-lace frosting. They crunched along over scattered, frozen pine needles, Gowan still holding her mittened hand, Elnora secretly thrilled.

"Are you looking for anything in particular?" she inquired after about five minutes. "The branches all seem identical to me."

"I'm searching for something specific. I'll know it when I see—*aha!*"

He'd stopped beside a small pine tree that barely reached to his chin. "I thought I might try something I saw one Christmas when a storm forced us to make port in Germany. The families there put up Yuletide trees decorated with candles and strings of fruit. This one should be perfect."

She frowned. "We usually just hung garlands in the doorways."

"Trust me," he said. "This will be the talk of your house party."

"Especially when the candles set fire to the branches."

"Little cynic," he said with a crooked smile. "The candles are lit only on Christmas Eve with everyone gathered round. I'll keep a water bucket handy if it will ease your mind."

Since the only thing that would ease her at that point was if he'd kept walking with her until they reached Gretna Green and an obligingly marital blacksmith, she just nodded.

When he knelt with the saw and began to hew the tree from its base, she surreptitiously admired the lean lines of his back.

"It's a pity to kill it," she said, harking back to his comment about the fish.

"It has plenty of brethren," he said. "Besides, a good husbandman knows he has to thin his plantings. And the tree won't go to waste after the holidays. Pine boughs make a fairly decent mulch."

"How do you know so much?" she said as she helped him bind up the branches with her twine. "I've had my nose in a book my whole life, and yet I seem to know so little compared to you."

He shrugged. "Perhaps experience is the most thorough tutor. It helps that my father is a nurseryman."

"August told me he once worked for the Bonvilliers."

"He was the steward at their estate outside Bristol. August and I were practically raised together. Then when my father came into a small inheritance, he went back to Wales to start his own nursery. Has a way with a shrub, my old da. He's done very well for himself."

Elnora thought he had done very well indeed if he'd

been able to elevate his son to the fringes of the gentry.

They carried the bound tree back to the gig—it was rather like an inert corpse, Elnora thought irreverently—and then returned to the woods to gather pine boughs. The whole time she kept wondering if she dared ask him about his own prospects in life. Could he afford a wife whose family was inches from financial ruin? Would he be willing to take on her ailing mother and her eccentric aunt?

They stopped at one point, and Elnora spied some holly bushes beyond a thicket of vines. The berries were a deep, vibrant red, and she thought the holly would look charming over the hall fireplace. She pushed boldly into the clump of vines—and found herself caught fast. Like a pea goose she'd forgotten about the nettles and thorns that always lay in wait for her whenever she ventured into the wild.

"Ahem," she said, trying to get Gowan's attention. He was busy trimming branches off a towering pine.

"*Ahum*," she coughed, more loudly this time.

"Coming down with *la grippe*, are you?" he said without turning.

When he did finally shift around, his arms now laden with boughs, he burst out laughing.

"I warned you," she grumbled, plucking fruitlessly at the thorny tendrils that had embedded themselves in her cloak. "Completely useless."

He dropped the branches at once and came forward. "You didn't notice that they were wild roses?"

"I was looking at the holly," she said, motioning with her chin to the tempting berries beyond her.

"You've got to watch where you're going, that's the trick to surviving out of doors," he said as he began to pry the vines away with his gloved fingers. "Easy now," he murmured. "Don't pull . . . you'll make it worse."

He cursed once, under his breath, when several

wicked thorns pierced his doeskin glove. Elnora could have died of remorse.

"Stop . . . *please stop!*" she cried. "I think I can manage the rest."

She ruthlessly tugged at the remaining vines and came plunging out of the thicket. She then made him remove his glove so she could wrap her handkerchief around his bloody finger.

"I think I'll live," he said, still merry in spite of the mishap.

Elnora looked up at him, unaware that she had curled her fingers around his bound hand and tenderly drawn it to her chest. He met her eyes, all trace of merriment fading from his face. He leaned down, never altering his intense, dark gaze, until his mouth was scant inches above her own. Time froze for an instant, and the trees around them grew hazy as Elnora waited, afraid to blink or even breathe.

The next instant, Gowan stepped back with a sharp, indrawn breath. "Then again, maybe I won't live," he muttered.

Shifting away from her, he bent and swept up the trimmed branches.

"Here, you take them," he said, shoving the boughs almost roughly into her arms. "*I'll* see to your holly."

She watched in a sort of daze as he skirted the wild-rose patch and gingerly lopped a few low branches from the holly bush. Together they trudged back to the gig, where Gowan seated Elnora before passing up the fragrant bundle of greens.

The whole way home she was assaulted by the rich tang of fresh-cut balsam, a scent so redolent with the aura of childhood that she wanted to weep. She was already feeling shaken and vulnerable after their frustrating encounter in the woods, and now she found herself nearly overwhelmed by raw emotion. The memories came flying back to her, all those childhood Christmases she had spent with her family at the

Chase. The merry parties with neighbors, the festive decorations, sledding and frolicking in the snow, the carols sung beside the hearth.

She hadn't wanted to go to London, she recalled now, but had cried bitterly the whole time while her parents rushed about preparing for the sudden relocation. How very odd that she had managed to forget that. And how fortunate for her doting parents that she quickly succumbed to the bustling charms of London.

She wanted to tell Gowan about this remarkable discovery—that she truly was a country miss at heart—and would likely flourish in the wilds of Wales. But before she could speak, he'd drawn up the gig a short distance from the gates of the Chase. She turned to him with a puzzled frown and was shaken to see that his face bore an expression of what could only be described as misery.

"I believe I will go home to Wales after all," he said, staring down at the reins knotted in his fist. "The doctors can have no complaint—I've never felt fitter. I should just make it in time for Christmas if I leave tomorrow." He did look at her then, but only for the briefest moment. "You've everything well in hand here, and . . . you see, Ellie, the thing is, I will be a bit out of my element once your illustrious guests arrive."

"Nonsense," she exclaimed. "I doubt you are ever out of your element. I've seen how you handle Mama and Tibby . . . you are kindhearted down to your fingertips. That is the essence of a true gentleman." She paused, and when he made no comment, she added with a sigh, "But of course you must go home if that is what you desire."

"What I desire this year," he said so softly she had to tip her head closer, "is not within my reach." He gave a dry chuckle. "But wasn't that so often the case with Christmas when we were young? We wished for the real pony and merely got the hobbyhorse."

Elnora was stricken. If only the man would stop being so dashed cryptic, she could pour out her heart to him. She wondered that any Welshmen ever managed to wed if they were all this averse to plain speaking.

"If it's any consolation, I'm not getting what I want this year either," she said at last, hoping that if she too resorted to speaking in code, he might just declare himself.

"You don't know that yet," he said with maddening density. "I have a feeling Kittredge will immediately fall under your spell. It's not hard to do."

Elnora wanted to scream in frustration. "Not for everyone, apparently. If you, for instance, were under my spell, I doubt you could leave us so abruptly."

He did look at her then, his dark eyes beseeching.

A stray gust of wind ruffled the hair at his brow, heightening the ruddy glow of his lean cheeks. He was handsome and rugged, wry and self-possessed, unfailingly thoughtful . . . and everything she'd ever wanted. Inexperienced as she was, Elnora understood for the first time the keen edge of longing that could cleave a woman's heart in two.

She was just about to throw caution out the window and cast herself into his arms, when her mother's voice rudely intruded on her vision of being passionately kissed by that warm, supple mouth.

"Look, Tibby, it's our Christmas angels returned from the greenwood."

The two women, bundled up against the chill, were taking their daily constitutional along the lane. They came up to the gig, full of good cheer and abuzz with wonder at the tree—and Elnora wished them both at Jericho.

The moment was lost, and she feared she would never have another chance to tell him how she felt.

They all returned to the Chase, and the three women busied themselves hanging greens in the drawing room while Gowan set up his small tree on a table by the French windows.

"He's leaving tomorrow for Wales," Elnora hissed to Tibby as, across the room, Gowan braced the trunk in a bucket of wet gravel. "He wants to see his own family."

She eyed Elnora sharply. "And you're just going to let him go?"

Elnora shrugged. "I can hardly hold him hostage."

Her aunt's eyes narrowed, and after a moment she called out, "Lieutenant Merthyr, I understand you are going to be leaving us shortly. Since you've worked so hard to get the house ready for the holiday, I believe we ought to have an early Christmas celebration tonight. In your honor."

Gowan's smile seemed a bit hollow. "I would like that very much, Miss Nesbitt."

Elnora wanted to hug her aunt—it was an inspired notion! Surely, mellowed with mulled wine, rum punch, and eggnog, her reticent Welshman would finally tell her how he felt.

Chapter Five

Elnora dressed with care that night, donning the gown she had originally planned to wear on Christmas Eve to coax Kittredge into a declaration. It was of a deep garnet hue with a sheer lawn tucker and a collar that rose in a charming ruffle about her throat. Demure and elegant, it turned her eyes the color of violets. If the nurseryman's son was immune to violet eyes, Elnora vowed she would eat her Christmas cracker.

Wills and the cook entered into the spirit of the night, providing a silver service polished to an impossible sheen and delicacies for the table that would tempt an anchorite. After the wonderful meal, they adjourned to the drawing room. Gowan went forward to light the candles he had carefully affixed to the ends of the tree branches. Tibby had called in all the servants while Mrs. Nesbitt blew out the remaining candles. As they gathered around the tree, a glittering, haloed beacon in the darkened room, Tibby whispered, "Sing for us, Gowan."

The Welshman nodded, standing there before his gift to the family, and in a clear, resonant baritone began to sing the familiar and beloved strains of the Sussex Carol.

God bless the master of this house, with happiness beside,
Where e'er his body rides or walks, his God shall be his guide.
God bless the mistress of this house with gold chain round her breast,
Where e'er her body sleeps or wakes, Lord send her soul to rest.
God bless your house, your children too, your cattle and your store.
The Lord increase you day by day, and send you more and more,
And send you more . . . and more.

He stepped forward then, among the breathless group surrounding him, offering brief kisses to the older ladies and warm handshakes to the servants. When he came to Elnora, she looked up at him, her eyes glazed with tears. He bent to kiss her cheek, but checked himself, and instead took up both her hands and squeezed them gently.

"Have a happy, blessed Christmas, Ellie," he whispered. "I pray you get everything you desire."

He turned away before she could reply, and busied himself pouring out drinks from the wassail bowl Wills had carried in. He made a point to keep his distance from her for the rest of the evening.

So much for wine and eggnog, she thought wretchedly. It was clear there weren't going to be any declarations that night. She decided the best thing was to drown her sorrow with endless glasses of the rum punch.

After Gowan had said his good-byes to the gathering, expressing his intention to be away quite early the next morning, Elnora went to her room and had a good, long cry. Tibby had been right—this acute longing in her heart was not an ailment that was likely to diminish in a few short days.

Once she had dried her eyes, she sat up on the bed

and wrestled with her problem. Why was it a given that the man had to be the one making the declaration? Plenty of women, she wagered, were not behindhand at letting their feelings be known to their chosen partners. But Elnora had never been comfortable expressing her emotions—except on the page.

With a determined frown she went to her desk and drew a sheet of paper from the drawer. If she couldn't actually speak her heart to Gowan, she would tell him the only way she knew how, with written words.

The instant she was done, she went out to the hall—before she lost her nerve—and made her way to his room, listing a bit like August's friend, the silly Filbert Dunlop. Kissing the note once for luck, she slid it under his door.

She might be making the biggest mistake of her life, but at least Gowan would know the truth.

She barely slept that night, fearing that every unexpected noise in the courtyard signalled Gowan's departure. Unfortunately, she finally did doze off near dawn and awoke some hours later to the sound of wheels on the gravel of the drive.

Springing from her bed, mindless of her throbbing head, she ran to the window and flung back the draperies. Sure enough, Gowan was tooling the gig toward the gate. But there didn't appear to be any luggage on the boot. Without even taking time to throw on a robe, she raced to his room and opened the door. His grooming set was still on the washstand and his dressing gown was draped over a leather ottoman. She fell back against the door, gasping with relief. That was when she saw her note, lying on the writing table. He'd not only refolded it, but had tied a length of red ribbon around it.

She quickly returned to her room to change, then hurried to find her aunt, who was putting the finishing touches on her "Battle of Agincur" mural.

"He's staying!" Elnora announced. "I wrote and told him how I felt and—"

Tibby's eyes sparkled. "I'd say it's about time."

"I told him how much he'd come to mean to me over the past two weeks—"

"And that you no longer had any interest in Kittredge?"

"*Err* . . . not exactly—"

"Or that you thought about him every minute of the day and dreamt of him at night?"

"No, not that either," she admitted, suddenly fearing that maybe she'd not been as forthcoming in her note as she'd intended. She was supposed to be an accomplished writer, for goodness' sake. Now, she could barely recall what she'd written. Had she been so addled with rum punch that she'd botched the job?

"I'm sure your note compelled him. But I believe he might also be staying on because someone sent him a message late last night, after you'd retired. I saw Wills carry it up myself. Some havey-cavey business that required your lieutenant to go off to the village this morning."

Elnora's expression of joy faded. "But my note . . ."

Tibby patted her hand. "I trust it was splendid, dearest girl. But you know men."

"It appears I don't, actually," Elnora lamented.

"I might never have married, but I wasn't exactly a nun in my youth. And one thing I learned is that men love nothing more than a little intrigue."

Elnora sank down onto the settee. "Well, so much for pouring my heart out."

"At least Lord Kittredge is due today," Tibby said brightly. "That's bound to make things . . . interesting."

Elnora shot her a sharp, sidelong glance. "What is that supposed to mean? I've been dreading his lordship's arrival."

"Just another thing you ought to know about young men," her aunt said. "You put any two of them together with a pretty girl, there is bound to be heated sparring." She grinned at Elnora. "And my money's on the Welshman."

Elnora was in the hall, arranging pine branches in a cut-glass vase, when Gowan came through the door.

"Change of plans?" she asked coolly without looking up. She'd decided that, in light of her outpouring to him, it was now his responsibility to make any further overtures.

"Something came up," he said in the most relaxed of voices. "I've just been to the village. I realized I would need Christmas gifts if I was staying on."

"That's hardly necessary," she said between her teeth. "I believe you've already given us quite enough already." To punctuate her words, she jabbed a long evergreen sprig viciously into the bouquet, nearly causing the vase to overturn.

Gowan was chuckling as he snatched up the vase and placed it out of harm's way on a nearby console. "Steady on. Something's put your back up. I thought you'd be happy that I decided to stay."

"I think it's a bit rude to get a jolly send-off and then not go," she grumbled.

He took a step closer, then stroked the back of his hand swiftly along her cheek.

"I had certain . . . inducements . . . to stay," he said, his eyes full of mischief.

"Yes, so I heard. A mysterious note arrived late last night."

"Come to think of it, it was a bit mysterious. The writer had clearly been over-imbibing."

Elnora blushed, right down to her slipper tips. So she'd written a mishmash of sodden sentiment after all.

"That is not the note to which I am referring," she said, bristling. "I meant the note that Wills carried up to you."

He shrugged. "A bit of business that needed my attention. No mystery there."

He chucked her once under the chin and went off, whistling merrily, to have a late breakfast.

Elnora watched him depart with narrowed eyes, wondering why she felt so angry. No, she realized, it wasn't anger, but disappointment that had soured her. She'd expected something more effusive from him, after her heartfelt note, than playful teasing and an avuncular chuck under the chin. She was forced to admit that his cavalier behavior this morning was fairly strong proof that she had jumped to a horrid and humiliating conclusion.

It was late afternoon, and Elnora was growing increasingly fretful. She'd changed her dress at least three times, at last settling on a simple brocade gown in dusty rose. Since the Kittredges weren't due to arrive for another few hours, she decided to take one last walk through the house to assure herself that everything was in order.

She had to admit the place looked reborn, a cozy, welcoming haven compared to the fright it had been the day they arrived. The furnishings were sparse, to be sure, but their sheer size made up for lack of quantity. And the crowning touch was the pine garlands and bright red ribbons that adorned each room on the two lower floors. Happily, Gowan had somehow soothed the ill will in the village, and the kitchen was now overflowing with baskets of provisions.

Yes, everything was just as it ought to be, the house oddly hushed, as though it were holding its breath in anticipation of the moment the guests would arrive with all the merry bustle that would ensue.

Gowan found her in the drawing room, in the

shadow of his tree, staring out at the drive through the French windows.

"I suppose they'll be here any time now," he said from the doorway. "And in case no one's said it already, you've done a remarkable job with the house."

She turned to him with a look of such entreaty, that he came at once to her side.

"You must know that this is not what I—" she began. "That is, I wasn't prepared for . . . I intended to call it off, you see . . . but Mama told the vicar and then—" She realized she was making absolutely no sense.

"He's not an ogre," Gowan said gently, "that you should be in such a quake."

She flung away from the window. "I hate waiting, especially now. It feels as though I am suspended over a high chasm . . . dangling by a rope . . . and there's a man with a sword—"

"Writers," he mouthed wryly, but with a warm gleam in his eye.

"You don't understand," she huffed. "*You're* the one with the sword. And if you let me fall . . . if I fall, I will crash down and never, ever—"

Elnora caught the unmistakable sound of a vehicle coming up the graveled drive and felt her throat close up.

Gowan took her by the shoulders. "You know what you've got to do," he said bracingly as he turned her toward the door.

She pushed away from him and put her chin up. "I assure you I can handle the baron."

"That's what I'm afraid of," he growled as he pulled her back and tugged her into his arms. He looked at her for one split second, dazzled her with his dark eyes, before he bent his head and kissed her.

It couldn't have lasted more than a few seconds, but she'd have sworn lifetimes blazed past inside her head while he bent her back and took her mouth.

She was reeling as he propelled her out the door,

whispering, "I'd never let you fall, Ellie . . . but don't you let me fall either."

When he shut the door firmly behind her, she wanted to fling herself against it, raking it with her nails until he opened it and kissed her again. And yet again.

Instead, she gathered what few wits she still had left and sailed off to welcome her guests to her immaculate home, the very model of a domestic divinity.

She was too dazed to recall much of the arrival. Kittredge looked quite pleased as he shrugged off his greatcoat, his bony scholar's face actually stretched into the semblance of a smile. Lady Kittredge, enveloped in furs, bussed Elnora promptly on each cheek, pronouncing her a clever puss for having re-created the very essence of her ladyship's own childhood home.

"Why, these furnishings bring me straight back to my youth," she proclaimed when Elnora led them to the small front parlor, where a brisk fire was burning. "The good sturdy stuff one rarely sees nowadays."

How ironic, Elnora mused, that now, when she no longer cared one whit if her ladyship approved, she'd ended up scoring such a coup.

There was a hasty introduction to the dowager's goddaughter, Miss Simsbury, a fresh-faced young miss with bouncing yellow ringlets.

"We do hope she is welcome," Lady Kittredge said as an aside to Elnora. "Poor dear recently suffered a disappointment of the heart. Then I thought, what better to cheer her up than a few days in the country with Dora Davenport?"

"What better, indeed?" Elnora said stoutly.

Ailing sailors, brokenhearted misses, it was all one and the same to old Dora.

Her mother and Tibby came downstairs to add to the general commotion, all the women instantly remarking on Town friends they had in common and possible distant relations they might share.

Elnora took a moment to slip downstairs and confer with Wills on the menu for that night—and came face to face with her cousin August in the dark passageway between the kitchen and scullery.

They both stood open-mouthed for about ten seconds; then August went racing off toward the door that led to the stable yard. After a moment of reeling in utter shock, Elnora went pelting after him. When she flung the door open, however, there was no one in the yard except the men unloading the Kittredges' coach.

"Now I'm having hallucinations," she muttered.

When she located Wills she asked him point-blank if August had been at the house.

"He would hardly be lurking in the kitchens, miss," said the butler with a frown. "Perhaps it was one of the workmen you mistook for your cousin."

"Then why did he run away?"

"I really couldn't say, miss."

She went off, grumbling, and completely forgot about discussing the menu.

She had fire in her eyes when she went down to dinner that night. Her temper faded somewhat when she got a glimpse of Gowan in the drawing room, quite at his ease speaking with Lady Kittredge. Somewhere in the wilds of Hartfordshire, he'd managed to find a top-of-the-trees dinner suit of deep black brocade with a waistcoat of fawn and gold. There was even a jet-and-diamond stud tucked into the folds of his pristine neck cloth. He looked like an elegant pirate.

Kittredge came to her at once. He guided her to the sofa, then seated himself beside her.

"You've made my mother very happy," he said. "I admit I had my doubts that you could manage a proper house party . . . your head's usually up on some lofty plane. And of course, I can see you had little to work with here, the house being sadly out-of-date. Still, it's charmed Mama. You've done well, my dear, very well indeed."

He patted her hand in a patronizing manner, and she nearly snatched it back.

He leaned in closer. "The thing is, Elnora, I'd be grateful for a private word with you after supper, if your guests can spare you."

Oh, here it comes, she thought with a sudden tightening of her chest. *He's not even going to wait until Christmas Eve to propose.*

Gowan drifted by just then. Elnora gave him a nervous smile, then turned to the baron. "You've met Lieutenant Merthyr?"

"Your aunt introduced us." Kittredge cocked his head. "Merthyr . . . *Merthyr* . . . now why does that name sound so familiar?"

Gowan's grin was puckish as he drawled with an exaggerated lilt, "Perhaps you've heard of my da, then? He's a nurseryman off in Wales."

Elnora watched as his lordship stiffened, nurserymen in remote districts being beyond—and doubtless far below—his normal circle of acquaintance.

"No, that's not it," he murmured.

Gowan was just moving on when Kittredge sprang up from the sofa. "By George, I've recalled it now. You're that Navy chap who got himself marooned on an island. The story was in all the papers, how you went overboard during a storm to help one of your mates caught in some fallen rigging."

Elnora's gaze flew to Gowan's face. He'd never said a word of it to her.

Kittredge, meanwhile, was pumping his hand vigorously. "Well done, there's a stout fellow. England is proud of all her brave fighting men on both land and sea."

Elnora wanted to gag. Kittredge had all but draped

himself in the Union Jack, clearly convinced that he was the perfect proxy for Britannia herself.

"Or *in* the sea, in my case," Gowan said with a chuckle. He nodded once to the baron, shot Elnora a smoldering look, then moved off toward her aunt.

"Curious sort," Kittredge remarked once he was out of earshot. "We get these self-made types in the service occasionally. Rising through the ranks in spite of their birth. Still, the man's a bona fide hero . . . if one can believe the tattle in the papers. Mama will find that entertaining."

Elnora scowled and firmly reminded him that he was, after all, discussing one of her guests. She wished she had the nerve to empty the nearest vase of greenery over his smug, self-impressed head.

How could she have ever envisioned marrying him? She must have been completely addled to have even considered it. Refusing him tonight was going to be a walk in the park.

That certainty didn't prevent her stomach from staying tied in a knot all through supper. She knew she'd be turning her back on a fortune without any real assurance that another suitor waited in the wings. To add to her woes, Gowan had by some mischance been seated beside Miss Simsbury and he spent the entire meal making her titter. Elnora hated titterers, especially when they had glistening blond ringlets.

Once the meal was over, the ladies adjourned to the drawing room. Kittredge caught up with Elnora in the hallway.

"I don't fancy making small talk with the sailor," he confided under his breath—and Elnora felt grateful on Gowan's account that he'd be spared his lordship's odious condescension.

He touched her sleeve. "I thought I might have a word with you now."

"Very well," she said a bit brusquely, and led him again to the front parlor.

She duly settled on a side chair, folded her hands, and gazed up at him expectantly.

His lordship, standing erect with one hand clasping his lapel, as though he were about to launch into a speech at Parliament, looked nothing like her notion of an ardent suitor.

"I have something to ask you, Elnora," he said. "Something quite important."

"Yes?"

"I recall thinking when I first met you, now here is a rare creature, a woman possessing the higher sensibilities and noble ideals of a man. It was beyond refreshing, and I can say from the depths of my heart that I have cherished your companionship."

"As I have yours," she said, wanting desperately to add, *Until about two hours ago, when you proved yourself to be a puffed-up nincompoop.*

"And so," he continued, "it is with the greatest confidence that I request your natural benevolence, your good and charitable offices—"

Oh, get on with it! she nearly growled. Gowan was likely falling end over teakettle in love with Miss Blonde Ringlets this very moment, and here she was trapped with the greatest windbag in the kingdom.

"—to take Miss Simsbury under your wing and groom her into the ideal wife for a cabinet minister. Which is to say, for myself."

"What?" Elnora had risen from her chair with no memory of having moved.

"I do realize it seems precipitate. Mama brought Miss Simsbury to town in early December, after her beau departed. She and I spent a great deal of time together, and I find her a complete delight. But she's so young, you see, and unformed. You, my dear Elnora, can instill in her the high-minded principles that we two share."

"I beg your pardon," she managed to get out in quivering tones, "but am I to understand that after ten months of paying marked attention to me, you are *not* proposing marriage?"

His lordship blanched. "Good heavens, Elnora. I am loath to point this out, but your family is hardly suitable."

"My mother is the daughter of a baron," she said between her teeth, bound by blood to defend her kin, even if she was fairly dancing on the inside at this turn of affairs.

"Miss Simsbury is the daughter of a viscount, and brings a sizeable portion." He cast a look around the room. "It's my guess that all you'll bring to your marriage is this drafty old shambles."

This drafty old shambles, she echoed silently. This house she had worked her fingers to the bone to make shine for him. The ingrate.

"I bring *myself* to a marriage," she declared with a firm jut of her chin. "And that's plenty for a . . . a discerning sort of gentleman."

He tugged at his neck cloth. "This is very awkward. I had no idea you were harboring any expectations."

Only me and half the bucks in the ton, she mused. According to August, the betting book at White's was full of wagers regarding the anticipated date of their betrothal.

"It's no matter," she said truthfully. "I was just a bit taken by surprise, is all. You and I have been so often in company together that people started to talk. I merely began to believe the common gossip."

"Elnora, no one can esteem you as greatly as I do."

"Now there I take leave to doubt. There is another who far outstrips you, at least I hope he does. A man with a strong back and a steady hand."

"You're making no sense."

"Indeed, I am making great sense for a change. I must go now, back to my guests. Let me wish you felicitations on your upcoming marriage—"

"There's one other thing. Miss Simsbury's aunt lives in Bedford and we're promised to her for Christmas."

"Lovely," Elnora said, making rapidly for the door. "Off you go then. Happy Christmas . . . healthy New Year . . . glorious Easter."

"Hold on a minute, you never answered my question. *Will* you take Miss Simsbury under your wing?"

Elnora paused at the threshold. "You know, Kittredge, I think not. I am hoping to be far too busy learning to cope in the wilds of Wales to give a figgy pudding for your fledgling bride. Sorry."

She found Gowan in the music room, surrounded by women.

"He sings like an angel," Miss Simsbury pronounced with a vast fluttering of her eyelashes. Lady Kittredge, meanwhile, was examining the "Agincur" mural with her lorgnette.

"Interesting . . . quite interesting."

Elnora pried him away from the piano.

"We need to have a talk, you and I," she said as she tugged him along the corridor toward the library. "A real talk, not in code, not couched in cryptic nuances."

"Then I am completely at your service."

"First of all," she said, swinging around to him the instant they got inside the door. "Why is my cousin skulking down in the kitchens?"

Gowan's eyes widened. "I really couldn't say."

Elnora blew out a breath. "Yes, that was exactly what Wills told me."

He reached out a hand to soothe her. "I expect you're overwrought after the arrival of your guests. Perhaps you imagined seeing him."

"And did I also imagine that you kissed me? And then made sheep's eyes all night at that simpering, ringleted schoolgirl?"

"I was merely being accommodating."

"To me or to Miss Simsbury?"

He was laughing at her now, under his breath, his eyes alight. "Lord help me, you're quite delightful in your wrath, Miss Nesbitt."

"Gowan," she growled warningly, "I have just whistled ten thousand a year down the wind. Or more accurately, it whistled me down the wind, but, nevertheless—"

"So he didn't propose after all. That's something then."

"He's to marry the ringlets," she said. "And I am left hanging by that rope again —"

"I know . . . over a deep chasm. You really ought to consult a lawyer, you know, see if you can't stick his lordship with a suit of intent to mislead or something like that. Ten months is a long time to waste on a self-inflated prig." He began backing her toward the corner of the room. "I'm actually thinking of going into the law myself—since my sailing days are over. You might want to think about hiring me."

He stopped advancing, having boxed her in neatly. He gazed down at her with a smug smile.

"I already hired you," she reminded him archly, "to look after the horse."

"Are we done sparring? Because as invigorating as it is, seeing your cheeks flushed and your eyes flashing, what I'd really like to do is kiss you again."

"Of course I'm not done . . . *Oh*!" Her mouth snapped shut when his last words filtered into her brain.

"There, that's better," he said, running his thumb along the crease of her mouth. He lowered his head, and Elnora closed her eyes. This time she would be prepared, maybe even contribute to the exercise. It would be lovely and delicious and—

She felt him draw back and at once opened her eyes.

"No, I think we'd better have a little talk first," he

said. "Get some things out in the open for a change. For instance, I'd like to know exactly how you feel about me."

"But that's why I brought you here . . . that's what *I* want to know."

"I think I've made myself quite clear."

Elnora nearly goggled at him. "*You?* You haven't said one word to me, Gowan Merthyr. And let me remind you that I am the one who wrote that note last night."

"Which is precisely why I require some clarification—rum punch and strong emotions not being a particularly reliable mix."

Elnora humphed. "You mock the sincere out-pourings of my soul?"

He set his hands on her shoulders. "Never. I'd just like to hear them from your own lips."

Oh dear, this was not going at all well. If only she could recall what she'd written and recite it to him.

He was watching her closely, some tension showing in his lean jaw as he waited. Finally when she didn't respond, his face darkened.

"Your feelings mustn't be very near the surface if you can't even give voice to them."

"I . . . I . . ." She felt the tears starting up, adding mortification to her confusion. It wasn't fair, having to speak first. Suppose she had misread him all along. What did it matter if he *had* kissed her? Plenty of men kissed and fled. Plenty.

She felt his hand cup her cheek, his thumb gently wiping away the lone tear that had managed to overcome her determination not to cry.

"Just say it, Ellie," he crooned. "You're so outspoken about everything else."

She turned her head to her shoulder. "It's not easy," she murmured. "You're supposed to help me, aren't you? Stand at my right hand?" She looked up at him beseechingly, her trusty Welshman, so strong and capable and kind. "Please, Gowan, please help me."

His eyes remained steely. "No. Not with this. This time you've got to stand on your own."

She drew in a steadying breath. How difficult could it be to speak her feelings? After all, in the past few weeks she'd made order out of chaos, acquired a knack for decorating *and* conquered country life—except for the occasional wild-rose thicket.

Best of all, she'd discovered something worth a deal more than wealth or intellect. She'd discovered her own tender heart. Surely she could find the words to tell him . . . without the Dutch courage of rum punch.

"I . . . I thought I knew myself so well," she began haltingly. "I honestly believed I could make a marriage with Kittredge, because we had the same goals in life. To see to the welfare of other people. For all his pomposity, he really is a good man. And to be absolutely truthful, I was relieved that he was wealthy enough to look after Mama and Tibby. Then you came along . . . and everything got scrambled inside my head."

She paused and gave a hollow laugh. "I don't have a single clue about what your goals in life are . . . except possibly to avoid living in London. And, you see, right there we have a problem. There's also all this debt we've incurred to impress the baron, which hardly makes me a bargain. I doubt the son of a nurseryman is equipped to take on such a responsibility. And Mama . . . she will surely not like it that you weren't born a gentleman.

"So I see nothing but problems looming between us . . . and yet"—her voice began to quaver—"and yet not a one of them makes the slightest difference to me."

She threw herself against him, burying her face in

his pristine neck cloth. "Because I fell in love with you, Gowan Merthyr. Practically from the second you wiped that bit of soot from my face."

He tipped her head back, his eyes glittering as he gazed down at her. "It's the oddest thing," he whispered hoarsely, "but I look back at that same moment. I touched you and my whole universe shifted." His arms tightened around her. "I would live in London for you, Ellie. I'd live in Timbuktu . . . if that's where you were." He stroked her face. "As for my humble beginnings, there's nothing I can do to change that. But I might have mislead you a trifle about my father. He's not just a village nurseryman. When his business prospered beyond all expectation, he bought up half the county. He's a proper squire now."

She gave him a little smack. "You could have mentioned that."

"I wanted you to choose me on my own merit. That's all any man wants."

"So did I pass the test?"

His dark eyes flashed for an instant, and then he smiled. "You did."

The Kittredge party left the following day at noon. Elnora discovered a startling fondness for them as they made their farewells, possibly because each of them had in some way hastened her toward Gowan.

Christmas was but three days away now, and she felt herself sink deep into the festive mood like a child into a feather bed. She'd finally gotten what she wanted—a holiday with only her loved ones around her.

They spent a merry afternoon shopping in the village and went caroling with the vicar's family. They crowded four across into the gig and drove off to visit all their neighbors. Elnora felt such admiration for her Welshman, who possessed a natural affinity with both the country gentry and the village shopkeepers. When they visited the local cottagers, he carried the food baskets into their homes without a shred of condescension and was immediately drawn into play with their children. He managed to express in action all the benevolent impulses she, who had such concern for the poor and the downtrodden, could only convey on paper.

Their meals at the Chase became a happy cacophony of bright chatter and relaxed laughter, and even her mother seemed to have reacquired her former vivacity. She also appeared surprisingly untroubled by the untimely departure of Lord Kittredge, and Elnora only found out later that Gowan had already apprised her of his expectations.

Yes, Elnora decided, everything was perfect. Well, nearly perfect. There was still no sign of August. No letters from London, no word from his solicitor, to whom Elnora had written in a fit of worry—and pique.

By Christmas Eve, she'd decided to put him out of her mind. August was likely at the home of one of his cronies, holding court at the dinner table, quite oblivious to the promise he'd made to aid her.

Though that wasn't like him—he might be mischievous and even manipulative at times, but he was never neglectful.

She was sitting in the drawing room, decorating the place cards for supper with bits of colored paper, when Gowan came in carrying a small baize sack. "This is one time I wish I were in London," he said. "The gift options in the village are rather limited."

She looked up with a warm smile. "You could give me an orange and a bag of peppermints, and I'd be quite content."

He grinned impishly. "That's a relief. Except it's a bag of licorice drops."

She reached for his hand. "You know I already got what I wanted for Christmas."

"So did I, Ellie."

He tugged her up from her chair and coaxed her to sit on the carpet close by the fire. "And it's a bit of a miracle, considering what you wrote in your note," he said as he settled beside her and slipped his arm about her waist.

She turned to him with a tiny frown. "I was quite specific about my feelings."

He pulled the creased piece of paper from his waistcoat—Elnora was instantly infused with tenderness that he carried it about with him—and wagged it under her nose. "You were a trifle bosky that night. Do you even recall what you wrote?"

"Not exactly, but you were leaving and my heart was breaking. It must have been something ardent."

"I'm not sure *ardent* is the precise word I would use."

"Here," she said, plucking it from his fingers, "let me read it . . . *My dear friend, I cannot let you go without telling you how much your aid and assistance has meant to me in the refurbishment of this house.*"

He looked at her over the bridge of his nose. "That's practically the balcony scene from *Romeo and Juliet,* don't you think?"

"Let me finish," she muttered, vowing to never touch rum punch again. "It has to get better." She coughed slightly, then read, *"Your strength of character and rare kindnesses have enriched these past weeks . . ."*

"A decent recommendation," he said, "if I were applying for a vicar's post."

Elnora set her jaw. *"And while I understand your reasons for leaving, please never forget that there is one who deeply treasures the man who stood at her right hand. Her greatest hope is that he might someday return to that place at her side."* She tossed the note down. "There, I'd say that's fairly clear."

He pointed to the bottom of the sheet, where her

signature had been underscored with a delicate flourish. "Except that you signed it 'Dora.' "

She snatched up the note and stared at the name in disbelief.

"I thought it might be 'Nora,' " he said reasonably, "but however I turned the page I couldn't make that D into an N. So who is this Dora and who is the man she was writing to?"

"Me, of course. And you. Oh, *bother*." She shifted around to face him. "You see, until recently I wrote a tiresome column for the *Ladies' Fireside Companion*, extolling the pleasures of the home and the joys of country life—"

He grabbed her by both shoulders. "Don't tell me *you're* Dora Davenport."

She gave him a sidelong glance. "I . . . I suppose I am."

His eyes were gleaming. "My mother used to clip those pieces and send them to me on board ship. Made me feel as though I were back in Wales, sprawled under an apple tree watching the harvesters at work in the fields. It was like going home. I came to look forward to those clippings every time we made port." He touched her cheek. "You have a gift, Ellie."

"But what about my real writing? My essays promoting the betterment of mankind?"

Then, in an instant, she understood that she needn't focus on uplifting the masses. She could do her part for mankind on a more personal, but equally effective, scale.

"No, maybe you're right," she said, tucking her head under his chin. "It seems that Dora knew something I only recently discovered—that a happy, contented home *is* worth extolling, because that is where we first learn charity and compassion . . . before we take it out into the world."

She nestled there against him, pleased with every

aspect of her future. But after a few minutes she pushed up from his chest with a grin. "So . . . what *did* you get me?"

He was laughing when he reached into the sack and drew out a foot-long wooden spoon wrapped in a red ribbon. He handed it to her, and she gasped softly when she saw how beautifully it was made, with swirls and arabesques carved deep into the lustrous wood.

At her questioning glance, he said, "It's a courting spoon . . . an ancient custom in Wales. When a man finds a tolerable girl"—he tickled her gently in the side—"he makes her a spoon and carves his sentiments into it along with the designs."

Elnora held it close to the light of the fireplace and murmured the single word embellished on the handle. "Enduring."

She shifted around to him. "But when did you make this, Gowan? It must have taken weeks. And we . . . we only spoke of our feelings three days ago."

He tipped his head until their brows touched. "I began it the day we met."

Once again they lit the Yuletide tree after dinner, and the four of them, Elnora and Gowan, her mother and Aunt Tibby, sang the Sussex Carol together.

Just as the song ended and they began blowing out the candles on the tree, there came a loud banging and clanging from out on the front lawn. They all ran to the French windows. Elnora's workmen were capering about, banging pots and pans in the light of several flaming torches. And coming up the drive was a caravan of wagons, with a suspiciously familiar figure holding the reins of the first one.

Elnora went racing out of the room toward the front door, with the others close at her heels.

"Happy Christmas, cuz!" August called from his perch as she flung the door open and stepped outside. "I've brought you a few trinkets."

"Is that my nephew August or Old Father Christmas?" Tibby asked from over Elnora's shoulder.

"Oh, my good stars," her mother was crying as she saw what lay in the first wagon. "It's my lovely dining table and your father's desk, Elnora . . . and my mama's favorite wing chair. August! You wonderful, wonderful boy!"

He leaped down and after all the women had embraced him, he went to shake Gowan's hand. "Thanks for covering for me."

"You knew?" Elnora said to Gowan, trying to muster a stern frown—and failing.

"He was my accomplice," August explained. "I told him I needed time to recover all your furnishings, but that someone had to come up here and help out. He volunteered."

"I couldn't help myself," Gowan drawled. "Not after he'd told me what a sharp-tongued little bluestocking you were."

"I warned him you were throwing yourself away on a prig," August said. "I had a feeling he might be just the sort of fellow to make you forget Kittredge."

She had an ominous glint in her eyes now. "You planned this whole thing?"

August shrugged. "I merely set the stage."

"And so it *was* you I saw in the kitchen last week."

He nodded. "I got up to Merrivale before the final shipment of furniture arrived and decided to stay in the village. Gowan came to see me the first morning I was here, to report on how things were going at the Chase. When he started describing the preparations for Kittredge's arrival, all I could think of was the delicacies the cook would be making and, well, the food in that inn is dreadful. So I rode over here and sneaked into the kitchen to have a taste."

She leaned up and kissed him. "You gave up all your comforts so that we could have this wonderful surprise."

"I managed to make do," he said with an expression of great fortitude. "The food was a scandal, but the landlord served an excellent claret. Smuggled, no doubt."

"And how did you locate Spackler?"

August glanced at Gowan. "Your lieutenant rounded up some of his shore-bound mates and along with some of my own . . . associates . . . they scoured London for traffickers of stolen merchandise."

"Your cousin has some good friends in very bad places," Gowan remarked dryly.

"We'll get everything unloaded tomorrow," August said, then spread his arms wide. "Come, ladies, come inside. It's freezing out here. We'll drink wassail and sing carols—"

"And eat roast goose and figgy pudding—" Elnora chanted.

"And don't forget the kissing boughs," August said wickedly.

"I believe I've already taken care of that," Gowan said with the utmost seriousness.

Elnora spun to him and threw her arms around his neck. "Bother the boughs."

And then she kissed him, feeling all the magic of Christmas—and family—shining around them as her reticent Welshman lifted her right off her feet and kissed her back.

"I guess she liked my gift," August murmured as he escorted Tibby and Mrs. Nesbitt into the house—leaving the young couple locked in each other's arms on the very spot where they had first set eyes on each other.

August carried a lone candle and his seventh glass of his late uncle's excellent port into the music room. It was quite late—Christmas morning, in fact—and everyone else had gone to bed. He sat at the piano and picked out a tune one-handed, an old carol he recalled from childhood. . . . *Good king Wenceslas looked out on the feast of Stephen.*

He felt rather like a benevolent king himself. Recovering his aunt's furniture, making sure that bounder Spackler took ship to America. At least the rogue would find plenty of good fishing over there to compensate for having to relinquish most of his ill-gotten profits.

And then there was the matter of throwing his childhood friend together with his favorite cousin. He couldn't be more pleased with the outcome. Gowan Merthyr would whisk Elnora off to Wales and doubt-less find a charming home for his new female relations, and then August's town house would be vacant again. Which suited him just fine, since he had a feeling he might be giving up his bachelor quarters one day soon. During his search for the purloined furniture he'd happened to stumble across an absolutely topping young lady, whose Dorsetshire father had purchased the stolen Agincourt Tapestry. She'd barely been out of his thoughts since then.

A trip back to Dorset was definitely in order.

He gazed across to the shadowed wall where the tapestry had formerly hung. There was a painting there now, some sort of mural replicating the original. One of Tibby's masterpieces, no doubt. Though as he gazed at it, he got the distinct impression that Henry V resembled nothing so much as a jowly English mastiff.

"That's done it," he muttered, snatching up his glass and emptying the contents into the nearest vase. "Definitely no more port for me."

A man—or woman—could so easily overindulge in Christmas cheer.

Christmas Cheer

Gayle Buck

Chapter One

The first snow fell softly during the night. Lady Hallcroft woke with a feeling of well-being that was only heightened when she received a note on the tray with her morning chocolate from Lord Hallcroft, suggesting a morning ride together. Lady Hallcroft sent back a reply in the affirmative. She finished breakfast and rushed through her toilette, anticipating the ride on horseback.

Lord Hallcroft awaited her downstairs in the wide entry hall. His handsome figure was already attired in a riding coat and breeches. He leaned against the finial at the foot of the stairs, one elbow laid casually across the top of it. At the sound of her hurried footsteps above, he straightened and looked up. When he caught sight of her running down the stairs, his mouth lifted in an appreciative smile. "There you are, my lady. I was afraid that you would wish to remain abed on such a chilly morn."

"Not I," exclaimed Lady Hallcroft gaily. She was still pulling on her gloves as she joined him. She was somewhat breathless from her dash. "I would not miss a morning ride with you for worlds."

"I am flattered." Lord Hallcroft swept her form with a swift glance, taking note of the heavy woolen cloak, tied at the throat, that covered her velvet-trimmed habit. "I hope you are attired warmly enough."

"I assure you that I am, my lord," said Lady Hallcroft, smiling up at him from beneath the brim of her plumed velvet bonnet. Her eyes sparkled like sapphires with the light of anticipation. "And if I should grow cold, I shall let you know."

Lord Hallcroft nodded, smiling again. "Then let us be off. I have our horses waiting in front." He motioned to a hovering footman, who helped him into his overcoat and handed him his beaver hat, which he put on, and his crop. Then he offered an arm to his lady, which she took with a slight inclination of her head.

They exited through the front door of the manor house. Lord Hallcroft solicitously held on to her elbow as they walked down the icy front steps. He waved aside the groom and helped Lady Hallcroft to mount her mare himself. She settled into the crafted leather sidesaddle, arranging the folds of her heavy cloak and habit skirt. Lord Hallcroft adjusted the height of the stirrup for her. "How is that?" he asked, looking up at her.

"It is perfect, my lord, thank you," said Lady Hallcroft, giving him a bright smile. She gathered her reins in her gloved hands. "I am ready now, my lord."

Lord Hallcroft turned and vaulted easily onto his own restive mount. He nodded to the groom, who was holding the reins of both horses. "You may let them go, Peters. We shall not need you today."

"Very good, my lord."

Lord Hallcroft and his lady set off sedately down the graveled drive. The snow was lighter under the canopy of bare tree branches that laced overhead and the horses' hooves clopped softly on the hard-frozen surface. Soon Lord Hallcroft turned off the drive and led the way into the surrounding fallow fields. The snow was heavier on the broad expanses and had blown in white drifts against the dark hedgerows and fences.

The riders' breaths frosted on the early morning air. Lady Hallcroft drew in a deep breath, enjoying how her nose and lungs felt seared by the cold. She felt terrifically alive. It was a lovely day. As she looked around at their pale surroundings she was struck by the stark beauty. "It is wonderful!" she said, puffs of white accenting her enthusiastic exclamation.

"Yes. Look there, at how the branches of the trees are encased in ice and how their clean surfaces glisten." Lord Hallcroft pointed with his crop. "And there, at those icicles. The light catching them like that makes them sparkle like fantastic earrings of diamonds."

Lady Hallcroft agreed with her husband's assessment. She privately marveled that a gentleman as distinguished as Lord Hallcroft could take pleasure in nature's simple wonders. She had seen how at ease he was in society and how well received he was by prominent hostesses and heads of state. Lord Hallcroft was an influential member of the House of Lords. His opinion was often sought on weighty matters and he seemed to enjoy such conversations. She was proud, of course, of his obvious intellect and the respect in which he was held. It had not once occurred to Lady Hallcroft that her husband might also possess an appreciation of natural beauty.

The horses' hooves were muffled by the deeper snow so that their progress was nearly silent. It was almost as though they were floating through the silent white landscape. Lady Hallcroft did not think that she had ever seen anything half as beautiful.

When Lord Hallcroft pointed with his crop at yet another lovely sight, reminiscing about his childhood, Lady Hallcroft looked over at him with a deep affection. She thought about how much she loved him and loved to be in his company in just such a fashion.

He talked with her in an open, easy manner that was at once relaxing and companionable. She was very glad that she had agreed to marry him. She had told him before that she loved him, of course, but it had always been in the sweet darkness of their bed. She wondered what he would say if she were to say the words now, and she unaccountably blushed.

Lord Hallcroft at once noticed her heightened color. "Your cheeks have turned rosy with the cold. Perhaps we should return to the manor."

"Have they? But I am not in the least chilled. Pray let us ride a bit further," said Lady Hallcroft, mastering her inexplicable confusion.

All at once Lord Hallcroft reached across the distance between them and caught her hand. "You look altogether lovely, my lady."

Lady Hallcroft felt her cheeks heat again. "My lord flatters me."

"No, I promise you. I speak but the truth," said Lord Hallcroft. There was a tender light in his eyes. He looked as though he wanted to say more and Lady Hallcroft waited with bated breath.

The horses stepped aside and their clasped hands parted, ending the moment. Lady Hallcroft regretted it, for she had felt a surge of happiness at the intimate contact. Lord Hallcroft had always been punctilious in his compliments and he always noticed if she was wearing a particularly flattering gown or hair arrangement. Yet it was the little things, like his spontaneous words just then, that made her heart sing. She thought that he must surely love her. He had not told her so in so many words, but she had accepted his reticence. It was simply not in Lord Hallcroft's nature to wear his feelings on his sleeve. However, it would be very nice to hear the words spoken aloud once in a while.

Lady Hallcroft was used to exchanging endearments. She had been raised in a large extended family with universal affection. It had been difficult to adjust to the more formal relationship of her marriage. But she had observed that Lord Hallcroft and his mother did not speak of their mutual devotion. Rather, it was shown in a longer handclasp or a kiss on the cheek or a solicitous word. She had assumed that was the manner in which Lord Hallcroft preferred to express his emotions and so she had adopted it for her own in order not to embarrass or disgust him.

Lady Hallcroft sighed. At such times as these, when she questioned the nuances of her marriage, she wished most to be able to confide in her mother or to solicit her father's wisdom. And how nice it would be to exchange confidences with her sisters and listen to her brothers' good-natured raillery.

"Are you wearied, my lady?"

She glanced over at her husband, startled out of her reflections. "Oh, no! On the contrary, it is all so beautiful and lovely that I was just thinking it is a pity that we cannot share it with all of our family and friends."

Lord Hallcroft pulled up his mount and looked around him. They had ascended a slight rise and were afforded a view of several miles. Though the gray clouds were low, the atmosphere was crystal clear. Sunlight shone on the snowy landscape, limning the tree edge line of the woods, and casting a glittering net over all the world. "Yes, it is a pity indeed. This is my favorite place. I do not believe that I could ever be as content anywhere else."

Lady Hallcroft looked over at him in surprise. His handsome profile was turned to her as he continued to look over the rolling lands. "But, my lord, you are an important man in the government. I would have thought that you preferred London or one of the other capitals."

Lord Hallcroft glanced around. A somewhat amused expression was in his eyes. "Is it so odd of me? To prefer the country?"

"Why, I suppose not," said Lady Hallcroft slowly.

She, too, contemplated the view before them. "I would like very much to share such wonder as this with my family. It is above all things more important to me than the whirls of polite society."

"Do you miss your family, Gwen?" asked Lord Hallcroft gently.

Lady Hallcroft glanced hastily at him, then away. "Of course. But then, I am with you and so I am vastly content."

"Prettily said, my lady," said Lord Hallcroft with a smile. "Now I think that we shall return to the manor. It is time that I returned you to a warm sitting room, while I must meet with my steward yet this morning."

"Very well, my lord," said Lady Hallcroft, stifling an instinctive protest. Obediently she turned her mare and set spur to its side. She did not understand why she should feel so bereft, but so it was. Despite what she had just said to Lord Hallcroft, she knew that it was not quite all of the truth. Ever since they had returned to England from their bridal journey she had felt an increasing restlessness, even a discontent. It appalled her. She was wed to the best gentleman in all of the world. How could she feel such traitorous emotions?

Lady Hallcroft did not want to dwell on such lowering reflections. She flashed a glance at her husband even as she pressed her heel against the mare's side. "I shall race you to the trees, my lord!"

She had a glimpse of Lord Hallcroft's startled expression before her horse swept her away. Almost instantly she heard the heavy thuds of his lordship's mount behind her. Lady Hallcroft urged the mare on, laughing as the cold wind whipped her cloak into flapping dark wings. It was exhilarating to race across the snow with the thunder of hooves in her ears and the leaping of the powerful animal beneath her.

When Lord Hallcroft's heavier mount carried him past her in a swirl of snow and clods of mud, Lady

Hallcroft laughed again. He had already pulled up at the edge of the woods when she raced up. Her cheeks tingled with cold and she felt chilled from the slap of the wind. But none of that mattered to her as she exclaimed, "That was marvelous!"

Lord Hallcroft was grinning. His eyes glinted with shared laughter. "Yes! I did not know you were such a hell-for-leather rider, Gwen!"

"Only wait until hunting season and I shall show you how I ride to hounds," promised Lady Hallcroft. She shivered suddenly, uncontrollably. The exhilaration and warmth she had felt from the race were fading, leaving her more vulnerable to the cold than before.

"I do not doubt that you will show us all the way, my lady. But for now let us return to the manor as quickly as possible, for I can see that you are chilled through," said Lord Hallcroft.

"I am rather," admitted Lady Hallcroft. "But it has been worth every moment."

"For me as well," said Lord Hallcroft softly. His glance and his smile were gentler than before and served to heat Lady Hallcroft's heart. She stored up the memory of such things because they seemed to her so much more meaningful than the polite expressions that a gentleman such as Lord Hallcroft would naturally utter.

It was just such a glance, accompanied by words that rang with sincerity, that had first won her heart. She had been much admired and courted, so much so that she had become used to flattery. Her heart had become armored against the smooth compliments bestowed upon her by admirers and she had learned to turn them aside. However, Lord Hallcroft had cut through all of her defenses with one stroke when he had looked at her just so, and told her that she was adorable.

Lady Hallcroft often wondered, especially of late,

where he kept that part of himself that had first inspired the spark of her love.

Lord Hallcroft led the way back on what Lady Hallcroft swiftly recognized to be a straighter path to the manor than that by which they had come, so that they came into sight of the house within a few minutes.

They dismounted at the stables and then walked up to the house, entering it through the left wing. Lord Hallcroft held his lady's hand tucked comfortably in the crook of his elbow even after they were inside. He kept up an amusing conversation, causing Lady Hallcroft to break into a peal of laughter.

At the merry sound, a stately woman came to the door of the sitting room. She smiled at the couple. "There you are, my dears. I was informed that you were out riding. How was it?"

"Cold and very, very beautiful, ma'am," said Lady Hallcroft. Her enjoyment of the moment was effectively extinguished. She suddenly felt as though she had been caught doing something of which she should feel guilty. She gently withdrew her hand from Lord Hallcroft's arm, covering the reason behind her action by making a slight curtsy to her mother-in-law, Lady Maria.

"Good morning, Mama. I trust that you slept well?" said Lord Hallcroft cheerfully.

"Exceptionally well, I assure you. Why, child, you appear to be perfectly frozen! Christopher, how can you keep Gwendolyn just standing about when she is shivering so?" asked Lady Maria. She contracted her brows in an expression of concern as she looked at her daughter-in-law. "I hope you do not contract a cold, my dear."

"Oh, I am perfectly well, ma'am," said Lady Hallcroft quickly. It seemed to her that her mother-in-law was casting blame upon Lord Hallcroft for her state and Lady Hallcroft didn't like it because Lord Hallcroft was always solicitous of her. Nor did she care for the implication that she was such a poor creature that she must naturally fall ill simply from an hour's exposure to the winter air.

"I am sending Gwendolyn directly up to her maid to change. She became chilled only towards the last when we indulged ourselves in a race against each other," said Lord Hallcroft. He turned to his wife and lifted her gloved hand to his lips for a formal salute. "Thank you, my lady. I enjoyed our ride very much."

"It was lovely, indeed," said Lady Hallcroft. She smiled up at her husband before turning back to excuse herself to her mother-in-law. Lady Maria graciously inclined her head in acknowledgement. Lady Hallcroft turned toward the stairs, while Lord Hallcroft stepped forward to greet his mother with a kiss on the cheek that her ladyship had upturned to him.

As she ascended the stairway and turned the corner of the landing, Lady Hallcroft sighed quietly. She always felt slightly uncomfortable in her mother-in-law's presence. It was difficult to discern what Lady Maria was really thinking behind her carefully preserved expression of civility. Lady Maria had never been unkind nor uttered a carelessly cutting remark to her daughter-in-law. But neither had her ladyship displayed the degree of warmth that Lady Hallcroft had hoped would be kindled in their relationship. It was just one of the many things that she wished that she could talk over with her own mother and father and ask their advice about. However, she was not likely to have that opportunity for any time in the foreseeable future. Lord Hallcroft had not mentioned the possibility of visiting her relations and Lady Hallcroft hesitated to bring up the subject, fearing that it would sound as though she were ungrateful for the position that she had attained through her marriage.

A letter was a poor substitute when what she really wished for was a comfortable coze, with her head lying in her mother's lap.

When Lady Hallcroft had finished changing out of her habit into a merino-wool gown with a shawl drawn over her shoulders, she returned downstairs. She discovered without surprise that Lord Hallcroft had already closeted himself in the study with his steward. That meant that she would be joining her mother-in-law in the sitting room, as she did on most days.

Lady Hallcroft sighed. She was accustomed to animated conversation and the warmth of shared hugs amongst her own family. It was still difficult for her to adjust to Lady Maria's less expressive nature. Lady Hallcroft interpreted it as a coolness towards herself and so she rather dreaded the hours that she spent in Lady Maria's company. Regardless of her misgivings, however, she made certain that she was wearing a cheerful expression when she entered the sitting room.

"There you are! I was beginning to wonder whether you had gotten lost," said Lady Maria with a slight smile. She had looked up briefly from her darning of white household linens with her tiny exquisite stitches.

Lady Hallcroft shook her head as she crossed the room. She was a little annoyed that Lady Maria would recall the single embarrassing incident that had happened shortly after her arrival at the sprawling manor. "I am quite conversant with the passageways now, ma'am." She seated herself in a wingback and leaned over the arm to open the basket beside it. She drew out her embroidery piece and the silks that she was working with.

"Isn't this pleasant! We are quite cozy before the fire, are you not, my dear?"

"Yes, indeed, ma'am," agreed Lady Hallcroft civilly. She bent her head over her embroidery hoop and began to draw the needle through.

Several minutes passed with only the tick of the ormolu mantle clock to mark the silence. At one point Lady Hallcroft reflected that it was a blessing that she enjoyed embroidering or otherwise the time would have crawled by for her.

"It will be a beautiful altar cloth when you are finished, Gwendolyn," remarked Lady Maria.

Lady Hallcroft looked up, surprised both by the compliment and by the opening gambit of conversation. "Why, thank you, my lady. I hope to have it finished by Christmas." She waited hopefully for what else her mother-in-law might have to say.

Lady Maria merely nodded, smiled, and returned her attention to her own work. However, as Lady Hallcroft quietly despaired of any further conversation, her ladyship surprised her. "I have had a delightful letter from Frances. She writes that William will be escorting her home from the seminary for the holiday."

"Indeed, ma'am? That will be a treat for all of us," said Lady Hallcroft with rising hope. Surely, with her sister-in-law and brother-in-law in residence, the days would not be quite as dull. Whenever she was with Lord Hallcroft, of course, she never felt the time weighing heavily on her hands. When she and Lord Hallcroft were so caught up in society during the months of their journey, she had never given a thought to what her life would be like when they returned to his home. However, once at the country estate, life had become like the gentle roll of the ocean— unceasing and with no end in sight. Lady Hallcroft knew that part of the fault was with her. She was used to being busy and there was very little for her to do with her time.

"Yes, indeed; it will be quite nice to have everyone gathered together under one roof again," said Lady Maria. She was smiling slightly and as she glanced over at her daughter-in-law there was a measure of understanding as well as gentle amusement in her eyes. "I suspect that you in particular will enjoy having some other company besides myself during the day. You are used to having a number of people about, are you not?"

Lady Hallcroft felt herself flush. Guiltily, she wondered whether her mother-in-law was something in the way of a seer. "It is true that I am looking forward to seeing Frances and William again. We did not have an opportunity to come to know each other very well before my lord and I embarked on our wedding journey. When are you expecting them to arrive, ma'am?"

"Oh, I expect it shall be rather sooner than later," said Lady Maria tranquilly. "Frances was always very good at dashing off a note at the last moment. I have already spoken to the housekeeper about making ready their rooms for them."

"I am very glad that your family will all be here for the holiday, my lady," said Lady Hallcroft sincerely.

"Why, thank you, Gwendolyn. And I am glad that you are become one of us, my dear," said Lady Maria.

Taken aback by her ladyship's gracious rejoinder, Lady Hallcroft stared for several seconds until she realized how gauche she must appear. Flushing again, she bent her head over her embroidery.

Chapter Two

Lord Hallcroft awaited his wife's presence with a small crease between his dark brows. He laid his hand on the shoulder-high mantle and leaned his weight on it as he contemplated the flickering fire. His thoughts turned again to the circumstances that had led up to todays interview. He had wed Miss Gwendolyn Harper six months before, in June. It had been a fine society wedding. He was well known in polite society and in political circles, while Miss Harper had been one of the reigning debutantes of the Season, so that their union had garnered much notice.

Theirs had been a traditional courtship. The parties had known of one another's antecedents. They had met in a social atmosphere where their every glance and word had been scrutinized. Their few private meetings after their betrothal was announced had been correctly chaperoned. Their wedding had been attended by all the pomp and ceremony that either of their families could devise.

Lord Hallcroft's stern features softened as he recalled their first spontaneous meeting.

She had been hurrying downstairs to return to her family's parlor, having been dispatched upon various errands before the dinner party, while he had just arrived and given his outer garments to the footman. Miss Harper's hands had been full with sundry things.

In attempting to make her curtsy to him, she had dropped her fan. "Oh!"

For an instant he had wondered if she had deliberately employed a stratagem to capture his interest, but he had as quickly dismissed the ignoble thought. Miss Harper was obviously aggravated with herself, and she was also obviously uncertain what to do since she was still holding a number of other items.

He had retrieved the fan, a delicate bit of painted parchment and carved ivory sticks. It crossed his mind that the fan was a perfect foil for her quiet dark beauty. Straightening to his full height, he had presented the fan to Miss Harper with a little bow. "Allow me, ma'am." Gently he slipped the fan between her fingers.

Miss Harper blushed. She accepted her fan with a small dignified curtsy. Raising her lovely blue eyes to his face, she said with a confiding air, "Thank you, Lord Hallcroft. It was so awkward for me, what with Mama's vinaigrette and my sister's shawl and my lovely flowers, also. I couldn't quite keep hold of everything."

"Yes, I see. Perhaps I can be of further assistance. I shall take your mama's vinaigrette and your sister's shawl and carry them for you," said Lord Hallcroft, smiling down at her. He had been struck by her grace and beauty when he was first introduced to her earlier in the Season, but in that moment when all formality was dispensed with he found her to be enchanting.

"Oh, there is no need to do so," said Miss Harper, her blush deepening. "I am really not as incompetent as I must appear."

"On the contrary, I think you appear adorable," said Lord Hallcroft. As her mouth rounded in amazement, and while he wondered where that totally unpremeditated compliment had sprung from, he gently removed the items from her slackened grasp. "It is no trouble at all, you know. Now, if you will permit me, I shall escort you safely to your mother."

Miss Harper stood indecisively. She bit her lip. "But I do not really know you, my lord. I doubt it is seemly for you to carry my things."

"My lamentable manners! I am Christopher, Lord Hallcroft and I am completely at your service," he said, making a courtly bow. "And you are undoubtedly someone of importance, for I find myself most anxious to serve you."

"Of course I know who you are! What I meant was, shouldn't you be properly announced?" Miss Harper cast a glance around and caught the attention of the butler. The wooden-faced butler, who had been waiting to one side during the impromptu meeting, started forward in order to perform his duty.

With a smile, Lord Hallcroft waved the man back. "I can conceive of no greater honor than for you to announce me, Miss Harper."

Miss Harper gave a small, delighted laugh. Her eyes sparkled. "I believe you are flirting shamelessly with me, my lord. I feel quite grown up. Pray do give me escort, for I cannot find it in my heart to gainsay such a gallant gentleman."

"So I should hope," he murmured, causing her to blush again and enjoying it.

After that accidental meeting, they had never again been alone in one another's company until their wedding night.

Lord Hallcroft's frown deepened with his reflections. He and Lady Hallcroft had embarked immediately upon an extended wedding trip, which naturally included calling upon every society hostess in each of the European capitals they had visited. It had all been very interesting and very merry because the late war had ended. They had enjoyed social engagements and dissipating entertainments without equal or number in half a dozen glittering settings.

Now it was fast closing on the holiday and Lord Hallcroft felt that he scarcely knew more about his lovely young bride than he had before they had been wedded. The question of what gift he could give to her had exercised his mind for some weeks, tangled as it was with a bigger question.

He was in love with Lady Hallcroft; he was perfectly certain of that. She was a lovely lady of grace and charm, warm and loving to those about whom she cared deeply. He was fairly certain that she loved him, but he suspected that she did not realize the depth of his own feelings for her.

Lord Hallcroft had attempted to express his feelings, but even in his own ears the words he uttered were clumsy. His tongue was never facile with the pretty phrases that dropped so readily from the lips of his wife's many admirers. He sometimes envied their easy discourse and wondered why he, a man of experience in politics, who had no difficulty delivering a speech or opinion, should suddenly become tongue-tied whenever he tried to expose his heart to one very dear lady.

Lady Hallcroft seemed content enough to be in his company whenever he escorted her to a function or to the theater. He had no reason to complain. However, Lord Hallcroft had noticed of late, especially since their recent return to England, that his lady wife seemed unhappy. It was nothing that she voiced or, indeed, anything even in her attitude. There was just a look in her eyes, gone the next instant, or an occasional trick of expression, that alerted him to the disturbing fact that Lady Hallcroft was not content.

Lord Hallcroft had been perplexed. He had given considerable thought to the matter. His imagination had supposed for him all sorts of causes. As the weeks had passed and the weather had grown steadily colder, he had tried to discover the reason for his wife's discontent. She had greeted his blunt question with an expression of amazement and dismay.

"My lord? Why, I am not unhappy. I do not know

why you should ask me such," said Lady Hallcroft. Her blue eyes were wide and incredulous.

Lord Hallcroft had hastily begged pardon and turned to an indifferent topic. But still he watched his lady. And she, made aware of his perception, had begun to behave with an unmistakable nervousness even as she showed him an all-too-eager will to please. There came to be an increasing discomfiture between the newlyweds.

Lord Hallcroft had resigned himself to the yawning chasm. He did not know how to bridge it. He honestly did not believe himself equal to the task of smoothing away his wife's megrims if she would not or could not confide in him.

Then he discovered what he took to be the key to the problem. He noticed how his wife's conversation began to turn increasingly on reminisces of her family.

It shot through him like a bolt of lightning. His relief was immense, and he set aside once and for all the ignoble suspicion that Lady Hallcroft was regretting their marriage because she was wearing the willow for some unknown gentleman who rivaled Lord Hallcroft in her affections. No, Lord Hallcroft thought, Gwendolyn was not pining for another gentleman.

Lady Hallcroft was homesick for her large extended family.

Of course, the approaching Christmas holiday had much to do with it. That, and the undeniable fact that he and Lady Hallcroft had not had an opportunity to establish a relationship of any depth either before or after they wedded. Theirs was a world filled with social obligations and niceties. It was not conducive to marital communication. In short, Lord Hallcroft and his new bride were not yet comfortable with one another.

Lord Hallcroft hoped that in devising his solution to alleviate Lady Hallcroft's doldrums, he would gain a greater place in her affections. Of course, he thought, one never knew exactly what notion a woman might take into her head. Perhaps he was going about the business all wrong. Quite unaccountably, he felt a sense of unease. Lord Hallcroft put a finger under the edge of his fine starched neckcloth to loosen it.

As Lady Hallcroft hurried down the hall, she wondered what was behind Lord Hallcroft's summons. He had never before sent for her to join him in his study. In fact, she had never set foot inside the room. Once she had dared to peep around the door at a time when she knew that Lord Hallcroft would be absent from the house. She had been hesitant to enter her husband's inner sanctum because she did not know what his reaction would have been if he were to find her there. The study was the place where Lord Hallcroft had begun to spend several hours each week attending to all the mysterious business involved in managing a large estate. Lady Hallcroft had almost begun to resent the study because it represented something that took her husband away from her side.

However, now she felt only a sense of anxiety and curiosity. Halting outside the heavy door, she put up her hand to knock on one of its panels. "Enter." Lady Hallcroft opened the door and stepped inside. She met the glance of her husband, who had turned from the hearth at her entrance. "My lord? You asked for me?"

"Yes, my lady. Pray be seated," said Lord Hallcroft, gesturing to the wing back in front of the fire.

Lady Hallcroft shut the door and crossed the floor, aware that Lord Hallcroft's gaze never strayed from her face. Warmth came up into her cheeks and she dropped her eyes. Seating herself, she composed her hands in her lap and looked up at her husband. Almost hesitantly, she asked, "Have I done something to displease you, my lord?"

Lord Hallcroft looked startled. "No, of course not. Whatever gave you that idea?"

Lady Hallcroft cast down her eyes. "You have never

summoned me here, to your study, my lord. I thought perhaps—"

"It was not my intention to make you nervous, Gwendolyn," said Lord Hallcroft. He shook his head. "Quite the opposite, actually."

She looked up at him again, puzzled. "I do not understand."

"I wish to host a Christmas party, Gwendolyn. And I wish you to handle all of the arrangements."

Lady Hallcroft was completely taken by surprise by Lord Hallcroft's blunt announcement. Her expression must have reflected her astonishment because Lord Hallcroft immediately launched into an explanation.

"Since we have returned to England and retired here to the estate, we have not had the opportunity to entertain. I thought perhaps the holiday would be a good time for you to entertain your first large gathering," said Lord Hallcroft. He cleared his throat. "What do you think, Gwendolyn?"

"Of course, my lord. I will be happy to take on such an agreeable task," said Lady Hallcroft quickly, anxious to please. "But—"

"Do you have some reservation, then?" asked Lord Hallcroft.

"Yes, my lord. What of Lady Maria? Surely it is more her place to act as hostess in this house?" asked Lady Hallcroft hesitantly. "I would not wish to usurp her position, my lord."

Lord Hallcroft nodded. "It is well thought of, my lady. However, you need not concern yourself. I have already spoken to my mother and she has expressed herself delighted at the notion. In fact, her exact words were that she was delighted to be relieved of such an onerous task. She has never been particularly fond of planning large events, preferring smaller gatherings to what I have in mind."

"In that case, I shall be happy indeed to fill that office, my lord," said Lady Hallcroft.

Lord Hallcroft smiled. The relief was evident in his eyes. "Thank you, my lady. I will tell the household to apply to you for all instructions."

"Whom shall we be inviting, my lord?" asked Lady Hallcroft curiously.

Lord Hallcroft waved his hand. "It will be a number of people with whom I am acquainted. You need not be concerned with that end of it. My secretary will attend to the invitations. You need only arrange for the dinner and the entertainment. In addition, I expect that several of the guests will wish to extend their stay for several days."

Lady Hallcroft's heart sank. It was obvious to her that Lord Hallcroft had it in mind to entertain several personages from political circles. Not having been raised with such connections, she knew few from that rarified segment of society. Nor had she had an opportunity to establish more than a nodding acquaintance with any of her husband's friends before they left England on their extended wedding trip. Now she was expected to put together an elegant function for all these unknowns. It was a difficult chore that Lord Hallcroft had set before her.

She did not want to fail Lord Hallcroft in her first foray into entertaining. Tentatively, she asked, "My lord, may I inquire what is expected? That is, I do not know precisely how you wish me to arrange this Christmas party so that it is most pleasing to your guests."

Lord Hallcroft smiled. "Why, I think it would be best for you to arrange things just as your own family would have done at this time of the year, Gwendolyn. You have often told me in these past few weeks what cheer your family enjoyed at Christmas."

Lady Hallcroft flushed. "I apologize, my lord! I did not realize that I was boring on in such a fashion."

"Nonsense. I did not find your reminisces boring in the least. On the contrary, I found them enlightening.

I hope that in planning our own Christmas party you will be less homesick for your family," said Lord Hallcroft gravely.

Lady Hallcroft was dismayed. Her eyes flew to meet his questioning gaze. She flushed fierily. "I am sorry. It is just that—"

"You do not have to explain, Gwendolyn. I should have realized earlier how difficult it must be for you to be away from your family, especially since we have returned to England and are not so very far from them," said Lord Hallcroft.

Lady Hallcroft pressed her hands to her cheeks. "I feel so ashamed. I know that I should not feel homesick! After all I am a married woman! I do not wish to insult you in such a fashion, my lord."

"You do not insult me, my lady," said Lord Hallcroft quietly. "It is your nature to care strongly for those for whom you have an affection."

Lady Hallcroft glanced up at him, then away. "Yes," she agreed in a smothered voice.

A little diffidently, he asked, "Would it please you if we were to plan on a long visit with your family?"

She looked up again, quickly, and this time the color that rose into her face was not due to embarrassment. Her eyes suddenly sparkled with unshed tears. "Oh, Christopher! Yes, it would please me very much!"

Lord Hallcroft let out his breath in a soft sigh. He smiled down at her. "Then that is what we will do. But first I shall ask you to direct all of your energies into our own Christmas party."

"I shall do so most willingly, my lord," said Lady Hallcroft, her fears and uncertainties fading before the glorious promise of reuniting with her beloved family.

Chapter Three

The following morning Lady Hallcroft wakened with her thoughts already revolving upon the awesome responsibility that Lord Hallcroft had laid on her. However, the first thing she did was delicately ask what Lady Maria's feelings were about her taking charge of the preparations for the large gathering. Lady Hallcroft had always been careful to defer to her mother-in-law and show the proper respect for Lady Maria's authority. Even though Lord Hallcroft had assured her that all had been agreed upon, she was not so certain of her footing with Lady Maria that she was able to accept his lordship's assurance with absolute confidence. Lady Hallcroft wanted to be perfectly certain that Lady Maria indeed regarded the arrangement with complacence.

At the question, Lady Maria laughed gently and shook her head. "My dear, of course I am perfectly willing for you to make all of the arrangements. I am a very poor creature when it comes to planning for huge parties. As you must already have realized, I am much more comfortable to leave even the mundane affairs of running this huge house in the hands of my capable staff. In fact, I have given instructions to Taylor and to Mrs. Simpkins that they are to take their orders directly from you."

"Are you quite certain, ma'am?" asked Lady Hallcroft anxiously. "I do not in the least wish to put you out."

Lady Maria laid a hand on her daughter-in-law's arm. With an unwavering gaze, she said, "My dear Gwendolyn, believe me, I infinitely prefer to leave everything to you. My son has expressed his complete confidence in you and therefore I know that I may rest easy."

Sensing the sincerity behind Lady Maria's words, Lady Hallcroft was able, without a twinge of guilt, to throw herself into devising a house party of splendid proportions. Lord Hallcroft had given her carte blanche, requesting specifically that she order all as her own family did. Recalling the wonderful Christmases of her girlhood, she began to feel a sense of excitement.

Lady Hallcroft set pen to paper, organizing her vision into a much-detailed plan. That very day she met with the butler, Taylor, and Mrs. Simpkins the housekeeper. In consultation with these worthies, Lady Hallcroft ordered massive preparations to be set in train. It was not long before Hallcroft Manor took on the air of a frenzied beehive. The twelve days leading up to Christmas were the most important, of course. The dinner menus were carefully chosen by Lady Hallcroft in consultation with the cook, but Lord Hallcroft chose the wines that would be served each evening.

Lady Maria suggested a small ball, which Lady Hallcroft interpreted to be a gently worded command. However, she was only too glad to incorporate Lady Maria's request into her list of entertainments. It nicely rounded out her own notions of what was due Lord Hallcroft's guests. Lady Hallcroft asked Lord Hallcroft's secretary to make arrangements for music for the ball, outlining what it was she required. She was soon informed that an orchestra, consisting of a pianoforte, a trumpet, a cello, and a violin, was engaged for the particular evening. Lady Hallcroft saw to a few other details, too, concerning the ball, which she considered imperative. Champagne was laid in; the silver was polished; a promise was extracted from the cook that a superlative confection treat was to be provided. The carpet was rolled up out of the ballroom and the floor was scrubbed and buffed until it gleamed.

A very busy week passed, during which Lady Hallcroft saw very little of her lord. She felt strangely bereft and could only be thankful that she had something with which to occupy her mind and her time. She tried not to mind the widening gap between them. She knew that Lord Hallcroft's hours were consumed with estate matters and, lately, some political question that was the focus of lengthy correspondence.

Lady Hallcroft realized that Lord Hallcroft had already given instructions for the invitations for the house party to be sent out because in a very short while responses began to trickle in. She never saw the respondents' notes, for Lord Hallcroft's secretary was quick to lay claim to them. She assumed, since Lord Hallcroft knew that she was not familiar with his friends and acquaintances, that his lordship preferred to leave that part of organizing the house party in the secretary's capable hands.

Lady Hallcroft did not mind that so very much since her time was completely taken up with the rest of the preparations. However, it would have been nice to have had the opportunity to discuss with Lord Hallcroft this personage's acceptance or that individual's decline, if only to have something more to talk about.

Despite Lady Hallcroft's enjoyment of making ready for the holidays and a Christmas house party, she could not quite ignore the cloud on her horizon. There was a new lack of interaction between herself and Lord Hallcroft. They met over breakfast and dinner, but they scarcely exchanged a word otherwise. When they did converse it was naturally over the details of the house party, which Lady Hallcroft was careful to relay to his lordship and which he seemed to enjoy listening to. However, there were no more companionable rides in the winter snow. Nor did Lord Hallcroft seem as likely to seek out her company as he had once had. He seemed content to spend the evenings with both her and Lady Maria.

Lady Hallcroft could not understand it. He had once tried to spend as much time alone with her as he possibly could. She could not quite set aside the slowly gathering conviction that Lord Hallcroft was becoming slightly bored with her.

Lady Hallcroft wanted to please her husband. She thought that if she did, he would naturally regard her with approval and wish to spend more time with her. It was the wish of a woman in love. Therefore, the inevitable anxiety that Lady Hallcroft felt over the house party and how well it would come off began to loom larger and larger in her mind.

One morning Lady Hallcroft started to enter the drawing room, but paused behind the half-open door when she heard her mother-in-law's voice lifted in remonstrance in connection with her own name.

"Christopher, I cannot quite approve of this plan of yours. It is not fair to Gwendolyn."

"I know, Mama. But it is only for a short while that she will be kept in the dark. Then she will know everything."

Lady Hallcroft bit her lip, uncertain of what she should do. She did not want to enter the drawing room after such an odd conversation. Her mind was already speculating over the meaning of what she had heard. Should she brazen it out and pretend that she had not heard anything, or should she retreat? The decision was taken from her when the housekeeper appeared and requested her aid in settling a minor household crisis concerning the upstairs maids.

"Let us go into the library, Mrs. Simpkins. I do not

wish to worry Lady Maria with such a thing," said
Lady Hallcroft quietly.

"Yes, my lady."

In the process of handling the problem and sending
off the satisfied housekeeper, Lady Hallcroft forgot
about the odd bit of overheard conversation. She did
not think of it again as she hurried off to check on the
progress of one of the tasks that she had set herself for
that day.

It was going on the hour before dinner when Lady
Hallcroft concluded that she had accomplished everything that could possibly be done that day and she
went upstairs to change her daydress.

An hour later, having dressed for dinner, she had
started downstairs when she heard Lord Hallcroft's
cheerful voice drifting up from the entry hall. She
glanced over the banister and saw that his lordship
was greeting two arrivals. Lady Hallcroft recognized
Lord Hallcroft's brother and sister and she realized
that Lady Maria's sanguine observation of not many
evenings before had proven true.

Lady Hallcroft hurried down the stairs, and then
stood hovering somewhat uncertainly to one side in
the entry hall because she did not want to intrude too
closely on what she saw was an emotional moment.

It was an exuberant homecoming, with both young
people throwing their arms about Lady Maria and
Lord Hallcroft in turn and talking animatedly. Observ-
ing the greetings among the family members, Lady
Hallcroft was astonished. She had never seen Lady
Maria display so much emotion, even wiping away a
few happy tears, nor was Lord Hallcroft the least bit
stiff with the physical display to which he was sub-
jected. He merely recommended that his younger
brother be more careful of the creases in his
starched neckcloth.

His brother laughed heartily. "Surely that statement
is more in my line, brother!"

"You would like to think so, at any rate!" retorted Lord Hallcroft.

William resembled his elder brother in face and frame. He was a handsome young man, still boyishly thin but nearly as tall as Lord Hallcroft. His taste in clothing ran to dandyism and he wore his starched shirt-points ridiculously high up on his ruddy cheekbones. Lady Hallcroft thought that he resembled her younger brother in manners and in fashion and she immediately felt that she could be comfortable with him. She turned her gaze upon her sister-in-law and did not feel quite so confident. There was nothing shy or retiring about Miss Hallcroft. Instead, the young lady appeared to be the epitome of fashionable élan. Lady Hallcroft felt certain that Lady Frances Hallcroft would never feel a second's anxiety about presiding over a house party consisting of a group of government influentials.

Lord Hallcroft's sister was a petite blonde with a curling mop of hair, speaking eyes, and a pert nose and mouth. Lady Frances was a veritable whirlwind of energy and there could be no more striking contrast than between her animated countenance and quicksilver movements and Lady Maria's studied elegance.

Lady Frances had already peeled off her kid gloves and was now undoing the ribbons of her fashionable bonnet, which she immediately pulled off of her head. She handed her possessions to the maid who stood a little to one side of her. "Whew! That is better."

"But what have you done to your hair, Frances?" asked Lady Maria, eyeing her daughter's short coiffure askance.

"I had it cropped. It is all the crack," said Lady Frances, fluffing her curls with her long slender fingers. "Do you like it?"

"I am not certain that I do," said Lady Maria judiciously, with a faint frown.

"Oh, Mama!" Lady Frances giggled and shook her

head with a tolerant, worldly air. "I assure you, it
simply was not possible to keep my past style! Why,
I would look a perfect quiz!"

Lady Hallcroft realized that her fingertips were
touching her own longer arrangement of cascading
curls and she hastily dropped her hand. She felt all
sorts of fool to have betrayed herself and she hoped
that no one had noticed her unconscious movement.

"I suspect that you will turn quite a few heads with
such a modish look," said Lord Hallcroft dryly.

Lady Frances's dimples peeped out on either side
of her mobile mouth. "So I should hope!" Her eyes
traveled past her brother's figure and settled on
Lady Hallcroft.

Lord Hallcroft, following his sister's gaze, appeared
to notice his wife's presence for the first time. "Gwen,
you have met my brother, William, and my reprehensible sister, Frances," he said, turning toward his wife
and holding out his hand to her. With a firm clasp on
her fingers, he drew her forward into the circle.

"Yes, of course. How do you do? I am happy that
you have come," said Lady Hallcroft politely, smiling
at them. She was anxious that she make a good impression because as she had recently told Lord Hallcroft, it was important to her to be well liked by all
of his family and friends. Of course, even after several
weeks she wasn't yet certain that Lady Maria really
liked her. Lady Hallcroft hoped her relationship with
these younger members might be easier to establish,
especially since they seemed to be more like her in
their outward expressions of affection.

"Well! You come in very good time, my dears. You
must go up immediately to put off your traveling
things, for we are about to sit down to dinner," said
Lady Maria, smiling at her younger children.

William rubbed his hands together. "Dinner! I shall
not be many minutes, I assure you!" With a bow in
Lady Hallcroft's direction he bounded up the stairs.

Lord Hallcroft laughed. "Will hasn't changed a bit. He still eats like a horse."

"Yes, I do not know where he puts it," said Lady Frances, shaking her head. She reached up on tiptoe to brush a kiss against her older brother's cheek. "I shall only be a quarter hour, I promise." She also ran up the stairs, followed more slowly by her faithful maid.

Lady Hallcroft beckoned the butler to her side and quietly instructed him, "Taylor, pray inform the cook to set dinner back."

The butler nodded and exited the entry hall.

Lord Hallcroft smiled at his wife and his mother. "We have cause to celebrate this evening, ladies. May I escort you both into the parlor where we shall await our two returned sojourners?"

"Indeed you may, Christopher. I am anxious to hear everything that William and Frances have to tell us," said Lady Maria, accepting her son's escort and tucking her hand inside his elbow.

Lady Hallcroft took her husband's proffered arm. She smiled up at him. "I am happy that your brother and sister have arrived in such good time, my lord. It will make the holidays that much more enjoyable."

"I am certain of it," murmured Lord Hallcroft with a smile.

Chapter Four

All the talk was for the upcoming house party. Lady Frances had initially bemoaned the fact that she was not to enjoy the society of her own friends during the house party; but after a short interview with Lord Hallcroft behind the closed door of the study, she suddenly stopped voicing her disappointment.

Lady Hallcroft felt sorry for her sister-in-law, interpreting the change to mean that Lord Hallcroft had sternly remonstrated with his sister. She therefore went out of her way to include Miss Hallcroft in her activities and to ask her advice on various things, so that a good understanding seemed to be developing between them.

As for the younger son of the house, William expressed himself fully satisfied with whatever preparations were being made. "I am just jolly glad to be home. There is the duck hunting and all sorts of sport to be had and meat pies and such to look forward to," he said. William liked the decorative fir garlands and red ribbons that had gone up, but it was the tantalizing scents of roasted goose and Christmas puddings wafting through the house that he most approved. He was seen more than once with his nose lifted high, sniffing appreciatively in a manner much akin to that of the hounds that were always following close at his heels.

Lady Maria was gracious enough to tell Lady Hallcroft that the manor house had never appeared more handsome than bedecked in its fragrant greenery, red bows, and tinsel. Lady Hallcroft glowed with the praise and she felt for the first time that perhaps Lady Maria did indeed approve of her. When Lord Hallcroft echoed his mother's sentiments, she felt herself to be quite in charity with everyone.

Everywhere one looked, there was the scent and sight of Christmas. Fir decorated the mantels in every room and was wound through the banister and up to the upper balcony. For days the sideboards had groaned with the scrumptious offerings from the kitchen—roasted fowl, hams, puddings, pastries, sweetmeats, and pies. The heady scents of the traditional eggnog and rum punch hung on the air. Everything that Lady Hallcroft could possibly think of to make the holiday more festive had been set in motion. She anxiously hoped that Lord Hallcroft's guests would not despise her efforts.

Lady Hallcroft still fretted over the ultimate success of her first attempt to entertain for Lord Hallcroft's set. When she asked Lord Hallcroft more specifically when he expected the house party guests to arrive, he was vague. She was forced to conclude that it was an unimportant detail to his lordship; however, it was of vital significance to her. She gave standing orders to the housekeeper to keep all the bedrooms in a ready state so that at any given moment guests could step into them and feel immediately at home.

Despite her insecurity, Lady Hallcroft was also feeling a keen sense of excitement. The Christmas holiday had always been one of her favorite times of the year and it had always connoted warmth and affection and family. She had written to her parents, conveying an open invitation to them and any other members of her family that might wish to visit. Her sense of joy was dimmed when she received her mother's disappointing reply.

She had unconsciously made a sound of dismay, which her sister-in-law was quick to hear. Lady Frances looked up from the ladies' magazine that she was perusing. "Have you received bad news, Gwen?"

"Not bad, precisely, but certainly unexpected," said Lady Hallcroft. She looked up from her mother's closely written sheets and managed to put a credible smile in place. "It seems that my parents have made other arrangements already for the holidays and so they have declined my invitation to visit us."

"I shouldn't mind it, Gwen, for my brother has made plans for the holidays that must meet with your approval," said Lady Frances offhandedly.

"Whatever do you mean? We are having this house party, certainly, but is there something else of which I am not yet aware?" asked Lady Hallcroft.

Flushing, Lady Frances just stared at her sister-in-law. Lady Hallcroft suddenly realized that Lady Frances was looking strangely guilty. Before she could pursue her question, Lady Frances scrambled up, allowing the magazine to fall to the floor. "Excuse me, I am certain that I hear my mother calling to me."

"Frances, pray tell me! Is there is something that I should know?" asked Lady Hallcroft, feeling the beginning of alarm.

Lady Frances' usual self-possession appeared to have deserted her. "Oh, I have said too much already! Pray forgive me! And pray, pray do not tell Christopher that I have!"

With that, Lady Frances whirled away and left the parlor, leaving Lady Hallcroft staring after her in lively surprise. Eventually it occurred to Lady Hallcroft that she had been unpleasantly left in the dark, and that thought brought to her recollection the tidbit of conversation that she had overheard between Lady Maria and Lord Hallcroft. It began to appear to her that Lord Hallcroft had apparently forgotten his solemn promise that she could visit with her family after the house party. Little by little, as she reflected upon her abortive conversation with Lady Frances, she grew angrier and angrier. Lady Hallcroft abruptly left the parlor and went upstairs to her bedroom, ordering her maid to deny her to anyone because she was laid down with a headache.

The hours that Lady Hallcroft spent alone in her bedroom did not bring her good counsel. She could not overcome the hurt that she felt that Lord Hallcroft apparently intended to break his word to her. Even more than the lost opportunity to visit with her family was the inescapable feeling that all Christmas cheer had been sucked out of her. Lady Hallcroft shed a few tears; but then, with the striking of the hour by the hall clock, she dried her face and made herself presentable for dinner. Then she slowly went downstairs.

Lady Hallcroft crossed the hall to join the rest of the household in the parlor before dinner. She paused in the doorway and glanced around. Here, too, the signs of the holiday were lavishly displayed. A kissing bough hung from the chandelier in the parlor, heavily laden with bright red apples and candies and tiny gifts and candles Mistletoe, lavishly ribboned, garnished the center of the bough.

The kissing bough was particularly hard to look at. It was unfortunate that she would not herself be the object of sweet gallantries under the same bough, came the traitorous thought. Lady Hallcroft suppressed it at once. It was simply not in Lord Hallcroft's nature to be overly demonstrative. Besides, she was not feeling particularly kindly toward her husband just then and she would almost certainly have rebuffed any such overture from him.

Lady Hallcroft spent the remainder of the afternoon in her room. More than once she started to go down to Lord Hallcroft's study and request a private audience with him. However, in the end she decided against such a confrontation. It could only serve to anger Lord Hallcroft and she did not feel so secure in his lordship's affections that she felt able to brave either his wrath or his rejection. After much reflection, she decided that there was little that she could do except pretend that she was still in total ignorance of Lord Hallcroft's perfidy.

Lady Hallcroft quietly greeted Lady Maria and Lady Frances with a smile and a gracious word as she made her way across the room. Ignoring Lady Frances' swift speculative glance, she took her place in a wing back before the blazing hearth.

"How are you, Gwendolyn? I understand that you suffered from the headache this afternoon," said Lady Maria.

"I am much better now, my lady," said Lady Hallcroft. She was aware of Lady Frances' stare and lifted her gaze to the younger woman, holding the glance steadily. Lady Frances was the first to look away, a slight flush rising in her face.

Lady Hallcroft calmly took out her embroidery and began adding delicate stitches to the exquisite design on the altar cloth. She listened with only half an ear to the conversation between Lady Frances and Lady Maria, responding as necessary when she was addressed. Otherwise she took no part in what was going forward, preferring her own thoughts to her companions' discourse.

At some point Lord Hallcroft and William entered the parlor, animatedly discussing a recent bout of billiards. Lady Hallcroft glanced up briefly, without forethought, to look at her husband. Upon meeting his smiling expression, she forced a tiny smile to her face. However, inside she was seething with resentment and hurt. She dropped her eyes and applied herself to her embroidery, using her handiwork as a shield against being drawn completely into conversation.

When it was time to go in to dinner, Lady Hallcroft

rose gracefully to her feet and accompanied her husband and his family into the dining room. It was the longest meal that she had ever partaken of and she was thankful when it was over. There was an unusual heaviness of spirit plaguing her and she was glad to return to the drawing room with the two other ladies. The gentlemen would naturally rejoin them after they had finished their after-dinner wine, and coffee would then be served. Lady Hallcroft settled down again with her embroidery and wished passionately that the unfortunate evening would pass quickly so that she could go upstairs to bed.

Lord Hallcroft and William returned. Lady Hallcroft acknowledged their presence with a smile and a nod, but she did not make any attempt to put herself forward. Once again she used her embroidery as an excuse to distance herself. Her reflections were somber.

The clock on the mantel struck the hour, startling Lady Hallcroft from her reverie. She heard the murmur of conversation, the occasional rise of laughter. The warmth of hearth and family were all around her, but she felt herself to be separated from the joyous spirit of Christmas. She did not understand her husband. She also did not really feel one within the Hallcroft household and she suddenly yearned for her own family, where she was assured of her place in their affection. Tears stung her eyes and she blinked them back so that she could see the flash of her needle.

Lord Hallcroft, who had more than once glanced in Lady Hallcroft's direction, rose from his seat to approach his wife. "It is the first of the twelve nights. We will light the first candle soon. May I interest you in helping me with that traditional task, my lady?"

Lady Hallcroft thought she could stand no more. She stabbed her needle into the fabric and rolled up the embroidery. Exercising self-control, when what she really wished to do was snap at him, she said quietly, "Forgive me, my lord. I am not feeling well and I have been thinking that I should like to go up early to my room."

"Poor Gwendolyn had the headache earlier this afternoon, Christopher. You must try to get her to rest, for I suspect that she has been going the pace too fast," said Lady Maria, apparently overhearing something of their conversation.

Lord Hallcroft looked down at his wife, concerned. He had not noticed it before but she did look to be a little under the weather. Certainly her generally sunny disposition had been rather subdued that evening. "I am sorry to hear that you are in distress, my lady."

"Are you? Are you really?" asked Lady Hallcroft hastily, her bosom heaving with her repressed feelings. Her eyes flashed as she jumped to her feet. "It is strange, then, that you have made it impossible for me to be aught else! When you promised me that I should visit with my family!"

Lady Hallcroft felt that she had to get away or otherwise she would probably say something that she would truly regret. She turned abruptly, but before she could make good her escape she was caught fast by the elbow. She looked up, astonished that Lord Hallcroft would so detain her. She was even more surprised by the grimness of his expression. "My lord!" She directed a meaningful glance down at his long fingers clasped about her forearm.

"I apologize for my heavy-handedness, my lady. However, I should like to hear what it is that has offended you so," said Lord Hallcroft. He gestured courteously with his free hand, as though requesting her company, but the pressure of his fingers left little doubt in Lady Hallcroft's mind that he was quite determined that she accompany him.

Lady Hallcroft threw another glance up at his profile when she realized that he was drawing her over to the settee against the wall. They were not even to go into a separate room, but would have this conversation with his family seated at the far end of the parlor. Humiliation suffused her; it did not occur to her that there would have been a great deal of speculation among his family if she and Lord Hallcroft were to precipitously desert the parlor.

"Pray be seated, my lady."

Lady Hallcroft sat down, perforce because she did not wish to make a scene, but she sat bolt upright with her hands held tight in her lap. Her eyes lowered, she said, "I do not wish to discuss this matter with you, my lord."

"Nevertheless, my lady, you may begin with your reference to your family. That is apparently the crux," he said quietly.

Lady Hallcroft rounded on him, stung out of proportion by his reasonable tone. "How could it be otherwise, my lord? At a passing remark from myself that I should like to see my family at Christmas, your sister tells me that you have made other plans for the entire holiday. Then Frances looked all shades of guilty and begged me not to reveal that she had said anything."

Lord Hallcroft regarded her with the dawn of understanding, which became swiftly intermingled with amusement. "Gwendolyn, I assure you that is not quite the way things are."

Lady Hallcroft was further incensed by the springing of laughter into his eyes. The hurt she felt intensified. "Oh, naturally not! I imagine that Frances was simply rattling away in her inimitable style and there is not a particle of truth in it!"

Lord Hallcroft had the audacity to laugh.

Lady Hallcroft rose hastily from the settee. "Excuse me, my lord. I must not neglect my duties. Lady Maria will wish me to pour the coffee!" She swept past him, her head held high.

Her wrist was caught in a gentle yet commanding grasp. Lady Hallcroft was consternated as she turned

to face her husband. More and more Lord Hallcroft
was surprising her, throwing her increasingly off balance. "Unhand me!"

"I do not think so, my lady. You have misinter-
preted my meaning and I—"

"Christopher, it is time to light the first candle on
the kissing bough. Pray do come do the honors."

Glancing briefly in Lady Maria's direction, Lord
Hallcroft stood indecisively. He wanted to finish the
discussion with his wife. He could scarcely believe that
such a quarrel had flared up between them. Indeed,
he was more than a little surprised that his meek and
biddable wife could be staring up at him with such
challenge sparkling in her blue eyes. In the end, the
decision was wrested from him as Lady Hallcroft took
advantage of his slackened grasp and freed herself
with a quick yank.

Lord Hallcroft watched as his wife walked swiftly
away, crossing the parlor with an angry sway to her
skirts. He saw that Lady Maria and his brother and
sister were beginning to realize that something untoward had taken place between the couple. All were
eyeing Lady Hallcroft's averted face and his own darkened expression. Lord Hallcroft made an effort to rid
himself of his frown. Unless he wished to initiate an
embarrassing scene, he had no alternative but to pretend that there was nothing amiss. "I shall be happy
to do the honors, Mama." He walked over to take the
brand that the butler ceremoniously offered to him. He
lifted the flame to solemnly light the first of the twelve
candles that symbolized the twelve days of Christmas.

Upon the candle being lit, Lady Frances laughed
and clapped her hands and William whooped. "Now
let's sing some of the old carols!" exclaimed Miss
Hallcroft, her eyes bright.

"Oh, let's do, by Jove! How jolly! Mama, will you
play for us?" asked William.

"Of course I shall, my dears," said Lady Maria, sitting down at once at the pianoforte. She began to play one of the joyous traditional songs and her two younger children began to sing along.

Lord Hallcroft reluctantly lifted his voice as well. Though he had never felt less like it, he was aware that if he did not participate there would be questions from his family that he might find difficult to answer. He glanced over at Lady Hallcroft and saw that she was standing at one of the tall windows, one hand holding back the heavy drapery as she gazed through the glazed panes. There was a forlorn air in her posture that made him want to go to her, but he suspected that she would not welcome the intrusion into her privacy.

For the next hour, Lord Hallcroft took note that his lady wife was careful to avoid him. After the caroling she served coffee, and even when she handed a cup to him, she did not meet his eyes. Then she initiated a game of charades with his brother and sister that kept all three thoroughly entertained until bedtime. Urged at first by his sister to join in the entertainment, Lord Hallcroft declined. He was certain, judging from Lady Hallcroft's sudden tenseness of figure, that his participation would have been a detriment to her amusement. It gave him a distinctly hollow feeling that his wife, whom he adored, did not wish to have anything to do with him that evening. He had badly misjudged in his dealings with her, that was abundantly clear to him.

Lady Hallcroft stared up into the canopy above her head. The long unhappy evening had finally ended and she had been able to escape to her apartment. She had half hoped and half feared that Lord Hallcroft would follow her. But he had not. She had assured herself that it was for the best and that she should feel better. However, nothing she told herself could quite erase the hollow feeling inside of her.

She and Lord Hallcroft had never quarreled before.

The brocaded bed curtains could be drawn at night to protect the sleeper from drafts, but Lady Hallcroft usually left one curtain slightly open so that she could see the fire, if it was still burning. This night shadows from the firelight played over the rosettes and vines carved into the headboard.

A small table beside the bed held a candle and flint. Her books were tumbled across the tabletop. She had read for a short time before snuffing the candle and sliding under the covers. She had still hoped that her husband would come to her after giving her time to ready herself for bed; but as the minutes ticked by, she had realized that Lord Hallcroft was not coming.

The worst thing was that after she had voiced her suspicion that he meant to break his word to her, she had instinctively felt an inner denial that he would actually do such a thing. It would have relieved her mind greatly to find out the truth.

Lady Hallcroft brushed a tear from her cheek. She could not sleep for thinking back over their quarrel. Finally, she concluded that it was easier simply to get up than to lie tossing and turning, feeling miserable and angry by turns. She reached out for the flint and lit her candle. The bedroom lightened, long shadows flickering across the walls.

Lady Hallcroft threw back the bedclothes and reached for her wrapper. She decided that she would go downstairs to the library and find another book to read in order to stop thinking back about the difference that had sprung up between herself and Lord Hallcroft. She belted the robe tightly around her small waist.

Shielding her candle flame with her cupped palm, Lady Hallcroft cautiously eased open the door, hardly daring to breathe when it softly creaked. The house remained quiet. She sped swiftly down the hall, her bare feet soundless on the carpet.

On the stairs, she moved more cautiously with one hand on the smooth banister as she felt her way down. Suddenly, a stair creaked loudly underfoot. She froze instinctively, her heart pounding. Straining her ears, she could detect nothing out of the ordinary disturbing the silent dark.

It suddenly struck her as amusing that she was reacting much as a housebreaker might, and on a breathless laugh she continued her descent. At the bottom of the stairs she turned, the candlelight flickering with the passage of air. She traversed the deserted great hall and walked quickly to the double doors of the library. Soundlessly she turned the knob and went into the darkened room, holding her candle high.

Moonlight filtered through a part in the drawn draperies so that even without her candle Lady Hallcroft would have had no difficulty in making out the placement of the furniture. A massive oak library table dominated the center of the room. Chairs of a bygone age, with wooden arms and carved backs and red velvet cushions, were placed around the table. Without needing to look, Lady Hallcroft knew that the walls were covered with floor-to-ceiling bookshelves, interspersed at intervals with several gilt-framed portraits of ancestors. The bust of a grim-faced predecessor stood in one darkened corner.

Lady Hallcroft set her flickering candle on the library table. The shadows danced and something seemed to move across the bust. Lady Hallcroft looked quickly towards the corner, her heart thumping a little, but she saw nothing untoward.

Then as her gaze became more focused, she perceived the figure of a man in shirt and breeches watching her from the shadows of the room. He was near the door that gave directly onto Lord Hallcroft's study. Lady Hallcroft gave a frightened gasp and started to turn, to run.

The man moved swiftly. With two bounds he was

beside her. A hard palm clamped over her mouth, stifling the scream that rose in her throat. He yanked her back against him, pinning her against him with his arms. "Softly, sweetheart. You do not want to raise the house."

Recognizing that low voice, Lady Hallcroft gave a sob and ceased struggling. Immediately the hand came away from her mouth and she was turned in the loosened arms so that she was folded close against Lord Hallcroft's chest. She reached up to clutch his lapel. "You frightened me horribly," she whispered. "I thought that you were a housebreaker."

"What are you doing down here, Gwen?" asked Lord Hallcroft.

"I—I could not sleep," said Lady Hallcroft, laying her head against his strong shoulder. She closed her eyes, a trickling tear escaping from under her lids.

His breath stirred her hair as he sighed. "Nor could I. My guilty conscience would not give me leave."

"I am sorry, my lord. I should not have behaved so childishly," said Lady Hallcroft in a low voice.

"No, do not apologize. I should have realized how it must have sounded to you," said Lord Hallcroft. He set her back from him a little so that he could look down into her pale face. "Gwen, I swear that I shall not renege on my promise to you. You shall be allowed to spend time with your beloved family."

Lady Hallcroft shook her head. "But that is just it, my lord! That is why I feel so low. I know that you would never break your word. How could I have doubted you, even for a second?"

Lord Hallcroft eased her securely back into his arms. "We made a misstep, Gwen. We do not know one another very well, it seems. But I should like to know you better."

It was Lady Hallcroft's turn to pull back, though she still stayed close within the circle of his arms. "I wish to know you better, too."

"Then let us make a pact, my lady. We must voice our feelings and our thoughts more to each other," said Lord Hallcroft.

Lady Hallcroft eyed him uncertainly. "Do you wish me to do that, my lord?"

"Indeed I do," he said firmly.

"Then pray take me back to bed, Christopher," said Lady Hallcroft in a breathy voice, feeling very daring.

Lord Hallcroft drew in his breath. "I shall be happy to do so," he said, his voice suddenly husky from feeling. He swept her up into his arms and strode swiftly out of the library.

Chapter Five

The well-sprung carriage rocked in a soothing rhythm. Lady Hallcroft was perfectly comfortable. She had a brick to warm her feet and a heavy lap rug tucked snugly over her legs. Lord Hallcroft sat beside her. The night of their quarrel had ended much better than she had anticipated and they had talked of many things. She should have been content.

However, Lady Hallcroft remained restive. She finally admitted to herself the reason why. She was uncertain of her reception at their journey's end. When William and Lady Frances had learned that Lord Hallcroft meant to take his new bride to meet their aunt, Lady Eagleton, they had both expressed amazed horror.

"I should not like to be in your shoes, Gwen," said Lady Frances with an artistic shudder.

"No, indeed! The old lady gives me a fright every time I see her," agreed William.

"It is very proper for Gwendolyn to make your aunt's acquaintance. Aunt Sophronia was ill at the time of the wedding, you will recall, and could not attend," said Lady Maria reprovingly.

"Are you going, Mama?" asked William pointedly.

Lady Maria had looked taken aback and even somewhat alarmed by the suggestion. "Why, no, I do not think so."

With a nod, William had turned to Gwendolyn. "You see? My brother is the only one that the old lady doesn't intimidate. Even Mama prefers to steer wide of Aunt Sophronia."

"Oh, dear," murmured Lady Hallcroft.

"Precisely," said Lady Frances with another sympathetic glance.

Now, thinking back on that conversation, Lady Hallcroft made a slight face. It did not ease her insecurity over the upcoming visit that Lord Hallcroft appeared to have sunk into a deep reverie. Even though they had aired the misunderstanding between them, Lady Hallcroft was hesitant to break into her husband's thoughts by engaging him in conversation. She gave herself over to the changing landscape outside the glazed window.

The journey was quickly done and the carriage drew up to an ivy-covered manor house. The front door opened and a footman ran quickly down the steps to open the carriage door and hand out the guests. Lord Hallcroft and his lady entered the house and their outer wraps were taken.

"I shall announce you, my lord," said the butler and went away with a stately tread.

Lord Hallcroft smiled down reassuringly at his wife. "You will like my aunt, I assure you."

"I am certain that I shall, my lord," responded Lady Hallcroft with an answering smile, but she still felt some inner trepidation. After all, she had heard quite a lot about Lady Eagleton from the younger Hallcrofts. The butler returned to lead them to Lady Eagleton and Lady Hallcroft took a deep sustaining breath.

When they were ushered into the parlor, Lady Hallcroft knew that her fears were justified. Lady Eagleton was seated on a settee with three of her lapdogs. The lady's sharp eyes were narrowed on the handsome couple that approached her. Lady Hallcroft felt that the lady's razor-sharp glance assessed and dismissed her in one and the same moment.

Lady Eagleton extended her hand toward Lord Hallcroft. She was smiling slightly, which served to relax her stern expression. "Well, nephew? Have you nothing to say for yourself? It is about time that you saw fit to visit me."

Lord Hallcroft gave a laugh. He took his aunt's hand and kissed her gnarled knuckles. "I knew that you would give me a scold, Aunt Sophronia."

"As well you might. Rumor has it that you returned to England weeks past. I take it in bad part that I haven't seen you before this! But then, your time has been otherwise engaged," said Lady Eagleton, turning her gaze to the lady on her nephew's arm. "Pray introduce me, Christopher."

"Allow me to present my wife, Gwendolyn, Lady Hallcroft," said Lord Hallcroft. He pressed his wife's fingers in a reassuring fashion before he drew her forward.

The two ladies exchanged polite greetings. Lady Eagleton pushed two of her lapdogs off of the settee, keeping just the one that remained on her lap. "Sit beside me, Lady Hallcroft," she commanded.

Lady Hallcroft did as she was bid, throwing a wondering glance at Lord Hallcroft as she did so. He looked amused, which served to bolster her confidence. Lady Hallcroft trusted that Lord Hallcroft would not throw her to the wolves, or in this case, the she-wolf. "I am happy to do so, my lady," she said civilly.

"Oho, you are, are you? Aren't you afraid of me, girl?" demanded Lady Eagleton, directing a fierce stare at her.

"To be sure, I have heard of your formidable reputation, my lady. But my lord holds you in high esteem and I trust in his judgment," said Lady Hallcroft steadily.

She was discomfited by the lady's high-handed manner, which bordered on rudeness, but she thought she knew better than to allow her discomfort to show. Her instinct was proven to be correct when Lord Hallcroft chuckled. "Bravo, my lady. You've quite taken the wind out of her ladyship's sails."

Lady Eagleton snorted, but she appeared pleased. "At least you are not a puling miss, as so many of the young women are these days. I can't abide mousey women who jump at their own shadows."

"Quite; but you do like them to turn pale with fear at receiving one of your basilisk stares," said Lord Hallcroft. He had seated himself in a wing chair facing the settee, crossed his legs, and was swinging one booted foot gently.

Lady Eagleton showed her teeth.

Lady Hallcroft assumed that her ladyship was expressing her amusement, an impression borne out by Lady Eagleton's next comment.

"I've always liked you, Christopher. You make me laugh." Lady Eagleton turned toward Lady Hallcroft. "Now tell me about yourself, Lady Hallcroft."

"I don't know that there is much to tell," said Lady Hallcroft, taken aback.

"Of course there is. You're a person, aren't you? You have talents and dreams, don't you? Tell me about your wedding journey. Where did you go? Whom did you meet?"

Lady Hallcroft threw a helpless glance toward Lord Hallcroft. She was embarrassed to be made the center of attention by the extraordinary old woman. But Lord Hallcroft gave the faintest of nods, as though he was perfectly at ease with his aunt's odd humor.

Little by little, Lady Eagleton drew out of Lady Hallcroft her impressions and observations about the six-month-long tour of the Continent, her efforts aided by Lord Hallcroft's contributions. As the two together recalled certain happenings and shared their mutual amusement in glances and smiles, Lady Hallcroft began to realize just what a magical time that it had been. She realized that she would always remember her wedding journey with Lord Hallcroft as one of the best of possible times.

Lady Eagleton was adept at extracting information. Lady Hallcroft did not know when or how it happened, but at some point she began to relate anecdotes about her family. Upon the realization, she abruptly broke off in confusion. "Forgive me, my lady. I did not mean to bore on in such a fashion."

"Nonsense! I am perfectly entertained," said Lady Eagleton.

"However, I realize that you cannot possibly be more than politely interested in personages you have never met," said Lady Hallcroft.

"As you will, Lady Hallcroft," said Lady Eagleton with a dismissive shrug.

Tea was served and it was a large, elaborate affair with plum cake and biscuits and fruits, but Lady Hallcroft scarcely noticed because Lady Eagleton began to reminisce about her own travel experiences. It seemed that in her heyday, Lady Eagleton and Lord Eagleton had been inveterate travelers, and they had been as far afield as the Levant and Egypt. Lady Hallcroft sat rapt, listening while her hostess spun magic tales of camels and shipwreck and vast pyramids.

At last, when Lady Eagleton announced that she was becoming hoarse from all of her storytelling, Lady Hallcroft sighed in contentment. "How I envy you, my lady. You make it all sound so very exciting."

"Indeed it was. I am glad I did it, so that I have the memories. Now I do not get around as well as I once did and it would be impossible for me to do even a portion of what we once accomplished," said Lady Eagleton. "I shall end with a bit of advice to you, Lady Hallcroft. Take pleasure in life as much as you are able. Then you will have few regrets."

"I never knew you to be a philosopher, ma'am," said Lord Hallcroft with a grin.

Lady Eagleton gave a rusty chuckle. "I'm not. I am merely an old woman with a vast amount of experience behind me." She gave an abrupt nod. "I shall tell you this, too, both of you. Do not allow convention or other people's opinions to dictate how you shall live, but instead be true to God and to yourselves."

"I shall remember all of it, my lady," promised Lady Hallcroft, taking it all to heart.

"See that you do," said Lady Eagleton. She reached over to briefly press the younger woman's hand. "I have enjoyed our visit tremendously, my dear. I hope that you will return."

"I would like that, my lady," said Lady Hallcroft with sincerity. She had begun by being slightly intimidated by Lady Eagleton, but now she liked her ladyship very well. Lady Eagleton's manners might be unfashionably abrupt, even rude, but her ladyship was obviously a woman of character. She saw that Lord Hallcroft had risen and she also got to her feet, realizing that they were ending their visit.

Lord Hallcroft took a cordial leave of his aunt and waited while the ladies exchanged civilities before he escorted his lady out to their carriage.

After they had seated themselves and the carriage door was shut, Lord Hallcroft asked curiously, "Well, was my aunt as bad as William and Frances led you to believe?"

"Indeed! Lady Eagleton was every bit as frightening as she was painted," said Lady Hallcroft, nodding. She thought that she had been too forthcoming and hastened to add, "However, by the end of our visit I could quite see how you could hold her in great affection, my lord. Lady Eagleton is a fascinating woman and I thought that she was very gracious to me. I cannot imagine that she found my stories to be particularly interesting but not once did she indicate her boredom."

"I do not think that my aunt was bored. On the contrary, I believe that she was quite taken with you, my lady."

Lady Hallcroft pinkened from gratification. "I do hope so, my lord. It must be an object with me to make myself agreeable to any member of your family."

"The wife I have chosen is approved by those whose opinions matter most to me," said Lord Hallcroft. "Can you doubt it, Gwen?"

Lady Hallcroft shook her head, wrinkling her brows. "Sometimes I do, my lord. Sometimes I feel as though I am living in a dream and one day I shall awaken."

"I trust that it is a pleasant dream, my lady," said Lord Hallcroft softly, glancing down into her face.

"So it is, my lord," said Lady Hallcroft, smiling at him with a sideways glance. She was recalling details from the night before. It would be wonderful were she and Lord Hallcroft able always to be in such agreement. Perhaps as she learned better how to relate to Lord Hallcroft's family, she and Lord Hallcroft would also become better companions to one another. Certainly she hoped that they would deal as famously together as Lady Eagleton and her lord had done.

"What are you thinking about now, my lady?"

Lady Hallcroft tucked her hand into the crook of Lord Hallcroft's elbow. She confided, "Only that I hope we shall be able to look back on our lives and be satisfied that we dealt well with one another, my lord."

Much moved, Lord Hallcroft lifted her gloved fingers to his lips. "So do I, Gwen. So do I."

Chapter Six

A couple of days later, with the exception of Miss Hallcroft, who habitually took her chocolate in bed, the family was enjoying breakfast together. The butler entered the breakfast parlor bearing a sealed note for Lord Hallcroft. Lord Hallcroft took it, nodding his thanks. He glanced at the penned address. "Why, it is from Aunt Sophronia."

Lady Hallcroft and William looked across the breakfast table at Lord Hallcroft in surprise. Lady Hallcroft's first thought was that Lady Eagleton had experienced some crisis in health.

It was left to Lady Maria to express Lady Hallcroft's unvoiced concern. She said with a tiny frown, "I hope that dear Sophronia is not taken ill."

"Not she! The old tartar is pluck to the backbone. She'll outlive us all," said William with conviction.

"William, pray speak more respectfully of your aunt," said Lady Maria with mild reproof.

William merely grinned at his parent and renewed his enthusiastic attack on his steak and kidneys.

Meanwhile, Lord Hallcroft had slit the seal with his knife and opened the sheet. He read it, an expression of mild interest on his face. When he raised his head he looked directly across at his wife. "Lady Eagleton requests that Gwendolyn visit her this afternoon."

William looked up, his expression one of astonishment. "My word!"

Lady Hallcroft was equally astonished. "I, my lord? Are you quite certain?"

A glint of amusement lighting his eyes, Lord Hallcroft nodded somberly. "Yes, I am certain. You do not mind, do you, Gwen? It would mean a great deal to me if you could cater to my aunt's wishes."

"Don't do it, Gwen," recommended William. "The old lady probably means to eat you."

"Really, William!" murmured Lady Maria disapprovingly.

"Don't be silly, William," said Lady Hallcroft. She turned back to Lord Hallcroft. "Of course I shall go. If you think that I should, my lord." Even as she acquiesced, she reflected on the multitude of things that still needed to be seen to before Lord Hallcroft's guests were due to arrive.

"I would greatly appreciate it, my lady," said Lord Hallcroft. With a smile, he added, "Despite William's disparate feelings on the subject, I do not suspect my aunt of having designs against you."

"It is just that the old lady always put me in mind of the conniving hag out of the village fables," said William cheerfully. "You know, where the wicked old woman lures the unsuspecting children into her hovel and then eats them."

"I knew that I should not have allowed that lax tutor for you," said Lady Maria, frowning at her younger son. "Now see what has come of it."

Lord Hallcroft and William laughed. Lady Hallcroft joined in, but even as she was laughing she hoped that the errand to Lady Eagleton did not take up too much of her day. There were so many details yet to be finished for the house party. She thought that if she set off directly after luncheon, she could probably wind up her visit to Lady Eagleton and return before the evening was too far along, especially since the moon was out.

*   *   *

Lady Eagleton received Lady Hallcroft in the parlor. "Thank you for coming, Lady Hallcroft. I am in your debt," said Lady Eagleton in a formal tone.

"Not at all, my lady," murmured Lady Hallcroft. She tried not to feel resentment and impatience over the situation, recognizing that her attitude would not be conducive to an agreeable visit. She was still wondering at the urgency of Lady Eagleton's request. She could not conceive why her ladyship had asked for her to come at all. She was not long left in suspense.

After Lady Eagleton had inquired after her wishes concerning hot tea and all was ordered to her ladyship's satisfaction, she dismissed the butler. When the door had quietly closed behind the butler, Lady Eagleton turned to face her reluctant guest. "You will undoubtedly think me to be naught but a foolish old woman. And selfish, too! But the truth is, it is lonely for me during the holiday. It is not like it was when Lord Eagleton was alive. We had no surviving children, yet we managed to be quite merry during the Christmas season because we surrounded ourselves with friends and neighbors. We always had the house beautifully decorated and we set a table that would bid fair to make one's eyes bulge from its extravagance."

Lady Eagleton was silent a moment as she reflected on past glories; then she glanced once more at Lady Hallcroft, almost apologetically. "It scarcely seems worth the effort to muster the household to decorate this great empty house and direct the cook to make up a menu when it is only myself."

"Oh, Lady Eagleton," said Lady Hallcroft, dismayed by the confidence. Her ready sympathies were instantly stirred. She felt that certainly no one should have to be alone during the Christmas holidays.

"I had hoped that, if I could impose on your good nature, you might help me organize for the holiday and then I could take more pleasure in the process," said Lady Eagleton, a bit gruffly. "I wished to have some of the neighbors in and of course I should like my tenants to have a Christmas feast as we used to do in the old days."

Lady Hallcroft's heart completely melted, and with it the last of her resentment disappeared. She leaned over to give Lady Eagleton a swift hug and smiled at her. "My dear ma'am! Of course I shall help you! You have only to tell me what you wish to have done."

Lady Eagleton had been startled by Lady Hallcroft's spontaneous show of affection, but she was by no means displeased. She quickly recovered her equilibrium. "Well, then! Let us have in my staff and not waste another moment of this wonderful day." She pulled on the bell. As she smiled at Lady Hallcroft, her faded eyes were sparkling with anticipation.

Having already been through the process once, Lady Hallcroft confidently set forth several suggestions that instantly found favor with Lady Eagleton. Her ladyship commissioned her upper staff to see that Lady Hallcroft's directions were followed to the letter. Soon messengers were sent to the village with orders for meats and cheeses and sundry other items that were needed for the tenants' feast. As for Lady Eagleton, she set herself the task of writing out in her beautiful copperplate all the invitations for a special evening to which she requested the presence of all of the neighborhood. Her invitation to her tenants was carried by word of mouth by her steward, who returned to report that her ladyship's message had generated much excitement.

The servants became worn out with rushing here and there, fetching and carrying, cleaning and polishing; but they caught the excitement. It had been many years since Lady Eagleton's household had seen such a bustle, and it quite reminded the older servants of better days before Lord Eagleton had succumbed to a long debilitating illness. Up went the fir garlands and bows and other symbols of the season, creating a festive air in the dignified house that had all exchanging smiles.

Lady Hallcroft was not unaffected. She loved the Christmas holidays and the cheerful season and all of its attendant celebrations. Between consulting with Lady Eagleton and seeing to all the details for the elderly lady, she had scarcely a moment for reflection. She thoroughly enjoyed herself.

When the afternoon had drawn on, Lady Eagleton pronounced it time for them to rest from their labors. "I am exhausted, my dear, but happily so. You have made such a difference and I am very happy with the result. It has been a long time since I have held a gala evening, but I hope to show my neighbors that I am still to be counted a superb hostess," said Lady Eagleton. "I trust that when my invitation arrives at Hallcroft, you and the rest of the family will attend."

"I am certain that Lord Hallcroft will be delighted, ma'am. He holds you in too much affection to do otherwise, as do I," said Lady Hallcroft with a smile. "As for myself, I am quite looking forward to it. I do love the Christmas season and the cheerful faces and lovely carols."

"You will drag William and Frances along with you, of course," said Lady Eagleton with a show of her teeth. "They have always been a bit frightened by me, you know."

Lady Hallcroft laughed. "I have no doubt of it, and perhaps Lady Maria is, too?"

Lady Eagleton cackled. "Oh, aye! I revel in a certain reputation amongst certain of my relations, but perhaps my Christmas gala will smooth their alarms."

The two ladies took a companionable tea together, at the conclusion of which Lady Hallcroft felt that it was time to take her leave. She informed Lady Eagleton of her decision and her ladyship nodded. "I shall ring for a message to be taken round to the stables for your carriage."

The ladies conversed easily for several minutes while Gwendolyn put on her pelisse and gloves. Then the door opened and the butler ushered in Lord Hallcroft's coachman. "My lady, the coachman wishes to speak to Lady Hallcroft."

Lady Hallcroft was surprised. She glanced at Lady Eagleton, who merely raised her brows. Lady Hallcroft turned back to the coachman. "What is it, Wheaton?"

"My lady, one of the leaders has strained a hock. I fear that if we are to set out directly that his lordship's horse will come up permanently lame," said the coachman in a respectful manner.

"Oh, dear! But when shall we be able to leave, then?" asked Lady Hallcroft, both concerned for the horse and dismayed that she would be getting back to the manor later than even she had anticipated. All of her forgotten anxieties began to seep back to her.

The coachman cleared his throat and said hoarsely, "I regret, my lady, but it would be best if the horse were to rest overnight."

"Overnight! It is not possible! I must get back before nightfall," said Lady Hallcroft, her dismay becoming full-blown.

The coachman shook his head.

"Perhaps I could borrow a horse from you, dear Lady Eagleton, and leave the lame one here to recover?" asked Lady Hallcroft.

Lady Eagleton and the coachman exchanged a swift glance that was impossible for her to interpret.

"I am sorry, my dear. It is not possible. My team are ill-tempered beasts and will only work in tandem with their own," said Lady Eagleton with finality.

"That be true, my lady," said the coachman quickly. "Her ladyship's horses are likely to kick out and maim his lordship's team."

"Could you not send me home in your own carriage, then?" suggested Lady Hallcroft.

Lady Eagleton shook her head. "I fear not. Tomorrow is always the date that I reserve to discharge my responsibility toward my tenants at this time of year. I have several visits to make beginning at first light. Forgive me, Gwendolyn, but I really cannot put off such errands as those."

"No, of course not," said Lady Hallcroft automatically. She looked at Lady Eagleton rather helplessly. "But then, what do you suggest, ma'am?"

"I don't consider the matter to be a problem, my dear. You must stay the night, of course," said Lady Eagleton coolly. "We shall allow the poor horse to rest overnight and in the morning it will probably be much recovered. Isn't that what you implied, coachman?"

The coachman nodded and turned his concerned gaze on Lady Hallcroft.

In the face of the man's obvious distress over the circumstances, Lady Hallcroft unhappily shrugged her shoulders. "I suppose there is nothing else to be done."

The coachman appeared immensely relieved and bowed himself out of the room.

"I understand that you are upset, Gwendolyn," said Lady Eagleton. "However, it is only a few hours, after all. My nephew will do very well without you for that long!"

"It is not that!" exclaimed Lady Hallcroft, turning impetuously toward the old lady. "My lord commissioned me to plan a house party for all of his influential friends. There is still so much to do! What if I should fail?" She unconsciously twisted her hands together.

Silence reigned for several seconds as Lady Eagleton regarded her guest with a blank expression. Under that unblinking regard, Lady Hallcroft flushed. In a suffocated voice, she said, "Forgive me, my lady. I should not have burst out in such a fashion."

Lady Eagleton nodded and held out her hand. "Come, my dear. I shall put you into the capable hands of my housekeeper. She shall take you up to your room, where you can rest before dinner."

Lady Hallcroft acquiesced to Lady Eagleton's suggestion, but she did not nap. After the maid had left her, she simply sat in front of the fire on a footstool, thinking. She turned over and over in her mind what had happened, and she kept coming back to the swift glance exchanged by Lady Eagleton and the coachman. It was almost as though they were coconspirators whose goal was to keep her at Lady Eagleton's residence. "But what nonsense!"

Lady Hallcroft felt stupid for even entertaining such a thought. However, the nagging suspicion was not quite stilled.

At dinner, Lady Eagleton exerted herself to be an amusing hostess. She began recounting several more of her youthful adventures, creating such fascination for Lady Hallcroft that she actually forgot her problem. It was not until Lady Hallcroft had retired to bed, attired in a gown borrowed from her hostess, that she again began to fret over her inability to return to Hallcroft Manor.

She did not think that she would be able to sleep. However, it had been a long day filled with activities and even her natural anxiety over being unable to return home could not keep her awake.

The morning dawned cold and with a lowering sky. Lady Eagleton invited Lady Hallcroft to accompany her on her visits to the estate tenants. Lady Hallcroft agreed, more out of civility than desire. However, by the time that she and Lady Eagleton had made the rounds and handed out the practical gifts that Lady Eagleton had prepared for each family, Lady Hallcroft was in a much better frame of mind. She understood that Lady Eagleton's feeling of obligation toward her tenants was deeply ingrained and that because of it her ladyship was well liked by them. In fact, at each small thatch-roofed dwelling it was obvious that the tenants and their families had all awaited her ladyship's arrival because without exception they had come out-of-doors as soon as Lady Eagleton's carriage stopped. Lady Hallcroft realized that from long-standing tradition the tenants knew what date that Lady Eagleton would come, bearing small gifts for them and their children and to talk with them. It would have been a bitter disappointment to all if Lady Eagleton had not appeared.

Lady Hallcroft was ashamed that she had harbored unkind thoughts over Lady Eagleton's refusal to put off her own responsibilities in order to lend out her carriage. She quite understood now the reasoning behind her ladyship's refusal. Lady Eagleton was all too aware what her absence on that particular date would mean.

But perhaps, thought Lady Hallcroft hopefully, since those obligations were now fulfilled, Lady Eagleton would be more amenable to the notion. Surely there could not now be any objection to the lending of the carriage for her use. Lady Hallcroft resolved to put the question to her hostess after they had warmed themselves up over tea.

However, the weather took a capricious hand in Lady Hallcroft's plans. Even before the ladies had returned to the manor house, the wind began blowing hard. It was bitingly cold and flurries of snow stung their faces even as the ladies hurried inside. By the time Lady Eagleton and Lady Hallcroft had put off their damp wraps and begun to warm themselves by the fire, waiting for tea to be served, the snowstorm was in full gale.

"I suspect that this weather will keep you tied here yet a while, Gwendolyn," remarked Lady Eagleton, sipping at her cup.

Lady Hallcroft hated to admit it, but she feared that Lady Eagleton was correct. When she looked out the window, it was only to see a curtain of impenetrable white. There was no way that her coachman would be able to see the road on such a day.

"I am sorry, my dear," said Lady Eagleton gently.

Lady Hallcroft summoned up a smile. "It is unfortunate, indeed. However, I trust that you and I shall pass the time well enough, ma'am."

"That is the spirit, girl," said Lady Eagleton with a slight smile.

The storm howled all night and then tapered off into a steady fall of snow. The day following was marked by weak sunshine and Lady Hallcroft's rising hope that the snow had at last run its course. She sent word down to the stables and was vastly relieved to learn that the lame horse was indeed fully recovered. At luncheon, when Lady Eagleton came down from her rooms, Lady Hallcroft announced that she would be leaving within the hour.

Lady Eagleton's sharp eyes shot to her guest's face, but her expression remained perfectly civil. "Of course, my dear. When my dresser brought me word this morning that the weather had begun to clear, I knew at once that you would be off. I have enjoyed our time together. I hope that you, too, have been amused?"

"Of course, ma'am. It has been a pleasant visit indeed," said Lady Hallcroft. She was more than a little sincere. Despite her restive desire to return to Hallcroft Manor, she had found much to busy herself with and to entertain her while she was marooned in Lady Eagleton's company. "I wish that you would come to visit us at Hallcroft during the holiday, my lady."

Lady Eagleton looked surprised; then her expression softened. A bit gruffly, she said, "Thank you, my dear. You have no notion what your invitation means to me, especially after such a trying time as you have had. I expect that some of your guests will have arrived already by the time you make your return."

Lady Hallcroft nodded, her unhappiness rushing back on her. "I fear so, my lady. I had so wanted to make certain of all of the details before the house party began."

"Never mind. Lady Maria is not completely useless. I have no doubt that she arranged all just as you had given orders for it to be done," said Lady Eagleton. "You have wrought a minor miracle here. Therefore I would be astonished indeed if your staff disregarded any of your superb direction."

Lady Hallcroft was heartened by Lady Eagleton's encouragement and was able to take leave of the inimitable old lady with good spirits. However, as the carriage set off and carried her ever nearer to the manor, her insecurities came creeping back. What if something had gone wrong? What if Lord Hallcroft was displeased with how the house party had been launched? And how could his lordship send her off at such a time, when he must have known how anxiously she had been planning the arrangements for his guests?

Snowflakes flashed past the glass, winking in the late-afternoon sunlight like so many bits of shiny tinsel. The white fields and hedgerows were marked by tall pristine drifts. It was an enchanting prospect, but Lady Hallcroft was not in the least appreciative.

When the carriage drew up at the front steps of the manor, Lady Hallcroft waited impatiently for the door to be opened and the iron step to be let down. She scarcely waited for the footman to help her down to the icy gravel before she swept up the front steps. She stopped when the door opened and Lord Hallcroft stepped outside, closing the front door behind him.

Lady Hallcroft eyed him somewhat resentfully. Lord Hallcroft did not seem the least put out that she had been gone nearly three days. She was still hurt that he had sent her away so easily on the errand to his aunt, especially on the eve of her debut as hostess. Nor did he express a particle of emotion at seeing her back.

A horrible suspicion raised its ugly head. Surely Lord Hallcroft had not fallen out of love with her. Surely he still felt some particle of affection for her! She thought it was despicable to have such creeping doubts at the holiday season, which had always been the most joyous time of the year for her.

"I hope that you enjoyed your little visit," said Lord Hallcroft. "It was a bit longer than I had anticipated it would be."

Lady Hallcroft nearly stamped her foot. With an effort she managed to speak civilly. "In truth it was becoming rather tedious, my lord." She was glad to hear how cool her voice was, but at the same she was saddened. Was she doomed for the remainder of her life to such cold exchanges?

Lord Hallcroft pulled a wide silk scarf out of his coat pocket. "I have a surprise for you, my lady, but I do not wish you to see it until I am ready to reveal it. Pray indulge me for a moment and allow me to blindfold you."

"You want to what?" asked Lady Hallcroft. She stiffened with outrage, her thoughts veering between disbelief and hurt.

"Please, Gwendolyn," said Lord Hallcroft softly.

She found that she could not stand against the appeal in his voice, nor the light in his eyes. "Oh, very well!" she said, and hated that she sounded petulant.

Lord Hallcroft did not appear to notice, but turned her around to tie the scarf securely over her eyes. "Can you see anything?"

"No, of course not," said Lady Hallcroft shortly.

"Then I shall lead you indoors now."

"Good; I am becoming chilled standing about," she said. One part of her was appalled by her sharpness, but she did not care. She was very, very hurt that Lord Hallcroft did not seem the least bit bothered by their separation. On the contrary, he wanted to play a silly game. Lady Hallcroft rebelliously thought that she was not in the mood for games.

Lady Hallcroft heard the front door open and felt Lord Hallcroft's hand under her elbow, guiding her. She stepped inside cautiously, her hands half raised in front of her. Lord Hallcroft drew her slowly forward and Lady Hallcroft heard the front door close behind her again. She thought that the footman must have shut it. Then Lord Hallcroft carefully turned her in a new direction and she realized that he was leading her into the drawing room. She heard a soft giggle, swiftly silenced, and she felt humiliated that she was being made such a spectacle of in front of the household. On the other hand, she was also becoming rather curious. Lord Hallcroft had said that he had a surprise for her. Lady Hallcroft could not imagine what it could be, but her heart began to beat more rapidly.

"This is far enough." Lady Hallcroft felt Lord Hallcroft's fingers working at the knot at the back of her head. She waited with bated breath until she could see again.

The silk scarf dropped from her eyes. Lady Hallcroft gasped. She was standing in front of a semicircle of her family, which crowded the drawing room from wall to wall. Lady Maria, William, and Frances were there, too. In unison the entire company shouted, "Merry Christmas! Merry Christmas!"

"Mama! Papa!" Lady Hallcroft shrieked, and rushed forward. She was engulfed in the arms of her family as they all began speaking animatedly together. Lady Hallcroft could not stop exclaiming at their unexpected presence. Lord Hallcroft stood a little to one side, enjoying the sight. He was included by one and then another, all of whom congratulated him on a successful surprise.

Taking advantage of a thinning in the circle surrounding Lady Hallcroft, Lady Maria went forward to draw her daughter-in-law into a gentle embrace. "Merry Christmas, dear, dear Gwendolyn."

"Thank you, ma'am," said Lady Hallcroft. Meeting her mother-in-law's smiling gaze, she realized that Lady Maria did indeed regard her with affection. Her already full heart overflowed. Lady Maria stepped back; Lady Hallcroft was once again engulfed by her family.

Eventually it dawned on Lady Hallcroft, as she listened to her brother and sisters and their spouses, that they were expecting to make an extended stay. Lady Hallcroft finally voiced the question that had loomed larger and larger in her mind, as she turned to Lord Hallcroft in confusion. "But I do not understand, my lord. I thought we were to have quite a different party of guests."

"It is my Christmas gift to you, Gwendolyn."

Lady Hallcroft looked around again at all of her loved ones, the shimmering tears in her eyes blurring their dear faces. She could scarcely believe it was true, that she was to celebrate the holiday with them all. And she owed it all to one person.

Impulsively she turned and flung her arms around her husband's neck. "I love you so!" she declared.

There arose indulgent, good-natured laughter all around. "Merry Christmas, Gwen!" shouted William.

Lord Hallcroft was seen to turn red, but he grinned also. "Then you do not mind now my subterfuge in sending you away from the house?"

"Oh, I did! And later I shall scold you monstrously for making me so very unhappy and confused," said Lady Hallcroft. She suddenly realized what he had said and her mouth rounded with astonishment. "Do you mean that Lady Eagleton knew—and that was why she sent for me?"

Lord Hallcroft looked a little uncomfortable. He regarded his wife's expression anxiously, unsure how she might react. "It was all an elaborate plot from the very beginning. I enlisted the help of my family and Lady Eagleton and your parents. My mother scolded me for employing such a stratagem. I confess, it was rather Machiavellian. Can you forgive me for causing you unhappiness?"

"Oh, I do! But I think—yes, I think that I shall punish you just a little, my lord," said Lady Hallcroft. She saw that Lord Hallcroft was looking both wary and uncertain. Her eyes gleamed with laughter. She gave a slow smile. "You are standing under the mistletoe bough, my lord." Thereupon she kissed him full on the lips, amid much laughter and hand-clapping. Fleetingly, she wondered what he would make of her patently public display of affection, but he surprised her.

Lord Hallcroft caught her up in his arms and proved that he was very much a man of the moment. Looking deep into her astonished eyes, he proclaimed roundly, "You are the one and only love of my heart, Gwen." Then he kissed her in a way that she would remember all her life.

More holiday romance from Signet

NEW YORK TIMES BESTSELLING AUTHORS

MARY JO PUTNEY

JILL BARNETT

AND

JUSTINE DARE

SUSAN KING

A STOCKINGFUL OF JOY

0-451-21595-8
penguin.com